THE CLEMATIS TREE

An accomplished first novel by the well-known politician...

The Clematis Tree opens happily, and deceptively, with a party in a sunny Surrey garden to celebrate the christening of Mark and Claire's new daughter, Pippa. Then, disaster. Jeremy, their young son, spots a wild rabbit racing across the garden. Giving chase, Jeremy forgets what he has been told and rushes through the main gate into the lane. A speeding car knocks him down, and although Jeremy survives he is now severely brain-damaged. His family are forced to cope with a catastrophe they never imagined could happen to them...

THE CLEMATIS TREE

THE CLEMATIS TREE

by

Ann Widdecombe

Magna Large Print Books
Long Preston, North Yorkshire,
BD23 4ND, England.

British Library Cataloguing in Publication Data.

Widdecombe, Ann
    The clematis tree.

    A catalogue record of this book is
    available from the British Library

O1116   ISBN   0-7505-1707-7

First published in Great Britain by Weidenfeld & Nicholson

Copyright © 2000 Ann Widdecombe

Cover illustration Photonica by arrangement with
The Orion Publishing Group Ltd.

The right of Ann Widdecombe to be identified as the author of this
work has been asserted by her in accordance with the Copyright,
Designs and Patents Act, 1988

Published in Large Print 2001 by arrangement with
The Orion Publishing Group Ltd.

Magna Large Print is an imprint of Library Magna Books Ltd.

Printed and bound in Great Britain by
T.J. (International) Ltd., Cornwall, PL28 8RW

For my Mother

Author's Note

Under existing parliamentary procedures, Sally Renwick's Terminally Ill Persons Act could not have become law. Rather than devise a complex scenario which would be of no interest to the general reader, I have assumed that Sally's bill is subject to the same procedures as a Government Bill. This may offend the purist but it assists the narrative.

1

The christening party was assembled on the lawn. Apart from Paul, Mark's brother, all the relatives were Claire's who assiduously attended family baptisms, weddings and funerals with the regularity and numbers of Galsworthy's Forsytes, contrasting sharply with Mark's nearest and dearest whose closeness was forged by the adamantine bonds of loving neglect.

'Are you going on Sunday?' Mark could imagine his mother asking Paul as surely as if he had been present. 'You are? Oh, good. I needn't bother then.' Yet Claire had one sibling and he five.

So now Paul circulated among the guests, an ambassador at a foreign reception, his tanned skin and dark rabbinical-style beard sorting oddly with the flowery dresses of Claire's aunts. Aunt Jane was looking at him as if he had done it on purpose.

Mark picked up two half-full bottles of champagne and advanced upon a group at the far end of the lawn.

'Lunch up any minute,' he remarked to the vicar as he passed him, and 'I like your hat,' to Aunt Isobel. Poor Aunt Isobel. Mark had never heard either Claire or her sister Sally refer to her in any other way. Similarly Claire's father generally referred to 'poor old Isobel' and Aunt

Jane to 'my poor sister'. As Isobel was certainly not at all poor in any material sense Mark could never understand the reason for the casual pity.

It might, he supposed, be a result of her having suffered what the family always described as a 'disappointment' when she was a young girl and never having married, or because she had given up sixteen years of her life to raise her brother's daughters, or merely because she had a vague, benevolent manner which suggested absence of mind and a propensity to be put upon. Yet she bustled about with joyful if ill-defined purpose and seemed to look with bright hope at a life which was largely behind her. Clever, cool, independent Sally adored her.

'Oh, that's a cheerful sight,' smiled Marianne as Mark approached with the champagne. 'I asked Peter to get me some ages ago but he said it was too hot to move.'

Mark grinned. 'Your new god-daughter's finding it too hot as well. Claire has just taken her inside to cool off.'

'Wasn't she good at the christening? But perhaps she's finding all those names a bit heavyweight in this weather.' Rupert Fiske, Aunt Jane's grandson and in his final year at Winchester, had only just begun taking liberties with his elders. He was a shy boy and the clumsy pleasantry sounded almost rude. Mark liked him.

'That was your Aunt Claire's doing,' Mark told him. 'Philippa Isobel Graine Ruth – a name we like, Claire's substitute mother, her real mother and my mother. You can take it as a declaration that our family is complete and we had to do our duty by everyone in one go.'

'I shall call my god-daughter Pip,' decided Marianne.

'We're calling her Pippa,' said Mark.

'No, Pip,' insisted Marianne. 'Pippa is a good little girl – you know, God's in His heaven, all's right with the world etc. With Sally as the other godmother the poor child hasn't a hope of being like that. She'll be a tomboy: Pip or even Phil.'

'I wish you wouldn't keep talking about Pip. It reminds me of the revision I haven't done for next week's Eng. Lit.' Rupert entered the conversation at a simultaneous charge and limp.

'*Great Expectations?* I hear you have too, young man. Place at Christ Church...' Peter, Marianne's husband, was saying in mock avuncular tones as Mark left the group and approached Sally, whom he could see under the magnolia tree talking to the latest in a surprisingly short line of boyfriends. As Mark looked at them he felt a shaft of unease.

Without being conventionally beautiful Sally, Mark's sister-in-law, was the most attractive woman at the gathering. She was sitting with her head slightly back, her hands on the ground behind her, and the thick hair which cascaded almost to her waist was a most unusual shade of deep red. By contrast a few wisps of auburn in an otherwise unremarkable head of mouse were the only evidence Claire gave of being Graine's daughter. Other than her eyes Claire had inherited all that was plain in either parent. She was taller than Sally but Sally's model-girl figure and elegant dress sense belied her average height.

11

It amused Mark now to remember that when he had first met her Sally had been a plain, skinny, awkward but determined child of twelve.

Mark's unease was on account of the boyfriend. Instinctively he did not like Oswald Bell-Porter, and not just because he found the name ridiculous.

'It must be a case of Doctor Fell,' Claire had commented after Bell-Porter's first visit, 'I don't know why I don't like him but I don't. He's polite, he's educated, he's got a good job and he's OK to look at, but he's not for Sally.'

'Polite but not kind, educated but without humility, good job and no concern for anything beyond the material, good looks and knows it.'

'Yes, that's it exactly. Clever Mark.'

But that was not it, thought Mark, though it was certainly a fair summary. His real objection was that Bell-Porter had a lubricious mouth and younger sisters-in-law were like younger sisters: you believed them pure, or at least wanted to believe them so. Even if the wish were not mother to the thought Mark would have risked a large wager on Sally's innocence. No, perhaps not innocence, rather on her chastity, he mused. Sally was far from innocent, surely. She occasionally drank too much, could swear fluently in her received English accent and in her teens had set out to shock her family with a string of blue jokes, but for all that she emanated a kind of puritanism.

Now his sister-in-law looked up at his approach and smiled. She was wearing a flame-red dress which should have clashed with her hair and did

12

clash with her politics.

'Hello, brother-in-law, you're making me feel guilty. Do you or Claire need any help?'

'A good time to ask, it's probably all done,' commented Bell-Porter as Mark briefly toyed with the idea of finding Sally a task just for the satisfaction of temporarily parting her from him. 'Yes it is,' went on the object of his unkind thoughts. 'There are Claire and Sam wheeling out the nosh.'

Mark repressed a feeling of irritation at Bell-Porter's familiar way of referring to his father-in-law, knowing it to be unreasonable and feeling sure that in any case Sam had invited the familiarity. He amused himself by imagining the expostulation which would follow if Bell-Porter were to take similar liberties with Aunt Jane and call her by her Christian name. Jane indeed!

'What's funny?' asked Sally curiously.

'Nothing. Mary, go and help Martha.'

Sally rose. 'That's elevating Ozzie to dizzy heights.'

'Don't blaspheme, my girl. The vicar might hear,' grinned Bell-Porter, slapping her bottom affectionately.

Mark turned away in disgust and headed towards Aunt Isobel.

'That's a nice young man Sally's got,' she greeted him.

'No, it isn't. He's ghastly.'

'Well, perhaps he isn't as nice as George,' agreed Isobel Renwick amiably.

George had been Sally's escort in her second year at Cambridge and Mark was not sure if

13

Aunt Isobel referred to him now because she had liked him best of Sally's boyfriends or because she had merely forgotten the two in between. Mark tried to remember George, managed a vague recollection of dark curls in an overlong style, and gave up.

'Who are the other godparents?' asked Aunt Isobel, removing her flower-trimmed hat and fanning herself with it. Her white wavy hair, flattened by hat and heat, lay limply but tidily round her temples. She was not yet sixty but already everyone treated her with that gentleness accorded to the very innocent elderly.

'Marianne and Peter Robson. Marianne was at Bristol with Claire. That's their son Michael playing with Jeremy.'

'Jeremy doesn't seem at all jealous of Pippa. That's nice.'

'For now at any rate he regards the baby as a bit of a curiosity, certainly not as a rival. Given that there's four years between them and that they're different sexes, it could just last.'

'Do you really like my hat?'

Mark remembered his earlier comment. 'Yes, I do. Especially in this sun. It makes all the colours glow.'

Aunt Isobel looked at it absentmindedly and began to play with the flowers which she had added to it in such abundance. Poor Aunt Isobel, thought Mark involuntarily.

Sally had been four and Claire fourteen when their mother, Graine, had died of cancer. Sam, then on the verge of the business success which was to bring him such wealth, could afford neither a housekeeper nor to abandon his business and bring up the girls himself. The result was that the young Claire began to assume responsibility for Sally and for the running of the household in addition to her schoolwork. Aunt Jane saw and volubly disapproved while offering no solution. Aunt Isobel saw and came to the rescue.

She offered to give up her small rented house in North London and come to Sussex and keep house for Sam until Sally should be grown up or Sam remarried or circumstances otherwise change. Sam accepted gratefully and was lectured upon his good fortune by Aunt Jane.

'You realise, of course, that my poor sister is giving up her own prospects for you and your family?'

As Isobel was uncourted, of modest means and in unremarkable employment, Sam felt he could live with the guilt. He loved his younger sister dearly, retained fond memories of how she adored him as a child and thanked Heaven that it was she rather than his elder sister who was free and willing to help.

Fortunately Jane was sufficiently fearful of becoming involved herself to be reluctant to interfere too much, and the arrangement proved more than satisfactory. Jane was not spiteful but she was sharp-tongued, severe and exacting. Her husband, good-natured, unambitious and thoroughly nagged to be otherwise, found what the family privately described as a merciful release in death while still in his sixties, after which Jane, younger than he by many years,

15

turned all her attention upon her only son Alex, who responded by leaving home and marrying at the earliest opportunity. His wife, Susan, was a match for her mother-in-law but was also diplomatic and a *modus vivendi* more amicable than Jane deserved had been established. She doted on Rupert, her first grandson, but otherwise remained unmellowed by age.

Meanwhile Isobel became the only mother whom Sally could remember, and to this day she called her Aunt 'Izzymum' to her face even though she called her 'Poor Aunt Isobel' to third parties. Sam's business prospered and Sally enjoyed a childhood marked by an affluence which Claire only shared in her later teens. Claire had attended the local comprehensive but Sally went to public school; Claire's first holiday abroad took place when she was seventeen while Sally was only seven; Sally's bicycles were brand-new, Claire's second-hand; Sally celebrated every birthday with a large party whereas Claire had only been allowed two friends to tea.

It was therefore a source of both surprise and relief to Sam and Isobel that there should have been not the remotest sign of jealousy or even wistfulness on Claire's part. Partly this was because the elder girl had developed a protective attitude towards her motherless sibling, partly because Aunt Isobel recognised the difference in the circumstances of the two girls and deliberately set out to minimise it, but mainly it was because Sally, far from growing up spoiled, had demonstrated a steely determination and a capacity for very hard work.

16

'She used to slog away till eleven or twelve at night when Aunt Isobel would insist she go to bed,' Claire had told Mark. 'She didn't get a scholarship to Cambridge because Daddy could afford private education – she got it through sheer grit plus a lot of brain power.'

Then, at the end of Sally's first year at Cambridge, Aunt Isobel startled the family by announcing that she wished to return to London and resume a life of her own. She had carried out her side of the bargain: Claire had long been married, Sally was grown up, away from home half the year, confident and successful. Rightly could their father consider his sister's duty done. Sam faced the fact that his life would be less comfortable and Sally protested that the house would be empty to come home to in vacations but to everyone's surprise Aunt Isobel stuck to her resolution and Sam, feeling both resigned and eternally grateful, bought her a small house in Hampstead. It was then to no one's surprise that Sally spent more of each vacation there than she did in the Sussex house, which Sam himself only occupied to sleep in as his business brought him his next million.

It had been that business which brought Mark and Claire together. She was then twenty-two, a new entrant to the Civil Service and commuting daily from the family home. Mark, twenty-five and established in a small firm of accountants which had served Sam's business from the start was reluctantly visiting him on a Saturday, that being the only day Sam would make himself available. Claire received him and poured tea,

17

Sally hovered outside the lounge door wanting badly to watch a television programme and willing them to hurry up. Sam was informal, affable and demanding. The day's business was concluded at ten o'clock and Claire offered supper.

'Sally tells me she is going to be a bank manager.' Aunt Isobel temporarily abandoned the flowers to break into Mark's recollections.

'Sort of,' agreed Mark with a small smile. 'She's going into a merchant bank.'

'I hope she will be kind to people.'

'Er ... I'm sure she will, but she won't be dealing with people in the way the ordinary banks do. I mean she won't be deciding about overdrafts and current accounts or things like that.'

'People shouldn't have overdrafts, dear, but merchants must sometimes if business is going through a bad patch.'

Mark, groping for a reply, was relieved to be interrupted by his father-in-law and amused to see that Sam was carrying a pint mug of beer from which he now removed a fly. 'Good,' he said, 'you found the beer.'

Automatically they looked over at Aunt Jane, expecting disapproval, but she was talking to the vicar and had not yet noticed the incongruity of Sam's pint among the champagne flutes.

'Claire's put on a good spread. Glad to see Paul here.'

'Sorry, Sam, I can see Claire signalling for help. I'll be back in a moment.' As he headed for the house he heard Sam say, 'Nice hat, Izz,' and smiled as he imagined Aunt Isobel's pleasure.

'Pippa's yelling,' Claire greeted him, 'and we need some more bottles opened. We'll cut the cake in a moment. Jeremy wants to do it.'

Paul joined them in time to overhear. 'I suggest Claire deals with the star of the show, you find Jeremy and I'll get to work on the corks,' he told Mark, who amended the proposal by assigning Pippa to himself and hurrying up the stairs, taking them two at a time as his daughter's cries became more urgent. Claire had put her in her cot in the boxroom which they had turned into a nursery, because Jeremy used the third bedroom as a playroom and Claire wanted to keep the fourth for guests.

Pippa quietened as Mark picked her up and held her on his knee. Her face was puce from the exertion of crying and she was dribbling from one corner of her mouth. Despite Rupert's assertion that she had 'been so good in church' she had bawled throughout the service and looked as if she were contemplating a repeat performance. Mark reached for a tissue and began to mop up mouth, chin and bib, the last designed to protect the christening gown. From the hall below Claire's voice reached him: 'OK?'

'OK,' confirmed Mark.

'Very OK,' he continued softly, gently dandling Pippa. 'Very, very OK. You're the sex we wanted, you're healthy and you complete our family. You're perfect and so is Jeremy. We've been lucky and you're lucky. You are loved, wanted and set one day to inherit part of your Grandad's fortune. Meanwhile, it's a great partnership

19

we've got, Pippa baby.'

He said the last sentence in a Bronx accent. Pippa closed uncomprehending eyes. 'You're fooling,' he said when he thought her asleep.

There was no response, her eyelids still firmly closed.

'No? I apologise,' murmured Mark as he returned her gently to her cot.

Downstairs he was greeted with a scene of happy anticipation. Paul, about to open another bottle of champagne, was standing outside with his back to the French window, pointing the bottle at Jeremy and Michael as his fingers slowly coaxed the cork. Jeremy had his hands firmly over his ears and was staring at the cork in giggling horror, Michael was trying to take refuge behind Marianne's skirts and Sam was getting ready to duck. To Paul's right Claire held a glass ready while behind her the vicar and both aunts watched the scene, Jane with condescending indulgence and Isobel with childish delight. Sally was smiling, Bell-Porter looked bored, Peter had paused with his fork halfway to his mouth, while Rupert Fiske looked first at Jeremy, then at Paul and then back at Jeremy as if following a game of tennis.

The cork popped, and as a fountain of froth followed it the adults cheered and the children screamed. Aunt Jane muttered something intentionally audible and predictable about expense and waste. Sally, suddenly finding her mane of hair too hot, fished an elastic band from her handbag and tied the red cascade back into a ponytail.

Michael and Jeremy were looking for the cork while Paul, who had seen it, called 'Warm', 'warmer' and 'cool' as they searched. Suddenly Jeremy saw it too, screamed triumphantly and raced towards it, intent only on possessing it before Michael. Aunt Jane turned round to tell him to be quiet, found him nearer than she expected, stepped back startled and upset her lunch over her new dress.

Instantly she was the centre of concern. Sally sped to get a cloth, Aunt Isobel dabbed ineffectually at the dress with paper napkins until irritably repulsed, Marianne picked up the plate, the vicar said 'Oh dear,' and Ozzie Bell-Porter smiled his only genuine smile of the day.

Red with anger, Aunt Jane waved them all away. 'Don't fuss, don't fuss, it really doesn't matter,' but her angry eyes promised plenty of fuss when the family was alone.

'Say "sorry",' Paul urged Jeremy sotto voce.

'Why? I didn't spill her silly food,' protested Jeremy between resentment at his spoiled fun and embarrassment at the scene he had innocently caused.

'Don't be rude,' interposed Sally firmly. 'Please now do as Uncle Paul tells you and say you are sorry.' Unlike Paul she had not lowered her voice, and Jeremy was miserably conscious that his father was about to intervene as well. He stomped off mutinously to Aunt Jane.

'Sorry,' he grumbled.

'That's quite all right, Jeremy,' declared Aunt Jane. 'You had been made far too excited, that's all.' She glared at Paul.

21

'My fault,' he called.

'Old cow,' muttered Jeremy now at a distance where he was blessedly inaudible to Aunt Jane but distressingly near the vicar.

Paul joined Mark. 'Sorry,' he said with a grimace.

'Not your fault. If only it had been anybody but Aunt Jane.'

'Oh, no. I wouldn't want to ruin anyone else's dress. Who's Sally's latest?'

'Ozzie Bell-Porter. He was two years ahead of her in the Cambridge Union. Also wants to go into politics.'

'Ozzie? Short for Oswald?'

'Yes.'

'Bloody silly name these days.'

'What's bloody silly?' piped up Jeremy, who had approached unseen as they talked.

'Jeremy! You're becoming a positive liability,' exploded Mark with a frantic but covert glance at Aunt Jane. 'Stop showing off.'

'Why don't you and Michael put on some old clothes and play in the orchard?' intervened Paul hastily.

'Michael,' called Jeremy. 'We've got to put on some old clothes.'

'You will have to lend him yours unless his mummy has brought some,' pointed out Mark.

'Mine will be too big for him. I'm four,' announced Jeremy proudly, oblivious to the fact that Michael would be four in a fortnight and was both bigger and stouter already.

Michael, certain that old clothes meant fun, was already racing towards Marianne. Jeremy,

22

catching his enthusiasm, gave chase. Relieved, Mark saw Marianne usher both towards the house, stopping for a discussion with Claire en route.

The afternoon wore pleasantly on. The guests sat and talked, some dozing in the hot June sun. Only the vicar left early, pleading a sermon to prepare for Evensong. Mark and Claire saw him to the car which he had thoughtfully parked where no one could block him. 'Didn't want to start a whole lot of manoeuvres on a Sunday afternoon,' he commented wryly.

Presently Eric Barton, the next-door neighbour, could be heard clipping his hedge, while further away a lawnmower droned. Aunt Isobel began to snore gently and Aunt Jane nudged her awake. The men had long since abandoned the formality of jackets and more than one woman had discreetly removed her tights on a visit indoors. Champagne had been replaced by soft drinks and most of the company now sat or lay in the shade, Marianne alone preferring the sun, conscious that a tan went well with her blonde hair. Rupert was looking at her appreciatively while Peter watched him with friendly amusement.

Mark, half asleep, was irritable when Jeremy once again appeared beside him, already tired of the orchard.

'Can we play in the stream?'

'No. You know that.'

'I can swim. I'm four.'

'Not on your own. Anyway, Michael can't swim.'

'We could just paddle.'

'No.'

'Why?'

'Don't argue.'

'Can we play in the front?'

'Only if you promise not to open the gate.'

'Promise.'

'Good. Off you go.'

'Can we take Rags?'

Mark sat up and looked around the garden but failed to locate Rags, Barton's small wire-haired terrier.

'Has Rags arrived?'

'No, not yet, but we can call him.'

'I think you should leave him alone. Mr Barton wouldn't like him to play in the front. He might get through the gate.'

'He wouldn't.'

'I am not going to tell you again to stop arguing.'

'I'm not arguing.'

Mark, who had settled back on the grass, began to sit up again in exasperation. Jeremy backed off, his small mouth puckered mutinously.

'Well, if we stay in the back can we call Rags?'

'No.'

'Why?'

'Because he will run around everywhere, knocking over glasses, breaking plates, disturbing the guests and probably jumping over Aunt Jane too, dammit,' whispered Mark furiously.

'You said "dammit",' accused Jeremy.

Sally began to giggle. Her father came to the rescue.

'Come on, lad. Your dad's wanting his rest. Go and play quietly in the front and I'll come and join you in a few minutes. Got to go inside first.'

'And don't stop at the Hole,' warned Mark as Jeremy prepared to run after Sam.

'What is the Hole?' asked Bell-Porter, immediately proclaiming himself an outsider, thought Mark with unreasonable satisfaction, for the Hole and its history were famous throughout the family. It had been discovered by Rags when Jeremy was two. Claire, having gone indoors for a few seconds, while the child was playing in the garden, returned to find him incoherent with excitement and barking coming from the other side of the hedge. Thereafter each time he went into the garden Jeremy had tried in vain to peer through the thick foliage and spot Rags until about a fortnight later when the small dog suddenly exploded through the hedge and ran around the garden pursued by an ecstatic and triumphant Jeremy.

'How did he get through?' asked Claire, who then watched to see how he would get back and thus discovered the small hole at the bottom of Barton's immaculate and lovingly tended hedge. It did not take Jeremy long to learn to bend down at the Hole and call Rags's name, upon which the terrier nearly always came, sometimes being let out when one of the Bartons heard the boy calling. Somewhat to the surprise of Claire and Mark, Barton faithfully preserved the Hole, which acquired a capital letter, occasionally clipping around it to enlarge the aperture to accommodate the terrier's slight growth and to

25

prevent nature obliterating it.

'He doesn't seem to mind,' Claire told Mark, wondering at her neighbour's attitude. 'It must be because he hasn't any children of his own.'

Sam's voice, the Yorkshire vowels still strong despite decades spent in London and Sussex, floated to them on the early summer breeze as he encouraged Jeremy and Michael. Mark was unsurprised when, a few minutes later, Rags rushed barking through the Hole and tore towards the party at play in the front garden. Presently he dozed, waking to the rattle of cups to see Claire and Aunt Isobel carrying tea and the remains of the christening cake. Around him his guests woke up, yawned, eased themselves into sitting positions and consulted their watches. The children and Sam appeared from the front, Rags at their heels.

In the distance a low rumble foretold a storm.

By half past five, when the sky had darkened and Aunt Jane was certain she had felt some rain, the guests began preparing for departure. Afterwards Mark was to view the heavy cloud and distant thunder as portents, but at the time he was preoccupied merely with getting crockery, rugs and loungers into the house before the storm broke.

Marianne scooped up a reluctant Michael while Rupert helped Aunt Jane into his aged Mini. She was to stay with friends near Winchester until the following weekend when Rupert, his last exam completed, would drive her to Yorkshire where she lived within a few miles of her son and his family.

Rupert looked mildly flustered as he walked round to the driver's door; his exeat expired at seven.

'You'll do it. You've got loads of time. Good luck!' called Mark, uncertain whether the last related to the expiring exeat, the forthcoming exams, the safety of his journey or merely the enduring of Aunt Jane within the confines of a Mini for a prolonged period.

Alec and Sue Fiske left next on the long drive to Yorkshire, while Paul marvelled at the concept of family duty which had brought them so far for a christening.

The thunder rumbled again and Rags crept inside to sit in the hall. Eventually only Sally, Aunt Isobel and Ozzie Bell-Porter, who was to drive both women to Hampstead, remained.

Sally was taking crockery and napkins into the kitchen while Aunt Isobel prepared to help Claire with the washing-up. As Bell-Porter helped Mark with the chairs and rugs, Jeremy ran up to them accompanied by a barking Rags who had re-gained his courage in the face of the impending storm. Suddenly Barton whistled from the other side of the hedge and Rags raced home to his supper. Jeremy stood still and Mark laughed at his desolate expression.

'He'll play later. Now everyone's gone and you can't hit cups and saucers, why not get your ball? Rags will like it when he comes back.'

'Can I play in the front?'

'*May* I play in the front? Yes, if the gate is shut. If not, ask Mummy to close it. All those people have gone out in their cars.'

27

Jeremy ran off happily, then suddenly turned and handed Mark a five-pound note which he had extracted from deep in his pocket. 'Grandad gave it to me,' he announced proudly. 'He said you would keep it safe.'

'I'll put it in Squawky,' promised Mark, referring to his son's money box on which sat a bird which shrieked when money was inserted in its beak.

The clearing-up completed, Mark offered the three remaining visitors a drink. Bell-Porter declined on the grounds that he was driving; Sally, thirsty, took a long draught of water standing up at the sink, while Aunt Isobel asked for a small sherry. Claire ushered her into the lounge and joined her with a gin and tonic. Through the large window they could see Jeremy throwing his ball, occasionally looking at the sky, fearful that rain would stop play.

'I don't envy you getting him to bed. He's terribly excited,' commented Aunt Isobel.

'Hopefully he is also worn out.'

Presently they saw the other three emerge from the back, go to Bell-Porter's car and raise the bonnet.

'Checking oil and water,' murmured Claire.

'It's always best,' said Aunt Isobel with conviction.

The thunder rolled as Mark walked down the drive to open the gate. It was still distant and there had been no lightning yet, nor had the rain materialised, but the clouds were dark. Claire saw Mark say something to Jeremy – a warning about the storm? A prohibition against straying outside the gate? She watched Mark wedge the gate open and walk back to Bell-Porter. Later she was to remember every detail of that innocent scene.

Aunt Isobel went into the hall and picked up her handbag, and Claire remained briefly at the window to signal to Jeremy that he must not play with his ball while the gate was open. Obediently he nodded and waved. She was out in the hall with Aunt Isobel when she heard the shouts, and, with prescient fear, ran outside.

It was Sally who had first seen the rabbit, a large, white, evidently escaped pet rabbit, sitting chewing in one of the flowerbeds. Jeremy saw it a split second later and sprinted towards it. Startled, the rabbit careered madly across the lawn, dashed into the rhododendron bushes, erupted out of them, veered towards the house, changed its mind and raced towards the gate with Jeremy in hot pursuit and a shouting Mark close behind.

Jeremy was well trained with balls and knew that if one went outside the gate only a grown-up could go and get it. It was a rule which guaranteed a certain amount of frustration and tedium but nevertheless he observed it meticulously. Going outside one's own territory for balls brought trouble, as he had discovered after an innocent attempt to squeeze through the Hole in order to retrieve one from Mr Barton's garden. Apparently this was yet another thing which grown-ups regarded as rude. He also knew and obeyed the rule which forbade opening the gate, but the gate was already open and rabbits were not balls. There was no 'don't' to cover the present situation even if he had not been recklessly intent on the pursuit.

Mark nearly caught him but Claire's relief turned to horror as her husband tripped just as he was reaching out. Later she would claim that his hand actually brushed Jeremy's teeshirt.

Mark was up again in an instant: in time to see the rabbit gain the safety of the other side of the broad avenue and his son in slow motion rolling back off the bonnet of the sports car which had hit him at sixty miles an hour.

He was standing stock still, disbelieving, immobile with terror, when Claire and Sally rushed past him to the small, still body in the road.

It was Bell-Porter who called the ambulance, Bell-Porter who quietly removed the keys from the young – too young, too drunken – driver of the sports car, Bell-Porter who calmed the driver's pretty, hysterical, even younger escort, Bell-Porter who fetched a rug to cover Jeremy, and Bell-Porter who fended off curious, distressed neighbours. Bell-Porter with a firm, purposeful mouth.

It was Sally who caught a fainting Aunt Isobel, who felt Jeremy's pulse and heart, who counselled against moving him till the ambulance arrived, who gave the first explanation to the police.

Mark himself did nothing, thought nothing, felt nothing. He found it hard to understand therefore why Bell-Porter and Barton, who had arrived at the scene, were holding his arms so tightly or why the young girl who had been in the sports car was again screaming and standing protectively in front of the young man. People were talking about rabbits, neighbours were coming and going. He understood none of it.

One thing he did however understand, and light-headedly rejoice over: Claire was saying again and again, 'He's alive, he's alive. Oh thank God, thank God, he's alive.'

2

As always Mark was surprised by the mellow warmth of the London evening, the sunlight sparkling on the Thames beneath Waterloo Bridge, a shaft suddenly illuminating the Royal Festival Hall as the chimes of Big Ben proclaimed half past six. Confined to his basement office all day, his lunch usually a sandwich at his desk, Mark frequently found the climate into which he emerged at six different from the one he left at nine in the morning. This morning it had been raining fairly hard and he had been wearing the mackintosh which he now carried over his arm.

His spirits lifting on account of both the fineness of the evening and his liberation from work, Mark experienced a brief joy, feeling his step lighten. He began to swing his briefcase gently in his hand. He knew the feeling would not survive his entry to Waterloo Station, much less the squash of the always overcrowded commuter train, so when a pleasure boat passed under the bridge he yearned irrationally to be on it.

His heart sank when he reached the concourse of the station and joined an even denser than usual throng of fellow commuters.

'...and all trains are subject to cancellation and delay. We regret...'

The announcer did not sound at all regretful, thought Mark resentfully. He struggled towards a telephone, finding himself at the end of a long queue – at least he assumed it was the queue, the general crush made it impossible to be sure.

'Sorry, darling, I'll be la-ate,' sang a voice near him. Mark turned irritably and directed a baleful stare at a young man earnestly and lovingly talking into a mobile telephone. He glanced in Mark's direction, caught his stare, blushed and turned away, jauntily continuing the conversation as if the embarrassment had not happened.

'...people for Bridge tonight. She'll be furious.'

'The second time in a week. It's a scandal. You don't get this in other countries.'

'I don't know why I do it...'

'Well, I just told 'im straight, didn't I? And 'e says...'

The meaningless snippets of vapid conversation fuelled Mark's fury. He glared contemptuously at the seething throng who stood staring expectantly at the departures board, which was still as bare of information as when they had entered the station. Some read their *Evening Standards*, turning back to the beginning when they had finished in the forlorn hope of finding something vaguely interesting which they had missed the first time. Others stood chatting either because they knew each other or because they were strangers temporarily united by misfortune; others still formed uncertain queues for the telephone, the lavatory, coffee or the *Evening Standard*. Mark merely stood and indulged a loathing of them all which he knew to be as unreasonable as it was uncharitable.

'...due to emergency engineering works on the Effingham and Cobham line...' explained the announcer.

'Effingham just about sums it up,' growled someone and those near enough to hear laughed. Mark felt himself relax at the joke as he shuffled a few inches nearer the telephone, but irritation began to return when simultaneously the departure board clacked, the loudspeakers crackled with an unintelligible announcement and there was a sudden surge in the crowd. With difficulty he stood still till the movement ceased, leaving him more space and further forward in the queue. There were now so few people ahead of him he could count them. Six. There was another announcement followed by another surge, a correction and a counter-surge. Four.

'Excuse me,' said a voice nearby, 'what did they say?'

Mark turned and saw a blind man with his guiding labrador and a young woman already answering his question.

'Not Woking yet, then?' He sounded serenely

acceptant, curious not cross.

'No,' replied the girl, 'not yet, but I'm going to Guildford so we can get the same train. That way you'll know you're on the right one.'

Mark turned away, refocusing his attention on the telephone queue, knowing he should feel shamed by the blind man's patience and by the girl's cheerfulness and ready willingness to help in contrast to his own moroseness in the face of his petty suffering. He was hot, bad-tempered, frustrated and faced the loss of his leisure time, but he was not blind. Yet the satisfying shame would not come, his mood continuing un-chastened as he longed to be out in the light, fine evening, not confined to this hot, dirty, over-crowded station.

'...Walton, Weybridge, West Byfleet, Byfleet and New Haw...'

'That's ours,' said the girl. 'Slow one I'm afraid, but I don't think it's worth waiting...'

They moved off, the dog disappearing in a sea of human legs. Mark watched them, reflecting on his selfishness and the repentance which eluded him and recalled an incident of long ago.

He had been a bachelor then, young, newly qualified, settling into his first job and on that occasion planning a quiet evening watching an epic on television: the full, original version of *All Quiet on the Western Front*. As he was preparing supper, which he intended having from a tray, he felt something in his eye and during the first hour of the film the condition got worse, refusing to respond to blinking, rubbing or bathing with Optrex. Unable to enjoy his supper, he tried to take his mind off his minor ailment by concentrating on the horrors unfolding before him, but found he could not. The unremitting death and destruction of that great conflict left him unmoved in his own immediate, trivial necessity, his sense of proportion untransferable from his intellect to his emotions. So tonight, too, he could not belittle his own misery by contemplating greater ones.

There were two people ahead of him now and, transferring his mackintosh to his other arm, he began to search for change. The man now in possession of the telephone was exhorting a child to 'fetch Mummy' in a tone which gradually changed from determined clarity to uneasy embarrassment then to weary despair as he failed to obtain the appropriate response. The woman in front of Mark shuffled impatiently, visibly if not audibly sighing. The man gave up the unequal struggle with 'Tell Mummy Daddy phoned. Tell Mummy naughty trains. Poor Daddy late. Naughty trains.' Mark could imagine the exasperated look on the face of the woman in front of him as his own temper worsened and he willed this patient, inoffensive father to finish his baby talk and hand over the telephone to those who would make quick, sensible use of it.

As his wish was granted he heard his train announced and saw its platform displayed on the departures board. Agitated, he began to compute the distance to the relevant platform and to calculate the probability of the woman finishing her own call quickly and of his getting through to Claire quickly. As he stood, irresolute, balancing

35

the desirability of making the call against the possibility of missing the train, the woman said into the receiver, 'Chaos, complete chaos. No sign of the train. Expect me when you see me,' and, replacing the instrument, moved off with a purpose wholly inapposite to the uncertainty she had just described.

Mark snatched up the receiver, dropped the fifty-pence piece he had been nursing, swore, left it unretrieved and tried to insert ten pence instead. The slot was jammed. He hit home a twenty-pence piece so hard he hurt his hand and punched out the number with a furious vigour and infantile wish to hurt the machine.

Hearing the engaged signal he slammed down the receiver, scrabbled ineffectually for the dropped fifty pence, gave up and ran, inwardly cursing, for the train. His mackintosh, trailing from his arm, slipped off and tripped him up. Several commuters exclaimed in sympathy but hurried on towards the train, only one throwing a guilty glance behind her. Mark got up, grazed and furious, and limped the remaining few yards before he could squeeze himself into the already vastly overcrowded train.

He had the discipline to make sure he had dropped nothing in the fall: checking season ticket, wallet, pen and keys in the confined space where he stood jammed against other commuters, scarcely able to breathe, almost savouring the misery of his cuts and torn kneecloth, his acute discomfort becoming absolute as he realised the smell of human sweat around him was mixed with stale cigarette smoke. He was in a smoking compartment and had no prospect of escape: the crowd would thin at the first major stop but even in normal conditions that would not happen for nearly half an hour.

In the event it was two hours before he found himself walking from his train to his parked car, his knees still stinging from the fall, in the dying twilight of a summer evening. He was momentarily soothed by his release from the purgatory of the train, the fresh air and the scent of stocks in the station flowerbeds.

Turning into his own drive he noticed the sprinkler on the lawn, the water on the lupin heads, an abandoned trug full of weeds near the garage door. Claire must have been gardening until the last moment. Shutting the garage door he looked up and saw the expected pyjama-clad figure of Pippa at the window of her bedroom. She waved when she saw him looking and he returned the salute. Glancing at Jeremy's window he noticed the absence of light and the drawn curtains and felt guiltily relieved.

Mark found his wife in the kitchen, flushed and busy although the room was immaculate and he could discern no immediate cause for activity. He dimly formed the impression that his lateness was bringing her a great deal of work and inconvenience which he could not at the moment identify.

'You look worn out,' she greeted him with matching weariness, 'We guessed it was trains again. Get Pippa over while I warm up your meal.'

Mark knew, shockingly, that the callous words exactly reflected his own mood. He thought of the father at the station. How long was it since he, Mark Wellings, had spoken to his daughter with natural rather than forced patience? If Pippa were ill or upset he was immediately and actively concerned but when she was well and happy, as she was most of the time, he was content to be dutiful rather than interested, to answer rather than to converse. When she misbehaved he snapped far more often than he reasoned. Lately he had come to notice a wariness in her approach to him, and he hated himself for it.

Tonight he sat on her bed for ten minutes, responding woodenly to her account of her day: ice cream for lunch, a minor injustice at school which seemed less minor to her, wasn't Rags wonderful and please could she have a cat? Oh and Auntie Marianne and Uncle Peter had come to supper and she stayed up late and played her recorder. Sadly Mark noticed she made no effort to detain him when, during a pause in her prattle, he got up to go.

His next duty was to look in on Jeremy. He found his son not yet asleep, unfocused eyes open, saliva at the corner of his drooping mouth. Mark made a small, unnecessary adjustment to the bedclothes, cleaned away the saliva with his own handkerchief, dropped a perfunctory rather than affectionate kiss on the top of his son's head and returned the room to darkness as he left.

In the kitchen he saw a gin and tonic awaiting him on the table and grimaced – tonight he favoured a large, strong, neat whisky.

'Marianne and Peter were here,' announced Claire, without turning round from the oven from which she was extracting a casserole.

'So Pippa said.'

'Marianne helped me get Jeremy to bed. They waited for ages but in the end we went ahead with supper.'

'I'm sorry. Tried to phone but it was hell at the station and then you were engaged just as the damn train came along. Why were they here?'

'Peter had to see a client in Petworth and Marianne has an old schoolfriend there so they made rather a day of it and then rang up just before tea to see if they could come over as it was so near.'

Mark finished his drink and, going to the lounge, came back with the glass filled with whisky. Claire looked disapproving but said nothing, leaving it uncertain as to whether she disapproved of the unwashed glass, the mixing of drinks or the volume of the one he was now consuming. Probably all three, thought Mark resignedly. He sat down at the table and summoned up his courage for the disagreement he knew he was about to cause and for the oft-fought battle that he now knew it was sheer compelling necessity to win.

'We need a holiday. Both of us. Soon.'

Claire did not reply. She placed a mat on the table and the casserole dish on top of it and went to a drawer to rummage for a ladle.

'Bread with it?'

'No. Please listen to me.'

'No, thank you,' corrected Claire absently, as

though she were speaking to Pippa. 'It can't be done. Not yet.'

'Not yet? We haven't had a holiday for three *years*. How yet is yet, for Heaven's sake?'

'No. Not after last time.'

'We must. Love, I can't take any more and neither can you, even though you won't admit it.'

'You're just a bit tired and browned off with the trains.'

'Claire, please listen,' begged Mark again. Leaning forward, demanding her attention, intent on his task, he failed to notice his tie brush his food.

'Mind your tie,' said Claire. 'There's enough washing and cleaning as it is.'

Mark gritted his teeth at the familiar nag but would not be distracted. 'I said listen. Just listen.' His own anger surprised him but he was rewarded with her equally startled attention.

'You're right,' he went on, 'I am tired. That is the whole point. I am so plain, dog tired that I no longer know what I'm doing. I can't relax, I can't enjoy myself and I have no interest in anyone or anything. Other people make me furious when I ought to be amused. Tonight I was fed up with a blind man for no better reason than his failure to make sense of all the chaos.'

'What are you talking about?' Claire sounded exasperated rather than bemused.

'I'm talking about withdrawal, retreat, preoccupation. About hating a man for the grand crime of talking into a mobile phone. About wishing another poor chap to the devil just because he couldn't make his child fetch his wife,

40

about despising some silly girl because she was boasting of giving her boss what for. A normal person would have wanted to help the blind man and would have found the others funny.'

Claire's eyes strayed to his drink, but it was on his food she commented. 'It'll go cold in a minute.'

He put his cutlery down, pushed the plate away from him, folded both arms on the table and faced her angrily. Just like Pippa in a tantrum, he thought, but at least she would recognise the signs.

'And then,' he continued with forced quietness, 'I couldn't put the right change in the blasted phone box, couldn't pick it up when I dropped it and couldn't even get to the train without tripping over my own mackintosh.'

'Did you hurt yourself?'

He would not be distracted. 'And then there's Pippa.'

Mark held his wife's gaze till it fell but she fought back. 'You have it all out of proportion. Everybody gets irritable in this weather. I do – in supermarkets, for example, when someone else's child is grizzling and whining. It's all perfectly normal. You know very well that you would have helped the blind man if you had to.'

'Of course. I'm not saying I'm a bad man, merely a tired one – a very, very tired one – but I shall deserve to be called bad if I go on neglecting Pippa.'

'You don't neglect her.'

'I do. You know I do. That is why you told me to "get Pippa over" when I came in.'

41

'All parents are bad-tempered sometimes. I tell you that you're making a mountain out of a molehill.'

Mark did not reply, letting the silence lengthen between them, trying to discomfit her into facing the issue.

'Why don't you stay up in London for the rest of the week? That way you at least cut out the train hassle. Then perhaps you could persuade Inglis to let you take a long weekend. You would feel much better.'

'No–' he managed to say it gently– 'No. I will stay up in town and I will take a day or two off but only as a stopgap between now and a proper holiday, not as a substitute for one.'

Claire played her final card: 'You could go alone.'

He shook his head. 'You, me, Pippa. As soon as term ends.'

'Who will you stay with this week? Sally?'

Mark fell in with the change of subject, knowing he had won as much ground as was likely in a regularly fought battle. He determined to book the holiday anyway, presenting Claire with a *fait accompli*, and somehow to do the same with arrangements for Jeremy.

'No. It's only a fortnight since the election. She'll be too busy. I'll give Aunt Isobel a ring.' Four of his own near relations lived in London but invariably he stayed with Claire's.

'Poor Aunt Isobel,' murmured Claire automatically. 'I'll ring now.'

'She'll be in bed. It's gone half past ten. We had better try tomorrow.'

Claire started, looked at the clock and, mildly cursing the trains, bemoaned the lost evening. Briskly resuming control over a situation in which for a while she had been at a disadvantage, she sought solace in organising. She despatched Mark to bed, hinted at work yet to be done in the domestic routine and began collecting up the dishes.

Mark complied, his offer to stay and help purely token. At the head of the stairs he paused and then gently opened Pippa's door. As he stood on the threshold watching her sleep peacefully in a tumbled, disordered bed, he wondered if she had heard them arguing as she fell asleep, if it worried her or if the sound of raised, irritable voices had become normality. Staring at the bed, lit by the light from the landing, he wondered what she had been playing. Somersaults? Tunnels? He crept nearer and saw her slide hanging loose in her short, sandy hair. He had not noticed it earlier, had not told her to take it out when he had settled her. Perhaps she had put it in with clandestine vanity when he was once more downstairs and she felt safe from grown-up interdicts. Pippa loved slides and ribbons and regularly pleaded to be allowed to grow her hair into plaits.

'When you are old enough to look after long hair,' Claire would invariably respond. 'It's very hard work, it tangles and hurts to comb and takes ages to dry.'

To which, equally invariably and with earnest entreaty, Pippa would promise her hair would not tangle. Mark tidied the bed as best he could without waking her. A cat, plaits. He thought how simple her needs were and yet how steadily they were denied. The guilt nagged him as he closed her door and went to listen at Jeremy's. In this room no bed would ever be tumbled, no wish for a cat confided to God, a bear or a pillow. He could hear his son's regular breathing which, as he stood there listening, suddenly caught, seemed to stop and then turned to a loud snore. Mark held his own breath and then expelled it slowly, afraid to analyse his own brief fears and hopes.

In his own room he undressed quickly and untidily, returning from the bathroom to gaze from the bedroom window at the moonlit lawn below, the shadows of the shrubs unmoving in the still night.

It was a habit he had formed while still at school, a child from a large, happy, freewheeling family. His mother, reacting against her own strict Jewish upbringing, had laid down few rules and applied little pressure for results at school. Meals were chaotic and he, his three brothers and two sisters came and went as they pleased. Granny Wellings, his father's mother, lived near enough to provide a peaceful house in which to execute homework and his own mother's one strictly applied rule was an insistence on no noise or music after nine thirty on weekdays. Thus the older children would return from their grandmother's to work in peace when the imminence of examinations called for long hours of revision. Their rooms were cleaned thoroughly once a week but in between cleans they could be as disorderly as they pleased so long as the untidiness was confined to their space and not their parents'. The Wellings children had more lenient coming-home times than their contemporaries, less supervision over their choice of television viewing and fewer compulsory family outings.

Consequently many of his friends, restricted, directed and disciplined by anxious or ambitious parents, envied Mark while he, unsure of himself and inclined to worry, in turn and to their considerable puzzlement envied them.

Even when he was young he knew he worried more than other children. He agonised over childish lies, lost goods, neglected schoolwork and being laughed at. He hated being different, being singled out for blame or praise, having to read, sing or recite in public. Then at about eight or nine he discovered the comfort of looking out at a dark garden.

At first it merely induced a sense of security – he was glad he was indoors, safe in a lighted bedroom, surrounded by familiar things and not out there in the mysterious dark shadows which danced in the garden. He knew he would never dare go out there to retrieve anything, not even his much loved bear; it even worried him to think of the cat walking about in such a menacing environment and he wished his parents would shut it in at night.

Later, when he was less afraid of the darkness, the same exercise of looking out on the night restored a sense of proportion. During the night nothing could touch him; not teachers, tor-

45

mentors, taunts, doubts, guilt, fear, nor any pressure for work, decisions or answers. The world simply stopped and became unimportant. The garden would be the same tomorrow night as tonight and would not alter because of something he had done in the meanwhile.

Later still, when confidence began to come to him and he worried less about difficult situations, he found the night a source of promise. The moon was majestic, the stars romantic: they had looked down on history and they would look down on his personal history. As he gazed at the dark shapes of bushes he savoured the memory of how they had been sun-dappled just a few hours before and reflected that nature was wonderful and powerful. At such moments he could believe he had a great destiny.

The great destiny was a redbrick university where he gained a degree which was satisfactory but unremarkable. In his first year he fell deeply in love and looking from the window of his hall of residence across the darkened acres of landscaped gardens he found first a promise of happiness, then solace, then a sense of emptiness and desolation. In the misery of rejection he was as likely to see the dawn rise as the moon. As his work suffered and his confidence plummeted he wondered if he would still be looking at these gardens the following autumn or if he would be sent down. He survived to share with the gardens a series of hopes and fears until finals released him to the wider world.

Now, nearly twenty years later, he reverted to the habit in times of stress. Sometimes when he looked out he found himself reliving that Christening Sunday of seven years ago.

Paul had been over by that tree, Sally sitting there with whatshisname – Ozzie, that was it – Aunt Jane glaring there, Aunt Isobel chattering by those rosebeds, but the images were fading, he could no longer have described an aunt's dress or sworn to Sally's hairstyle. In his memories the dresses were of modern cut, Claire's hair was as now, the shrubs in their present state of growth, Rags no longer a young dog. He knew that he was recreating not remembering and that it was no longer spontaneous. The only image which never altered was that of the mangled body of his son, and the voice which said over and over again 'Thank God he's alive', was always that of a younger Claire.

The present-day Claire came into the bedroom, said 'Bed' in a peremptory tone and disappeared towards the bathroom from which shortly emanated the sounds and scents of a bath. Mark took his small weekend case down from the top of the wardrobe and mentally packed it, while putting off the task till the morning. He picked up his clothes from their untidy trail and indiscriminately piled them in the laundry basket, vaguely justifying his action by the necessity to 'Go away clean' as his grandmother, mother and now Claire put it. He put his suit over the back of the chair, recollected the undone work in his briefcase and the necessity of buying Aunt Isobel a present and wearily got into bed, pulling the duvet over him and yearning for the simplicity of a childhood the miserable complexities of which he had long since forgotten.

Presently Claire would come in and he would ask her if she had remembered the sprinkler and turned it off. She would say of course, someone had to remember these things and she had hoped he might be asleep by now and then she would get in beside him, turn off the light and back to back they would fall lovelessly asleep. He had it in his power to make it a false prophecy but was too weary to try.

In the morning Claire gave him a string of messages for Aunt Isobel as she packed his case and he lacked the energy to suggest she tell Aunt Isobel all this herself when she telephoned her, a task she had now reserved for herself. At breakfast Pippa rummaged through the corn-flakes for a plastic toy, the presence of which was promised on the packet, earning herself a rebuke from Claire who then relapsed into silence as Pippa fought back tears. Mark fetched a bowl, emptied the cornflakes into it and handed Pippa a green elephant.

'Conservation cereal,' he murmured, a remark neither understood by Pippa nor responded to by Claire. He turned up the radio news and Claire began chivvying Pippa. When he left for the station, Claire had still not alluded to the subject uppermost in their minds and they parted with their son's name still unmentioned between them.

3

'But what will you do about Jeremy?'

'God knows.'

Aunt Isobel gazed at him anxiously, but he thought that beneath the anxiety he could detect an uncharacteristic hint of censoriousness – though whether the reproof was for the blasphemy or for his failure to reassure her he did not know.

'It's so difficult,' mused Aunt Isobel vaguely.

'Yes, after last time.'

'I wouldn't mind staying with him, but with this awful back of mine I couldn't lift him alone any more.'

'No, he's a very big eleven.'

There was an embarrassed pause during which Isobel Renwick visibly wondered how to respond. Eleven years of age was not a stage of development readily associated with Jeremy.

'But thanks for the thought, Aunt Isobel,' Mark saved her. 'We couldn't ask it of you anyway. It's a hell of a responsibility.'

Too late Mark regretted the expletive but Aunt Isobel did not react. 'We could ask Sally, if it's in recess,' she suggested, her face bright with hope that she had discovered the answer.

They could ask Sam any damn time, thought Mark angrily. He might be older than Aunt Isobel but he was strong and fit and easily as capable of lifting Jeremy as any of the women. Now that he was leaving the management of his business to a highly capable chief executive he had plenty of time and regularly observed that he did not know how to fill it. Such a thought, however, would never occur to a Renwick. There was women's work and men's work, and the care of the sick and dependent fell firmly to the women.

He had arrived an hour ago and they were now sitting in Aunt Isobel's kitchen which was small, modern and determinedly old-fashioned. Mark, gazing at the woolly teacosy, wished sadly rather than fervently that the pot it concealed would metamorphose into a whisky decanter. Aunt Isobel's idea of a drink was a small sherry unsuitably cast in the role of nightcap. A ready supply of brandy had been Aunt Jane's one saving grace, in Mark's memory of her. In a far corner of his mind nagged a small thought that he looked to drink too often these days, but he repressed it.

He began to toy with a tassel on the teacosy. 'It wouldn't be fair. Not even in recess.'

'Well, why not employ a full-time nurse and I'll come down and stay? True, she wouldn't have much to do most of the time.'

It was a possible solution and one he had thought of. Claire would not hear of respite care after the disastrous episode when Jeremy was eight and they had left him behind for the first time while they took their summer holiday. His decline was now nearly complete and he was becoming too big to carry far with any ease, but they were not the reasons Claire had decided he should be left at home. She was worried about standards of health care in Kenya, about the difficulties of taking a child in a wheelchair on a safari holiday and about the doctor's warnings of the effect on Jeremy of a severe stomach disorder. There was also the embarrassment of Jeremy's propensity to grunt loudly for hours on end, which Claire did not want to tackle in the confines of a plane crowded with passengers wishing to sleep.

Social Services recommended a home with an excellent reputation, but it was full and so were the next four they tried. The sixth, also fully approved by Social Services, was not. It was friendly and although all the regular clientele appeared to be elderly, the proprietor assured them that all ages came for respite. The nurses were very experienced. They checked again with Social Services. The care manager was kind and reassuring: Jeremy would be in expert hands.

Claire was uncertain but Mark pressed her into agreeing. It was a good arrangement and Pippa could have three weeks' individual attention from them. They could ask someone to call in occasionally and see if Jeremy was all right.

The holiday was a success: Pippa took inexpert photographs of rhino, elephant, lions and wildebeest and Mark enjoyed his new camcorder. They went on safari in the Masai Mara and the Aberdares, travelled four hours out of Nairobi into the bush to see an African village, accompanied by a diplomat whom Mark had known at school, and ended with five days of sun and swimming in Mombasa. They returned refreshed and ready for the year ahead. Pippa was longing to tell Jeremy all about it despite the impossibility of either comprehension or response.

As soon as they arrived at their house the neighbour, a kindly and practical mother of five, who had volunteered to call on Jeremy came to tell them of her misgivings. They were due to pick him up the following day. As a consequence of what she had to say they went to the home that night and a lengthy battle with Social Services began, for while Jeremy had been fed, bathed and changed regularly, he had also been left in bed for the whole three weeks.

It would have made no difference to Jeremy. They all knew that, even as their sense of outrage grew. Blanket baths, regular turning to prevent pressure sores and adequate nutrition – all of which he had received – would have answered all his needs. Even as he shuddered away from the thought of those three weeks in Jeremy's life Mark asked himself the brutal question: For whose benefit was his son regularly transferred from bed to wheelchair to sofa and back again at night? Why all the effort to dress him, bring him downstairs, push his wheelchair to the table at mealtimes? Originally they had done this from some vestigial hope that it was Jeremy they were helping, that the television images which moved before his unfocused eyes or the noise of family laughter, no longer interpretable by his brain, were nonetheless sources of stimulation; that something they could not see was thereby kept alive.

Because the deterioration had been gradual, acceptance of its totality when it was complete had been delayed, both by a natural resistance to such a fate and by a never entirely abandoned hope that the fate was reversible. So they convinced themselves that one day Jeremy might still need the skills of dressing and eating at table. Mark had long since recognised that the only reason now for continuing these rituals was that a simple human routine confirmed the humanity of the being long bereft of visible human faculties: it insisted on normality in the face of abnormality; it sent out a cry to the world that this was still their son. Yet the world had never disputed it. Once, tired and angry, he had told Claire they were as concerned with their own consciences as with Jeremy's comfort and dignity. It was one of many things he wished unsaid in their now troubled marriage. He did not even believe it – surely even to think it was to betray Jeremy – so it discomfited him that the Judas thought occasionally returned.

It was Pippa who comforted them with her unquestioning love of Jeremy. She spoon-fed him, chattering away oblivious to his lack of response. She deposited her bear in his lap when she left for school, turned his chair – now with some effort – to face the window or the television or anything which caught her own interest, and introduced him to all her friends, none of whom looked uncomfortable. Most greeted Pippa's brother with uninhibited friendly curiosity but some, Mark noted, looked back sadly as they left and he blessed their early sensitivity and hoped life would be kinder to them.

One who never entirely gave up hope was Sally, who spent a lot of time on her visits rustling brightly coloured foil in the hope of stimulating her nephew, however minimally. Pippa, who accepted Jeremy's condition without aspiring to change it, would look at her as if she were mad, and Mark smiled faintly as he recalled the look of superior wonder she bestowed on her aunt last time, a look which had made Claire very angry on Jeremy's rather than Sally's behalf.

'What's funny, dear?' asked Aunt Isobel. Mark looked up, startled, recalling himself to the present.

'I mean, I can't think of anyone else we can ask,' said Aunt Isobel. 'Claire always says we must have someone who can lift in an emergency. Well, a nurse or one of those care people can do that, and I'll be there to make sure everything is as it should be. If we can get the right person she can move all his muscles and stimulate him and things.'

At any rate, thought Mark with grim humour, she was not going to suggest asking one of his own family: the Renwicks in general gave the impression of not quite believing his relatives existed, though they had filled three pews when he married Claire.

'I'll talk to Paul,' he said, initially to entertain himself with her reaction, and was surprised to find himself immediately convinced that in his brother he had found the solution.

While Aunt Isobel struggled to find a response appropriate to this unexpected suggestion he added, 'He has a spare room, a downstairs bathroom and a non-working wife.'

Aunt Isobel blinked. 'But would his wife love Jeremy?'

'She's an ex-nurse,' evaded Mark.

Aunt Isobel refused to be deflected. 'Yes, but would she want him? She's got a family of her own and she can hardly know Jeremy very well. It needs a very special sort of coping, dear. You wouldn't just be asking her to look after Jeremy in practical terms. It's not like parking a pet for the holidays.'

At once she realised the construction he might put on her words, and blushed.

Mark spared neither her nor himself. 'An animal would give more trouble.'

Surprisingly she rallied and fought back. 'That's exactly what I mean. A pet would demand affection, would make its needs known. Jeremy can't, and therefore whoever looks after him must love him.'

'All I want is an arrangement that will work or I will never get Claire away again. Also we can't always be asking the same people year after year. Amy will go back to work when the children are old enough, so now is the time to ask her and Paul. We'll impose on your kindness and later on Sally's another year if the offer stays open. As it is it's still going to be difficult to get Claire to agree.'

'Go to Cornwall.'

'What?'

'Holiday in this country. Phone Paul or Amy every other day. That way Claire will feel she can

55

return at the drop of a hat and you'll be getting regular reports. It will hardly be the African bush.'

She was right, thought Mark, but not Britain with its uncertain weather, dirty beaches and jammed roads. France. He would see Paul for lunch on Friday and he could consult Amy over the weekend. France. Vineyards, chateaux, sun. Pippa could try out her embryonic French.

'France,' he told Aunt Isobel, and appreciating the possibilities, she beamed happily at him, 'Why don't we have a small glass of sherry to celebrate?'

He said nothing to Claire in the two telephone conversations he had with her before Friday. She did not know Paul well and Amy, his wife, she hardly knew at all. With something approaching shock he realised Claire had only met his brother's children once. She was therefore certain to raise objections, as she had for the past three years, to whatever was proposed. If he was to win now he would have to present her with a watertight solution.

He met Paul in a City wine bar packed with lunchtime drinkers. One corner was taken over entirely by what was obviously an office farewell party, in another a few tables placed very close together were laid for lunch. They had to raise their voices to hear each other and Mark felt inhibited by the awkwardness of the favour he was about to ask.

Paul listened sympathetically, then sadly shook his head. 'Sorry. Another year I'm sure Amy would be delighted. We both would. But no can do this time. We're going to Australia for six weeks as soon as the kids break up, to stay with Amy's sister. The company have let me go with their blessing on condition I do a bit of work while I'm out there.'

He talked of Australia with enthusiasm. The children were looking forward to kangaroos and koalas, Amy had not seen her sister since she emigrated ten years ago, he had always wanted to go to the Sydney Opera House... So sorry, any other year and they would have helped...

Mark's resentment was not soothed by his utter conviction that the reason for refusal was genuine; he had been relying on this brother and had been let down. His eldest brother Christopher was unmarried, the next, John, had a working wife and a fifth-floor flat. His twin sisters, Rachael and Ruth, shared a London flat with two other working girls and a young man whose presence was a constant source of prurient speculation among their friends. His own parents were older than Sam and in any event Claire would never have consented to entrust Jeremy to Mrs Wellings' easy-going, laissez-faire household. Only Paul could have helped. Irrationally he blamed his mother for marrying *out*. In a traditional Jewish family he could never have been so deserted.

Paul saw his disappointment, and although Mark pretended to rally the conversation continued strained until they parted with relief at twenty to two.

Arriving at work Mark told Inglis, the senior partner in the tiny firm, that he was taking the afternoon off. If Inglis would have preferred a polite request he did not say so, and Mark returned to Aunt Isobel's house to discuss the only arrangement left to him – the acceptance of her offer. He then went to a travel agent and booked a three-week holiday in France on the spot. He would have preferred to take home brochures, discuss the options with Claire, share the excitement of decision, but he would give her no excuse this time. The plan must be irrevocable, its abandonment must involve a disappointed aunt, the forfeit of a hefty deposit (he had persuaded an incredulous travel agent to take fifty per cent rather than ten) and, above all, a disappointed child. Guiltily but resolutely, he planned to tell Pippa before Claire. His wife would be justifiably outraged at his using his daughter in this way but he would not be thwarted and Pippa was his strongest card. It only remained to register his request with a nursing agency and get the interviewing process under way.

The afternoon's activity coupled with the need to return to the office to pick up his suitcase meant that he returned home at his normal time. Pippa flew down the drive to open the gates for him and he wound down his window to talk to her.

'I got ten today for English and Mummy says if I get ten next week I can have a kitten. I know some ginger kittens. Mummy says they look just like little tigers...'

She prattled on while Mark was first astonished and then angry. He need not, it seemed, have been worried about Claire's reaction to his using their daughter since his wife was now being equally unscrupulous. A newly acquired, untrained kitten could not be left so soon. It was another difficulty in the way of a holiday. Doubtless Pippa would hate the thought of leaving it.

'I shall call it Marmalade,' his daughter told him happily, 'or Orlandy.'

'Orlando,' corrected Mark. 'Just remember you have to get ten first.'

'I will. I'm good at spelling,' Pippa assured him with no trace of smugness but with plenty of excited anticipation.

'Spell Orlando then,' challenged Mark, and to his amusement she did. He became resigned to the prospect of the cat and reflected that at least Aunt Isobel would love it. Despising himself, he made his own pre-emptive strike.

'We're going on holiday. To France. You can swim and speak French and stay up to supper.'

'Can we take Marmalade?'

'It wouldn't be kind so we need a dear old lady to look after him. Shall we ask Great Auntie Isobel?'

Pippa, who adored Aunt Isobel, shrieked her assent. She raced in to tell Claire while Mark, grimly satisfied, put the car away. By the time he was locking the garage door he was feeling ashamed. He had always despised parents who used their children as pawns in divorce arrangements and now he and Claire were making a pawn of Pippa within marriage.

Claire greeted him tight-lipped and without the

usual perfunctory peck on the cheek, but she was as guilty as he and both knew it. He ran through the arrangements and with enforced patience answered each objection. Pippa listened with growing excitement until Claire suddenly said, 'We had better get the cat after we come back. It isn't fair to poor Aunt Isobel.'

As Pippa wept and pleaded Mark stared furiously at Claire. Then he turned to Pippa and said quietly, 'We'll get the cat as soon as you get ten. And if you get two more tens, you can have plaits.'

Pippa's tears turned to excited joy but she looked uncertainly from parent to parent, sensing the tension, dimly aware that she was the cause of it but not understanding how. Suddenly she sobered and walked out of the room looking older and somehow burdened.

Claire fought back tears as Mark groaned and put his head in his hands. She came to him and put an arm tentatively round his shoulders, fearing a repulse. Instead he reached out suddenly and they held each other, shocked into long-forgotten closeness by mutual shame and self-loathing.

'We must never do that again,' whispered Claire. 'Never, ever again. You're right – we do need a holiday, but, Mark, if it's only France surely we can take Jeremy? Then I wouldn't worry.'

'You can still get holiday tummy in France and you know what the doctor said. He wouldn't be able to shake it off like the rest of us. Then there's the grunting. I've booked a hotel. What do we say when the people next to us complain? And don't suggest self-catering. We need a *holiday*.'

'There must be ways.'

'There are. Special places...'

'No.'

'You can't have it both ways. If we're going to be too snooty to others then we must expect that is how others will treat us.'

She moved sharply away from him, the temporary closeness shattered. 'It isn't a question of snootiness,' she said tightly.

But it was, thought Mark, as she busied herself with the preparations for supper, studiously ignoring him. He contemplated another con-frontation and then abandoned the idea with a mental shrug. They did not claim the non-means-tested attendance allowance nor invalid care allowance because Claire proclaimed that no Renwick had ever depended on the state and that they did not need it. The latter was true but the former was the driving motivation. Jeremy was attended by private nurses at great expense because Claire would not avail herself of care assistants whom she insisted on regarding as second best. She drove a ninety-mile round trip each day for two years because she regarded only a private special school as right for her son, until she exhaustedly withdrew him on the doubtless valid grounds that they could provide as much at home for Jeremy as any school could.

Mark stood up and began to lay the large farmhouse table where they took most of their meals. Claire still had not spoken nor Pippa returned when the task was finished and he went

61

in search of Jeremy, whom he found lying on the lounge sofa, his head propped sideways so that his unfocused eyes could gaze uncomprehendingly at a video now playing on the television screen. *Jack and the Beanstalk.* He had loved the story as an infant, before a drunken driver had robbed him of the capacity to enjoy anything again.

Mark pulled up his wheelchair and lifted him into it, then, switching off video and lights, he pushed him towards the kitchen, calling Pippa on the way. Claire had already served the meal and they assembled round the table, Pippa's air of uncertainty as completely evaporated as if it had never existed. She talked of Marmalade and France and took her turn at gently inserting the spoon into Jeremy's mouth.

Halfway through the meal Jeremy started grunting and Pippa, endeavouring to concentrate on a complex tale of kittenhood, was uncharacteristically irritated. 'Hush!' she commanded and resumed her story. Jeremy's grunts grew louder and as both Claire and Mark turned to soothe him, Pippa lost her temper.

'I'm talking. It's rude not to listen. Why does he always spoil things?'

'Don't speak to us like that,' said Claire sharply.

Pippa pushed her plate away and stood up. 'It's not fair,' she shouted, tears spurting from her eyes.

'Sit down,' ordered Claire, trying to quieten Jeremy with a spoonful of food.

Pippa instead stamped out, wailing loudly and slamming the door. 'Leave her,' said Mark.

'We're all under the weather. If you try to insist on an apology now it will be hopeless. She'll miss her pudding and come back.'

'She needs a smack, not pudding.'

'She needs attention and hasn't been getting it.'

'Then perhaps you should stay at home all day and give her some.'

They were bickering again, thought Mark. The truce had lasted less than half an hour. The rest of the evening was no more successful. Pippa did not return for dessert and was still complaining when Claire put her to bed. When he went up to read her a story she pulled the blankets over her head and told him snufflingly to go and read to Jeremy instead because it was Jeremy he loved not her. Taking over the task of bathing Jeremy, who grunted loudly throughout the operation, he was frustrated by his son's immediately soiling his clean pad. By the time he ventured into the garden for some late watering he found the summer gnats had arrived in force. They went to bed early, neither looking forward to the weekend.

On Saturday morning, when Claire had taken a subdued Pippa to her riding lesson, Sam telephoned. He had decided to float his company, sell his shares and retire on the proceeds.

'Reckon seventy is the time to go. The old business has done pretty well. Never thought I'd be floating it one day when I started it in Tom's yard. Wish Graine had seen it. She was always telling me to get a proper job so we'd know what the wages would be and your Aunt Jane wouldn't right own me as her brother. But it's champion now.'

Mark listened to the reminiscences with fondness. Sam had been good to them when they were starting the marriage and no request for help had gone ungranted when they embarked on the long course of expensive treatment following Jeremy's accident. He also knew that a flotation would mean long hard hours for his own firm, which Sam still used despite the huge growth in his business even if he had for many years also used other firms for explicit tasks. He would resign before he sacrificed his holiday, he told himself fiercely. Miserably he recognised that her father had unwittingly handed Claire another weapon to add to her armoury of resistance.

Sam chatted on for some time until it was Mark's turn, when he seized the opportunity to tell him about the holiday. Sam approved vociferously, although adding that he never could see why folks would not be content with their own shores. He and Graine had had some champion holidays at Scarborough.

'Hope the flotation doesn't get in the way,' Mark murmured, trying to sound casual.

'Eh? Oh, I see. No, I'll tell Inglis...'

Mark grinned. His father-in-law had been quick on the uptake as usual, and he knew Inglis was putty in the hands of the man whose custom now accounted for over half of the firm's business.

Claire and Pippa returned at lunchtime, the latter making a beeline for Jeremy to tell him about her ride, now seemingly oblivious of the grunts which last night had so upset and frustrated her. After lunch Claire changed Jeremy and settled him in his chair under the lilacs. Pippa had invited a friend for tea and they paddled in the stream at the bottom of the garden. Claire kept an eye on them as she gardened. Barton began to clip his hedge. Predictably Rags wandered through the Hole and joined the girls in the stream, who shrieked delightedly as he hurled himself in and splashed them. Jeremy's grunts ceased as he fell asleep.

Mark, sharpening a pair of shears in the garage, heard the telephone ring again, briefly debated whether to answer it, then went inside. It was Sally. For a while they chatted about Sam's forthcoming flotation and her impressions of Parliament, he passed on news of Aunt Isobel (poor Aunt Isobel, said Sally) and she rejoiced in the forthcoming holiday and the proposed acquisition of Marmalade. After ten minutes Mark still had no idea why she was ringing, then she said, 'There is something I think you should know.'

Mark felt an uneasy premonition of bad news.

'I came second in the ballot for Private Members' Bills,' went on Sally. 'I've decided to do one on legalising euthanasia.'

4

'Apparently it's purely to deal with the terminally and painfully ill who are mentally able to make a decision.' Mark had delayed telling Claire about Sally's call until well after Pippa's bedtime. Now he sought to reassure her with an answer to a question she had not asked. 'It's voluntary euthanasia and only voluntary euthanasia.'

'How could she?'

'Presumably because she believes in it.'

'That's all very well. What about us? It's not as if she were doing a Bill on the Little Puddleton Relief Road. It will be big, emotive, high-profile stuff and it will take the press all of five minutes to find out she has a handicapped nephew. You must realise that?'

He had been thinking of little else since Sally's call and Mark's principal reaction now was relief that he did not have to explain the consequences of the Bill to Claire, that she was so quickly alert to its implications.

'We shall simply point out that Jeremy is not affected by any of this. Of course it's always possible that they may focus on Graine's death instead. If so, Sam should be more than a match for them.'

Claire rarely spoke of her mother's death and when she did it was usually in terms of its effect on the infant Sally. Unable to find the words to ask what he knew he must he paused, hoping she would answer it anyway. She did.

'Mother suffered for a long time. He won't want to relive all that.'

Mark absorbed the statement in silence. Claire sat watching him, her mouth tense and resentful as she thought of her father. He knew she was unhappy but she looked merely sulky, as if she were about to nag, not cry. Dutifully rather than sympathetically he put out a hand to cover hers but she snatched her own away. It did not hurt him although he knew it should have done so: her action was an honest acknowledgement of the state of their marriage. Today, in the garage, before Sally had telephoned, he had been thinking of making a similar acknowledgement and forcing her to confront the issue. Now he could not.

'Sally said something about a press announcement on Monday. I hope she's thought to tell Aunt Isobel, otherwise she might get upset.' Aunt Isobel was still as protective of Sally now as she had been when bringing her up and Mark was uncertain as to how she would react when Sally became the object of fierce, public criticism.

'Oh, she probably told her Izzymum before she told her father. You're right about Aunt Isobel but it's him I'm thinking of. I wish Sally had consulted us all first. She hasn't been very thoughtful.'

'I'm not sure we're being very thoughtful if it comes to that. We might try thinking about your sister. It takes courage to introduce that sort of Bill – courage and conviction.'

67

'Courage can sometimes be destructive – and so can conviction,' Claire was retorting, when the telephone rang and she sprang to answer it, leaving the lounge door open as she went into the hall. Mark listened to her opening responses and was relieved the call was not from a member of the family, but from a friend of long standing who regularly kept Claire on the telephone for anything up to half an hour at a time. Claire frequently lamented the length of these calls while giving every impression of enjoying them while they lasted, chiefly, Mark thought, because they consisted of scandal about mutual friends. He shut the door quietly and made a guilty visit to the drinks cabinet.

Courage and conviction or destructive recklessness? A generation ago, the debate would have raged in his own family when his mother married *out*. That, he reflected, took courage – the courage to hurt loved ones, to forsake the comfort and safety of a wealthy home, to take a risk in an age when women took few risks. But would he apply the same word to her calling her first four children by the most aggressively Christian names she could think of? Was that not rather mere bravado, ostentatious defiance?

He remembered his maternal grandfather: gentle, occasionally playful, looking at the world through sad rather than angry eyes, and was glad that a reconciliation, commemorated in the names of his twin sisters, had been effected before he died.

Sally now faced the world with courage. Of that, despite her sister's anger, he was convinced.

It remained to be seen whether she would avoid the pitfalls of recklessness as she carried through her resolution.

Courageous was not an adjective he could yet apply to any of his own siblings and certainly not to himself. Paul had once grown a vast, long beard and shocked his relatives, to say nothing of Claire's Aunt Jane, but it betokened conformity with rebellion rather than rebellion against conformity and disappeared at the first hint of promotion.

As for him, Mark Wellings, he hadn't the courage to tackle his wife on the subject of their deteriorating marriage. He did not want a divorce while Pippa was so young but he saw no prospect of even a comfortable, quiet *modus vivendi,* much less the rekindling of a once bright flame. He dared not ask himself if he still loved Claire because he was afraid of the answer and its challenge.

Claire returned, frowned faintly at his too-obviously replenished glass, and began to relay scandal. Mark allowed the topic to be exhausted and then, with a steady determination which soon became genuine enthusiasm, he began to talk of their holiday. His wife listened as he waxed lyrical about the Loire Valley and sun-drenched beaches, hearing him out before embarking on a long list of preparations they must make. It was all work, her tone implied, and work which she herself would have to do in order to gratify his selfish desire for a family holiday. Refusing to rise to the bait he patiently commented on passport renewals, currency transactions, washing, packing, stocking the refrigerator for Aunt Isobel and the nurse, getting the car serviced, house-training Marmalade... She was in the middle of rehearsing all the instructions she would have to leave for the care of Jeremy when the telephone shrilled again and Mark went to answer it.

'What a lass we've got, eh? She's got guts, our Sal. Wish her mum had lived to see it,' boomed Sam, and Mark was surprised to find himself not relieved but resentful. So he had wanted Sam to pressure Sally into dropping the idea for her Bill, had wanted him to feel it inappropriate, to tell her it was not in the best interests of the family. Instead he was happy and excited about it. Claire would feel cheated of her concern on her father's behalf. Mark felt obliged to ask if Sam had thought about the press but he did not mention Graine, and if she was in Sam's thoughts he concealed it well.

'Aye, they'll want to know everything. No harm in wanting, lad, but I'll not be giving 'em owt.'

Easy to say, thought Mark as he called Claire and heard her greet her father cheerfully. Seconds later her voice took on an irritable tone, then a positively belligerent one. Evidently she too was affronted by Sam's equanimity. To avoid an argument when she had rung off he began to tidy the lounge for the night, pulling back the curtains, plumping up cushions, unplugging the television, but his precautions were unnecessary for she called out 'I'm off to bed' and left him to his own company.

He knew he should go to comfort her but it

seemed too great an effort. Slowly, giving her time to get to bed and fall asleep, he began to lock up the house for the night.

After that they talked little of either Sally's Bill or the holiday as the summer term neared its end and the heat and commuting wore Mark's patience thin. At work Mark became immersed in Sam's flotation and persuaded Inglis to take on more staff for the autumn, at school Pippa obtained three more tens and at home Claire resigned herself to both cat and plaits. Returning late one Friday evening Mark went to say good-night to his daughter and found a small ginger cat on her bed. Pippa, instead of being ecstatic, was in tears.

'It's my cat,' she sobbed. 'I can call him what I like.'

Mark, unwarned by Claire and sensing danger, trod warily. 'I thought you were calling him Marmalade.'

'That's a stupid name. I hate it.'

'Well what about Orlando?'

'No,' wailed Pippa wretchedly.

'What do you want to call him?'

'Jeremy, and Mummy says I can't. It's not fair.'

'Well, it might be a bit confusing having two Jeremies. I mean if Mummy says "Jeremy" how do we know which one she means?'

'Lots of children have the same name as their parents,' countered Pippa. 'They don't get muddled.'

Mark stared. Had she really just thought up that argument on the spur of the moment or was she copying something she had heard a grown-up say? Briefly he glimpsed the future in which ten years hence Pippa would argue with him and Claire on equal and sometimes conquering terms. Tonight, however, he must win.

'Why don't we call him Jem or Jimmy? Something nearly the same but a little bit different?'

'No. It's *my* cat. You said I could name him.'

'Why do you want to call him Jeremy?'

'After Jeremy. He will never be able to have a little boy to call Jeremy. Mummy says so.'

'Well, you can call your little boy Jeremy when you are a mummy.'

'My husband might not like it,' said Pippa gravely and was immediately offended by Mark's mirth, which was renewed helplessly when he repeated the conversation to Claire.

'Oh she's always saying that these days,' Claire told him. 'It's her standard response if I tell her she can do something or other when she's a lady. Somehow I don't think our daughter will be much of a feminist.'

'We can't let her call the cat Jeremy. People might misinterpret it.'

'Don't worry. By this time tomorrow it will be called Tiddles or something.'

He believed her, knowing she had a way with Pippa when talking her out of something on which she had set her heart, but what, he wondered, had caused the sudden rejection of Marmalade and Orlando?

'The discovery that there were already two Marmalades and one Orlando owned by members of her class, to say nothing of a Marmaduke, an Alphonsus and an Obadiah. I reckon I've heard the names of every pet of every child in the school. One even has a snake called Schweppes.'

There was something wrong, some underlying anxiety beneath the light-hearted talk, something which had probably stopped her taking an interest in the names Pippa's classmates had inflicted on their pets, thereby contributing to his daughter's distress. He wondered if the subject of white rabbits had come up, but not even that would account for his wife's preoccupation. However much constraint there was between them now, there were habits of closeness which did not die and each could always sense when the other was tormented.

He watched and waited but her conversation remained superficially cheerful.

'What is it?' he asked gently.

She threw him a startled look but said nothing, tossing a salad with unnecessary vigour and stiffening when he approached her. Undeterred he turned her to face him and suddenly she gave in, burying her face against his chest while a tiny moan turned to deep-drawn, shuddering sobs. It was some time before she pulled away, sniffing, to locate a handkerchief. She made to sit down at the table but Mark stopped her, guiding her instead to the pair of rocking chairs by the Aga. She sat on the edge of one, her feet firmly on the ground, leaning forward, tense, watchful. Mark adopted a similar position.

'What is it?' This time he spoke insistently.

'There is to be a new child at Valence Towers in September.'

She did not elaborate, waiting for him to deduce the rest, but he could not. He assumed there would be an entire new year's worth of children at Pippa's large, mixed, preparatory school and he knew of no child who had ever made his daughter's life difficult.

'Philip Cooper.'

The name did nothing to clear his confusion. It was an unremarkable, solidly English name. He might have known a dozen Philip Coopers or none. He thought he knew none.

An exasperated edge entered Claire's defeated tone. 'Son of Robert.'

He felt the shock as a physical blow. Robert Cooper. He remembered him as he had last seen him, nineteen years old with a place at Oxford but destined instead for prison. He remembered his white, pinched, shamed, face as the judge sentenced him to two years while his parents wept quietly in court and Paul cried out with audible anger and a fierce expletive that it was not enough. The judge, turning to reprove the bearded, noisy individual who had the temerity to comment so profanely on his sentencing, saw he was with Mark and Claire and visibly swallowed his ire.

Even then Mark knew that it was enough, that the judge had got it right, that the young man in the dock faced a life sentence from his own conscience, but he hated him then and he hated him now. Robert Cooper, the killer in all but death of his son.

Neither of them had seen him since, although he was from an address only four miles from them. In court it had emerged that he was the younger son of a senior civil servant and a gynaecologist who practised at a London hospital. The following autumn he would have taken up a scholarship at Christ Church, Oxford, where he would have been a contemporary of Rupert Fiske. On that Sunday he had been celebrating the birthday of his girlfriend. They had both had too much to drink and argued with each other and with his parents before driving off furiously in his elder brother's sports car without his permission. Young, privileged, irresponsible, heedless of loving advice from their families, they had been catapulted into responsibility in the most horrible way.

'He can't have lost much time when he came out,' commented Claire bitterly, 'though he wouldn't have done the whole two years, I suppose. Whose side is the law on? I wonder if that awful girl is the mother? She may have waited for him.'

'I doubt it. As I recall it she was only sixteen. How did you find out about Philip Cooper?'

'Another parent who knew him and knew what had happened told Jake James when she found out he had accepted him. He's horrified. Had no idea.'

Jake James was the name of the sixty-year-old headmaster who ruled the school with old-fashioned discipline, firm purpose and a huge sense of humour. He was a religious man who believed in redemption and forgiveness, and

75

Mark could only imagine his present torment.

'What is he going to do?'

'He asked me to discuss it with you and speak to him tomorrow. Dear God, Mark, what is there to discuss?'

'Plenty.' Mark's mouth twisted.

During the ensuing silence Claire got up and dragged herself back to the salad. 'I'm not hungry,' she said. 'Are you?'

'No. Leave it. Come back here. First of all, if we decide to protest I'm coming with you to see Jake James...'

'If?' Claire's voice rose hysterically.

'If. Let's try and work it all out. We have nothing against Philip Cooper himself, have we? He's only four or five and he has as much entitlement to be educated at Valence Towers as Pippa. He will be three years behind Pippa and she won't be mixing with him. Indeed but for the good offices of your friend we might never have known. Against that there lies the probability that sooner or later we will run into his father at Speech Day or at a parents' evening. Well, if we all know that's a risk we can doubtless enlist Jake James' help in avoiding it, or we can simply face up to it. Nothing obliges us to speak to Cooper even if we do run into him. The real problem is probably Philip Cooper's. Other children can be cruel and they may find out his father went to prison.'

'How can you be so cold-blooded? What about Pippa? Supposing she finds out? Supposing some obliging little busybody points at darling Philip and says "His daddy ran over your brother". What then?'

'We shall already have told her. Before next term. We shall tell her in somewhat more comprehensible language that the sins of the father are not to be visited upon the next generation.'

Claire was watching him in outraged disbelief. 'Your grandfather might have said otherwise.'

There was a dreadful silence. Never had he thought the taunt possible – and nor had she, as he realised when she blanched and crumpled miserably. He stayed calm but was appalled to find he was looking at her without sympathy. Another precious jewel of their marriage lay shattered.

'I'm sorry,' floundered Claire, running her hands distractedly through her hair. 'I didn't mean that. I don't know where it came from.'

'From a desire to hurt. It worked.'

'I'm sorry.' It was a whisper, low, ashamed, shocked.

He refused to give comfort but returned to the subject in hand. 'We shall not object.'

She could not oppose him now though she wanted to with every fibre of her being. She twisted in her chair, guilty, humbled, furious. He had sufficient pity to say more, but he spoke coldly.

'Consider this. If we object and they kick up a fuss there could well be a controversy which would drag in Pippa. Oh hell...'

Suddenly they both saw the implications, realisation triggered by the word 'controversy'. Sally's Bill. The press. If they started chewing over the details of the accident, tracing the parties involved, they would assuredly find out that the victim's sister was at the same exclusive, expensive school as the perpetrator's son. For a moment hostility was suspended by shared horror, then Mark called them back to reality.

'This is all nonsense. The Bill is about fully competent, terminally and painfully ill adults, not about the Jeremies of this world. Sally is Jeremy's aunt, not his mother. We are letting our imaginations run riot. I will phone Jake James tomorrow and suggest he has a quiet word with Cooper, pointing out the possible problems for his son. If he still decides to go ahead we will live with it. The Coopers are local: we haven't run into them yet, but we might any time. We will merely be living with an enhanced risk of that.'

'You talk like a calculating machine.'

'I apply my mind. I think we should sleep on what I've just said. You may wish to take other advice.'

'I beg the calculating machine's pardon. I should have said you talk like a bad lawyer. "Other advice"!'

They were raising their voices. Mark thought of Pippa, repeated in lower but urgent tones 'Let's sleep on it', and went to pour a nightcap.

Claire followed him. 'You're drinking on an empty stomach.'

He ignored her. She came close and touched his arm: 'Mark, I'm sorry. I didn't mean what I said about...' Her voice trailed off but she looked at him pleadingly.

He did not shake her off, but he stood stiffly unresponsive until she turned from him with a small, inarticulate sound of misery. She did not follow him upstairs for a long time and he waited at the window, looking out over the garden, hating and pitying himself and his wife, no longer finding solace in the prospect of a holiday which would throw them upon each other's company all day every day for three weeks.

Eventually she came upstairs and took the cat from Pippa's room. He heard her go down again, talking to it, and wondered irrelevantly how she addressed it when it had no name.

When finally she came to bed she said, 'You're right about the holiday. I need it too,' and, not waiting for a response, switched out her lamp and closed her eyes. Mark, looking down at her sleepy form, trying to love her and not succeeding, knew that sleep would elude him for most of the night.

In the event neither of them was blessed with an untroubled night. Pippa was sick and called Claire at two and again at four. The cat jumped on Mark and purred happily. The telephone shrilled at five and when Mark fearfully picked it up a voice demanded a taxi. By breakfast Pippa was too ill to go to school, Claire worried, tired and snapping, and Mark facing a day's hard grind of which he did not then feel remotely capable.

The telephone on his desk was ringing when he arrived. Jake James. Claire had reported Pippa sick but had dodged the issue of Philip Cooper. Mark explained the position and the Head promised to let him know the outcome of his conversation with Cooper. Emerging from a meeting at eleven he was accosted by the secretary he shared with two other partners.

'A Mr Cooper telephoned. He said he'll call back.'

Mark stared at her, mentally denying what he had just heard, shock temporarily robbing him of speech.

She consulted her notebook. 'Mr Giles Cooper of Cooper, James and Cooper.'

He relaxed momentarily until he thought suddenly that Giles and Robert could be related. The older brother? Angrily he took himself in hand. This was just a coincidence, he told himself, but even when he was proved right his hand continued to shake. He knew his colleagues looked at him oddly and it was no surprise when Inglis summoned him in the early afternoon and asked if he were all right.

He told him the whole story because it was less effort than prevaricating and Inglis said he must go home, of course, and help Claire with their sick daughter and sort out the unfortunate business with the headmaster and recover from such an unpleasant experience and get some sleep. Mark replied that he was grateful but there was no need to take up this kind offer: there was no emergency with Pippa, the Head would telephone in due course and he would prefer to stay at work.

Inglis said he quite understood but if Mark changed his mind he should not hesitate to say so, after which conversation – as pointless as it was insincere – they both applied themselves to Sam's flotation and it was eight o'clock before anyone left the office.

Yet he returned home happier than he had left, for Jake James had rung to say the Coopers were horrified to find that Pippa was at Valence Towers, that Philip had been accepted in another two schools and that they would now be choosing one of them. They had asked particularly after Jeremy and he, James, had told them what he could. Mark listened relieved to the first part of this news and to the second part unmoved. He wished the Coopers no active harm but neither had he any forgiveness to offer.

At home Claire told him that Pippa's stomach upset was worse and she was banned from seeing Jeremy. He, Mark, must not disturb her as she was now asleep. Oh, and the cat was called Montefiore.

'Montefiore?'

'After Bishop Hugh. He was pontificating away about something or other on the television today and Pippa kept asking me what his name was because she couldn't say it properly. Then I bet her that no one at school had a cat called Montefiore. We giggled over the name a bit and Bob's your uncle and Montefiore's your cat. Before you ask, yes she can spell it.'

'I'm all admiration,' declared Mark, and meant it.

'At my tactics or her spelling?'

'Both.'

'Mr Barton thinks it's a pretentious name.'

'Did he say so?'

'Gracious, no. It was just the expression on his face when I told him. I wanted to warn him

81

about the cat because of Rags.'

'Well if you call your dog Rags, you probably do find Montefiore a bit of a mouthful. Perhaps we can call it Monte for short.'

'*Verboten*, I'm afraid. By Pippa. I tried.'

He laughed. He was laughing at Pippa and her choice of name, at the prospect of calling 'Montefiore, Montefiore' and imagining the expression on the Bartons' faces, at their fears about Cooper and his own nervous reaction to today's coincidence, at the sudden unity in the wish for a holiday and the thought of Pippa earnestly building sandcastles, at Inglis's unctious tones, at the way everything had changed from dark to light in twenty-four hours.

He repressed the memory of Claire's cruel gibe but could not quite repress the small, inner, nagging voice which, even as he laughed, told him things also went from light to dark with equal speed.

5

Pippa again had a bad night and was now missing the last day of the summer term. Her consolation was Montefiore, who spent most of his time in her room, a happy arrangement for Claire.

He had arrived already half trained and was proving a lighter burden than she had expected. Twice when Claire looked into Pippa's room she found them both asleep, but at midday the kitten wandered into the kitchen and appropriated one of the rocking chairs by the Aga.

Thinking her daughter might be feeling deserted Claire again went to her room, but she was still asleep. Frowning, Claire glanced at the Paddington Bear clock by Pippa's bed. Twelve forty. She crept to the bed and gently laid her hand on the child's forehead, finding it hot. Pippa stirred, woke and was immediately and prolifically sick. She began to cry. Claire decided to call the doctor, who arrived shortly after lunch.

Pippa's temperature had soared, she was too weak to get out of bed and the sickness was now accompanied by diarrhoea. The doctor was reassuring: there was an infection going round, lots of children had caught it, including two of his own and half the top class at the local primary. It was nasty and had worried many a parent but it was harmless. Pippa would feel better in a day or two and would be completely normal in three or four days. She should drink lots of water meanwhile.

However it was an infection, he emphasised gently, and not just an upset, so they must continue to keep the children apart. Pippa must not be allowed near Jeremy for at least two more days. Then, as was his habit when called to the Wellings household, he asked to see the boy.

Jeremy was lying on his activity mat in the playroom. By his side lay the foil and bells which Claire had been rustling and ringing earlier in the day. A huge mobile of rabbits and hedgehogs swung above him. In the background a cassette played 'A Windmill in Old Amsterdam'. Inert, oblivious, dribbling, the child was bathed in a sunbeam.

If the doctor knew that Claire's heart was broken afresh each time she entered this room he gave no sign. He knelt down beside the child and began to feel his muscles: he stretched and bent each limb, examined his eyes, ears, throat, gently tested the jaws for any hint of a swelling which might have indicated a painful tooth, removed his pad and examined the deposits, held a thermometer in Jeremy's mouth. It was a thorough, professional, concerned performance which left nothing to chance.

'It all looks OK. No sign of infection. He still eats?'

Claire nodded. She dreaded the day when Jeremy might need to be fed by tube. She was assured he still had movement above the neck but his head always hung slackly and he could not chew. He could no longer suck through a straw. She had not known him sniff in months and the small twitch which would occasionally afflict his eyes or his mouth had similarly disappeared. All that was left was a capacity to swallow safely liquidised food with the head held at a certain angle. Not that there was much active swallowing now. There must soon be a real danger of choking and that would mean the final indignity of a tube. Then only the grunts would be left, those meaningless, intrusive, often seemingly unending sounds which irritated them all. Dear God, don't let him ever stop grunting.

They talked of the holiday arrangements. By

chance the doctor knew the nurse and warmly approved the choice. Aunt Isobel must feel free to ring him at any time and he would come immediately. Jeremy would be safe, loved and well cared for.

He, Neville Harris, could guarantee it. It was imperative that Claire and Mark should relax and give some full-time attention to Pippa. Few of his patients more deserved a break.

Claire heard him gratefully. Once when a well-meaning friend had suggested that they should move away from the house with its daily reminders of the accident, the gate, the garden, the road, and start afresh somewhere completely new, Claire had cited Doctor Harris as a reason not to do so and had never repented of the decision.

When she opened the front door for him, he parted from her with a light pat of encouragement on her shoulder.

It rained all afternoon, huge drops running in rivulets down the window panes as she read to Pippa, who was now too fractious to enjoy it, and attended to Jeremy. Montefiore remained resolutely by the Aga, opening one eye to look at her when she entered the kitchen. As she was just beginning to contemplate preparations for the evening meal Mark rang to say that if he was to clear his desk by the following Tuesday, his last day in the office before their holiday, he must work late, probably very late. She should go ahead and eat. He would not require more than a sandwich. As he spoke she could hear the laughter of colleagues in the background and the clack of word processors and, reflecting that the office had become a lively place with the impending flotation, she wondered how many more evenings there might be like this.

By eight o'clock both children were asleep, Pippa restlessly.

Claire put Pippa's soiled bedlinen in the washing machine, switched it on, gave Montefiore his feed, cut Mark's sandwiches, wrote him a note saying she had gone to bed early, security-locked every window and the back door and went upstairs.

Pippa and Jeremy were still asleep. She looked in on them once more when she emerged from her bath.

She was woken by Mark saying, 'Quick! Jeremy! Wake up!' She struggled towards consciousness, blinking in the light Mark had turned on. He was in his pyjamas and she realised that he must have been home for some time although neither the headlights of his car nor the sounds of his entry had woken her. By the time she was sitting up, absorbing that it was gone four in the morning, Mark had left the room. Then she remembered what he had been saying and with icy fear ran to her son's room.

By the time he woke Claire, Mark had already extracted the vomit from his son's throat, laid him in the recovery position and called an ambulance. He had not had time to deal with the effects of the diarrhoea which had struck simultaneously but he had felt the heat coming from Jeremy's body and knew him to be running a high temperature. Now as Claire appeared he said, 'Get Pippa up.' They would both have to go with the ambulance and could not leave her alone, ill or not.

While Claire dressed, then woke and wrapped up Pippa he set about cleaning up his son. He considered carrying him downstairs but on reflection preferred to leave him for the ambulancemen to move. They would be here any minute. When Claire returned he went to dress, listening grimly to Pippa's moans of protest.

Twenty minutes later there was still no sign of the ambulance, Pippa's moans had turned to a long grizzling whine and Claire was going distractedly from one child to the other though their separation now seemed superfluous, with the certainty not only that Jeremy was already infected but that he and his sister would shortly travel in the confines of the same ambulance.

Deciding to risk both moving Jeremy and putting the children together, Mark assembled them all in the hall. Pippa twisted in the blanket Claire had wrapped round her, whimpered miserably and was sick.

'It's no good,' said Claire, despair in her voice. 'She'll have to stay and one of us will have to stay with her.'

They both looked at Jeremy, remembering the repeated warnings they had received about any sort of enteritis, neither wanting to stay behind, both knowing it must be Claire, that she was the parent Pippa would want when ill. Resignedly she gathered Pippa up and prepared to take her upstairs.

The ambulance had still not arrived when Claire came down to report Pippa peacefully asleep.

'Where the hell is it?' she demanded, uncharacteristically profane in her anguish. 'It's nearly an hour since you rang. What did they say?'

'They said they would send one as soon as possible. I'll ring again.'

'You did tell them Jeremy is special?' Claire's tone was sharp with an anxiety born of dawning realisation which suddenly crystallised into horror as Mark hesitated.

'Mark! Half the children in Surrey are down with this. Neville Harris said it had frightened umpteen parents. They probably think you're fussing. Oh, God, ring again, ring again!'

Mark was already doing so. In truth he could not remember exactly what he had said the first time, although he had certainly indicated danger to his son's life. Surely the law stipulated that the ambulance must come merely because it had been called? This time he left no room for doubt. He had telephoned over an hour ago. No ambulance had come. His son was severely handicapped and his immune system would not be up to coping. Did they want a death on their conscience and in the press? As soon as possible would no longer do. He must know precisely.

'Twenty minutes,' he told Claire.

'Should we take him ourselves?'

'No. It will only mean a major hassle at A and E.'

'His temperature is awful. I'd better take it.'

Claire went upstairs for the thermometer, leaving Mark to wonder why she wanted to know what was bound to increase her anxiety but which she could not remedy, even as he put his hand on Jeremy's forehead and grimaced at the heat. 'Come on,' he urged the distant ambulance.

Montefiore appeared and walked to the door before turning to look at Mark. They had not yet let him out and Mark did not want a further worry to add to the day ahead. He picked up the kitten and took him through to his litter box in the utility room.

'One hundred and three.' Claire took the thermometer from Jeremy's mouth as Mark came back into the hall.

A siren wailed faintly in the distance and Claire ran to open the door. Mark walked to the gate listening to the sound becoming louder and nearer, praying that it was for them and not a source of false hope.

'I'll try and join you later,' called Claire as he climbed into the ambulance. 'I'll ring Nurse Allen.'

Nurse Allen came twice a week to help with Jeremy, bathing him, weighing him, applying ointments at the slightest sign of pressure sores, trying new methods of stimulation, dreaming up new foods to meet his dietary requirements, above all remaining with Jeremy for hours at a time so that Claire could leave the house with confidence. She had once been a full-time nurse in the children's ward of the local hospital but was now a mother of a small child herself. The child, Melissa, had Down's Syndrome.

At the hospital, where they put Jeremy in a side ward and attached him to a drip, Mark realised it was Claire who should have come as he struggled to answer questions put by a doctor who, though calm even after a fraught night, was having difficulty concealing his frustration at Mark's inability to provide information. In the end he took a note of Claire's telephone number and went off to obtain from her the details of Jeremy's meals that day, the last time she had checked him that night and what the pads had contained when she last changed him.

The paediatrician arrived half an hour later, having been called from his bed. Mark did not know him. Every three months Claire took Jeremy to London to consult a top consultant at exorbitant cost because she believed private treatment guaranteed better quality. Now that their son was bigger and more difficult to transport, Mark went too. He had never particularly liked the London paediatrician although he was undeniably clever, competent and kind, but he liked this man instantly. He introduced himself as David Trotter, examined Jeremy, held a sotto voce conversation with the doctor and then gently advised Mark that Claire might like to be with him.

Large lumps of ice moved about in Mark's stomach. He stared down at his son who looked as he ever looked. No. No. No.

Claire arrived an hour later. Mrs Barton had heard the ambulance arrive and had come to see if they were all right. She was sitting with a still sleeping Pippa until Nurse Allen arrived at nine.

Aunt Isobel would be on her way soon and that would then mean they were covered all the time. Pippa loved Aunt Isobel and she would not be alarmed at finding either Mrs Barton or Nurse Allen there when she woke up. However Claire hoped Pippa would not wake up until Nurse Allen had arrived, because she was by no means sure how Mrs Barton would cope if Pippa were sick or had the other thing. After all, the Bartons had never had children of their own...

Mark heard the arrangements with scant attention. He was wondering how to tell Claire what he feared.

'They're very worried.'

'I know. They wouldn't have asked you to call me in otherwise.'

'He looks peaceful enough.'

'He can't look anything else, can he?'

They sat throughout the long morning, holding Jeremy's hand, telling him in soothing voices that he would be fine, moving away from the bed when the nurses came in, watching anxiously when the doctor did so, listening to the paediatrician telling them what they knew already: that Jeremy's immune system was weak and that any enteritis must be taken seriously. He must be closely watched for several days and must stay in until the last of the infection had gone. His diet would have to be severely re-stricted thereafter.

Claire groaned in protest. It already was restricted. He had too little variety already. More restrictions were just more limitations on an already limited quality of life. There were some

91

things she specially liked blending for him because she knew he had liked them when he was little. He had so few pleasures... Trotter was sympathetic but firm. Claire, exhausted and anxious, wept.

As the morning wore into afternoon Mark began to distinguish the nurses and to like one in particular. Nurse Kenward was a large woman with a Midlands accent, a red face and thin wispy hair. She prattled away to Jeremy as oblivious to the lack of response as Pippa, brought Claire a cup of tea, and when Mark was returning from the lavatory on one occasion he saw her making a child on the main ward laugh uproariously despite being bandaged in all four limbs and covered in head dressings. Had he met her casually he would have thought her a good-natured school dinner lady.

He had no confidence at all in Nurse French, who leaned on the ward desk talking to the others of boyfriends and nail varnish and whom he often saw glancing at the clock. At three o'clock the shift changed and he had to get to know a new collection of faces, voices and attitudes.

At teatime Aunt Isobel phoned and Claire went to take the call at the ward desk, leaving Jeremy in the care of a young, dark-haired Irish nurse, a breezy, pert woman who amused Mark. Jeremy's temperature was being taken every hour. It had been something he and Claire had first watched with fear, dreading a worried look, a hasty exit and then a sudden surge of activity, but as these fears failed to turn into reality they grew less exercised by the hourly routine, and Mark almost missed the slight shadow of concern which crossed Nurse Leahy's face. Almost.

'What is it?' he asked sharply.

She gave him a bright professional smile. 'A small rise, that's all. Just wait a moment now.' She left the side ward with studied unhurriedness. She wants to run, thought Mark, and the ice moved again. He looked at Jeremy in disbelief and then he was moved gently away as the ward filled. The doctor came and asked him to wait outside because the ward was so small, but by that time he had already heard someone say 'Peter Langley' which he knew was the name of the Intensive Care ward, after a famous local benefactor.

Helplessly they sat and waited, wretchedly noticing the increase in quiet, controlled activity. Claire said Pippa was better and pleased to see Aunt Isobel and Mark was startled to realise that he had scarcely thought of Pippa all day, that he had almost forgotten she too was ill. Guiltily he forced himself to enquire further but his eyes were on the closed door of the side ward and his anxious mind on the scene beyond it. What was happening? It was their son, dammit. They had a right to know. Why didn't someone tell them?

A small party emerged from the ward and the doctor sat down beside them. 'We are going to move Jeremy to another ward. We need to increase some of the treatment. We are putting him in Intensive Care.'

'What's happened?' Claire's voice was quiet but Mark had felt her tremble.

'Jeremy is running a very high temperature. There is nothing to worry about now, but for a very little while he stopped breathing. We need to monitor everything for a while. It's a sensible precaution.'

Euphemisms, thought Mark, our armour against fear, against acknowledging reality, the grim precursors of death itself. 'Did you tell them Jeremy is special?' Claire had asked him as they waited for the tardy ambulance. Special? They had never used that word, having decided early on that it was patronising. Handicapped, they had insisted even to Aunt Isobel. Yet tonight, in fear, Claire had herself taken refuge in the rejected word. 'A slight rise,' the nurse had proclaimed as she departed to raise the alarm. Now the doctor was talking of sensible pre-cautions when he meant a last throw of an uncertain dice.

If you wanted to know if someone were dying you had no need to look at him, only to listen to the language of those around him. He wondered if Claire had noticed. Just as he was sure their son was dying or at any rate in severe danger of doing so, he was also sure that no one would tell them until certain that they already knew themselves.

'Intensive Care?'

'Yes, for a while.'

'And after the while?' Mark heard the aggression in his own voice and saw Claire's surprise. She touched his arm lightly and then they both turned as Jeremy was wheeled from the ward on a trolley.

'They're doing their best,' she whispered.

After that it was no very great surprise to Mark that the doctor earnestly advised them to get some rest. They had been up since four. Nothing was going to happen tonight – he looked at Mark as he said this – Jeremy would be quite safe in Intensive Care and they would be called at once if there was any change. If, all that notwithstanding, they felt better staying they should take it in turns to do so. In this day and age there were proper facilities for parents to remain with children but Jeremy would be in for at least another week...

The week became two weeks. Acting on the doctor's advice they took it in turns to maintain a twenty-four-hour vigil. Jeremy moved out of Intensive Care and then back in again. Pippa went to stay with Mark's mother in lieu of the now aborted holiday; Mark regretted the size of the lost deposit and excused himself from work, knowing that Inglis would once more regard him as unreliable. Aunt Isobel ran the house without anyone bothering to enquire what was happening to her own, and a steady stream of Renwicks visited the hospital. Claire made friends with the nurses and some of the children on the main ward, with whom Sam became a firm favourite. By contrast Sally came only to see Jeremy and remained at his unresponsive side for hours. Aunt Isobel, Rupert Fiske, Mrs Barton and Nurse Allen all came bearing get well cards and toys which filled the side ward to which Jeremy had once more been moved.

'My, you're a popular young man,' Nurse Leahy told Jeremy.

Arriving three days after Jeremy had come out of Intensive Care on the second occasion, Mark found him in a bed on the main ward. A large picture of Beatrix Potter's Mrs Tiggywinkle adorned the wall over the bed. Looking round, Mark saw a different character over each bed and correctly guessed that this was how the nurses distinguished between patients. 'Nil by mouth in Tiggywinkle,' he could imagine them saying.

'He's very much better, Mr Wellings,' Nurse Kenward greeted him. 'Temperature normal, breathing normal. Holding down his food. Mr Trotter is very pleased.'

Passing the side ward Mark had seen a new occupant and briefly he wondered whether he ought to believe Nurse Kenward, whether in fact they had moved Jeremy to the main ward because they needed the bed in the side ward, but her pleasure seemed genuine and he dismissed the thought as unworthy.

'We can take him home in a few days,' Claire told him. 'They just want to do some more work on the diet. Make sure it's absolutely right.'

Mark looked at her, his waning anxiety on Jeremy's account suddenly growing on hers. She had been getting no more than four or five hours' sleep for two weeks, her eyes were red-rimmed and her skin grey, her mousy hair lank, the lines on her face deep etched. There would be no holiday now. Soon they would resume their normal lives, Jeremy would be home, he would be back at work and Aunt Isobel would be in London. Everything would be as it had been before Jeremy was taken ill – except that they would be more tired and even less able to cope than before.

'You need to sleep,' he said gently. 'And so do I.'

'Like Jeremy. He's slept all day.'

'Is that normal?'

'Yes. Aunt Isobel says Pippa did when she was better.'

They looked at their peacefully sleeping son and agreed in whispers that tonight they would leave early and get a full night's rest. They could go at teatime. There was no longer anything to worry about.

A small child wandered over to them and they smiled at her. Her name was Alice but the character over her bed was Jemima Puddleduck and to her delight she had been nicknamed Puddleduck by the other children. Mark was not sure why, because every other child was addressed by Christian name, but even the nurses adopted the habit.

'Hello, how are you today?' Mark gently stopped her from climbing on Jeremy's bed.

'Better, thank you,' she said primly. 'If Jeremy is asleep I can have Freddie.'

Claire decided it was not her business to correct the child's manners and handed over the large green cuddly frog which Sally had brought. Alice took it with a happy 'Thank you' and presently its croaks filled the room as Alice pressed the button in its stomach.

'Shh! You'll wake Jeremy,' warned a boy of about eleven whose bed was presided over by a picture of Squirrel Nutkin.

'No I won't,' retorted Alice, 'Jeremy can't hear.'

Apparently he could not, reflected Mark, watching him sleep through the din. A small baby would wake and cry at sudden noise but a loud bang behind Jeremy would produce no reaction at all. 'We just don't know what he hears or sees or feels or why one day he grunts and the next he doesn't. All we can be certain of is that he cannot respond, cannot communicate.' That was as much as the expensive London consultant had ever been able to tell them.

Had he really felt nothing over the last two weeks, been unaware of the heat which burned through him and the sweat which poured off him? Of the pain and taste of being sick? Had he sensed none of the fear, none of the affection with which he was surrounded? Had he not known, not drawn comfort when they held his hand? Did he not even know when they were there and when they were not?

'Yes, he can hear,' another girl entered the argument. 'If he couldn't hear people wouldn't spend all day talking to him. It would be silly. So leave the frog alone, Puddleduck.'

Alice, outnumbered, turned to Mark and Claire. 'Can he hear?' she demanded.

'We don't know,' said Mark.

The older boy looked embarrassed but the others stared at Mark in surprise.

'You could ask the doctor,' suggested Alice practically.

'Oh shut up, Puddleduck,' the older boy said angrily.

Alice slammed the frog down on Jeremy's bed.

'Horrible frog. I don't want it anyway.' She stomped back to her own bed, sulking, her bad temper persisting till her parents arrived.

Jeremy was still sleeping when they left for the night. Nurse Leahy was glad to see them going early.

'He'll be fine now. There's no need to come till tomorrow afternoon. We'd let you know at once if there was any change.'

At home they began the preparations for the return to normality. Aunt Isobel was to return home next day. Mark would start work next week. Pippa would be collected at the weekend.

'Spoiled rotten, no doubt,' sniffed Claire.

'More likely benignly neglected,' said Mark.

'Well let's sleep while we can,' suggested Claire. 'It's the first time we've had neither of them at home.'

They did not set the alarm and it was with surprise and a shadow of shame that they did not wake till ten the next morning. Aunt Isobel had already left. A note on the kitchen table told them Montefiore was fed and that there was a casserole in the fridge for their lunch. She hoped Jeremy would stay well and that Pippa would enjoy the rest of the summer. She had had a lovely time and she thanked them very much. This last made Mark laugh. It read like a child's bread-and-butter letter.

They took the rest of the day at a similarly easy pace. Claire went alone to the hospital in the afternoon and Mark in the evening. They again retired early, turning off the light before ten. Mark began to wonder if a series of early nights might not be a substitute for a holiday.

He awoke to the sound of the telephone. The bedside clock told him it was 2.00 a.m. A drunken voice asked if they could send a taxi. Mark snapped 'Wrong number' irritably and put the phone down. Claire fell back with relief and slept immediately, but Mark did not. Instead his mind started to re-run the last two weeks. He relived coming home just before midnight, creeping softly so as not to wake Claire as he moved from bedroom to bathroom and back again, waking up in need of the bathroom several hours later, creeping carefully again, pausing outside the children's doors in turn, listening to their steady breathing, turning back towards his own room and suddenly hearing the gurgling rush of vomit in Jeremy's. If he had not got up, had not gone to the lavatory, had not paused to listen... If Jeremy had been taken ill earlier or later in the night... Mark began to sweat at the thought. Remorselessly the events continued to play in front of his mind's eye: the innocently brutal Alice, the perceptive, kind eleven-year-old, the nurses, the smell of the Intensive Care ward, the tasteful black and gold sign 'Peter Langley' which they followed along the hospital corridors.

Hot, uncomfortable, eventually giving up the struggle to sleep he went downstairs to the kitchen for water. Montefiore greeted him sleepily.

Mark put some ice in a tall glass and filled it with Perrier. He drank deeply but the effect on his thirst was negligible so he repeated the exercise, growing wider awake as he did so. He unlocked the back door and stepped out into the night, finding it hot and sultry, not refreshing as he had hoped. Montefiore came out too, rubbing around Mark's legs. Aunt Isobel had trained him in the use of a cat flap and he now came and went as he pleased. Apparently he and Rags had twice met on each other's territory without ill effect.

On impulse Mark went inside, poured himself a whisky and took it out on to the lawn. He was barefoot, but to have gone upstairs for his slippers might have woken Claire and the only footwear downstairs consisted of wellingtons. He located a garden chair. In the stillness of the night he could hear the stream and thought fleetingly of paddling his feet in its chilly water, but it was at the other end of the garden and it was too much effort. Perhaps he was tireder than he realised.

He awoke to the redness of a summer's dawn and Barton's low voice: 'Are you all right, Mr Wellings?' Although neighbours for thirteen years they had never progressed to Christian names, even on Christmas cards. Claire was certain Barton would consider it vulgar.

Mark reassured him, ruefully convinced Barton must think him mad to be sleeping in a chair in the garden in his pyjamas with his house open to any passing robber. He stood up reluctantly, grateful that at that distance his neighbour was unlikely to detect the stale whisky which stained his pyjamas and thus come to a conclusion that insanity might not be the problem after all. He must have still been holding the glass when he fell asleep. He could only hope Barton would not tell Claire. Presumably he had seen Mark from an upstairs window as he went to the bathroom, for it was not yet five and he could scarcely be getting up.

Claire did not stir when he rejoined her, and when she woke nearly three hours later she had no reason to suppose he had not been there all night. They were both lighter in step and spirit and this happy feeling was augmented at the hospital when they were told that Jeremy would be discharged the next day.

The plan was changed abruptly that evening, as two emergency admissions were made to the children's ward and Jeremy was sent home to make room. Mark was at the hospital when the decision was made, a decision he accepted without fear or resentment. Jeremy was now quite well and would have been discharged the following morning anyway. He telephoned Claire and sat outside the ward while the nurses got Jeremy ready.

It took a long time because the nurses were busy and preoccupied with the new admissions. Throughout the bustle he could hear the croaks of Freddie the Frog and deduced that Alice wanted attention. He decided to make her a present of Freddie. Nurse Kenward passed him on her way to the nurses' room and paused to say goodbye. He gathered she had been supposed to go off duty at three but was prevented from doing so by the emergencies. Other staff had now been drafted in and she was off, and not before time.

By the time Claire arrived they had still not got Jeremy ready but were unwilling for her to help.

They both sat and waited as patiently as they could, longing for this episode in their lives to be over, knowing that they would briefly miss some of the nurses or wonder about the fate of Alice and the other children but that soon the hospital, the ward and the people would fade into the shadows of the past, to be recalled occasionally into sharp focus by a scent, a half-remembered face, a dream. For now it was still very real, very present and very dominating.

Mark wandered a little to stretch his legs and ease the tedium of waiting. Claire too got up, and began to study the children's drawings on the walls as if seeing them for the first time. In the course of this aimless passing of time they drew nearer to the nurses' room. From it they could hear Nurse Kenward grumbling pleasantly. Then the voice of another nurse, this time unrecognised: 'And that poor little boy in Tiggywinkle isn't ready yet.'

'No,' came the Midlands reply, 'Doctor Bonneaud says he must see the parents first and he's tied up with that baby...'

Mark grimaced. It looked as if he and Claire were in for a long wait. Perhaps they should hunt out the canteen.

'They look dead,' the unknown nurse was saying. 'They've been in all day every day.'

'Poor little scrap, not that he looks that little. His mother must have her work cut out.'

'I thought we'd lost him last week, he was so poorly. His poor parents!'

'Perhaps, poor mite, it would have been better.' The nurses pondered that in silence while

Mark stood rigid, trying to come to terms with what he had just heard. Claire flew past him like a whirlwind and threw open the door of the nurses' room.

'That's my son you've just wished dead, Nurse.' Her cry echoed round the ward reception area.

Nurse Kenward began to stammer apologies and reassurance but Claire cut through them with fury, her voice alternately loud with anger and low and hissing.

'I want him now,' Claire demanded. 'Now, now, now. You shouldn't be looking after children. You are not fit to do so ... Get him ready now. Now!'

Mark knew he should intervene, that his wife had lost control, that she was probably now frightening not only the nurses but the children on the ward. He remained still, unable to react.

The other nurse was now operating professionally, trying to soothe what she doubtless saw as a case of hysterics brought about by stress and fatigue. In the ward a child began to cry. Mark continued helpless as he had been helpless on that other occasion, seven years ago, when some vaguely remembered character by the name of Oswald Something-Something had taken charge. He saw his helplessness as if observing that of a stranger, and he despised it without being able to overcome it.

A doctor with a calm voice despite a harassed expression appeared on the rapidly escalating scene. Somehow he detached Mark and Claire and persuaded them to accompany him to a small room near another ward. They left behind a tearful Nurse Kenward, her face red and blotchy. Mark wondered how he had ever liked her.

Claire remained standing, ignoring the chair offered to her. 'We mustn't take up your time, Doctor. I know you're busy this evening. I expect my husband is dying with embarrassment so just give us Jeremy and we'll go.' The stilted words, aggressive, sarcastic, challenging, met with a gentle smile.

'I'm not embarrassed. I'm proud of you,' said Mark and meant it.

He looked at the doctor, who now introduced himself as Bonneaud but whose Welsh accent belied the French name. He was young, good-looking and complete with white coat and stethoscope. Doctor Kildare, thought Mark.

For the next five minutes Bonneaud engaged their attention on Jeremy, the new diet, the checks he wanted made, what the hospital would be telling Neville Harris and what Harris would be likely to do. He forced them to concentrate. Then with equal insistence he spoke to them of their own welfare, about the toll the last two weeks had taken, about the toll of caring for Jeremy generally and the availability of help, of respite care, of self-support groups. He asked about a holiday and Claire, now meek, described the aborted plans. Persistently, like a terrier, he extracted from them a promise to take at least a short break.

Only then did he turn to the issue of Nurse Kenward. She was an excellent nurse, fond of the children she cared for, who had given unstinting care to Jeremy. Of course she should not have spoken as she did but she had not intended them to hear, she was very tired after hours of unexpected overtime and she was trying, however clumsily, to express sympathy for Jeremy.

Claire snorted and Mark, to avoid another row, belatedly exerted himself. They would not be making a complaint, but it must be in all their interests to take Jeremy away as soon as possible. They would like to thank the staff on Peter Langley Ward and he hoped that when they returned Jeremy would be ready. It might be better if Jeremy were brought down to the main door to avoid their having to return to the ward. Of course they would always be grateful for what had been done for Jeremy over the last fortnight and they would be writing to Trotter to say so.

The doctor agreed and waved to them as they turned at the end of the corridor. He smiled, looking even more like Doctor Kildare, and Mark thought he probably had a great future in front of him, in his profession and with women.

Claire was still sufficiently angry to recount the whole episode to Aunt Isobel when she rang next morning and was made even more angry by Aunt Isobel's reaction: 'That was a bit unkind of her, dear, but there are people who think like that.'

Claire had looked for something less mild and more condemnatory but Mark knew the response was reasonable. He also knew now why he feared the Euthanasia Bill. It was because indeed there were people who thought like that, plenty of them, and their views would be aired through press and media. He utterly accepted Sally's view that the innate decency of the British people

106

would prevent any extension of the Bill to encompass involuntary euthanasia but that was not the point. It was not Jeremy the Bill menaced; it threatened people like Claire

6

In the small basement cloakroom which served the male staff of Inglis and May, Mark stared into the tiny, cracked, faintly-dirty mirror over the washbasin and remembered the scene in *The Picture of Dorian Gray* when Wilde's fascinating, beastly character, fortified by new resolutions, looked hopefully at his portrait and saw only the lines of the hypocrite. For a week or more that was all Mark, in his conscience-stricken imagination, had seen in his own reflection.

Claire's fierce anger had enabled her to get over the scene at the hospital and Mark believed she now barely remembered it, certainly in any active sense, and that it was relegated to that dark trunk in the attic of the mind where human beings are wont to store those memories they do not wish to recall but from which dark place occasionally the recollections nonetheless burst forth, often bearing a different appearance, sometimes more and sometimes less bearable, from when they were put away. Occasionally so pleasingly altered is their aspect that they are dusted off and kept on display.

For Mark, however, there had been no furnace

of anger in which to burn future reflection and he had begun to think of Nurse Kenward if not with shame then certainly with awkwardness. Had he himself never reflected that if Jeremy were taken, as Aunt Isobel would have put it, he would pass into a peaceful oblivion, a place where he was no longer alien to his surroundings? Mark had lost belief long ago, he discounted any notion of Heaven and used it only as a gentle way of introducing Pippa to news of death but, whether there were any sort of afterlife or not, this life could mean nothing to Jeremy. If he felt pain he could not tell them and must suffer, and if he could not feel pain then he probably felt nothing at all and lived in name only. Was it not true that he had occasionally listened outside Jeremy's door and, hearing his breathing catch, had felt hope as well as fear? Had not even Claire agreed that if Jeremy were to pass peacefully away they would not insist on a life-support machine? Had she not once said that it would be cruel to force him back to a world in which he could play no part?

Yet they had condemned Nurse Kenward.

He knew now that they would insist on a life-support machine, that there was nothing half-hearted about the way he had willed his son's survival, that he had felt as fiercely protective towards the helpless, slack Jeremy lying in hospital as he had towards the equally helpless small bundles of fist-waving life and energy that had been Jeremy and Pippa in their prams. Claire had always felt thus; he had now caught up with her.

That did not, however, give him the right to condemn Nurse Kenward.

Now he was back at work, lamentably failing to pull his weight and he knew he was ineffectual, a liability, someone who might well be dismissed but for the influence of his father-in-law. He was too tired to function properly and indeed was now working in what would have been his holiday period had things gone according to plan, but there had been a number of loose ends left by his sudden absence when Jeremy was ill and he had come in to clear them up, to show willing, to try to rescue some small part of his tarnished reputation. At least he had the honesty to recognise that he had no career, just a job, a steady job, a well-paid job, a respectable job, but just a job all the same, not the dazzling career he had once promised himself.

Somewhat to his surprise Claire had agreed that they should honour their promise to Bonneaud and take a short break, but she would not accept they go together. One must stay behind in case Jeremy had a relapse. Mark would go first and he decided to retrieve a bit of the lost holiday and spend the week in Paris. A little later Claire would go to Scotland and the long-suffering Aunt Isobel would come and look after the children and Mark.

At the last minute Mark abandoned Paris for Estoril, sundrenched Portugal being more to his taste than the heat and dust of Paris. He made a half-hearted offer to take Pippa, but she was already excited by the programme of outings and activities at home which Claire had arranged to compensate for the lost holiday.

In his cramped office he day-dreamed, scarcely believing that in a few days he would be doing nothing more exhausting than lying on the beach. His plans were more ambitious, of course. He would go to Cascais to look at the fishing boats and Lisbon to visit Mr Cork where he would select cork products as he enjoyed the shopkeeper's drink. He would photograph the Ponte Salazaar at night. For the first few days, however, he had promised himself nothing except laziness. Sam had thought it very odd to go so far for so little.

He finished washing his hands, ran a wet comb through his hair to combat the August stickiness. In his office the fans were set at full speed. He looked out on to a small patio, formed well below street level, where plants grew half-heartedly in boxes and no sun ever really reached. He had worked here for eighteen years and was still a junior partner and never likely to be anything else. Two new partners had been taken on in that time and the firm now occupied the ground floor as well, but Inglis steadily refused any suggestion of better premises. He preferred profits and had no ambitions to rival Touche Ross. May was but a distant memory but his name remained because, it was humorously rumoured, Inglis begrudged the money it would cost to alter the signs.

Initially Mark had thought to make progress in the firm and then to move on, perhaps even to set up on his own, a project enthusiastically supported by Sam. He qualified well and the early years were promising but then Fate took an unhelpful hand. He contracted glandular fever and was ill for months afterwards. Recovered, he returned to find three of his main clients had transferred to other members of the firm but that the most important had left and gone elsewhere. Mark knew Inglis blamed him, however unfairly. He knew Inglis did not want to entrust him with Sam's work but on that fateful Saturday he had not had any choice. Afterwards the marriage to Sam's daughter secured his position and gradually he had worked his way back into favour. Then had come Jeremy's terrible accident and Mark's near nervous breakdown which followed it. As his son's condition deteriorated he had taken him to the States, to Canada, to France. They had spent Sam's money on the best specialists the world could offer but to no avail.

Everyone had been sympathetic; they carried his workload without complaint and Inglis uttered no demur even in the year he had been away for six months, but promotion was for ever out of the question. Once the flotation was over he must choose between making the break with the firm or going on like this for another twenty-five years. It was one of many things he promised himself to think through to a conclusion while soaking up the Portuguese sun.

For today, there was the brimming in-tray which Mark contemplated without enthusiasm. At eleven the shared secretary put a cup of coffee on his desk and he looked at it with similar disfavour. It was slopped in the saucer and he knew it would be lukewarm.

'Thank you, Karen.' He immediately despised himself. Why did he not tell her he wanted it hot and in the cup not the saucer?

'The new girls start next week, Mr Wellings.'

'New girls? Are you leaving us?' He tried not to sound hopeful.

'You won't get rid of me so easily,' she smiled, causing Mark to wonder if she had read his thoughts. 'I mean the extra staff we need to deal with the flotation. We've got two secretaries starting.'

Mark forbore to comment. The staff had been expected in the autumn and there had been no talk of bringing that forward a couple of weeks ago. The work must really have gathered pace while he had been away during Jeremy's illness.

'Where are we putting them?'

Karen described arrangements which made Mark wonder if either girl would stay more than twenty-four hours, especially as one was not a girl at all but, according to Karen, a fifty-year-old who prior to her marriage and children had run her own small secretarial agency. The other was a working holidaymaker from Australia who would only be with them two months. Karen described her as an outdoor type and Mark revised his estimate of twenty-four hours to twenty minutes. He wondered if the arrangements were legal under the fire regulations.

With rigorous application, he left an empty in-tray behind him on the Thursday evening. On Friday he drove the sixteen miles to the nearest Snoezelen which Jeremy attended once a fortnight. Whenever Pippa was on holiday she went too, thoroughly enjoying the changing colours which swamped the walls and ceiling. Watching her delight Mark had sometimes wondered which child was getting benefit from the exercise. Jeremy lay on a soft mat while the colours played and changed around him. From time to time Mark sat him up and held his head upright so that he could see the ever-changing kaleidoscope designed to soothe and stimulate. Pippa gurgled and chuckled like a tiny infant.

Usually the task fell to Claire, and that pleased Mark because it was the only time she came into contact with other parents of children like Jeremy. She spurned self-support groups because it upset her to hear the complaints of those with children so much less disabled than Jeremy.

'Don't they realise how lucky they are?' she had cried on her return from one such group. 'All they can do is talk of how there is too little provision for this and not enough of that and how other Local Authorities are better than ours and what the Government ought to do.'

Mark tried to tell her it could not be typical, that she should join another group. In misery she refused. He found another, went to a meeting, talked to the other parents, but Claire would not be persuaded, her resistance undiminished even when one of the parents visited their house bringing a teenage child half Jeremy's size and – at that time – with less than Jeremy's then remaining ability.

In the end Mark had given up, but he knew her attitude must mean increasing isolation. However limited his faith in the Snoezelen, he valued

113

it just for the company it provided for Claire. When Jeremy's session was over he took the children to the large room used as a day centre by Social Services. Several of the staff and parents recognised Jeremy but they were strangers to Mark, who had last accompanied Jeremy at Christmas. He went to the small servery and obtained a Coca-Cola for Pippa, a weak orange squash for Jeremy and a coffee for himself. Pippa took her cola off to another table to join a girl the same age as herself, whom as far as Mark could ascertain she did not know previously. Admiring her easy sociability, he draped a towel round Jeremy and holding his head at the right angle spooned in a fraction of the squash.

There was no swallow. Mark bent him forward and the pathetic amount dribbled out. He tried again with the same result. A care worker approached.

'He was all right at breakfast,' said Mark.

'Perhaps he doesn't want it,' contributed a woman from the next table. Mark looked at her. She was a heavy woman with too short a skirt, several layers of make-up and peroxide blonde hair. Beside her was a very dirty pushchair. A slattern, thought Mark, and was immediately ashamed. Had she not the same trouble as he had, and with only a small proportion of the wit and resources to cope?

'I only wish he could take charge like that,' replied Mark quietly.

'Needs a tube then,' said the woman in the tone of one stating an obvious fact. This time Mark hated her without shame.

114

'I don't think I'll try again,' he told the care worker who introduced herself as Annie. 'If he won't swallow he could choke.'

Won't swallow. Can't swallow.

She chatted to him for a while, sympathetic, interested, but with no realisation that a bit more of his son had just died.

Pippa had been too preoccupied with her new friend to notice. She came charging over to him to ask if Kylie could come and play one day during the holiday. Mark forced himself to concentrate, told her to 'watch Jeremy' and went to introduce himself to Kylie's mother. Pippa immediately joined him and, turning, he saw Annie with Jeremy. Reassured, he gave his attention to his new acquaintances. Kylie Grant was the eldest of three children, the youngest of whom, Lee, had cerebral palsy. Kylie was eight, Dean five and Lee two. Kylie's father had left when she was one. Her mother's current boyfriend, Wayne, was a father to them all.

Mark's heart sank. Kylie, Dean, Lee, Wayne. A single parent complete with boyfriend though possibly still legally married. They probably lived on a council estate and drew benefit. He knew only too well what Claire's reaction would be. It would not matter that the mother, Eve Grant, was clean, presentable and devoted with clean, presentable, well-mannered children. Then he thought he saw a way to give Pippa her wish and fixed a date with Mrs Grant for a Saturday after his return from holiday and before Claire's. Pippa and Kylie were delighted. They exchanged addresses.

The Snoezelen served the population for miles around, but Kylie's address was within eight miles of theirs. Still, it was a fair distance and Claire would be able to extricate herself if she thought fit.

Mark left the day centre with his peace of mind thoroughly disturbed. There was a tube at home, unwrapped, and they both knew how to use it. Thank God at least there were no sudden arrangements to make, just the shock to overcome. Just the shock! He almost physically shrank at the thought of telling Claire.

Once outside he took Pippa to task. 'I told you to watch Jeremy.'

'Annie watched him.'

'Who? I've told you not to call grown-ups by their first names. It's rude.'

'She told me to call her Annie.'

'Then call her Auntie Annie.'

'She's not my auntie.'

'Don't argue and don't ever again leave Jeremy if I tell you to watch him. It's dangerous.' Mark opened the back door of the car and manoeuvred Jeremy in, clicking the seat belt into place and adjusting the angle of his head. It was an operation that always took a few minutes, and usually Pippa had climbed in beside Jeremy and put on her own seat belt by the time he had finished.

Today, however, she did not do this and he looked around for her in a mixture of irritation and mild anxiety before spotting her on a bench, sobbing with indignation and self-pity.

'Come on,' he called. 'Mummy will be getting lunch.'

She turned from him with a petulant shrug and began to wail her protests aloud. Wearily he walked over to her, trying to coax her towards the car, but when she refused with words of defiance he began to take her from the bench by force. She screamed, holding on to the back which bore a brass plaque announcing that one Gwendoline Jane Walters had donated the seat that the elderly and infirm of the town might find rest. Grimly Mark loosened her grasp and carried her still screaming to the car, her roars and struggles attracting rather more attention than Mark found comfortable. As he pulled the seat belt round her writhing form he heard a small child observe to his mother that Pippa was a 'very naughty little girl'.

'Hush,' she replied in a stage whisper. 'She's not very well. That's why her daddy brings her here.'

To her startled embarrassment Mark turned and said, 'Oh, no. She's supposed to be the normal one.'

The woman reddened and hurried away, the child with her still looking behind him at Pippa. Mark slammed the back door shut, opened the driver's and then slammed that too. It was rude to slam doors, he had so often told Pippa, but if she thought of reminding him she had the wisdom not to do so. Instead she whined and complained and occasionally screamed the entire sixteen miles, refusing to get out and open the gate when they arrived home. Claire, peacefully gardening, turned, appalled at the noise.

Mark, exhausted, anxious, angry, said, 'Leave

117

this to me,' extracted a still howling Pippa from the car, carried her bodily up the stairs and put her in her bedroom, threatening retribution if she appeared until told to do so.

He found Claire by the car with Jeremy's wheelchair and together they lifted him out. Mark held him, warm and dear, before putting him in the chair. He began to wheel him towards the lilacs.

'No,' called Claire, 'not there. I heard bees this morning.'

Instead Mark wheeled him under the shade of the large cedar standing majestically at the top of the slope which fell away to the stream. Unbidden there came into his mind the scene at Pippa's christening when Jeremy had caused Aunt Jane to spill her lunch. He had been running under this tree, racing Michael for the champagne cork, a lively, laughing, innocent four-year-old. Mark's eyes filled with tears which he tried urgently to blink away as Claire came up to him, but she had seen and was now looking apprehensive.

'What is it? What's happened?'

'He can't swallow.'

She went on looking at him, saying nothing. In the background Barton's ever active shears were at work. Then: 'Are you sure?'

'Yes. Unless it was something very temporary, he just doesn't swallow any more. I tried twice.'

'I must get Nurse Allen over. I can't do it for the first time alone, even if I do supposedly know how, and he'll need fitting right away.'

'I had better stay with you next week.'

She shook her head. 'This holiday is jinxed. You must have it. You need it. Daddy's been telling me exactly what is involved in a flotation. It's different for me. Aunt Isobel can't be expected to manage the tube.'

'The nurse can. Harris told you she was good. We must see if she is still free.'

'Don't let's argue. I'll phone Nurse Allen, but first tell me about Pippa. Is it because of Jeremy's swallowing?'

'She disobeyed me and was then mildly rude and argumentative, then threw a king-size tantrum when I ticked her off. But at root, yes, I was preoccupied with Jeremy or I suppose I would have handled it better.'

'She never seems to forget quickly like other children. Once upset it goes on for hours. I can't seem to break her of it. Reasoning doesn't work and neither does punishment.'

Jeremy began to grunt, the sounds growing louder and longer, carrying across the stillness of the summer's day. Barton's shears paused and then stoically carried on. Mark cheered and Claire whispered, 'Thank God.'

In her bedroom Pippa heard the cheer and, feeling excluded, wept anew. She could not know that the cheer was a declaration of despair, not triumph, as her parents thrashed through the sea of their drowned hopes to clutch a tiny, golden straw of life.

7

Refusing Sam's offer to subsidise a stay in the Estoril Sol, Mark had booked into the much cheaper but still very comfortable Hotel Londres, reflecting with deep satisfaction as he unpacked that despite its name it had none of the characteristics of London. Now, as he looked forward to a long swim and a lazy afternoon by the pool, the only cloud on his horizon was the phone call Claire would be expecting him to make to report safe arrival. He could see no necessity for it and resented the forthcoming conversation with what he knew was unreasonable vigour, mentally casting round for excuses to avoid it.

His last hours at home before departure had been fraught with argument and recrimination when his plan to induce Claire to allow Eve and Kylie Grant to visit failed catastrophically, sending Pippa into yet another long, drawn-out tantrum and causing Claire to sit tight-lipped and furious throughout the drive to Heathrow while their daughter sulked in the back seat. A long delay at roadworks which had them glancing at their watches every few minutes destroyed their remaining self-control, already frayed by heat, bad temper and Jeremy's long, loud grunts which caused the occupants of slowly passing cars to stare. When Pippa began to whine and tell

Jeremy to be quiet, Claire turned and snapped at her, making her cry.

Mark was not surprised when Claire made no effort to accompany him to the departure hall. When he got out she immediately moved into the driving seat and waited while he extracted his luggage from the boot. Pippa refused to kiss him goodbye.

Jeremy was grunting, dribbling and smelling of sweat and pads which needed changing as Mark bent to bid him farewell, but at that moment he was the only one for whom Mark felt active affection. He turned from them all willingly, his step light as he approached the check-in desk, unashamed to be looking forward to their absence from his life for one whole, too-short week, already fantasising about extending the holiday.

The mood had continued throughout his journey. Marvelling at the patience with which his fellow passengers dealt with bored or fractious children, noting without envy or wistfulness the closeness of many of the couples, watching business travellers attempting paper-work in their small, cramped spaces, Mark unfeignedly rejoiced in the absence of both work and family, knowing he should instead be missing the little group now somewhere in a car on the way home.

He did not make the telephone call, deriving satisfaction from his poor conduct, knowing Claire would be waiting and eventually worrying. He guessed she would herself in the end ring the hotel and, when he had enjoyed a protracted swim and a doze in the shade by the pool, he guiltlessly decided to go and explore the beach, where she would be unable to reach him.

The beach was less crowded than he expected and he chose a spot as far from his fellow humans as he could manage. As he alternately read and dozed snatches of conversation drifted into his consciousness, incomprehensible French, some German he could have translated had he been wanting to concentrate, lively Spanish – or was it the native Portuguese? Glad that it was all unconnected with him, that no one would be demanding his attention, he eventually began to look about him and observe the activity on the sands. Two children were belabouring each other with spades but attracting no adult intervention, a suntanned couple were entwined upon a loudly patterned towel, both inelegantly asleep with their mouths open. while on an equally garish towel a few yards away another couple behaved indecently. The young woman caught Mark's eye and he looked away grinning.

He sat up to apply more suntan lotion and saw two children with their backs to him spinning pebbles on the sea with mixed success, their happy exclamations reaching him when one or the other managed to make the stones bounce. Some unhappiness stirred within him and he lay back to doze before it should take shape, before he should picture a very different Jeremy and a happy Pippa spinning pebbles, before he began to resent every active, happy child on the beach.

Something horribly cold and wet landed on his bare stomach, shocking him out of sleep, causing him to sit upright with a strangled shout while not yet fully awake. Mark stared at the gooey, pink, prolific ice-cream which now ran from his midriff into the sand and also, less pleasingly, into his trunks, then looked up into the embarrassed eyes of a girl of about eight.

At once he looked away again, himself embarrassed, and then met her eyes squarely trying, vainly, to pretend he had not noticed the hideous portwine stain which covered the left-hand side of her face. He looked at the ice-cream again and grinned. Relieved, she giggled as a boy of about eleven or twelve hurriedly joined them, gaping at the mess which Mark was making worse by endeavouring to rub it off. Mark recognised them now as the children he had been watching throwing pebbles.

'Gosh!' exclaimed the boy. 'I'm awfully sorry, sir. My sister didn't mean to do that.'

Gosh? Sir? Were there still children who talked like that? Mark was about to respond when the girl spoke.

'He may not speak English,' she advised her brother solemnly.

'Yes he does, silly.' As he spoke, the boy indicated the book Mark had been reading. 'Oh, dear, Sarah, there's ice-cream on that too.'

'It doesn't matter,' said Mark. 'But I'm afraid it's an awful waste of an ice-cream.'

'You had better wash it off,' Sarah told him, 'or a wasp might sting you. Are there wasps in Portugal, Fritz?'

Mark felt himself intrigued by the boy's name as, taking Sarah's advice, he headed for the sea.

He had seemed so very conventionally British, so very public school, that the name was incongruous, rather as if the heir to the throne had been called Wayne. Returning, he buried the ice-cream remains, wiped the residue off his book and mentally debated the merits of a swim. While he was still deliberating he noticed Sarah standing once more at the water's edge before being joined by Fritz and a woman who must be their mother. Mark watched her with happy approval as she attached water wings to Sarah and immediately he decided to swim. She was tall with long blonde hair, an excellent figure and a joyful smile. Above all there was no tiredness or irritability in her movements, and she ran into the sea with the healthy liveliness of a young girl.

'Hello,' called Sarah as he approached. 'Mummy, that's the gentleman I spilled the ice-cream on.'

'On whom I spilled the ice-cream,' corrected Fritz, then hastily submerged himself as Sarah tried to splash him.

'I gather you were very kind about it, especially as Sarah tells me she woke you up. I should have taken a decidedly jaundiced view if someone had dropped a great cold lump of ice on my tummy.'

The children giggled. Mark smiled, said it did not matter and introduced himself. She responded that her name was Smith Jackson, which he at first assumed to be a double-barrelled surname but she explained, to renewed laughter from the children, that Smith was her Christian name.

There had been no mention of a husband.

To hide from his own thoughts Mark turned to Sarah and asked how long she had been trying to swim, with a vague idea of helping her to manage without water wings, suppressing as he did so the memory of how unwilling he had been to bring Pippa, of how the job of teaching her to swim had been resolutely left to Claire. Somehow he could not see Sarah having a tantrum or sulking for hours in her room. The unworthy thoughts hurt and disturbed him, but still they forced their way into his consciousness.

Two other children, chatting to each other in French, swam up to Fritz, who tried some elementary conversation in that language, telling them when they learned his name that he was Anglais not Allemand. They had no English whatever but laughter, splashes and races proved a more than satisfactory substitute, and Mark noted that Smith only occasionally looked round to check she could still see Fritz. He admired her relaxed approach and was soon admiring even more Sarah's dogged determination to swim, declaring that in a few days they would have the water wings off.

A few days? Did he really intend to spend half his holiday with this family, entertaining two children he had known for less than an hour? He guessed alarm bells had rung with Smith too, for presently she asked with an assumed casualness which did not fool him: 'Is your wife on the beach?'

So she had noticed his wedding ring, a thin gold band which now would not come off except with the application of very soapy water. He felt

125

both disappointment and reassurance.

'She's not in Portugal at all. We have a permanently sick son and one of us always needs to be on hand.' Permanently sick? Jeremy was rarely ill. Why on earth had he chosen that phrase?

'I'm sorry,' said Smith gently. 'What's wrong with him?'

'He had an accident at four. He's paralysed from the neck down and severely brain damaged, but the real problem at the moment is that he is recovering from a nasty dose of enteritis. My wife didn't feel she could leave him. She will get away for a bit when I return.'

Smith made no comment but he found himself adding defensively: 'There was nothing else for it. We haven't managed a holiday in three years and my wife won't touch respite care with a ten-foot bargepole.'

'I'm sorry,' said Smith again. 'These things put one's own problems into perspective.'

He glanced at the disfigured child dog-paddling a few feet away. 'People always say that. I suppose some would say that was Jeremy's purpose on this earth.' The anger in his tone communicated itself to Sarah, who looked at him, startled. To cover up the awkwardness he encouraged her to try to lift her feet up more, hoping to refocus her mind on her swimming.

She was not to be deflected. 'Why are you cross with Mummy?'

A denial rose to his lips but Smith said, 'Because Mr Wellings is very worried about his little boy and Mummy can't make him not worry.'

'Oh,' said Sarah and dog-paddled away, her anxiety removed.

He wondered why he and Claire were not more direct with Pippa sometimes instead of offering fatuous explanations which they protectively but condescendingly expected her to believe.

'That was very clumsy of me,' apologised Smith.

'No, I just need this holiday, that's all. What about you? Is your husband here?'

'He died last year.' She spoke quietly but her eyes filled and she turned so that Sarah should not see.

'I'm sorry.' He tried to find the right words but she said with friendly mockery:

'Now I've put your problems in perspective.'

'Yes,' he smiled bleakly. 'Life can be pretty rotten.'

'He was a wonderful man, brilliant with Sarah. I know it's silly after all this time but I'm still fragile.'

Brilliant with Sarah. He wondered what epitaph Claire would give him if he were to die. Certainly it would not be 'brilliant with Pippa' nor with her brother. 'Good to Jeremy,' would be the most his ghost could hope to hear.

A sharp scream, near at hand, rang out, causing both those in the sea and on the beach to look in their direction. Smith turned her head abruptly and Mark saw a small girl swimming speedily away from Sarah, bawling for her mother.

Sarah turned calmly towards them. 'I think my face frightened her,' she announced matter-of-factly and resumed her swimming.

127

Mark swore and Smith shot him a disapproving look. 'You mustn't be angry, Mark,' she whispered. 'I've taught her not to be. I want her to face life confidently so first she must be serene. Anger won't do anything except screw her up.'

He stared, marvelling, mildly surprised by the vulgarity of her last words, utterly admiring of her sense, thinking that if a child had to suffer Sarah's indignity she could not do better than have a parent like this. He sighed, recollecting how inadequately he was dealing with Pippa's lesser Calvary.

Smith, watching him, raised an enquiring eyebrow. He shrugged and then laughed: 'I think Sarah has just put my daughter's problems into perspective too. My wife's aunt may have a point when she tells us to count our blessings every day, although I've never found it much of an antidote to whatever has been bothering me.'

After that the conversation lightened though Mark could not have said later of what it was they talked. Fritz eventually splashed back to them full of tales of duckings and splashings and how he could open his eyes underwater here with only a little stinging afterwards. Sarah stopped her attempts to swim and rested on her water wings, legs hanging idly in the water. When Smith said it was time they all went back to the hotel he found the courage to ask where they were staying.

'The Estoril Sol. And you?'

'Nothing so grand. The Londres. Will you have dinner with me there?'

'I can't leave the children.'

'Of course not,' said Mark. 'I meant bring them too.'

He had not, of course, meant that, but he felt rewarded by the children's enthusiastic response. Obviously not much had been planned for them that evening or they would hardly be keen to sit politely at a dinner table with a strange grown-up. A time was arranged and when he finally retrieved his towel and book and pulled on shorts over his wet trunks it was with rising spirits and happy but ill-defined expectations.

At the hotel he was surprised and somehow vaguely affronted to find Claire had not rung. Childishly he felt a reinforced determination not to ring her. Instead he shaved, showered and inspected the limited wardrobe he had brought on holiday.

He had one pair of decent slacks which he selected, together with an open-necked shirt. He had brought no suit and only a dull tie. He found himself yearning for the casual elegance of a tropical suit or even just a jazzy cravat despite the fact that he possessed neither and at home would have found the tie acceptable.

Standing before the mirror he took stock: handsome, classic Jewish features with little suggestion of his Wellings forebears, flecks but not yet streaks of grey at the temples in his still-thick dark hair, a summer tan already well developed despite days of hard slog in his basement office, a flat stomach despite the absence of exercise in his normal routine. With satisfaction he saw nothing which might repel Smith Jackson.

He had never been unfaithful to Claire. In a panic he picked up the telephone and dialled their number. He let it ring a long time before accepting there was no reply. Puzzled, he replaced the receiver and tried again in case he had misdialled, but the result was the same. The panic tightened its grip, Portugal suddenly seeming too far away from home, from his son. He would not be able to get a flight if anything had happened. His mind busied itself with mental maps of an overland journey.

Calming himself as best he could, knowing he was reacting illogically, he tried to remember what Claire's arrangements had been. When was Aunt Isobel coming? He told himself not to be a fool. Of course Claire was not normally out in the evenings, but that was because he himself was expected home for dinner. There was no reason why she and the children should not be visiting or something.

He resumed his dressing but his mood was destroyed. He cursed Claire, blaming her for the cloud he now saw hanging over his evening. Then it occurred to him that if anything were wrong Sam or Aunt Isobel would know and he could ring them. An ingrown toenail would set the Renwick bush telegraph working. Then he could always phone the hospital itself to ask if his son had been admitted or, for that matter, Neville Harris. Indeed, if anything were seriously wrong surely any of those people would phone him?

Soothed by so many sudden solutions to his problem, he found himself no longer worried and availed himself of none of them.

At least now he could say he had tried to telephone. There was no need to try again until the morning. For this evening he could be charmed by Smith Jackson, even if regrettably accompanied by her children. Briefly he indulged a fantasy in which she arrived alone, brightly declaring she had used the hotel babysitting service because the children had decided they would be bored by a grown-up dinner. Something in the way she said it would indicate that really it had been her idea to leave them, that she had cajoled or bribed them perhaps to stay behind, that she had her own notions of what grown-up things might be happening. He knew he deceived himself: the children were her chaperons, her armour against any situation which might not be to her liking, her excuse to leave early.

He decided not to have a drink in the hotel bar before they arrived and felt disproportionately virtuous. Instead he browsed through the many leaflets in his room advertising excursions, wondering what might be suitable for children of eight and twelve and what perhaps just for adults. Of course he did not know what the Jacksons had already done and seen, he did not even know how long they had been in Estoril. Indeed, it was not at all certain that they would not have their own arrangements for the rest of their stay which did not include him.

He wondered what he should tell Claire, doubting that he could even begin to explain why, when he had come to Portugal expressly to relax and escape the pressures of everyday life, he

131

should immediately assume responsibility for two strange children, one of whom was burdened by gross disfigurement. That, to Claire, would be a greater betrayal than his consorting with a beautiful widow. Perhaps he should not mention the Jacksons at all.

In the half-hour before they were due to arrive Mark consulted his watch every few minutes, getting up from his chair to put his room keys in his pocket, checking his wallet, combing already perfectly tidy hair, then returning to the chair to sit unrelaxed until he should begin his next false departure for the foyer. With two minutes to go and his hand on the door knob he turned back into the room and rang Claire, feeling annoyed and frustrated when she answered. He looked at his watch, knowing that now he would keep the Jacksons waiting – if they waited. Suppose Smith used his tardiness as an excuse to escape an engagement of which she might now be becoming wary?

In an agony of impatience he told Claire curtly that he had a good flight, was settled in and due at dinner shortly. Was all well with her? His nerves frayed as she began to chat, possibly from guilt at the coldness of her farewell at the airport. She began to detail the exploits of Pippa and Montefiore, to reassure him as to Jeremy's welfare. He felt obliged to make a perfunctory enquiry about the tube and learned that it was all a false alarm, that Jeremy's swallowing reflexes were back to normal. He should have danced for joy; instead he consulted his watch and wondered how to end the conversation, resenting her questions about the hotel and had he been to the beach yet and what was the pool like and was it all abominably crowded?

The call had taken a full ten minutes and he ran down the stairs, looking round the foyer with fear. They were not there and his heart sank: they had not waited, they had gone. He ran outside to see if they were still visible and saw them walking towards him, just arriving. Sarah smiled and waved and he felt a fool, unable to think up any reason for his sudden eruption into their path.

'Sorry we're late,' Smith greeted him.

'I was late myself. I came out to see if you had given up and gone.'

'Gracious, you must be a stickler for punctuality. We're only a few minutes past the appointed hour.' Smith was teasing him but her eyes were watchful.

To reassure her he mentioned his conversation with Claire as the reason for his lateness, but when she smiled he knew she saw through his words. It occurred to him that Claire, who had been married to him for thirteen years, knew him less well, was far more easily gulled than this woman he had met but a few hours ago, and a small voice within cried Judas. He confronted and crushed his conscience; it was a time for taking, for irresponsibility, for self-indulgence, he did not seek to dress them up in any other terms or to make excuses for them, merely to let them take over for as long as he willed it, unfettered by that tiny nagging voice. With St Augustine he could have prayed for deferred virtue, had he any faith in prayer at all, but then Sarah put her

133

small, trusting hand in his and he felt himself a satyr.

They went straight into dinner as he thought the children might be hungry and bored at the prospect of lingering over drinks in the bar. The dining room was very full, mainly of package tourists talking over the day's excursions and, as the waiter led them to a table in the far corner of the room, he felt heads turn, heard conversations falter and then start again. As they took their seats there were more glances, not of open admiration for Smith's good looks but of covert curiosity and repulsion at Sarah's. Undaunted, but Mark felt not unaware, she chose the seat facing into the room, saying she wanted to watch what everyone was doing, meaning instead that she dared them all to watch her. It might have been courage or it might have been bravado; Mark, still a stranger to her, could not be sure which.

Smith asked after and about his family, he returned the curiosity and learned there was a third child, Maisie, left at home in Somerset with Smith's parents because she was too young to come. She was not yet two, and Mark realised that Smith must have been widowed with a babe in arms, realised too that she was only a little on the wrong side of thirty and must have married while still in her teens. Life had scarcely been kind to her, yet she seemed genuinely serene.

He asked about her unusual Christian name and the children rolled their eyes at each other as she embarked upon the explanation they must have heard many times before.

'My father is German' – so that explained Fritz – 'and when my mother was expecting me she bombarded him with every name she could think of because she was terrified he might want to call me something German and my grandfather would have created the most awful fuss because he still hadn't got over the war. She thought he might disown her altogether if I were a boy and was called Hans or something. So she produced name after name day after day from the moment she knew I was coming. In the end he got so fed up he shouted, "Ach, call it Smith. Everybody in ziss country is called Smith."

'So for the rest of her pregnancy they referred to me as Smith and the nickname stayed with me when I was born. I think they meant to drop it later but never did. I liked it because it was different and so I didn't drop it either, and now I'm just too used to it.'

Mark raised a politely inquisitive eyebrow.

Smith smiled: 'Lucy Ernestina Maria. Maria is after my German grandmother but my other grandfather could not be sure.'

Mark laughed. 'I prefer Lucy, but it's hardly a conversation piece like Smith.'

'And Mark?'

He could take the hint or ignore it. He decided to take it and described his mother's rebellion. The children began their own sotto-voce conversation, giggling at someone or something elsewhere in the room.

When Mark had finished his potted family history Smith was silent, her face sweetly grave, the light in her eyes dying a little.

'What is it?' asked Mark.

'I was lust thinking – our grandfathers might have hated one another.'

'Yes, but the world has moved on.'

She glanced at Sarah. 'Has it?'

Mark thought of Jeremy, of Nurse Kenward, of Sally's forthcoming Bill, of Claire's reaction to Eve and Kylie, but he said stoutly, 'Yes, surely we must believe that. If human beings aren't making progress, aren't creating a better world, then we might as well give up.'

She shook her head but, to his relief, changed the subject. Soon the conversation was once more light and trivial, the glimpse she had just afforded him of her soul almost forgotten, the small but dense cloud of pessimism gone. He knew she had wanted to talk, to share with him her fears for Sarah, but he wanted no burdens and he justified his reaction with the reflection that they could not have spoken of those fears and doubts with Sarah there.

He no longer wanted to pursue this friendship, to take them all to Lisbon or Cascais, to teach Sarah to swim properly or to feel Smith leaning on his arm as they took long walks together. As for the rest, how could he have even thought of it? He wanted Smith to entertain him, to imbue him with her calmness, her serenity, her steady philosophical acceptance of the terrible. He did not want to be her prop, to have to reassure her and show her hope. He began to think of excuses in case she should suggest another meeting.

The children jumped up with alacrity when it was time to go. Smith had already ordered a taxi.

He realised that he had made little conversation with them, had left them to their own devices, ignoring them save when discussing the menu. Good. That would repel her. She surely would not like anyone who cared so little for her children. Yet he was sorry too, for they had been no trouble and deserved better from him.

His impatience grew as he waited in the foyer while they made use of the lavatories. He wanted them gone.

Smith hesitated as she said goodnight, perhaps hoping for some suggestion for the morrow, but then gave him a social hug and a light peck on his cheek. He briefly scented her perfume, her hair, her.

'Will you be on the beach tomorrow?' he asked.

'Yes.' No longer wary, perhaps yearning.

'See you then.' He handed her into the taxi. They all waved and he turned, undecided, towards his lonely room.

8

He struggled to wake up, to escape the dream in which he knew something terrible was about to happen, that there was some horror lurking in the sea, but the dream held him, mocking. It had not started as a nightmare but pleasantly, excitingly, as he pursued Smith along the sand, overtaking her long-legged strides. She had turned to laugh at him when suddenly he saw her no more but was instead in the sea, not the warm Portuguese sea but a cold, inhospitable sea in which he could not touch the sand beneath. A child was there in water wings but it was not Sarah, nor were these wings like any he had seen, growing large and green from Pippa's arms, culminating in great, sharp points yards above them. He struggled towards her and the wings enveloped them both as they were dragged down. Down, down, down. Pippa was laughing and he was swimming again, alone, towards the shore, where at the water's edge lay something he did not want to see, the thing which was driving him to try to wake up. Something pale, something over which the seaweed straggled menacingly. Jeremy.

It was not the present-day Jeremy, but Jeremy as he had been at three or four, Jeremy hideously disfigured by a livid birthmark which spread over a face cracked like that of the doll his mother had had as a child and which his sisters had refused to discard. Smith was coming back along the beach and he wanted to run because he was afraid of her, of evil. This time his frantic struggles availed him and he came out of the dream into his dark bedroom, grasping for the light switch by the bed. He found it and clicked it but nothing happened, no comforting light bathed the room. He clicked again with the same result. He got out of bed in too great a hurry, tying himself up in bedclothes, struggling to free himself, racing for the switch of the main light, terrified he might not reach it before whatever was waiting in the room grasped him malevolently. Again the light refused to respond, and now he knew he was still dreaming. He tried to pull open the door but it stayed shut; he shouted but no sound came.

This time he did wake, did light the room with the bedside lamp, sinking back against the pillows, sweating, conscious of the flight of residual fear. For a while he lay still, absorbing the normality of his unremarkable room. Had he really shouted and struggled, disturbed other guests? The smooth, unruffled sheet reassured him. In his dream he had become entangled with sheets and blankets but his real bed was blanketless: equipped for hot summer nights, not nightmares.

He sat up, aware that there was still a shaking in his stomach, forming a half-hearted intention to walk round the room in order to complete his awakening, to drive the bad dream into oblivion, but he was too tired. Instead he reviewed the dream, most of the details of which he could no longer remember. It was all nonsense: Pippa had never used water wings and would have scorned them as babyish, she swam well; Jeremy had never looked like that; and as for Smith, no one could call that lovely, serene face evil.

The logic did not quite reassure him enough to turn off the light. He tried to sleep with it on, eventually turning it off in irritation when he was nearly slumbering anyway.

In the morning he was ashamed: he had behaved like a child with night terrors, it was a wonder he had not called for Nanny. Nor did he need a dream analyst to tell him that he was suffering from a bad attack of conscience rather than mere indigestion or even anxiety. His affair with Smith was betraying his children. Affair? There was no affair, would be no affair. Men like him were too nervous of affairs, they went through life worrying, shouldering responsibilities, seeing things through. They were not more moral than others, merely more burdened, more tormented. Anxiety gave them foresight and they avoided temptation because the consequences were too much trouble. Claire, he recalled, had not featured in the nightmare.

At breakfast a package tourist and his wife at the next, closely-placed, table engaged him in conversation and he found himself responding willingly, trying to take an interest in those around him in order to take his mind off his own unsatisfactory life.

They came to Portugal every year, alternating Estoril with the Algarve. Their grown-up children thought them mad because there were so many places to go and see. They kept saying go to France, go to Spain, but why should they when they liked Portugal so much? They had been to Calais on a day trip and did not think much of France. What about him?

Mark obliged with a summary of his own travel experiences, talking of Kenya, India, the Far East, Italy and Tangier. He could tell they were wondering what brought him to a modest hotel in Estoril without the family he had mentioned, so he told them that too. They exclaimed together.

'Oh, the poor mite!' said the woman, of Jeremy.

'Poor you!' said the man, of Mark.

If either had noticed him with another family the previous evening neither said so now. There were some further exchanges on the heat, the day's plans, the qualities of the hotel, then they rose and said they would doubtless see him at supper that night.

Mark half rose from his seat, but did not stand, as the woman got up. Alone, he ordered more toast to postpone the moment of decision between spending the morning by the pool and going to the beach where Smith would expect to see him. He decided on the beach to avoid disappointing the children, but when he came back down from his room he went to the pool instead.

He read, swam, wrote postcards, swam, ate lunch, read and swam. He would have been relaxed, his tensions easing their grip, if he had not been so aware they were waiting for him on the beach. Later he took a hot shower and returned to sip the hotel's special cocktail by the pool. On his way into dinner the receptionist handed him a message which had been taken down in abysmally spelled English but well enough to convey its meaning.

'Sorry we mist you on beech. Desided at last minut to go to Lisbon. Diner heer Wensday queshon marck. Love Smith.'

So they had never been waiting on the beach, the children had been excitedly enjoying Lisbon instead. Mark felt both relieved and irritated, but pleased at the prospect of forty-eight hours without the same dilemma. Presumably Smith

141

wanted space too. He wondered if she also had felt guilty at not being on the beach.

His spirits lifted and he chatted to the tourists on the tables to either side of him, this time learning their names: Robert and Clare to whom he had been talking that morning and Desmond and Jane, a young, giggly, mildly furtive couple who pretended to be married. Mark was unsure whether they did so for their own amusement or out of deference to the other tourists, most of whom were comfortably into middle age.

A long walk, some photography of the fishing boats against the night sky, a drink at an outdoor café; he felt renewed, undriven, on holiday, capable of making decisions tomorrow. Yet the next day and the day after he found himself on the beach, ostensibly relaxing, in fact looking for Smith. On the Wednesday he was there again, counting the hours before dinner. In his return message he had said he would be at the Estoril Sol at eight and he was now wishing he had made it earlier. To appease himself he made a decision to leave Inglis and May after the flotation. He would set up a one-man practice within ten miles of home and cut out the commuting. He did not bother himself with any practicalities nor with questions about what would happen if this did not work: it would be a very long time before his family would be driven to starvation and he had no doubt Sam would help anyway. He suppressed the inevitable stab of guilt which rebuked him for having designs on Sam's money at the same time as actively thinking about betraying Sam's daughter.

He had begun to miss Jeremy and Pippa, to want to hold Jeremy and feel his passive warmth, to listen to Pippa's chatter and watch her fondling Montefiore, her face bright and innocent, but he did not, could not, miss Claire. His indifference to her alarmed him. Surely even divorced people missed their former partners occasionally? Had some vague longing? Some regret at the parting? The years before Pippa should be grown-up, more emotionally independent, better able to accept their parting, yawned before him, a terrible chasm of wasted opportunity. What was grown-up? Fourteen? Sixteen? Twenty? Depressed, he began to calculate his own age at these possible points of freedom.

He sat up and looked round the beach, seeking some distraction from his hardly encouraging thoughts, and saw Smith approaching carrying towel and beach bag but without either of the children or their impedimenta. His spirits soared.

She greeted him happily, then spread her towel beside his. He noticed it was one of those bright, violently patterned ones apparently designed to be seen from several miles away. He felt a growing dissatisfaction with his own: a faded, dull affair with pale green stripes which he could remember using to wipe Rags with when he ran into the stream in winter and Claire said Barton would worry the dog might catch pneumonia. He had almost used it for protective covering of the dining-room furniture when they were last decorating, and now he wished he had. It was not the sort of towel on to which to invite a lady.

'What's funny?' asked Smith, as his reflections caused him to smile.

'My ancient towel,' he said, deadpan.

Smith looked at it, puzzled. 'It's conventional,' she pronounced judiciously, and they both laughed.

'Where are the children?'

'Gone out in a fishing boat with some other children from the hotel and their parents. Then they're all off to some late-night market. I was told to expect them when I see them but not before ten.'

So they would dine alone but that was all. The children would be back at ten. Yet it was more than he had hoped for even if much less than he wished for. He could of course suggest returning to the hotel early, but something, perhaps a fear of rejection or perhaps a faint wariness in her manner, deterred him.

For a while they fell silent, watching the sea, listening to it as it lapped the shore. Neither felt like swimming and presently, when Smith struggled to apply her suntan lotion to her back, he offered to rub it in for her. She lay compliantly on her stomach while he did so, but he could sense her tension and made it a briefer contact than he had intended. Seeing himself through her eyes, he saw a married man off the leash for a week and his conscience told him it was not an unfair picture, that only the absence of opportunity and perhaps an unwillingness on Smith's part had this time preserved his unbroken record of marital fidelity. With insight he knew she wanted him but that she herself was

144

yet faithful to the husband of whose death she still could not speak without tears. Fragile. That was the word which she had used of herself. Fragile. Handle with care. He knew it was not in his nature to damage anything fragile.

He subsided on to his own towel, relieved and disappointed. Later they swam. Without the children to restrain her she proved a strong, adventurous swimmer and they stayed long in the water, returning exhausted and exhilarated to collapse in contented but individual sleep. When they woke, Smith suggested he came to the Estoril Sol for a drink before dinner and they agreed to meet at seven.

They took the drinks out into the garden of the big hotel and found a seat among the bright flowers and shrubs. Smith asked if he had heard again from his family and he told her he had not. She said she had spoken to her mother the previous night and Maisie was fine. They began to talk of their children to satisfy each other's hungry curiosity about lives which each wished were connected but knew were about to be separated for ever. Fritz and Sarah were both clever and their natural abilities were being supplemented by rigorous and expensive education. She expected both to do well, and hoped that the world would be kind to Sarah.

When they spoke of Jeremy, however, Smith was not inclined to accept the certainty of the bleak picture Mark described, one with which he and Claire had long since intellectually come to terms and with which emotionally they never would. Jeremy would be loved and looked after

145

throughout their lives and if he survived them his grandfather's money should ensure a high standard of care thereafter. They were luckier than many in their position.

'Medical science moves very fast these days and Jeremy is still a child. He may yet have a quality of life which at the moment none of you can imagine, just as one day they may just be able to laser away Sarah's disfigurement.'

Mark shook his head. 'No,' he said emphatically, 'not in Jeremy's case. It's too absolute. But let's just suppose they do have that sort of breakthrough in say thirty or forty years' time, where the hell does that leave Jeremy? I know they say life begins at forty, but it can't be done literally. You remember that phrase of Thomas Wolfe's? That we are the sum of our experiences? So what does that make Jeremy? You can't go from four to forty or fifty with nothing in between.'

Nor could he and Claire, he thought savagely. Whatever sort of nightmare would that be in their seventies or eighties or even nineties? Yet if medicine offered the chance, could they deny it to their son? Surely not.

'I'm not convinced you're right,' said Smith gently. 'Obviously he would not suddenly find himself a normal fifty-year-old with two kids, a mortgage and a company pension scheme, but that is not the meaning of life. If he could move, see, hear, enjoy affection, learn elementary communication skills, that would be enough to bring you huge joy, wouldn't it?'

'Montefiore can do all that.'

Smith looked blank.

'The cat. I mean, of course we'd be over the moon if that happened or if any little bit of it happened. Dear God, if only it could. What I mean is Jeremy still wouldn't be Jeremy, wouldn't be whoever he would have been if that bastard hadn't run him over. That is what I meant by not being able to start at forty. He must for ever be a vague shadow of himself because life hasn't shaped him. Seeing, moving, hearing, even talking, would be things he could do, but they wouldn't be *him*.'

'Have you forgiven that bastard?' asked Smith unexpectedly.

Mark stared at her warily, his eyes suddenly drawn to the small crucifix at her neck. He did not want a lecture or an analysis of his own psychology, however gently phrased.

'No. I never will. He was young, silly and he's been punished by the law and doubtless still is being punished by the knowledge of what he did. But that doesn't make it any better. I don't wish him any harm but I can't forgive. If I saw him suffering I suppose I would even help but I still hate him. He left Jeremy an empty shell, and stole from him all the purpose of his existence.'

'No,' said Smith kindly, 'not all the purpose, only some of it. You love him, your wife loves him and your little girl loves him. Other children like him, enjoy pushing his chair, playing with him even if in a limited way. That's purpose.'

'So Jeremy's purpose is to be an object for other people's indulgence?' He heard the bitterness in his voice but she was unperturbed.

147

'Aren't there thousands of people who live for others? Why do we always think that it has to be something active, self-sacrificial? It is just as possible to live for others passively, and just as beautiful. Maybe it is even more beautiful, because at least it is not done to earn gratitude or plaudits or to receive love in return. And in this case the inability to *give* love in return means there is no underlying bargain, just purity.'

He looked at her in amazement, but she did not notice because her own gaze was fixed on a distant tree around the trunk of which grew a large fiery plant, its tendrils already entwining the lower branches. She turned to him.

'You see that tree? The one with the plant all round it? It reminds me of my own garden at home in Somerset. I used to have a large sumac tree which turned fiery red each year, a bit like the colour of that plant, and it seemed to light up the whole garden with glory, even though it only lasted a couple of weeks. People used to stop and admire it and for years it was our pride and joy. Then it just started to die and we were heart-broken, but my husband would not have it taken down. He just cut it right back and year after year we looked for any sign of life but there wasn't any. Even so I couldn't bear to destroy it, so we trained a clematis round it and now, each May, it is a spectacular sight. The tree has become beautiful through the clematis and the clematis is more beautiful because the tree makes it unusual – normally you would expect to find it climbing a wall or a trellis or something.'

Smith paused, but he did not interrupt. She

went on: 'You see, Jeremy is like the tree: passive, but giving beauty, and the clematis is all that love which embraces him and grows stronger and more beautiful. That tree will always have a purpose now until the last bit of it is dead, and its purpose is to light up its surroundings. These days people stop to admire the clematis tree, so it isn't a sumac in any recognisable form any more, just the shell or the shadow of one, but that has not destroyed its purpose.'

It was very quiet in the garden. 'Thank you,' said Mark, and he kissed her, not the Judas kiss he had contemplated that afternoon, but a chaste, gentle, humble kiss of a gratitude deep as the sea.

He looked again at her crucifix. 'You have faith?'

'Yes. Do you?'

'No.'

'Because of the accident?'

'No. I don't think I ever had much. My father ensured we were all baptised, but that was about it.'

'And Claire?'

'Yes. She's practising C of E. Goes to church every Sunday without fail, takes both children, sends Pippa to Sunday School, supports the church fête. The vicar has become a family friend. He was very supportive after the accident.'

'Why do you say it like that?'

'Because the peace of God appears to have made her shrewish, nagging and snobbish. She's a good mother and I still love her but I no longer want to live with her. I only stay because of Pippa.' He knew his words were ugly, harsh and brutal. Smith would think less of him.

'Not Jeremy?'

'Jeremy doesn't know whether I'm there or not,' retorted Mark bitterly.

'Are you sure?' It was gentle, not challenging, but Mark remembered the conversation with Puddleduck on the children's ward and winced. The garden was still quiet but no longer tranquil.

Then Smith asked, 'Have you spoken to the vicar about Claire?' Mark looked startled. 'The vicar? No. I've spoken to the doctor more times than I can count but he just says have a good long holiday, and so we would have done but for the enteritis. We had planned a pretty comprehensive tour of France.'

'It would help.'

'Only a little. The situation is way beyond being rescued by a mere holiday. Anyway, why the vicar?'

She shrugged. 'You said he was a family friend, and presumably to Claire he is also a spiritual guide?'

It was Mark's turn to shrug. 'God knows,' he said dismissively, unconscious of the irony.

'He probably does,' observed Smith drily, smiling at an elderly couple who had just wandered into that part of the garden.

'Where is everyone tonight?' Mark suddenly became aware that the silence of the garden was not a normal attribute of a large hotel in the height of the holiday season.

'Special kids' entertainment probably due to

end any minute now. The adults will be grabbing some peace somewhere. It's the sort of time people shower and change for dinner.'

They got up, stretching, and began to make their way into the hotel, but Smith took his arm and turned him to face the tree which hosted the fiery plant. They both looked at it in silence. Then he put his arm round Smith and led her in to dinner.

He was grateful that she kept the conversation light for the rest of the evening, and they were both surprised at the passing of time when the children came in exuberantly just after ten. In deference to the other diners Smith moved them all out into the lounge for coffee, and in Mark's case a brandy as well. There were five children in the group, and Mark could not help noticing how utterly unaware they seemed to be of Sarah's appearance, though he also noted with less favour the covert glances of some of the other holidaymakers in the lounge. He supposed being conscious of this was a habit born out of accompanying Jeremy, or perhaps he was merely too sensitive, too willing to find fault in those who did not share his difficulty, who had damnably perfect children. Smith appeared to have no such resentment, her attention too focused on the bright faces of the children to be diverted to others' reactions.

Perhaps it was not only Claire who had grown ungenerous towards half the human race. The thought unsettled him briefly but it was too chastening a reflection on which to dwell, so he applied himself instead to Fritz's cork purchases

151

and Sarah's enormous sponge.

'Do you know,' he asked Fritz, 'that some shops in England won't sell real sponges because they think it's cruelty to living organisms in the sea?'

Fritz laughed and Mark, looking at his happy countenance, his earnest interest, his sometimes quaintly grave, grown-up mannerisms, thought of how he was only a little older than Jeremy and was miserably conscious of the acute pain of loss.

Smith, as if sensing his sadness and longing, looked up from the children and met his eyes. She smiled understandingly and he smiled back, soothed. How long since there had been such moments with Claire, such unspoken tenderness, such a meeting of souls?

Yet there had been such a union, such an understanding once, when he had no need to explain his thoughts to share them. Now such knowledge of each other was no longer their haven but just part of the stormy sea on which their love had been tossed and wrecked, on which they were being torn asunder. It was a long time since either had sought a lifeline to offer hope, to unite them, to pull them out.

He said he would walk home, despite the distance. The children did not want him to go, he suspected because they feared the departure of their mother's guest would almost certainly herald bedtime. He smiled, patted their heads, admired a cork artefact he had missed and which was now offered as a delaying tactic. Smith told the children to pack up their purchases and went with him to the door.

They made no arrangements to meet again.

She was leaving on Friday morning and he on Saturday. Nor did they exchange addresses. Their kiss was one of close friendship, their hug tighter than on the previous parting, but as he walked home, savouring the night air and its scents, pausing to look out over the coast, he knew they would probably never see each other again. He conceived a wild intention to scour all the Somerset telephone directories for an L.E.M. Jackson, to hire a private detective to track down a clematis tree in a Somerset garden, to forge some link with the major public school to which Fritz had told him he would be going next year.

He stopped to look out over the sea and to face reality. For the second time that evening it was the reality of loss, of the pain of missing and longing. He knew Smith had given him courage, philosophy and hope. She had given him the lasting present of the image of the clematis tree whose glories grew from the withering sumac. He had given her nothing in return. He had been the passive parasite of her strength.

Mark, who had neither belief nor a desire for belief, prayed to the Estoril sky that, if it held a benevolent force which intervened in the affairs of mere mortals, Sarah should find happiness. It would, Mark informed the Deity grimly, be some small compensation for the suffering He had allowed to be inflicted on his own family.

That night he wept for Smith like a lovelorn teenager, feeling no braver or wiser than a small boy lost in a hostile environment, but he dreamed of the clematis tree and woke with a measure of peace.

9

Mark struggled through the throng of package tourists to reach the hotel reception desk. The foyer was full of luggage, people, harassed couriers and porters. Amidst the departure of the holidaymakers for Gatwick and for Paris, the remaining tourists were anxiously enquiring which were the coaches for the day's excursions. He wondered that he had not foreseen this mêlée and timed his own departure better. Around him the hotel's departing guests were lamenting the end of their holidays, trying to remember if they had left a gratuity for the chambermaid, urging children to keep together and wondering what the weather was like at their destinations.

His own formalities completed, Mark located the taxi which, despite the delay, was reliably waiting for him and leaned back in relief, leaving the driver to stow his suitcase in the boot. He was leaving Portugal without regret, knowing Smith was already back in Britain, somewhere in Somerset. He thought of apple orchards and Bath stone.

With less willingness he tried to focus on his own homecoming, on the return to work on Monday, on Claire's own forthcoming holiday. None of it yet felt real, nor did so when he was in the aeroplane watching Portugal fall away beneath him. He could think only of Smith.

At Heathrow he regretted that he had arranged with Claire to make his own way home: Pippa hated waiting at stations and airports and was prone to grizzle if forced to endure a long delay. As he took his large holdall from the carousel he dreaded the tube and train journeys ahead. It was with real pleasure and surprise, therefore, that he found them all waiting to greet him. Pippa flung herself on him and, when he took Jeremy's wheelchair from Claire, his daughter walked beside him talking non-stop. Claire came behind with his holdall on a trolley, but each time he turned to see how she was managing Pippa impatiently reclaimed his attention. The wheel-chair guaranteed high standards of politeness and people got out of their way, shifting luggage to facilitate their path. Claire, with a mere trolley, was less lucky. Mark remembered a time when no man would have allowed a woman to push a trolley of luggage without offering to help, regretted its passing and decided he must be growing old.

In the car he persuaded Pippa to let him 'talk to Mummy for two minutes' and asked about Jeremy. Still swallowing, said Claire. No sign of the enteritis. All well. So was all the family. Montefiore was developing great character and was each day growing more of a cat and less of a kitten.

'I've got some things done while you were away,' Claire told him.

He thought he detected a note of uncertainty but any enquiries he might have made were pre-empted by Pippa's impatience to tell him of school uniform purchases and the latest computer games. There was no mention of Kylie Grant and he concluded Claire had stood firm. At least Pippa seemed to have lost her faint wariness of him, and he inwardly formed a futile resolution to give her no cause to renew it, but he sensed Claire was tense though he could not tell why.

Enlightenment came when he opened his front door. There, immediately inside it, was a new wheelchair, identical to the one he knew to be in the back of the car outside. He stared at it, puzzled.

'What's up with the wheelchair?' he called to Claire as he parked his holdall and went outside to help with Jeremy.

'Nothing, but it's useful to have a spare for indoors. This one makes dirty tracks all over the place when it's raining or he's been on the grass.'

'Which is why we use the kitchen entrance.'

'Mark, it's an effort. Don't you understand? He's getting bigger every day. I'm not a world weight-lifting champion. Getting him into the kitchen, out of the chair, cleaning up the wheels, getting him back in again, wheeling him to where I want him to go, getting him out again, taking the chair back to the hall: it's all work. You don't have to do it all the time like I do, because you're not here until Jeremy goes to bed.'

'But why such a complicated thing if all you want it for is inside wheeling? It doesn't need to go up and down pavements or brake on slopes or anything. Why not a basic one?'

'It can double as a spare if we need to send the

156

other in for repair.'

Mark did not reply. He lifted Jeremy bodily from the car and, ignoring the wheelchair Claire had unfolded, carried him into the house. On his way to the lounge he stopped, staring at the foot of the stairs in disbelief before continuing on his way, putting Jeremy on the sofa and switching on the television. Turning, he saw Claire in the lounge doorway.

'It's the other side tonight,' she said quietly.

With no sign of impatience, Mark turned Jeremy round and placed him with his head at the other end of the sofa, before adjusting the position of the television which stood on a castor-wheeled table, enabling it to be stationed wherever it was needed for Jeremy's line of possible vision, the imperative to avoid pressure sores dictating frequent changes of his position. This task completed, and assured of his son's comfort, he returned to the hall and once more stared at the chair and electric cables which were now affixed to the staircase. Claire came and stood beside him.

'It's necessary,' she said in a voice between a plea and a whine. 'He's getting so big, Mark. I won't be able to carry him upstairs much longer and I don't want him to have to sleep downstairs; I want him living as the rest of us do.'

Mark stared at the Stannah lift, hating it. It spoke of further separation from his son, of the time when even he would find him too heavy to carry up and down stairs regularly, when he would not feel the familiar warmth as he lifted him in his arms. He swore.

Claire misunderstood. 'Mark, be reasonable,' she began, but he cut her off.

'Anything else?'

She muttered something about the spare bathroom. Mark took the stairs two at a time and arrived at the bathroom door already with an accurate idea of what he would see: a bathroom converted for the utterly paralysed, including a large, expensive hoist. As the original bathroom had been made out of a former bedroom it was an ideal size for such a project, the bath now standing in the middle of the room.

He returned downstairs and found Claire in the kitchen doing nothing very purposeful. They faced each other from either end of the farmhouse table.

'How much?'

She coloured. 'Daddy's paid.'

'You told him I didn't know?'

'I said it would be a surprise.'

'When?'

'What?' She looked at him uncomprehendingly.

'When? You didn't get all that complex stuff designed, ordered and installed in the space of one miserable week. You must have been planning this for ages.'

'So?'

'So a man likes to know what is going on in his own home. He might also have views about whether or not his father-in-law should be scrounged from when he could well afford to pay for something a bit simpler.'

'I didn't want anything a bit simpler. I wanted what is right for looking after Jeremy.'

158

'Then you could have tried persuading me that it was right.'

'Your choice of words sums it up: "tried persuading you". That's exactly what it would have been – a challenge to see if I could make you change your mind and face up to reality. It would not have been a discussion. It would have been a trial of wills. If you are so concerned about what is going on in your own home you could always spend more time in it and see. Then you might understand what I have to put up with and cope with day after day.'

He looked at her without speaking, taking in the grey which was now replacing the mouse colour of her hair, the thickening waistline, the lines too deeply etched at the sides of her mouth, the hands perpetually stained with gardening, slightly ragged nails, flat shoes, presentable but unremarkable clothes. Fastidious in so much, she was nevertheless neglecting aspects of her appearance which only a couple of years ago would have been the object of fierce pride. She looked less cared for than Eve Grant.

Certainly she would cut a poor figure beside her younger, energetic, beautiful sister, and he could not help wondering how many of the ever-watchful Renwicks had noticed. Perhaps they thought he neglected her. He suppressed any comparisons with Smith.

He tried reasoning. 'Look, it may well be that we needed some of these things or even all of them. I can't ever remember refusing you or Pippa or Jeremy anything which you needed, but Jeremy is my son, not Sam's. As far as possible I

159

want to provide for all of you myself. That's not pride. It's just a matter of being the breadwinner not the pocket-money earner. When it was a matter of taking Jeremy halfway round the world to see all those specialists that was different, but this sort of thing we should sort out ourselves.'

'Daddy doesn't grudge it.'

'That is not the point. We are very well off as it is. When did we last have any money worries? A lot of people face our problems without two halfpennies to rub together. What the NHS and Social Services don't provide they don't get, full stop.'

'I can't see what that has to do with us or with Jeremy.'

'It should have more to do with us than you let it. You have cut yourself off from all those other parents who might value your moral support, brains, shared experience or whatever. Perhaps even a limited amount of help with money occasionally.'

'Like Eve Grant? That woman at the Snoezelen?'

'She's just one example.'

'The sort of example you want to set Pippa? Come on, Mark!'

'Pippa cannot grow up believing that the whole world lives as well as we do.'

'She can have as many poor friends as she likes providing they have decent morals. If she wants the other sort when she's older that's up to her.'

'I'm not going to argue. I can't force you to see it my way, but we both need to do things a bit differently if we are to go on together.'

160

He saw the alarm in her eyes. It was the first time either had openly acknowledged the possibility of their marriage failing, and ruthlessly he pressed home his advantage.

'I'm leaving Inglis and May once the flotation is over and I'll set up on my own somewhere around here. That will mean no commuting, no hours wasted on trains and no fretting and fuming when the damn things don't run. I'll be here more often and take more of my share. I can work at my own pace. It also means that I shall earn less, at least in the early years.'

Claire did not look enthusiastic. 'What brought all this on?' she asked sceptically.

'Having time to think it out.'

'You said both of us needed to do things differently.'

'Yes.'

He wanted to tell her to be less isolated, to nag him less, to react less dramatically to occasional failures like the respite home and the parent support group, to make an effort to enjoy her life instead of filling it with causes of complaint, but he said none of these things, waiting for her to make the first move. She shrugged.

'Well?' she demanded when the silence had lengthened still further. It was both a challenge and a promise of non-cooperation. Mark rose to neither and suddenly she looked haggard, as if her lines had deepened even while he watched her. He pitied her and wondered what her life would be if he did leave, if even the undoubted support of Sam, Sally and Aunt Isobel could rescue her from the emotional prison she was constructing for herself.

'You also said "if we are to go on together". What did that mean?'

'Are you happy?'

'Oh, for God's sake,' she snapped, too late seeing Pippa appear in the doorway. The child had been so quiet Claire had forgotten to be wary. Mark, seeing her start, turned and saw Pippa too. He had been home less than half an hour and already they were bickering.

'You two are always arguing,' Pippa informed them in the exasperated tone Claire used when intervening in quarrels among visiting children. She rolled her eyes heavenwards and wandered away again.

'That statement at any rate is unarguable,' observed Mark when both were satisfied that Pippa was out of earshot.

Claire had begun to look afraid. 'Mark, what are we talking about? Just now we were all together, happy; at the airport, in the car. Now you stand there and seriously talk about divorce, at least that's what I think you're talking about. What about Pippa? And above all what about Jeremy? Are you really just going to walk away and leave me to cope with him alone?'

Mark knew that was how the world would see it. He could imagine the Bartons talking to each other in scandalised tones: 'And after all that he just left her with that poor little boy.' He also knew he must not be blackmailed by it, that she must know he would not be blackmailed by it.

'I didn't mention divorce. I talked about trying to make the changes which will avoid it, which

162

will mean we all stay together. I want that as much as you, but not at any price. I'm not happy, you're not happy, soon Pippa won't be happy. You yourself have just demonstrated one of the problems.'

'What do you mean?'

'When we had a single bad experience with respite care your reaction was to ban all holidays. It would have been for ever if you had your way. When you tried that lousy parent support group you wouldn't try any others. When I point out that there's something rotten in the state of our marriage you talk dramatically of divorce and desertion and prepare to play the role of the tragic abandoned mother, struggling to bring up her handicapped son with only an adoring Daddy and a few million to fall back on. You asked just now what I wanted you to do. Well, I want you to grow up.'

He had not intended his homecoming to be like this and was not sure how the quarrel had even started, much less developed into this catalogue of recrimination. He was searching for a conciliatory form of words which would nevertheless reinforce rather than weaken his position when the telephone rang. Neither moved, each unwilling to appear the first to back away from the confrontation, until eventually Pippa picked up the upstairs extension. There was the sound of an indistinct conversation then Pippa leaned over the banister and yelled, 'It's Grandad.'

'OK,' Mark called back, forbearing to rebuke his daughter for shouting, uncomfortably aware

163

he had not been setting much of an example in the last few minutes. He turned towards the hall.

'Mark...' Claire's tone was half plea, half warning.

'Don't worry,' grumbled Mark, 'I shan't take it out on him.'

Claire stood beside him in the hall while he thanked Sam for his 'surprise'. Sam, who loved to give others pleasure, spoke happily about the work it would save.

'It'll save the lass no end, and that chair lift will do for me in old age, right champion.'

Mark laughed and began to praise the bathroom, trying to match Sam's enthusiasm. As he waxed lyrical about the hoist, deplored indignantly muddy tracks across carpets and exaggerated Jeremy's heaviness he felt Claire begin to vibrate with suppressed laughter. Turning, he caught her eye and felt his own irritation dissolve in rueful amusement. When he thought her overwhelmed by mirth he wickedly handed her the phone and mocked her in gestures as she spoke, before returning to the kitchen.

When she eventually followed him they both wanted to sustain the mood but, unsure how, were awkward with each other. The situation was saved by Pippa who, reassured by the substitution of laughter for anger, hastened to join them, thereby providing the imperative for at least the appearance of harmony. Mark, mentally casting about for a means of maintaining peace, toyed with the idea of offering to take Claire out to dinner to avoid the near inevitability of a mealtime quarrel but, as so often in the past, was deterred by the unlikely prospect of finding last-minute arrangements for the care of Jeremy.

He took heart from learning that she still intended to take her own holiday, never having been entirely convinced that she would not cast about for excuses once he had returned from his. She spoke, however, as if she were looking forward to it and detailed the arrangements which she had been able to confirm while he had been away. These were expensive but thorough and Aunt Isobel would be present throughout. Sally would also come for two nights, but Aunt Isobel would look after her and if he, Mark, had to work late that would not matter – Sally had said she did not mind. Mark began to wonder why he needed to be home at all and thought that they could have holidayed together as originally intended. It was a thought he kept to himself as he knew Claire attached importance to one of them being on hand, but it occurred to him that he had no idea how long she might insist on this or how far in the past Jeremy's enteritis would have to be before she relaxed the rule.

For the time being it was enough for him that Claire was at last about to have a holiday, however short, and that the evening passed peacefully after the earlier arguments.

At supper Claire asked him playfully whether the beach had been full of pretty girls and he said truthfully that he had not noticed but, seeing his opening and thinking he had an opportunity to pre-empt any unwary remark he might make in the future, he assumed a playful tone himself and told her that he had met a beautiful, wealthy young widow. She was not alert, he thought, as he watched her reaction: she trusted him implicitly, took his fidelity utterly for granted despite their difficulties and he was at once guilty, amused and irritated. Pippa wanted to know her name and he was surprised to hear himself reply:

'Lucy Jackson.'

For some reason he did not want to share her name with others albeit it was the only one she used. He described Fritz and Sarah, then went on to talk about Robert and Clare and Desmond and Jane so that he should not seem to dwell on the Jackson family.

Claire raised her eyebrows when he mentioned Sarah's disfigurement and Pippa said her friend had a horse called Fritz but there was no other comment. He managed to convey the situation between Desmond and Jane to Claire without being explicit enough for Pippa to understand.

He himself did not understand and looked quizzically at Claire when, later, as Pippa was going upstairs to get ready for bed, she called out, 'On your own feet, please' in firm and warning tones.

'She goes up on the Stannah if I don't watch. The first day it was in she gave all her bears a ride, then tried to persuade Montefiore to go up on it and got very frustrated when he kept jumping off.'

Mark laughed. He said he needed an early night and Claire replied tartly that he must be worn out enjoying himself but when he asked if

166

there were any jobs he should do she said no. Conscience eased, he topped up his glass with the Portuguese wine they had been enjoying at supper and prepared to retire. In the hall he called Claire and, putting his glass on the chair, pressed the button to send it aloft.

'I knew it had a use,' he joked.

He had intended it to be a light-hearted gesture of reconciliation, to indicate that he accepted the wretched installation after all, that he did not really resent it and all was well, but as his wife watched the drink make its journey she said:

'I'm surprised you can bear to be parted from it for so long.'

Then he looked at her with a mixture of hurt and hatred and knew that his marriage was doomed.

10

As Mark stood expostulating in his small office, staring in disbelief at the extra desk crammed into an inadequate space between a filing cabinet and the wall, he reflected that his return appeared to be bedevilled by physical alterations, his space thoroughly invaded, first at home and now at work.

'We had no choice,' Karen told him placatingly. 'The fire people got really nasty with Mr Inglis and we do need the extra staff.'

'I cannot have a secretary in my office,' Mark

told Inglis in a raised voice. 'I can't concentrate with all that clackety-clack stuff and I can scarcely have a sensitive telephone conversation with a client.'

'Half the world works in open-plan offices these days,' reasoned Inglis mildly.

'That is not an open-plan office. It is a glorified broom cupboard.'

'But the principle is the same as far as telephone conversations and clackety-clack stuff are concerned.'

'But why not have secretaries sharing with secretaries?'

'We have, as you will see if you take a look round. We've done our best but there was still one over.' Inglis made the secretary sound like a digit unexpectedly remaining after an unsatisfactory decimal calculation.

'And I wasn't here so I drew the short straw?' fumed Mark.

He knew Inglis wanted to retort that no, he had drawn the short straw because he was the least indispensable, knew also that he would not do so and that he, Mark, would be unwise to choose this moment to announce that he intended to leave after the flotation anyway. He wondered if he was to share with the former proprietor of a secretarial agency or with the working holiday-maker, and was not surprised to find it was the latter.

'This is Miss Bunter,' Karen told him a quarter of an hour later and he was as gracious as he could be.

'Ginny,' she said.

Mark looked at her, his heart sinking, taking in her Australian accent, informal manner and too-short skirt. If he must share an office he would have preferred someone quiet, efficient and self-effacing. Had the workload been less demanding he would simply have prepared to be amused and to watch the clash of cultures between this girl's informality and the pretensions of Inglis and May. It would not surprise him to learn that she had already called Inglis by his Christian name, whatever that might be. In the midst of pre-flotation pressure, however, he simply wanted quiet efficiency.

Karen told him that she was temporarily helping another partner and that Ginny would be looking after him for the time being, said he must let her know at once if there was anything she could do and then departed, leaving Ginny to settle in as best she could. Settling in appeared to consist of making her desk as chaotic as possible and Mark viewed her with increasing disfavour. If, instead of running a home, his mother had managed an office, her desk would have looked like Ginny's.

At eleven o'clock he was somewhat mollified by the appearance of his coffee, served unslopped with a tissue separating cup and saucer. By twelve he was impressed by the speed and accuracy of her typing, by half past she had reminded him of his lunch engagement and given him the short brief to go with it, by four he noticed she had subtly improved some English in his dictation though she claimed merely to be out of practice with transliteration from shorthand,

169

and by five he had twice heard her deal with difficult clients on the telephone not merely with diplomacy but with an assurance which seemed born of an intimate knowledge of the workings of Inglis and May, despite her having been with the firm less than eight hours. He felt the straw was not after all so short, and at six offered her a drink at a nearby wine bar.

He was disproportionately pleased when she accepted and he looked forward to a pleasant half-hour, hearing of Australia and her experiences in Britain, which he was sure she would describe entertainingly. In this he was not disappointed and it was with a jolt he suddenly realised two hours had passed.

'That was a long first day,' Claire greeted him on his return and he felt not guilty but exhilarated. Ginny had lifted his spirits and utterly distracted him from thoughts of both work and home, amusing him with exploits which carried him to another continent and another generation, showing him the world through as yet unjaded eyes, a perspective which these days he rarely enjoyed.

It was the beginning of a period in which he actively looked forward to work, to going to the office. Relying on Ginny's efficiency, infected by her enthusiasm, he slowly started to recapture some of the ambition and optimism with which he had once been wont to look at the world. By contrast, home became a place of burden, duty, anxiety and tension. One evening, when he had been enjoying what he had described to his conscience as a quick drink with Ginny and four of her friends, three of whom were also working holidaymakers and as relaxed and carefree as she, he was invited back to the flat of one of them for dinner. He accepted without telephoning Claire, knowing she would presume him at work and not wanting to tell her a direct lie.

He should have hated the evening, with the pop music which played incessantly in the untidy flat, the loud Australian voices, the amateurish cooking, the conversations which often excluded him because he did not know the people or their families, the homes and towns which were being discussed. Instead he revelled in it all, despite suspecting that they wondered what he was doing there and would probably laugh at him when he left.

It was Ginny's and not his own sense of responsibility which ensured he caught the last train from Waterloo. He told Claire he had worked late, then had a bite to eat because he did not want to impose upon her so late. Her reaction covered Alexander Bell, the invention of the telephone, the even later invention of mobiles, the nature of the meal which she suspected to have been largely liquid, the long day's work she also had faced, his grossly inconsiderate behaviour.

'And it's no good dressing it up as concern for me. You often eat around midnight and you've never been surprised to see a meal on the table at that time before.'

Mark refused to argue, knowing, but unabashed by the knowledge, that she was justifiably aggrieved. He felt irresponsible, enthusiastic, although about what he could not have said, and light-headed not, as she thought, from drink but from an unaccustomed freedom. It was illusory and he knew it, but he was finding the sensation too pleasant to repel with the claims of reality. He had felt freer tonight than in that whole week at Estoril with Sarah and Fritz the ghosts of his own waiting responsibilities and Smith still so unhappy, so untouchable.

Smith! He thought of her grave, sweet ways, of the clematis tree, of the way she looked at Sarah, and he was angry with himself for the comparison he had just made, ashamed that he was abandoning her so soon. The irony that it should be Smith, not Claire, who prompted the still small voice within was not lost on him, but he ignored it. A greater irony still was that he had begun to dread the time of his wife's holiday when his obligations to Aunt Isobel, the nurses and his children would force him to be at home as much as possible. The prospect of dutifully-caught trains immediately after work was too dull to contemplate, and his spirits might have been dampened but for the lucky recollection that duty was optional not, as he had always thought until now, imperative.

Buoyed up by a determination to behave badly he interrupted Claire's remonstrations with a firm 'goodnight' and headed for the stairs. Claire followed with angry protests and to irritate her further he turned into the lounge and poured himself a whisky he did not want, before sinking on to the Stannah and letting it take him to the landing. Claire stared with disgusted incredulity.

172

He wanted to giggle.

In the bathroom he poured the unwanted drink into the washbasin, and glancing into the mirror above it saw the reflection of Claire watching him from the doorway, her expression changed from anger to anxiety. For a moment they stood looking at each other's reflections, then Mark turned and faced her.

'What is it?' she asked softly. 'Why are you carrying on like this?'

There was no point in asking 'Like what?' other than to gain time. Rational people did not pour drinks for the purpose of disposing of them down the bathroom sink five minutes later. Responsible husbands did not arrive home after midnight with no excuse and then walk away when their wives protested at meals cooked but uneaten. He was most satisfyingly unashamed. This must be how Pippa felt when embarked, full of glee, on some forbidden activity: daring, defiant, giggly, free, longing to shock, afraid of the consequences of so doing. Presumably long ago in his own childhood he too had felt like that, had felt as he felt now.

'Like a child,' said Claire echoing his own thoughts.

He looked at her sharply, some fear in her voice reaching him. It was his turn to voice unease, to ask 'What is it?'

'Are you ill?'

He understood then and was sobered into reassuring her, remembering the silly, argumentative moods he had inflicted on her in the months after Jeremy's accident when, as the

173

extent of the injuries and the future itself became horrifyingly clear, he had deserted her in all but his physical presence, retreating into a world of bitter protest and black clouds. He remembered the worried contempt in Sam's eyes, the bewilderment in Aunt Isobel's, the hard haughtiness in Aunt Jane's, the exasperation in Sally's and the unwavering, defensively protective love in Claire's, then reciprocated, now so long unsought and unoffered. He recognised too her own long, slow breakdown under strain, manifesting itself in a different sort of unreasonableness, endured rather than addressed.

It was not, he knew, the right time to invite her recognition of this. Like him, she must in her heart know that she was changed into something she did not really want to be and that she no longer controlled the new being but was instead possessed by it. It might have been better if they had both tried less hard, had depended more on others, had given up early and been coaxed back to competence. Instead everything that was precious was being stripped away in pieces so small as to be unseen.

Quietly he told her the truth: that he had left work tired, been taken for a drink by a group of young, carefree, boisterous Australians, had found their fun surprisingly infectious, had stayed to dinner; of course he should have phoned, of course he was culpable and of course he knew that at the time, but he was light-headed and somehow he wanted to be irresponsible.

'Can you understand that? I wanted to be irresponsible. I suppose it sounds crazy, or, as

174

you rightly say, childish. Anyway, crazy or childish, it was indefensible.'

Surprisingly, she smiled. 'Like my shopping trips.'

'What?'

'My shopping trips. When I ask Nurse Allen to stay an extra couple of hours so that I can go shopping for things I don't need.'

'What things?'

'Oh, things for Jeremy mainly. His bedroom drawers are full of clothes he'll never wear and the playroom of toys he'll never use. Boy's things. Nothing that would do for Pippa.'

'Lots of these things? Really lots?'

'Yes. If we weren't so well off I would have ruined us by now.'

'Have you told Neville Harris?'

'No. I can't. No one must start thinking I'm unfit to look after Jeremy.'

'They wouldn't, couldn't. You're the one who is suffering from this, not Jeremy. But surely the nurses know? They must notice when they're looking after him. And what about Pippa? She can hardly not know what's in the playroom.'

'I lock those drawers and cupboards. The nurses have free access to all the rest. I tell them I keep sentimental things in there from before the accident and that I lock them up to stop Pippa or her friends pulling them out and playing with them. I've told Pippa the same.'

Mark pulled her to him. 'Why didn't you tell me?'

'Because you're always so controlled and dutiful and so damned responsible. I didn't think

175

you would even begin to understand.'

'I understand that these things are better faced than brushed under carpets. Listen, I want you to tell Chris Sands. He can't tell anyone if you bind him not to. Then on Saturday we'll take all the stuff out of the cupboards and give them to the church. Leave the locks off in future. All that may be enough to stop it. If not, we'll go to Neville Harris together.'

He did not believe his own words, that obsessions could be so easily cured, was not even sure that it was a practical solution which Claire sought rather than the unburdening of her spirit. He resolved to confide in Nurse Allen if necessary and to ask her to be less accommodating when asked to work overtime. If she welcomed the opportunities financially he could make up the loss.

In the night he woke with the sudden conviction that none of it was true, that it was a device to keep him, to play on his sense of responsibility; that her supposed confession sprang not from any reassurance occasioned by his own poor conduct but rather from the argument between them on the day of his return from holiday when they had spoken of divorce for the first and only time.

He left the bed carefully, pausing every so often to reassure himself, by her steady breathing, that she was still asleep. In the playroom he switched on the lights and began to examine the cupboards. Two were locked. Turning, he found her immediately behind him and he jumped as if confronted by a ghost, just suppressing a shout, his heart racing.

'I thought I might have dreamed it,' he lied gently.

'Or that I had, Mark? If you want proof I'll fetch the keys.'

He shook his head penitently, but she was already on her way back to their bedroom and another piece of the rock on which they had founded their marriage and which had once seemed strong enough to withstand any tide, crumbled and fell irretrievably into the sea.

Yet the following Saturday when they emptied the cupboards he found himself covertly inspecting the clothes to see if they had been accumulated over time, if they were different sizes, last year's fashion. He knew then that she had spoken the truth and, sorrowing, tried to comfort and encourage her but she was resentful and distant. In the playroom it was different and, as he piled on the floor toys and games which he knew would be any boy's treasured possessions, they both wept and held each other for comfort as Jeremy, oblivious, lay on the activity mat, his huge mobile swinging unheeded above him.

Chris Sands, the vicar, to whom Mark not Claire had explained the reason for the large amount of unused goods about to be donated to the poor of the parish, calmly accepted nine full black plastic bin bags as if such largesse arrived at the vicarage door every day, but when he and Mark had their heads in the car and Claire had stopped by the doorstep to stroke the vicarage cat, he seized the opportunity to invite Mark to look in that evening for a gin and tonic. He

177

always said gin and tonic when he meant simply an evening drink, just as he always said a sherry when indicating a drink at lunchtime. On either occasion Mark would find not only his preferred drink of whisky but unfailingly also his preferred blend waiting for him. Claire argued that it was no odder than calling one's vacuum a Hoover even if it was a completely different brand.

He told Claire the truth about where he was going when the time came and she nodded, telling him not to hurry back. Obviously she was relieved to have matters taken out of her hands and for that he was grateful. He thought of Smith and of how right she had been about the potential role of the vicar, and reproved himself for not having thought of it earlier.

He walked to the vicarage, partly to enjoy the early September evening and partly to enable himself to accept the offered drink. Neither he nor Claire drank any alcohol when driving, needing no Government advertising campaign to convince them of its dangers.

With the vicar he had an easy friendship, although he suspected Sands was not as acceptant as he contrived to appear about Mark's lack of faith.

'I was going to suggest we took it out on the lawn – in a couple of weeks' time it won't be possible again until next summer. But then I thought you might prefer to be inside.'

Mark did prefer it. The vicarage was large and old-fashioned with substantial grounds, and the Church was beginning to find its upkeep unmanageable. Mark had no doubt that anything said on the wide, sloping lawn would be unheard by any except the uncomprehending birds, insects and cat, but he chose the greater certainty of the cluttered study in which to discuss his wife's illness. Had it been his own illness he might have been less careful, but the Renwick pride demanded absolute secrecy.

'You didn't know?'

'No. I had no idea until I behaved so crassly that she felt it safe to tell me what she had been doing. It's been going on a long time.'

'But the expenditure?'

'She handles the household accounts. I never check individual items. We don't need to be that careful, although in general we are not big spenders. At least I thought we weren't.'

'She'll see someone? A specialist?'

'If it doesn't stop.'

'Let's assume it's a cry for help, as they say. Is she now getting that help? I don't know why she should stop otherwise.'

Mark pondered that uneasily.

'I don't know. She's very tired and naggy but won't take more than a short holiday, and you have no idea of the dramas there have been over even that. The only outside help is practical rather than psychological and recently Pippa has been giving us hell with tantrums, most of them when we have to give too much attention to Jeremy. As you know, Jeremy's been ill recently, and even though that's been over for weeks she's still edgy. But none of that explains it. It's been going on for at least two years. I still can't believe it.'

179

'Is your marriage happy?'

Mark stared into his glass, absent-mindedly swilling the amber liquid round inside it. He looked up, not at the vicar but at the vicar's clock, a large, Victorian, loudly ticking, very accurate clock. As he looked at it the minute hand moved and Mark had an absurd desire to seek Sands' views on time. What came before or after time? Did God create time? If so, what had God existed in if not time? Was the life everlasting outside time and space?

'No,' he answered quietly.

Sands looked sad. 'I've wondered for some time, but Claire never said anything and I scarcely liked to ask. I'm afraid I have probably failed her in that.'

Mark shook his head. 'I doubt it. Renwicks don't discuss such things. She wouldn't have wanted to talk about it.'

'Renwicks? Ah, I see. Certainly they're a large and impressive family.'

'Nothing like as large as mine. It's just that they give the impression of being an army. But they're impressive all right. Sam made a million and then several more from a scrap-metal business he started with a friend in the back yard of a Yorkshire two-up-one-down and outside loo. That's not what's impressive though. It's the fact that he's never been brash or cocky or cheated anyone or become arrogant to obtain or maintain that success. Then there's poor Aunt Isobel giving up half her life to bring up Claire and Sally and doing it all with a minimum of fuss despite being so vague she couldn't tell you what day of the week it was. And finally there's Sally, cleverer than any man I know and ambitious to match. She'll probably become Prime Minister and Aunt Isobel will go and look after her every need at Number Ten.'

The vicar laughed but did not speak. He waited for Mark to go on.

'Mark you, Aunt Jane was a bitch, but she did that well too. At her funeral we all stood dutifully around with not a single tear in a single eye. Even poor old Isobel's hanky stayed firmly in its pocket. Pippa was too young to know her and I tell Claire that must have been the work of a fairy godmother.'

Again the vicar laughed and again he waited. Mark had already seen the trap.

'That leaves Claire,' he conceded, 'who is really very ordinary compared to the rest of them, but I do not honestly think that is the problem. She thinks, not without cause, that she is cleverer than poor Aunt Isobel and better educated than Sam. As for Sally, Claire is more like a mother to her than a sister. She's never been jealous, in fact she rather revels in Sally's success.'

'Nevertheless, when you were happy she had something none of the others had. Sally and Aunt Isobel have not yet found someone to share their lives with and Sam has not remarried, if I remember correctly. She alone had a husband and children and since she tells me she gave up work on marriage, presumably that is all she wanted from life. Now that is going wrong. No wonder she is unhappy.'

Mark thought back. How long had their

181

marriage been empty? Three years? Four? He looked again at the clock. It was not the sort of question which could ever be answered with a precise span of time.

'Is it rescuable?'

'I don't know.'

'Do you want it to be?'

'I don't know that either. There isn't anyone else. No eternal triangle. I don't suppose I'll actually walk out while Pippa is so young, though she must be aware that we argue a great deal. It's just that I don't feel driven to keep it going any more.'

'You still love her?'

He remembered his harsh words to Smith but he could not use them now, whether because he felt inhibited by the disapproval they might generate or because his attitude had itself softened he did not know. He merely shrugged.

'Forgive me, but isn't it time you both took charge of things with a bit more will?'

'What do you suggest?'

'For a start Claire needs more outside contact, more stimulation, but I think we both know she won't do anything about it. When she comes back from holiday, present her with a *fait accompli* of some friends coming to visit. It will give her something to organise other than the endless family routine, and create a situation in which you will both have to behave and not argue.'

'Perhaps. I don't mind trying, but it's hardly a long-term solution.'

'It's a start.'

'You could help too, surely? Find her

something to do in the church?'

'I've tried. She says she cannot commit to anything because of the demands of looking after Jeremy.'

'Jeremy? What has Jeremy to do with any of this?' Mark's pent-up anger suddenly spilled over. 'Jeremy! The eternal, convenient, ready excuse for anything that goes wrong. Of course we're as miserable as hell about what happened, but we've had seven long years to come to terms with it. Jeremy is Claire's excuse for the existence she leads: no holidays, no interests other than the garden, no going out to dinner or the theatre, no friends, all help repulsed in the name of independence. We play no part in Pippa's school and although the house is always full of Pippa's friends I don't think Claire would even recognise half their parents. But none of that is down to Jeremy. We have the money to pay for nurses, babysitters, respite, nannies, anything else you can name. The fact is that if Jeremy were a normal little boy off to school each day Claire would still lead an insular existence.'

'Did she?'

'You mean before the accident? She gave up work as soon as we married, as you said, but there were still the remains of her single girl's existence around for a bit. Friends stayed in touch. Sally was still young and came and stayed a lot in the holidays. I think it was Jeremy's birth, not the accident, which changed her – or perhaps I should say which brought out those character-istics which had always been there.'

'Some people are happily insular. She might

183

have been, I suppose, but something is making her unhappy, and if it is not Jeremy then what is it?'

Mark did not answer and after a short silence Sands asked: 'You work long hours. Does that worry her?'

'No. Oddly it never seems to. I think that is the effect of having grown up with Sam as the male role model. She would probably think me an idle provider if I didn't have periods of virtually living in the office.'

The vicar smiled sadly. 'But it leaves her alone even more than usual. I'm not going to suggest counselling as I can just imagine what you would call the Renwick reaction, but I think we should all contrive to blitz her solitude for a while.'

Mark nodded. 'I'm grateful for what you're doing and for this evening.'

'I'm afraid I won't be doing it much longer. Not here, anyway. That was one of the reasons I wanted to talk to you.'

Mark groaned incredulously, 'You're leaving?'

'Yes. I have been offered a living near Exeter and as I always planned to retire to the West Country anyway it will fit in well if my last incumbency is down that way.'

'Congratulations,' lamented Mark.

'It's never the right time for a vicar to leave, Mark,' Sands pointed out gently. 'There is always someone who needs his care.'

'I know. It's what my sister-in-law says about politicians' pay rises – that it's never the right time. Do you know who your successor will be?'

'No. The PCC can't do anything until I tell

them formally that I'm going but of course they know about the offer. I think they're interested in a chap from London who has stood in for me occasionally.'

'What's he like?'

'Theologically an Anglo-Catholic, but he's an odd mixture because he is also a fire-and-brimstone-style preacher and his flock come from miles around just to hear his sermons.'

'Dear God,' whispered Mark.

'Dear God would help if you called on him a bit more reverently,' retorted Sands tartly as, too late, Mark remembered his deep-rooted objection to casual blasphemy.

'I'm sorry,' he apologised. 'What's he like as a pastor?'

'By all accounts a good one, but all this is very premature. He may not even apply, though I hear he has expressed tentative interest.'

'What's his name?'

'Ernest Fisher. Rather a good one for a preacher, don't you think?'

Mark managed to smile, but he knew another important source of support for Claire was about to be cut off. Sands had baptised both Jeremy and Pippa, had helped in the aftermath of the accident from the time he returned to their house that evening and had been a constant friend since. He doubted Claire would be prepared to put the same degree of trust in any successor.

The vicar read his thoughts. 'I am going to preach to you now, Mark. You won't like the sermon but I'm relying on our friendship and another glass of whisky in hoping you won't

185

actually walk out.'

He smiled gently to take the sting from his forthcoming words.

'You have told me you don't know whether you are still interested in saving your marriage but I can't believe you aren't interested in the best thing for Pippa. Indeed, you tell me she is the reason you stay. Well, the best thing for Pippa is a stable, serene mother and a happy, interested father. At the moment it sounds to me as if she has neither. Putting that right requires effort – a lot of effort – before she really starts to understand what is going on. Your effort. Not just my effort, or Fisher's effort or Neville Harris's effort. Yours. Not yours alone but yours principally. Claire has effectively asked you for help. She deserves to have it and if she doesn't get it next time you may not be so lucky. Instead of buying half the shop she may steal it.'

The vicar let Mark absorb this while he poured him another drink. When he came back Mark noticed it was a large measure and reflected that had Claire been present it could hardly have escaped her censure.

'Thank you,' he said.

'For the drink, presumably, rather than the sermon?'

'For both.'

The vicar grimaced. 'That's generous because I'm not at all sure I've helped. There's something else worrying me which I think I ought to mention.'

'What is it?' asked Mark warily as the other hesitated.

'Several of my congregation have pretty elderly parents. One or two are in homes. The lady who does the flowers has a husband with advanced senile dementia and she looks after him at home. I visit several couples who are spending their last years on this earth unwillingly separated because one or other can no longer be cared for at home and the other has been assessed by Social Services as not in need of residential care.'

Mark looked puzzled. 'I'm not sure I follow you. You want Claire to get involved with the parish elderly?'

'No. I'm talking about the Euthanasia Bill. A lot of them don't like it at all, and I'm afraid everyone knows that Sally is Claire's sister.'

Mark felt on safer ground. 'Look, you're telling me that this band of worthy Christians will take it out on Claire? Well as it happens, she likes the Bill no more than they do, though for different reasons.'

'What reasons?'

'She thinks it could affect Jeremy. She's wrong. She also thinks the Bill is misconceived, that many people and particularly the elderly will be put at risk if it is passed, that we should be warned by the Dutch experience.'

'And you?'

'I don't agree. It can't affect Jeremy and I rather share Sally's view that the innate decency of the British people will be proof enough against any proposals for involuntary euthanasia. However I dread the sort of views we will be reading and hearing when the debate gets under way. People will talk about quality of life and the burdens of carers as if the destruction of human life were on a par with putting down an animal. Nobody should have to justify a human life. It is enough just to be.'

'And the principle of voluntary euthanasia?'

'If someone is drawing to a natural end anyhow and is suffering, then I don't see why that person should be prevented from speeding up the process, providing only that it is his decision and no one else's.'

'And the role of the doctor?'

'According to conscience.'

'Like the '67 Abortion Act? How many gynaecologists do you know who can find work and promotion while refusing to touch abortion? Let this Bill become law and it will soon be the same for geriatricians who won't touch euthanasia.'

Sands sounded angry and Mark did not feel like an argument.

'This is Sally's Bill. Not Claire's and not mine. It is Sally's job to consider all these arguments. I am however grateful for the warning about feeling in the parish. I'll pass it on, but it really is essential Sally and Claire are regarded as individuals. They're sisters separated by ten years, not Siamese twins.'

The vicar took the hint and they talked of more general subjects before Mark left, more troubled than when he had come: the challenge to himself, the looming departure of Sands and the Euthanasia Bill all nagged at his mind, but overarching them all was the terrible prospect of Claire's spending deteriorating into stealing, of the slow but steady advance of irrationality.

He wanted to protect them all: Claire from herself, Pippa from the friction between them, the three of them from the emotions generated by Sally's Bill. But above all he wanted to protect Jeremy, the perceived cause of everyone else's problems, the innocent scapegoat, the focus of excuse.

11

By unspoken agreement they did not mention the trip to the vicarage until Pippa had gone to bed. Then Mark gave Claire a truthful but necessarily censored account. Pitying her, wondering how much more she could take, he broke it to her as gently as he could that Chris Sands would soon be leaving and that feeling was growing over Sally's Bill. Smith had called herself fragile and he had treated her accordingly, yet here was much greater fragility and he had not even noticed.

Claire shook her head when, with care and circumlocution, he suggested that the difficulties in their marriage had caused the shopping expeditions.

'No. I started just after I hit Jeremy.'

Anger, amazement, incredulity, contempt: he knew he must show none of them, that if he did she would never confide in him again.

'Tell me,' he spoke calmly, knowing she was

189

watching him, that she sensed his shock.

'You remember, about two years ago, when he could still chew and used to roll his eyes and move his head a bit?'

Mark nodded, dreading revelation.

'Well, Pippa had been a real pain all day and finally I snapped and sent her to bed early without any supper. She was lucky I didn't smack her as well, especially as she screamed the place down, but I hardly ever do smack and that's what made it so hard when ... when...' she faltered miserably.

Mark got up and went to her, sitting on the arm of her chair.

'Then Rags came in and put paw marks all over the place. I let some milk boil over and it all started getting to me but I calmed down, shut Rags out and cleaned up the stove. Then I started to feed Jeremy, talking to him all the time, telling him what a good boy he was and how much I loved him, but he just refused to chew. Every time I put food in he opened his mouth and let it fall out. So I prepared something else, with the same result. It was frustrating but I thought he was off his food, possibly feeling sick or going down with flu or something. So I gave up and opened his mouth to make sure there was nothing left in there for him to choke on and he bit me.'

'What?'

'He bit me, quite deliberately and quite hard. He had never done it before and I don't know why he did it then. I suppose he had no other way of indicating his own frustration. It was horribly painful but that was nothing compared to my hurt feelings. I had been so loving, so patient, had tried so hard, and he bit me. I wanted to cry and I wish now I had but I didn't. I shouted at him and then I hit him.'

Mark sensed there was more to come but she sat, with head bowed, saying nothing.

'You smacked his hand?'

Her face twisted and she shook her head, her voice muffled by a sob.

'No. I was wild with pain and anger. I unstrapped him, yanked him out of his chair, put him over my knee and spanked him. Then I put him firmly back in his chair and left him there while I washed up. I had no mercy, no care that he couldn't move or rub himself to ease the pain. I felt it was I who was hard done by. He couldn't even wail, but he could cry. It was the last time I saw him cry. When I came back from the sink, starting to relent, there were tears on his cheeks and his nose was running. No sounds. No sniffs. Not even the grunts. Just tears. I hadn't seen any tears for months. I didn't even know he could still cry. I just took it for granted he couldn't.'

There was a silence while Mark absorbed the implications of his son's distress.

'You see,' she continued, 'it meant he knew what was happening. His feelings were hurt. It was after that time he got sunburnt – you remember? – when Pippa moved him out of the shade to enjoy the sun, as she put it. He must have been in awful pain then but he did not cry. It wouldn't have been the pain that made him cry like that: I hurt his feelings. He thought I

191

didn't love him.'

'All children feel like that for a bit when their parents have flipped. He knew you loved him and if he can know anything he knows that now. What did you do?'

'I held him and cried a bit myself and tried to comfort him, telling him I was sorry and that I didn't mean to do it, but he couldn't understand, could he?'

'If he could feel the smack then by the same token he could feel the cuddle. You are tormenting yourself unnecessarily. Jeremy knows you love him.'

Claire leaned against him and Mark put his arm around her, pulling her closer, trying to comfort her, his duty requiring it, his heart cold. She must sense the absence of warmth, must feel as abandoned as she believed Jeremy had felt.

'After that I tried frantically to make it up to him. If only he could have smiled or actively snuggled up to me when I held him I would have known it was all right, but he couldn't. So I started trying to please him by buying him things, quite sensible things at first, toys with bright colours and noise and movement. A new one nearly every day.'

She paused again, looking at Mark desolately, wanting comfort, fearing condemnation, forcing herself to go on but finding the relief she had sought from the confession elusive.

'Then it just escalated until I was buying him anything and everything, things he could never have made any sense of, which offered no stimulation at all. I actually managed to stop for a few months but then they cut another lot of foods out of his diet and I felt he wouldn't understand, that he would think I was punishing him, so I started buying him things again, only this time it got even worse than before.'

'It doesn't matter any more, love. It's over. Quite over. You should have told me before.'

He did not need to ask why she had not and she did not bother explaining. Mark held her until she stopped shaking and had pulled away from him, shriven but defeated.

'I can't believe Chris Sands is going. He's been a tower of strength. Who am I going to talk to?'

'The new chap may be just as good.'

'I don't know him.'

'You do have me, you know.'

'Yes. Thank you.'

It was a formal reply, less convincing even than a promise to write soon exchanged at a chance meeting of former acquaintances. Their marriage was in deepest winter and neither expected a sudden spring.

'Why didn't you tell Neville Harris?'

'He would have called in Social Services if he thought Jeremy was in danger.'

'But Jeremy has never been in danger. He could not have a better mother or, come to that, sister.'

Claire gave a watery smile. 'Yes, Pippa's very good with him. You aren't too bad yourself.'

Mark tried to match her emerging mood with a grin. 'When I'm here. And that's not often enough. That's why it really is imperative that I give up commuting.'

'Mark, do you know what's involved in setting

up on your own? I don't remember seeing much of my father.'

'That was different. I'm not trying to become a millionaire like Sam. I merely want to carry on the same trade a bit nearer to home. That's all.'

'All!'

He wondered if her resistance would dissolve if she knew about Ginny.

The thought surprised and absorbed him so much that he did not hear the rest of Claire's reply. Ginny? He denied it strongly to himself, at first with detached amusement and then with mild alarm. His secretary was half his age, free, perhaps wild. Beneath his feet yawned a common, vulgar trap.

Mentally shaking himself, Mark saw Claire watching him quizzically. He realised she had been speaking to him and that he had not heard.

'For that matter I could always work from home.' It was the first thing which had come into his head and the last thing he wanted to do.

It was with relief that he watched her reaction, a firm shake of the head.

'No,' she said. 'No, Mark. It's lonely at home.'

He was spared a reply by the ringing of the telephone and the necessity of going into the hall to answer it, wondering as he did so why he so often answered the instrument's summons when it was nearly always a Renwick for Claire on the other end. Tonight was no exception and after a few polite exchanges he called Claire to talk to Sally. She came, looking drained and unhappy; he wished she would unburden herself to her sister, to Sam, to Aunt Isobel, to anyone.

194

Later she said that she was tired and went to bed before him. Mark lingered downstairs, finding small tasks he did not need to do. When he drew back the kitchen curtains and extinguished the lights the room was still faintly illuminated by a beam from the Bartons' house. His elderly neighbours were still up, perhaps watching television, reading, talking, finding quiet pleasure in their declining years. He and Claire, with half their lives still ahead, had given up and sought to escape their misery in sleep. An image of Ginny and her noisy young friends danced before him. He felt he could almost reach out and touch them, laugh with them, dance with them, abandon all with them.

In conscious rebellion against the temptation he now believed her to offer, Mark sought to find as much fault as possible with Ginny's work, but there was little to find and his own irritability provoked none from her. Her steady cheerfulness and sometimes noisy sense of humour became assets in an office burdened with more work than it could sensibly cope with as Inglis stoutly refused to engage more staff, a parsimony difficult to counter when there was patently no room to accommodate any more.

Mark began to consider whether he could get away with asking Sam privately to farm out some of the work elsewhere.

It became rare for anyone in the office to leave before eight in the evening and Mark found himself catching ever-earlier trains in order to snatch an hour or so at work in the morning before the others arrived and the telephones started to ring. With Claire's holiday drawing closer he knew he would not be able to do his duty by Aunt Isobel and when Sally rang to say that there was, after all, no possibility of her sparing two days he knew that Aunt Isobel and the nurses would have to cope unaided. It was with relief, therefore, that he found Claire still willing to go on holiday providing only that they engaged a nurse for the evenings too.

Claire insisted on driving to Scotland, reasoning that if she had the car at her disposal she could return at any time in an emergency, 'at two or three in the morning if necessary'. Mark fervently hoped that would not be necessary, that she would relax and enjoy herself and rediscover trust in others to look after Jeremy. Her decision meant that he had to leave his own car at home for the daily use of Aunt Isobel and take the bus to the station. He did not dare to propose staying in London instead as he knew Claire would insist that he keep an eye on Jeremy, even though his son would be in bed when he returned each night and not yet up when he left in the mornings.

On the appointed Saturday they all assembled in the drive to wave her off, Pippa unperturbed by the temporary separation and looking forward to being spoiled by Aunt Isobel. Nurse Allen held up Jeremy's arm and made it wave, while Pippa performed the same function with Montefiore's paw. Barton laid down his shears on the top of the hedge and waved also.

As the car disappeared from view Mark could feel only relief and was shocked to sense much the same reaction in Pippa, who flew from one to the other of them with happy predictions of all that she would do in Claire's absence. Suddenly she turned to Mark and asked, 'Can Kylie come and play?'

He looked at her in surprise, wondering what had prompted the thought until he recollected that Claire had taken Jeremy to the Snoezelen recently and that Pippa and Kylie had probably met up again.

He shook his head and hated seeing her face fall as he formed the word 'no', but he knew that he must never let her play one parent off against the other and that Claire would be unlikely to be persuaded to go away again if she knew that her absence would be used as an excuse to defy her wishes. Both considerations were proof against the onslaught of pleading and threatened sulking from Pippa and he was grateful when Aunt Isobel distracted her before the argument degenerated into recriminations and a tantrum.

The rest of the weekend passed peacefully enough and Mark was able to get sufficient work done from his bulging briefcase to feel fully on top of everything when he set out for the office on Monday morning. Claire had rung twice and been reassured, the nurses had performed their duties with efficiency and settled seemingly effortlessly into the routine Aunt Isobel imposed. Pippa enjoyed the extra attention she was getting and Aunt Isobel employed a great deal of time in singing to Jeremy. Montefiore, with an enlarged choice of laps to curl up in and an increased chance of snacks between his regular feeds, purred his satisfaction, and it was a tranquil house which Mark quitted to catch the bus.

There were four people ahead of him at the bus stop and for the rest of the week he was to find them there in the same order each day. Occasionally one would pass a remark to the person in front or behind him and invariably the comment and answer would be about the likely temperature of the day and the lateness of the bus. The foremost position in the queue was taken by a young woman with dyed hair, a short skirt, preposterously high heels and a cigarette, the end of which she always reached as the bus pulled up when she would flick away the stub into the road, an action she also performed with her bus ticket when arriving at the station. The older woman behind her looked disapproving but said nothing. She was immaculately but inexpensively dressed with flat shoes and permed grey hair and as the bus appeared would switch her handbag to the other arm and delve in her pocket for her season ticket.

Behind her stood a young man in jeans and teeshirt and behind him a man of Mark's age in the uniform of the City commuter. At the station all but the young man caught a train. Mark never had any conversation from any of them beyond a grunted hello from the City type and he would often afterwards wonder if they all still stood there in the same order.

At the office he handed his briefcase to Ginny and pulled his in-tray towards him with little enthusiasm.

'My, you've been working, Mark,' said Ginny

approvingly as she emptied the case and stacked the work on her desk. 'It must be because you're a grass widower.'

She looked up and smiled at him.

'It's because I've a houseful of bossy women so I keep out of the way,' grinned Mark.

'Tough,' sympathised Ginny.

He hoped she'd had a good weekend and she replied she had been to Cardiff with two other working holidaymakers. As Mark listened to her enthusing over the castle, over Wales and over the funny accents which she mimicked well, he found himself nostalgic for the weekends of his own early twenties when he had been unencumbered by family and property to look after. He rebuked himself for his childishness but the yearning remained.

'What is it?' Ginny was looking at him almost anxiously.

'Nothing.' He pulled himself together, resisting the temptation to unburden himself.

'You looked sad,' she persisted.

'No, I was just a bit distracted. What were you saying?'

'I wasn't. I'd better get on with this,' Ginny indicated the piles on her desk and Mark applied himself gratefully to his own labours. Yet he found himself watching the clock, willing the day away until he could offer Ginny a drink and be alone with her.

Conscious of her presence, he wondered if she could sense it, if she knew his gaze lingered on her hair as she bent over her work, her hands as she wrote, her legs when she moved about, her

199

breasts when she reached up to a shelf. Would she mind? Would she think of him as an adventure on her way through Britain or as just another married man taking advantage of his wife's absence? Would she let him down gently or angrily? Or would she feel sorry for him?

Even as he resented the last possibility he knew that he was feeling sorry for himself. He lusted for comfort, not excitement, considering Ginny with neither great affection nor compelling attraction but with a child's longing for escape to somewhere warm and reassuring. He had neither the amused detachment of the philanderer nor the ardent longing of the besotted: he wanted only the illusory comfort of affection without responsibility.

With an accountant's eye he could see the balance sheet and knew well the possible consequences, yet at seven, when the exhausted workforce of Inglis and May was beginning to end the day's travail, he telephoned Aunt Isobel to say he was working late and would not want dinner. No, there was no need to keep anything warm or to leave sandwiches. He would have something at his desk. Nor should she wait up for him. Oh, by the way, the switchboard had gone home half an hour ago so if she needed him she should use his mobile number.

An hour later, as she was putting on her coat, he invited Ginny to dinner knowing that she had heard his lies to Aunt Isobel, and when she accepted he picked up the phone and calmly booked a table at the Savoy Grill.

Ginny looked amused.

'Pizza will do.'

'It will not do for me. Not tonight.'

'Josephine,' murmured Ginny.

Over the meal he relaxed and was pleased to find no wariness in her own manner, appreciating in her the life force which had been crushed out of him. The world in her eyes was still full of promise, excitement, enjoyment.

When they talked of Jeremy she was concerned, sympathetic and blessedly free of well-meant advice; she evinced no alarm over Pippa, saying all kids had tantrums and grew out of them, she herself had 'given her parents hell'. She grew earnest, however, when they talked of Claire, saying Mark must just force more company on her, must insist on getting her out of the house. It was imperative she was not left alone night after night during the flotation.

Then she talked of her own family, which turned out to be nearly as large as Mark's but among whom there was a great deal more contact. She spoke with particular affection of a younger sister.

When she spoke of home Mark began to yearn for the open spaces, clear sky and uninhibited attitudes of Australia, yet he suddenly found himself transported in his imagination to the summer heat of a Portuguese garden in which Smith walked looking at the flowers. He saw her bend over one to smell its scent and then she looked up and smiled at him gravely.

'You're miles away,' protested Ginny.

'In Australia,' lied Mark.

'But I'm in Cardiff,' she laughed, and he

realised he had heard nothing she had just been saying.

On a visit to what he coyly referred to as the facilities, he looked at himself in the mirror over the washbasins, his reflection lit by the harsh, all-revealing strip light. He looked reassuringly normal, perhaps just a little flushed with drink but certainly with no tell-tale lines which would proclaim him an adulterer.

Returning to their table, he was disconcerted to find Ginny talking into his mobile. She passed it to him.

'It's your wife. I said you would be leaving the office soon, that we were just finishing off the last piece of work,' she told him in lowered tones.

Mark felt the sweat break out on his forehead. Dear God. The background noises would not be clear on a mobile. She could not know he was in a restaurant, but could she sense anything? Different atmospherics from usual? He began to blab something about the line being bad.

Claire told him she could hear him perfectly as he walked with the instrument across the restaurant to the corridor, aware a disapproving waiter was hovering and other diners were glaring. As he walked he wondered how much of Ginny's false assurance had been heard by others at nearby tables. He imagined them smiling knowingly at him when he returned.

Claire wanted nothing in particular. She was just 'checking up', an unfortunate phrase in the circumstances. She was sorry he was working so late, he must not overdo it. Between irritation and guilt Mark assured her he would not. She suggested gently that it was not fair to Aunt Isobel to abandon her so completely and asked if he could not take work home. He said yes he realised and yes he would try before yelling that his battery was low and bringing the conversation to a blessed close.

In the restaurant Ginny had ordered coffee and the bill. She asked what time the last train was.

'I'm sorry,' said Mark helplessly.

'So am I,' said Ginny.

12

The rest of the week brought no reduction in frustration. On Tuesday the entire office worked till nine and Ginny said she was too tired to do anything other than go home and sleep, on Wednesday she had a long-standing engagement with a girlfriend to go to see *A Little Night Music*, on Thursday his sister, Ruth, rang Mark and said she would like to take him for a drink after work. In his surprise he accepted at once and offered her dinner, this time ringing Aunt Isobel with the truth.

'I hope everything is all right, dear,' worried Aunt Isobel. 'I hope nothing's wrong with any of the family.'

Ginny looked disappointed when he told her but was diverted by his curiosity as he explained that the Wellings brood hardly ever saw each other. He had last seen this particular sister two

Christmases ago. Then she too expressed anxiety but Mark replied that Ruth had not sounded at all worried, if anything she had sounded excited. Nevertheless he would have telephoned Paul had he not still been in Australia.

They met in L'Amico's, a small restaurant in Horseferry Road, much frequented by politicians and journalists, where Mark half expected he might see Sally who had first taken him there. She was not, however, among the diners but Ruth was already at their table, rising to embrace him affectionately.

'Sorry about the drink,' said Mark, who had been obliged to cancel that part of the arrangement owing to Inglis's demanding to see him just as he had been about to leave.

'*Pas de problème*. I'm sorry work is so awful at the moment.'

They exchanged such news as they had of their family. The girls tended to keep in touch with his parents more than did his brothers. Ruth enquired after Jeremy and Pippa. She did not know Aunt Isobel, having met her only once at his wedding to Claire. Mark found himself marvelling that someone so vital to his immediate family was virtually unknown to his larger one.

By the time she told him the reason for their meeting he had guessed it, alerted by something in her manner, a new happiness, an inner glow, an increased calm and serenity. She was engaged to be married. It would be announced in next week's *Times* and *Telegraph*. Sadly Ben could not come tonight to meet him.

He asked about Ben and she said he was a widower, about Mark's age, with a son whose Bar mitzvah she was about to attend.

'Bar mitzvah! You mean...?'

'Yes. Very much so. Very practising.'

'That's marvellous. I can't believe it. I wish our grandfather had lived to see it.'

'So do I. Oh, so do I. He must have been so sad when Mum rebelled.'

'But this would have made him happy. I'm so pleased for you, Ruth.'

'Mum's pleased too, though she pretends to be quite casual about the whole thing. Can you see me as a wicked stepmother?'

'As a very good one.'

'We shall have Friday nights, of course, and I can't just watch from the outside. I'm going over completely. It's easy as Mum's Jewish.'

'Yes. And that is how you will bring up any children?'

'Naturally. We both want a large family. He and his first wife did too.'

'What happened to her?'

'Car crash. They had two small daughters who died too.'

'I'm sorry,' whispered Mark, appalled.

'So am I. For him. I would give anything to bring them back, even though that would mean I couldn't have him. Does that sound daft?'

'No. It sounds like love.'

Mark was suddenly ashamed of his own tawdry feelings towards Ginny, which starkly contrasted with the purity of his sister's love. He could only hope Ruth had no disillusionment to face in some dark future lurking ahead of them in time.

She showed him her ring, tasteful and expensive, sapphires and diamonds, returning it to her handbag with a lament that she could not wear it until the following week. Ben had a large house in Hendon and they planned an engagement party. Mark must come.

His sister seemed in little danger of being poor, thought Mark. Of his married siblings only John lived with noticeable modesty, his wife working to help with the mortgage rather than for any career satisfaction.

When they parted and he had waved off the taxi which bore Ruth away, he felt happier than he had in many years. His little sister was in love and marrying *in*. That night as he looked out over the darkened garden he felt once more the stirring of hope, the lifting of a weight, that the world could still give as well as take away.

On Friday Mark told his colleagues firmly that he would not work late, flotation or no flotation, and saw the disappointment in Ginny's eyes, simultaneously feeling guilty and relieved. He did not know whether it was observation or imagination which suggested his coffee was placed in front of him with loving rather than professional care, tissues produced with solicitous rather than efficient alacrity when he spilled a tiny amount of ink, hands brushing by design rather than accident. Reassured, flattered, alarmed, he fled the office a good half-hour before he had intended with Ginny's wishes for him to have a good weekend hastening him on his way. Elated, he despised himself.

Claire's return the next day heralded an unexpected period of calm, even the fatigue of a long journey failing to disguise the positive effects the break had produced. She looked healthy, relaxed and as close to serene as her temperament was ever likely to permit. She made a fuss of Pippa and looked approvingly at Jeremy, was happily grateful to Aunt Isobel and presented Montefiore with some loch fish. She brought presents for them all and supper was accompanied by a hilarity which had become rare in the Wellings household.

'Let it last,' prayed the atheist Mark. 'Dear God, let it last.'

It began to look as though it might as the next few weeks passed in near tranquillity. Pippa returned for the autumn term, her thoughts already focusing on Christmas. The Wellings family kept in uncharacteristic touch with each other as the first preparations began for Ruth's wedding. Barton ceased clipping his hedge for the winter and Rags began to act with the slow dignity which presaged the onset of old age.

Only Ginny suffered from Mark's new-found happiness as his withdrawal from anything he might have had in mind became more pronounced. Subconsciously he relied on her happy-go-lucky nature to sustain her, consciously he justified his new conduct on the grounds that he had never really encouraged her very far anyway. A small voice somewhere told him he had discarded her, but he argued with it that at least the discarding was before and not after use. Virtuous at now resisting temptation,

207

relieved at his escape from a danger into which he had always promised himself he would not be led, he rejoiced in the rediscovery of married life but could not disguise from himself his recognition that Ginny was still an escape route willing enough to be used should he ever again feel the necessity.

Resolving to take nothing for granted, Mark invited Marianne and Peter, Pippa's godparents, to spend a weekend with them, hoping to reinterest Claire in the pleasures of company. If she nagged about the extra work it was only a gentle nag and Mark, heartened, began to trust the future.

Chris Sands left the parish and the interregnum was filled by an elderly colleague recently retired from a neighbouring incumbency. Claire was not visibly affected by the change and Mark's clandestine inspection of drawers and cupboards revealed no evidence of inappropriate or excessive shopping.

Jeremy continued to swallow.

Claire announced that Marianne and Peter would be accompanied by all three of their children and mentioned neither the extra work nor the unhappy association of Michael with the day of Jeremy's accident. Mark began to wonder if even Kylie Grant or Philip Cooper would be welcome and saw with real pleasure the falling away of Pippa's wariness. Oddly, he also found himself thinking of Smith, picturing her in a Somerset garden, and of her parable of the clematis tree.

Pippa's godparents arrived on a wet Friday

night and for the rest of the weekend the rain continued heavy and unremitting, hurling itself against the windows, driven by a gale-force wind which howled around the garden, making any outdoor play impossible and cancelling two proposed outings. The children, excited by each other's company, played noisily and energetically about the house, while Claire lit an early fire in the drawing room before which most of the adults spent their time, Mark withdrawing to work in his small study for some of each afternoon.

Of the visitors' younger children, Sarah was six and Elinor five, causing Pippa to revel in the novelty of having younger children in the house. 'She'll probably try bossing them about,' Mark had predicted accurately.

Michael, however, found himself in no man's land between three small girls and the grown-ups and alternated between them in his quest for companionship. On Saturday night he arrived in the lounge to watch the six o'clock news, to the considerable admiration of Mark and Claire who commented, when Michael had rejoined the girls, what a pleasure it must be when children began to have common interests with their parents.

'Don't be too fooled,' laughed Peter. 'His reaction to the news last week was to drape a towel round his head and proclaim himself Yasser Arafat.'

'It can get worse,' added Marianne amidst the general laughter. 'He and his friends produce some awfully sick jokes about things in the news.

When you tell them off they just roll around helplessly repeating the foul stuff.'

'At least we appear to be past the lavatory joke stage,' observed Peter. 'With any luck the girls won't go through it.'

'At the moment what they're going through is playing with the Stannah,' groaned Marianne, getting up to put an end to the recreation.

'No, leave them,' said Claire. 'They'll soon get fed up because it travels so slowly.'

Marianne subsided and then jumped in fright as Michael bounded into the room in full pursuit of Montefiore, who took refuge under an armchair.

'Calm down!' ordered Peter in angry exasperation. 'Leave the poor animal alone.'

Michael pulled a face of disappointment, then went out of the room with his arms stretched out and imitating fairly convincingly the noise of an aeroplane. Peter got up and shut the door firmly behind him.

'Grown up, indeed!' snorted Marianne. 'Mentally defective would be more like it.'

There was a short silence.

'Oh God,' breathed Marianne, 'I'm sorry. I didn't mean...'

'Forget it,' said Claire quickly. 'We are not so sensitive.'

Later she wept her sensitivity at the dressing table as they prepared for bed, with Jeremy already asleep in a makeshift bed beside theirs, his own room occupied by Michael, but it was not for Marianne's careless remark that she cried.

'I keep thinking of them playing together when they were little,' she told Mark, 'and now look at them. It's not...'

'Fair,' supplied Mark as she stopped short of completing the familiar childish complaint she heard from Pippa nearly every day. 'No. It isn't, so you needn't be afraid to say so once in a while.'

'I would give anything for Jeremy to wrap a towel round his head and call himself Yasser Arafat. I'd even put up with lavatory jokes.'

'I know.'

'I don't think they know how lucky they are.'

'They do. That's why this weekend is difficult for them too.'

'Michael ignores Jeremy completely.'

'He's only eleven. He doesn't know what to do. It's different for the girls – they are too young to be embarrassed.'

'They're a bit too much the other way. Elinor climbed on his lap and she's far too heavy.'

Mark's thoughts strayed as he wished Montefiore would occasionally climb on to Jeremy's lap when they had him propped in the wheelchair, but he never did. It was as if the cat knew that the least resistant and most consistently available lap in the house was incapable of active rather than passive warmth. It hurt Mark with a surprisingly intense chill each time he made the observation afresh.

Claire was asleep when Jeremy began grunting in the night, fortunately not loudly enough to disturb the other occupants of the house. Mark reached over the side of the bed and located his

211

son's hand, holding it for comfort, himself comforted by the warmth. As the grunts subsided Jeremy's breathing caught and Mark's eyes opened fully until, within seconds, it returned with the steadiness of slumber. He knew that a gentle slide into oblivion might spare his son and all of them much that was to come, but he knew also that he could not bear the hand he now held in his to be withdrawn by the coldness of death, or the dearly heard grunts to fall silent for ever. In a rush of possession and protectiveness he gripped his son's hand tightly, so tightly that had he been able Jeremy must have cried out. He relinquished his hold only when sleep overcame him.

He slept well into the next morning, rising at ten, embarrassed until discovering Peter still in his dressing gown. Claire and Marianne were preparing the lunch. Michael was still in bed, foreshadowing the habits of a teenager, in contrast to the girls who had been up and noisy since half past six. Montefiore was now in permanent hiding under an armchair.

By lunchtime the girls were fractious. Sarah complained that Michael had more Yorkshire puddings than she, Elinor said she was too tired to eat and demanded to know why she could not be fed like Jeremy, while Pippa seemed incapable of sitting still on her chair. Mark was relieved when the end of the meal dismissed them to their own pursuits and mentally resolved to warn his sister against having a large number of children. Claire, remarkably, seemed to take it all in her stride. For the first time he wondered if Neville

Harris might be prescribing for her, unable to credit to a single week's break so remarkable a transformation, but the absence of any evidence to this effect belied his conclusions.

At five o'clock their visitors departed, running through the rain to load the car, urging Pippa to come and stay some time and calling irritably for Michael who had suddenly disappeared from the farewells. Mark found him bidding goodbye to Jeremy, solemnly shaking his hand and addressing him as 'mate'. Unbidden, the image of Fritz rose in his mind. He was sure Fritz would have said 'old chap'.

Clad in a Barbour, Mark held the gate while the car went through and disappeared from view bearing a final glimpse of Sarah and Elinor already arguing. He pushed the gate to with relief and hurried up the drive out of the rain.

'My God!' said Claire, and Mark had no idea whether she prayed or blasphemed.

'Are you going to church?' he asked, prompted by the association of ideas.

She shook her head. 'No. No time now to get ready. I'll just have to be a heathen.'

Together they turned towards the lounge, Mark shedding his rainwear on the way, and fell exhausted into armchairs.

'Never again,' moaned Claire.

'Do you mean that?'

His wife turned to him and smiled. 'No,' she said, 'It was fun, really.'

He glanced towards the ceiling.

'It's OK,' she assured him, 'Pippa's wholly engrossed with the game they gave her.'

213

His glance switched to the garden.

'No one can see,' she said, already tugging off her jersey. His hesitation was only fractional before they relived a time prior to the arrival of Jeremy, witnessed only by two eyes from beneath an armchair and the uncomprehending gaze of their son.

There was nothing uncomprehending about the look Ginny gave him the following morning. Just as he had known before Ruth told him that his sister was engaged, so Ginny knew him to be in love with Claire and Mark in turn guessed that she knew. He felt for her, felt sorrow at her disappointment and guilt at the part he had played, but he consoled himself that he had in truth done very little to arouse her hopes and had no doubt that she would recover quickly from her present downheartedness, which was scarcely manifest at all except in some increased quietness of manner.

He felt no great surprise when she said she was leaving Inglis and May, that she found the hours more than she had bargained for, that she had enough money to fund further travel and had no immediate need to work and that some of her friends were proposing to work in the Scottish Highlands. She would therefore travel with them and explore Scotland.

Mark accepted the resignation, pretending to take it at face value, flattered to know she would have worked all hours if only she could have relied on his continuing interest, worried only at the prospect of training someone else when the firm was so busy. It might have been worse: she could have demanded a move within Inglis and May, thus rousing suspicion where Mark was sure none existed. Suddenly the mere thought caused his hands to shake. He saw how impossible it would have been to have escaped detection at work for long, how very quickly Sam might have heard rumours. He had played with the proverbial fire and he could only be humbly grateful that he had escaped the proverbial burning.

When Ginny said goodbye at the end of the following week his relief was such that he held her in a tight hug and kissed her cheek paternally, seeing, with sadness and a guilty gratification, the tears spring into her eyes. His colleagues raised their glasses in a toast to someone who had fitted in with such impressive efficiency that Inglis had departed from his usually rigorously enforced rule that temporary staff did not merit leaving parties. Mark watched her legs disappear up the basement steps with only a small twinge of regret.

It was therefore with disbelief as well as a profound unease that Mark saw Ginny walking up the drive one Sunday afternoon when Sam, Sally and Aunt Isobel were visiting unexpectedly and the entire family was gathered in the lounge for a tea of toasted muffins and a rich chocolate cake Sally had brought, ostensibly to please Pippa. Mark had noticed with pleasure that Sam was appreciating the change in Claire, while Sally was as usual devoting herself to Jeremy. He wanted no intrusion, and particularly not from Ginny.

Hurriedly Mark went to forestall Ginny on the doorstep with some vaguely formed notion of turning her away. He knew she must not come into the house.

'Hi, Mark,' she drawled. 'We were this way and I said I just can't be this near without looking up my old boss.'

'We?'

'Sure. The usual crowd. They've gone to look at Petworth. Going to pick me up later. We had to postpone Scotland for a bit.'

'Ginny, it's awkward,' Mark was protesting when, with sinking heart, he heard Claire's voice as she came into the hall.

Unwillingly Mark introduced them and Ginny immediately repeated her story, to be invited for tea by an innocent Claire. Full of foreboding which threatened to turn into something akin to panic, Mark shut the door and followed the women to the lounge. As the introductions were made and the room filled with Sam's Yorkshire vowels and Ginny's Australian ones raised in social greetings, Mark felt his insides shake. Why had she come? For a last tormenting glimpse of him, of his happiness? Or for revenge? To destroy that very happiness?

With an effort he took a grip on himself. He had lied to Aunt Isobel, Ginny had lied to Claire. He could say the first was genuine, he had intended to work but had become too tired and suggested dinner rather than change the arrangement and give inconvenience to Aunt Isobel. Ginny's lies to Claire could be put down to panic as she suddenly realised an innocent arrangement might not bear an innocent appearance. Why somewhere so expensive? He wanted to show Ginny the best London had to offer. Why had he not told Claire until now? He had forgotten. The event was not important enough to remember.

Mark felt the sweat on his palms. It would not need Sherlock Holmes to demolish such transparent nonsense. 'In this day and age a man and a woman dining together means nothing, so why all the secrecy? Tell me, Mark, why all the secrecy? Why not tell Aunt Isobel you were giving Ginny dinner?'

He came out of his desperate thoughts to realise that Claire was offering Ginny muffins, not interrogating him. Sam was looking at him.

'Penny for 'em?' teased his father-in-law.

Mark coloured and saw the curiosity enter Sam's eyes. He knew he must pull himself together if the curiosity were not to become suspicion. He had, in the end, done nothing and he must rely on that. The road to Hell, after all, was paved with good intentions, not bad ones.

Then Ginny turned to him and laughed, 'I couldn't believe it when I saw where we were. I said, "This is where that boss lives, the one I've told you about. The one who worked me half to death and couldn't remember my name and kept calling me either Karen or Eileen." Then Rich just dared me to call and when I got the betting up to twenty pounds I couldn't afford to chicken out.'

Mark felt the fear leave him in a rush of relief. Whatever had inspired Ginny to call, it was not

217

vindictiveness. He reverted to the alternative theory of self-torment, and pitied her.

Then, when he was allowing himself the luxury of being amused by his earlier fears, the conversation turned to politics. Sally, not wanting a busman's holiday, left most of the conversation to Claire, who inveighed heavily against the unions and environmental lobbies. Ginny asked Sally about her experiences in the general election which had taken place in the early summer, but did not mention the Euthanasia Bill, although Mark had confided to her his doubts about its effect on all of them. Again he was grateful for her discretion, and wondered that he could have so misjudged her intentions.

Ginny's next words blasted his complacency to atoms.

'Actually I vote Labour at home.'

The words themselves meant nothing. It was that they were aimed not at Sally, although it was in her direction Ginny was looking, but at Claire. Under no circumstances could such a statement be expected to provoke Sally, who would be used to it as a daily occurrence and who, though she might occasionally feel frustrated by such sentiments, was highly unlikely ever to be shocked by them. Claire was different. Her conversation had just revealed her passionately, and perhaps intolerantly, Conservative. Ginny had not spoken lightly as in jest, or even neutrally as one stating a fact; she had instead adopted a provocative tone, deliberately seeking to irritate her victim.

Mark's heart thudded and to avoid looking at his in-laws he asked Pippa if she needed a flannel to mop up the evidence of chocolate cake around her mouth. Claire, tight-lipped, rose to get one and Ginny, conscious only of social error and momentary childishness, turned the conversation and began to engage Pippa on the subject of koala bears.

With any luck they might merely think Ginny rude, unable to control her irritation and probable contempt inspired by Claire's right-wing monologue, but Mark relied on no such good fortune. Such an explanation might well have imposed upon Aunt Isobel but Sam and Sally were sharp and quick-witted. Both would wonder at this secretary who appeared out of the blue with such an evident dislike of her boss's wife. Claire, mercifully, was less likely to see anything more than evidence that the young were as ever politically unreliable.

His mood spoiled and peace of mind thoroughly perturbed, Mark could hardly contain his impatience for Ginny to be gone and when a distant car horn was heard, telling of waiting companions at the end of the drive, Mark had to force himself to move with seeming reluctance rather than rude alacrity. He prayed no one would suggest inviting the other Australians to join them, acutely fearing the sociable instincts of Sam.

Not wanting to walk to the gate with her in case suspicious minds thought he wanted to be alone in her company, and fearing equally not to do so in case those same minds should ask why he denied her a courtesy he never failed to accord anyone else, he compromised by standing on the doorstep until she had disappeared from view. He marvelled that she went without once looking back, though convinced she sensed him still watching her, and hoped he would not have to see her again, a hope destined to be realised. Over the coming months he would sometimes calculate how much longer she had before her visa as a working holidaymaker ran out, longing for the time when he could reasonably assume she was on the other side of the world and unlikely to bother him again.

Before the trio of Renwicks departed, Sam drew Mark aside to congratulate him on Claire's new-found health and tranquillity.

'It's right champion what that break's done for our lass. I wouldn't have believed it were possible until I saw it with my own eyes today.'

'No. Nor did I expect a change like this. I even thought she might be taking something, but apparently not.'

'Will it last?'

'We can only wait and see, but it should be easier in future to persuade her to go on holiday. Maybe next time we'll manage it together. We've shown her Jeremy can be well cared for without us, because I was working so damn hard I might just as well not have been here at all.'

'Aye.' Sam hesitated and Mark, with premonition, dreaded his next words.

'Reckon she's lucky you've been so patient. There's many who would have given up by now, divorced or played away or summat.'

'I've never played away, Sam,' Mark told him with much accuracy and no truth, and then realised too late that the assurance was in itself a confession, that Sam's comment had called for no such response.

'Aye.' Sam sounded sadly unconvinced.

Mark knew that he could only set his father-in-law's mind at rest by telling him the truth, and he liked Sam enough to want his peace of mind.

'Never.' He looked straight into Sam's eyes. 'I'm not saying that when things were very bad I was never tempted, but in the end I never did. It just didn't turn out that way. And I can't claim that I never threatened divorce either but, again, it didn't come to that.'

Then, when he saw with relief that Sam believed him, he added what he did not necessarily himself believe: 'Claire will always be able to count on me, Sam, and so will you.'

He saw that Sam received that more dubiously – even as he thanked Mark for the promise – and respected afresh a perspicacity in which no wish ever mothered a foundling thought.

When Aunt Isobel wandered vaguely into the back garden where they had been talking Mark made good his escape. The conversation had begun with his feeling like a schoolboy caught pilfering tuck and had ended with his feeling like a ham actor whose tragic lines had produced howls of mirth.

'I can't be bothered with a meal tonight,' announced Claire when their guests had gone. 'Why don't we just collapse with something out of the fridge?'

The evening passed peacefully until, just as Mark was going to propose retiring, Claire picked up the remote control. The third channel she tried offered a discussion on the forthcoming Euthanasia Bill, the second reading of which was now only three weeks away.

Claire abruptly switched it off. 'I'm too tired for politics,' she announced with an exaggerated yawn. 'Let's go to bed.'

Mark agreed, but lingered longer than usual when looking into Jeremy's room. A low rumble of thunder sounded and Mark, remembering the storm on the day of the accident, could not repress a feeling of its being a bad omen, a herald of doom. He shrugged off the superstition at once, but, as lightning illuminated the room and his sleeping son, he knew he needed no portent to tell him that ahead of him and Claire lay a time of trial.

13

Sam must have put on a three-line whip for the debate, thought Mark wryly as he surveyed the assembly of Renwicks who had turned up to watch Sally introduce her Bill. Knowing well how difficult it was to obtain seats in the Strangers Gallery, he wondered at the organisation which had produced almost half a row of Sally's family on this Friday morning.

Sam sat in the middle, tense, proud, excited.

Beside him Aunt Isobel was merely tense. Rupert Fiske had come from Oxford and his parents, Sue and Alec, were there too, having travelled from Yorkshire the previous day. Mark and Claire brought the number to seven. They had debated whether to take Pippa from school for the day, but had decided she was likely to be quickly bored.

Below them the chamber was packed. Mark recognised half the Cabinet and somewhat less of its shadow equivalent. Some Members were looking through sheaves of notes, others sat watching and listening. Mark looked up to where, opposite him, lobby correspondents had similarly packed the press gallery. The Speaker was in the Chair and as the petitions ended and the Clerk read the title of the Bill, the atmosphere was electric with expectation.

'Mr Speaker,' began Sally. 'Let me begin by saying today what this Bill is not. It is not, contrary to ill-informed and alarmist reports in the press and media, a licence for one person to decide on another's right to live, nor is it a licence for anyone who is permanently sick and disabled to take his life with the assistance of the medical profession. It is quite specifically limited to those who are not merely incurably ill but who are in the terminal stages of their disease. In other words death must be imminent. Those terminal stages must also be painful and not susceptible to relief from pain. In other words it is insufficient merely to be in the final stages of one's life. Those stages must be rendered intolerable by pain.'

A Member opposite rose to intervene and

Mark recognised a prominent pro-life campaigner, who had been seen and heard a great deal on the media denouncing Sally's Bill with evangelical fervour.

Sally did not give way, promising to do so later when she had set out the parameters of her Bill. Her opponent sat down with a shrug and Mark, guessing he had been about to question the definition of intolerable, wondered how Sally would have responded.

'Thirdly,' Sally was saying, 'any individual taking advantage of this Bill must be fully competent mentally. It will not, for example, confer any rights on a relative holding Power of Attorney, nor will it be able to be invoked by a living Will drawn up when the individual was mentally competent. He or she must be fully in control and fully competent at the time the decision is taken. Finally the proposal, not just the decision, must, as far as can reasonably be ascertained, emanate from the individual and not from a third party.'

'Unenforceable,' commented several Members loudly.

'Order!' called the Speaker.

'In particular it will be a criminal offence for a doctor, nurse or other medical practitioner to propose such a course of action.'

Again there was a susurration of protest.

'I turn now to what this Bill will do...'

For several minutes Sally outlined the purpose and provisions of her Bill. She spoke well and commanded the attention of the House. Remaining dispassionate in her passion, she did not draw on any experiences of her own or of those she loved, but her voice trembled slightly as she spoke of suffering and pain and the unhappiness of those who had to witness it. That emotion was replaced by anger as she demanded to know by what right Members of the House condemned their fellow human beings to suffer so appallingly when those very human beings cried out to be allowed to end their misery. Not once did she use the phrase 'to die with dignity' nor 'quality of life'.

It was a confident, assured performance during which Sally fielded with courtesy and sometimes humour the many interventions which came from both sides of the House. Watching her audience, Mark was sure there were many MPs still undecided. When she finally sat down there was applause from the gallery, and white-tied-and-tailed officials moved down the gangways to utter rebukes and warn against any further unseemly behaviour. Sam grinned.

The enthusiasm for the speech was not universal, and Mark spotted three nuns two rows in front of him telling Rosary beads.

Sally was followed by the Member who had first tried to intervene, and whose name was Guy Mortimer. He too delivered a *tour de force*, pouring scorn on the measures to protect the vulnerable of which Sally had made so much in her own speech.

'Let us imagine two people side by side in a hospital ward. Both are near death and both in agony, but one is mentally competent and the other retarded. For how long can we sustain a situation in which one of those people has the right to die and the other does not? The pressure to relax the safeguard of mental competence would, I submit, become irresistible, and then where would it all end?'

A Conservative Member called Francis Middleton tried to shoot that fox.

'But the Honourable Gentleman will acknowledge that to relax the safeguard would actually require a change of the law? This House would have to be convinced that it was right before any such change could be made? It cannot just happen?'

'I've heard that sort of thing before,' declared Mortimer. 'Let any Member who believes that this sort of law will be observed to the letter look at what happened to the legislation of the sixties. Let us first consider the 1967 Abortion Act.'

'Irrelevant,' shouted a Liberal Democrat.

Mortimer continued unperturbed. 'We were assured it would not lead to abortion on demand, and does anyone seriously believe that is not what we have now got? We were told it would end the scourge of child abuse and also of illegitimacy, and now we have record levels of both. We were told the law would be strictly applied and since then we have had more than five million unborn children killed. Or take the 1969 divorce legislation. We were told it wouldn't lead to a breakdown in respect for marriage, but would merely give relief to a few hopelessly troubled marriages. Now more than forty per cent of all marriages end in divorce. Then what about Abse's Equality for Homosexuals? I urge

Members to read that debate. This House was told there would be no open displays of such feeling...'

The House stirred in protest but Mortimer raged on.

'And now we have *Gay News* on every street corner. The point is not whether any or all of these results are good or bad. The issue is not whether honourable Members believe in abortion on demand, or easy divorce or open homosexuality. It is that these things were not foreseen as consequences of those laws by their promoters. History teaches us to beware this Bill. I do not question for a millisecond the good faith of the Honourable Lady, I do not question her sincerity in believing that her Bill will not lead to widescale abuse, but the lessons of the past fairly scream at us to foresee the unthinkable.

'This Bill is no more able to be insulated from human emotions, from desires for quick solutions, from the effects of human greed, than any other Bill. Some relatives will want relief from caring or paying others to care, some will simply callously wish to inherit, others will accept a tentative proposal to die too readily, creating guilt and moral pressure for the wavering, some from the best of motives will pressurise doctors who may have doubts. If this Bill is passed then in ten years' time no granny will be safe.'

A buzz followed this speech, and it was succeeded by a series of thoughtful but much less spectacular ones. A female Conservative Member believed it posed too much threat to the medical profession, whose right to a conscientious refusal to participate in such deaths she did not believe sustainable. She too prayed in aid the 1967 Abortion Act.

'Once doctors had to explain why they would be willing to perform abortions, but now they have to explain why they won't. It is hard to make progress with a career in gynaecology if you will have nothing to do with abortion. Why should this Bill be different? What it will mean is that in future it will be hard to have a career in geriatrics if you will have nothing to do with euthanasia.'

It was the first use of the word 'euthanasia'. Mark saw several Members shudder and exchange glances. He remembered that Chris Sands had used this very argument when they spoke together and the vicar had warned him about feeling in the parish. But why just geriatrics? All ages could avail themselves of this Bill if it became law. He wished he were in the chamber and could put the question.

Two Members spoke movingly of terrible suffering in their own families. Then a Labour Member, bitterly and angrily opposed to the Bill, took up the theme of abuse. Once the House started allowing quality of life as a reason to institutionalise suicide, and assisted suicide at that, it would become impossible to hold a clear line between black and white. Grey areas would appear and when those had been encompassed by the misplaced compassion of a gullible society the line would be pushed further back still. Already disability was a reason for abortion, so why not for euthanasia? Already children with disabilities were passed over for treatment and operations available to other children, as the House would recollect from the Hinds case. How small a step it was from that to a so-called merciful release.

Some ignored abuse and challenged the very philosophy behind the Bill. Some told of miraculous recoveries, of misdiagnosis, of sudden medical advances.

The Secretary of State for Health concentrated on the practicalities of applying some of the definitions in the Bill. When he sat down nobody could have told if he were in favour or against. His shadow supported the Bill personally, but entered similar caveats. Certain Irish MPs sought assurances that the legislation would not be extended to cover Northern Ireland, while some Scottish MPs sought for a guarantee that it *would* apply to their home country.

One Member passionately quoted Dylan Thomas:

Do not go gentle into that good night...
Rage, rage against the dying of the light.

Another quietly retorted, 'But there are some who have no light to die.'

Mark looked down at the Member who had just spoken, a grey-haired man of about sixty who in ten words had conveyed as much pent-up emotion as others had in twenty minutes, and wondered what private grief had moved him.

He and Claire met each other's eyes. Mark remembered Smith and, thinking of the parable

229

of the clematis tree, knew he had the secret of Jeremy's light.

Finally, at half past two, the House divided, being as packed for the last speech as it had for the first. It gave the Terminally Ill Persons Bill a second reading by three hundred and two votes to two hundred and six. Sally's supporters waved Order Papers.

It had, thought Mark, been Parliament at its best, and amidst the mix of disappointed and jubilant spectators there was a common appreciation of what they had seen and heard, a feeling of being better people just for having been there, or a sense of having been present on an historic occasion. Some were silent as after a moving play, others volubly excited. For Mark, the over-riding reaction was simply one of certainty. The Bill would succeed and become law.

14

The Sunday following the debate on the Euthanasia Bill saw two major sermons, reports of which dominated the press on Monday. At Westminster Cathedral the Cardinal Archbishop told one thousand Roman Catholics that Britain had lost its claim to be a Christian country and that it was the duty of all Catholics to make their views known to their Members of Parliament. Only half an hour separated his homily from the sermon of the Archbishop of Canterbury, who informed his flock that the Bill threatened the old, the confused and, in due course, doubtless the severely disabled too. Equally uncomfortable for Claire were the pulpit strictures of the elderly cleric who was bridging the gap between Chris Sands and his successor. These at least went unreported, much to his disappointment.

The Church of England was divided by lunchtime and by Sunday evening half a dozen bishops were appearing on news bulletins to voice their disagreement with their Archbishop. In one case the bishop devoted all his disagreement to his superior's prediction that the Bill might ultimately affect the severely disabled. Representatives of the Hospice Movement debated fiercely with representatives of the Voluntary Euthanasia Society. Sally went with increasing weariness from news studio to news studio, and on Monday's *Newsnight* was aggressively interviewed by Jeremy Paxman.

'What possible guarantee can you give that this Bill is not just the beginning of a very slippery slope?'

'The Bill is very tightly drawn and also...'

'Isn't that what they said about the abortion law?'

'And also,' continued Sally unperturbed, 'the innate decency of the British people...'

'Who are now very worried about your Bill.'

'No. Who are worried by the distorted version your profession is giving them.'

'They are worried about a slippery slope. What can you say to reassure them?'

'Look,' snapped Sally, exasperated, 'I of all

231

people would not want to see the severely disabled in any danger.'

'Why you of all people? What does that mean?'

Mark held his breath as Claire clung to him in agonised anticipation, crying 'No!'

Almost as if she had heard her sister's plea Sally forbore to present her credentials, but Mark guessed that the damage was done.

'It's Jeremy's birthday on Wednesday,' whispered Claire. 'They'll all know by then.'

They knew by the following morning. Drawing back the bedroom curtains at seven fifteen, Mark saw two people standing just outside the gate. As he was about to call Claire the telephone shrilled, and he walked to the bedside table to pick up the receiver.

'Good morning, Mr Wellings,' came the stately tones of Mr Barton, 'I thought you should know there are two gentlemen by your gate. I fear they may be press.'

'In which case they are probably not gentlemen,' snapped Mark, before adding, 'Thanks for the info anyway' in much calmer tones.

'Would you like me to tell them to go away, Mr Wellings?'

Mark toyed with the entertaining possibility of watching a confrontation between his pedantic neighbour and what he suspected were the representatives of the less respectable press, but felt an obligation to Barton to decline the offer.

As soon as he replaced the receiver the telephone rang again, the call this time being from Sally.

'I don't know whether you saw *Newsnight?* Oh,

you did. I'm sorry, Mark. I should never have faced Paxman when I was so dog-tired. He never misses a trick.'

'It was bound to come out some time. I shall stay at home today and ring every editor in Fleet Street.'

'Then you won't be ringing many these days.'

'I was using Fleet Street figuratively. Jeremy is a private person. I'll go to the Press Complaints Commission if necessary.'

'A toothless bulldog if ever there was one. They just tell the editors to say sorry nicely after the event. Has anyone turned up yet?'

'Yes. There are two in the road outside.'

'Three,' amended Claire who, alerted by the frequency of the telephone bell so early, had come into the room to ascertain the cause. 'Three in the road, that is. Number four is halfway up a tree. I hope he falls out.'

The curse was uttered mildly and Mark was grateful for her calm. He told Sally he would call the police.

'No,' urged Sally. 'There is nothing they can do providing there is no trespass and no obstruction. Get dressed, then go out and talk to them. They can't go back to their editors empty-handed, so give them something and they'll go. The crucial thing is to decide what you will give them and then stick to it.'

'Damn Paxman.'

'No. He's a very good interviewer doing his job. I just screwed it up, that's all. Mark, all those pressmen are also doing their jobs, but they all have wives and children or elderly parents or

233

something and because life's tragedies don't bypass journalists one or two will know all about disability as well. Just go out there, tell them the bare facts and plead for privacy. That will give them something to take back.'

'They'll want photos of Jeremy.'

'Just be firm. Say no. He's a private person who has nothing whatever to do with his aunt's Bill. They'll realise that short of a forced entry into the house they're on to a loser.'

'You have more faith in the gutter press than I have.'

'You don't know they're from the gutter, or even from the tabloids. My bet is that a broadsheet or two will arrive ere long, if they are not there already.'

Mark groaned. Sally repeated her advice to 'give them something', and Mark was surprised to find Claire in agreement.

'It's worth a try. Wait till there are a few more, then go out and talk to them on condition they leave afterwards. Meanwhile we can put on the answering machine and say we will not return press calls. But we can't let them see Jeremy. God knows what sorts of cameras they have these days but I'm not taking any chances. I'll keep his curtains drawn.'

'OK. I'll take Pippa to school. We need to brief her not to talk to them.'

By the time Mark went to get the car out of the garage, four neighbours had been accosted by the swelling crowd of journalists. One simply said 'No comment'; one said 'Leave them alone, they've enough to cope with'; one mentioned the police; and Barton gave an interview.

Not that Barton would have described it as an interview. He was just trying to help Mr and Mrs Wellings by persuading the press invasion to go away, by explaining to them what a nice family the Wellingses were, how lovely Jeremy had been as a little boy, how good Pippa was with him now, how much Rags loved him. He found his audience polite, respectful and attentive, and began to enjoy himself. Of course he remembered the day it happened...

Ignorant of his neighbour's garrulity, Mark walked down the drive to the gates with anger and dread. He found the press surprisingly co-operative when he said that he was now taking his daughter to school and that as she was a private person he hoped they would take no photographs of her. If they did not, he would talk to them on his return. He did not add that it would be impossible anyway to photograph Pippa as he had already arranged for her to hide under her school mackintosh on the back seat.

His return was greeted with flashbulbs and a considerable jostling, but the unwelcome visitors stayed outside the gate while he put the car away and then, as promised, walked down the drive to speak to them. He kept his comments to a minimum. He and his family were private individuals, they had nothing whatever to do with Sally's Bill; yes, they did see Sally from time to time but no, they did not discuss politics; the Bill did not affect any of them.

He wished he had avoided that emphasis on 'any' but his audience did not appear to notice

235

and he was surprised that they made no effort to detain him when he concluded with a polite but decidedly firm request for them to leave. He would have been less surprised and a good deal more alarmed had he known that even as he spoke a representative of the Press Association was happily ensconced in an armchair next door being plied with fresh scones by Mrs Barton while her husband proudly showed off an album of photographs of animals they had owned throughout their fifty-five-year marriage.

The Press Association man could not help regretting that Rags had quite so many predecessors, but he was patient and, as his grandmother had so often reminded him, patience usually paid more than its own reward. By the time he left he was reflecting how right Gran so often was.

Meanwhile the little crowd outside the Wellingses' gate dwindled but the presence of just the one or two who remained throughout the day was enough to persuade Claire to keep not only Jeremy's bedroom curtains drawn but those of every room downstairs as well. Mark protested it was over the top but she insisted. It was he who drove to the shops to purchase supplies for the next day's festivities and who, contrary to his sister-in-law's advice, visited the local police station to say press would not be welcome at his son's birthday party or at the gates, intimidating small guests and their parents.

The officer to whom he spoke explained the law to him and Mark insisted on speaking to his superior, who promised a policeman would attend the event. Relieved, he returned to Claire, making clumsy efforts to help with the preparations, and was grateful when the necessity to collect Pippa enabled him to escape.

A solitary photographer witnessed his return while Pippa innocently giggled under the mackintosh, enjoying the adventure and looking forward to telling all her friends about it. Excited at the prospect of the coming party she ran noisily about the house, alternately amusing and irritating her parents, bothering Montefiore until he hid in the airing cupboard and swinging on the back of Jeremy's chair.

'Be quiet,' said Claire firmly at supper. 'Have you wrapped up Jeremy's mobile?'

'You've given it away, you stupid thing,' yelled Pippa furiously.

'Don't speak to Mummy like that,' said Mark quietly. 'Say sorry and answer Mummy properly.'

'She's given it away,' wailed Pippa, beginning to cry.

'She is the cat's mother,' observed Claire. 'Now calm down and don't speak until you can say something sensible.'

'You've given it away,' screamed Pippa.

'For pity's sake, grow up,' snapped Mark. 'You know very well that Jeremy doesn't understand.'

Pippa looked at him, shocked into silence, as he realised chillingly that he had just destroyed a precious piece of innocence – he, who had always rejoiced at the way Pippa prattled to Jeremy seemingly oblivious at the absence of reaction. Father Christmas did not exist, there were no fairies at the bottom of the garden and Montefiore would not understand the significance of the new toy which would be faithfully produced on each anniversary of his arrival in their household and which they would celebrate as his birthday. He assumed Pippa realised all of this but he and Claire always pretended otherwise, as part of that elaborate game in which adults pretend in order to protect childhood and children in turn pretend in order not to hurt their elders' feelings, or perhaps because they fear that to reject a myth is also to reject the security the myth creates.

Now he realised that his assumption that Pippa believed conversation with Jeremy to be a one-way flow was wrong. Either she did not appreciate Jeremy's lack of comprehension or she had simply refused to acknowledge it consciously. For that matter, what he had just said contradicted earlier statements that no one knew whether Jeremy could hear or not.

Pippa attempted a mouthful of food, choked, burst into fresh tears and ran from the room. Neither parent sought to stop her flight.

'My, what a day,' sighed Claire.

'I'm sorry. My fault. She is only seven.'

'I've a feeling tomorrow may be worse.'

'I'd like to say I disagree but I'm pretty sure it will be. What time is Sam coming?'

'For lunch, or at any rate for a snack. Will you go to work?'

'Not unless he can come earlier. I'd be home early in any case.'

'Daddy can't come before lunch. I had already asked, for different reasons, but it really doesn't matter. I can deal with the press if I have to.'

Mark shook his head, imagining Inglis's displeasure.

Later, he was reassuring Sally on the telephone that none of them had spoken to the press beyond his own few, uninformative words, when he heard a bell clanging in the background and she cut the conversation short saying she must vote. Turning from the phone, he went to stand at the window.

As far as he could make out in the dark there was no one waiting now at the gate. The last had given up and gone home. He stood for some time looking out over the darkening garden, at the shapes of the shrubs and the rosebushes, thinking wistfully of a tree stump covered by a clematis tree, wanting to share the comfort of that thought with Pippa, knowing she was still too young to understand. He wished he could believe so that he might pray for Smith.

Just before midnight, when they had turned out the light and were hovering between wakefulness and sleep, Sally rang. She had picked up the first editions of Wednesday's papers from Victoria Station on her way home after the House had risen, and thought they should know about what was in them and about one in particular.

Unfortunately there was little in the way of competition for news that day, and three of the broadsheets ran the story on their front pages, though low down, and inside was the same photograph of Jeremy as a toddler with Rags. Two chose to comment in their leader columns on the dangers of exaggerating the implications of the Bill. It was about the terminally, painfully and fully mentally competent sick, not about inconvenient and senile grannies and much less about disabled children. Both concluded with the pious hope that the Wellings family would be left in peace for the duration of the rest of the Bill's passage through Parliament. Mark snorted.

The third ignored the issue in its leader column but ran a large article on the grievous dangers of this Bill. There was a difference between suicide and doctor-assisted dying. It drew in some detail on the experiences of Holland, pointed to what it described as anomalies in the Bill's provisions, claimed to have no doubt as to Sally's good intentions but reminded the public of the old adage that they paved the road to Hell, and then painted a graphic picture of the perdition to come, with no sick person safe. This time it was Sally who snorted, commenting that clearly it would be dangerous to have the flu if she had her way.

The fourth broadsheet gave the discovery of Jeremy two short paragraphs on page four, and neither named him nor displayed any photograph.

Two of the tabloids ran the story across two pages though in neither case did it feature on the front page. There were also several photographs, including one of the house with so many curtains drawn, one of Mark leaving the gates in his car, several of Jeremy with Rags. Neighbours' comments were given some space while a great deal was accorded to the reflections of Mr Barton. Mark cursed.

Neither paper supported the Bill and both managed to imply, without actually stating it as fact, that in the long run it posed a threat to people like Jeremy. Today this little boy is lovingly cared for in a safe and caring society, pronounced one, but what sort of society would he be living in when he was the age his aunt had reached?

'It wouldn't make any damn difference,' snapped Mark on having this read to him. 'It's his family who look after him, not society.'

It was the third tabloid which worried Sally, and she prepared them for 'very bad news'. This alone had dared to carry a picture of Jeremy after the accident, in his wheelchair, aged about seven or eight and, inevitably, with Rags but also Pippa. That, however, was the least of it. The headline was THE LITTLE BOY HIDDEN FROM THE WORLD. The story related how Jeremy lived behind drawn curtains, was never taken out and never seen in the neighbourhood. The implied reason was that his family was ashamed. Sally had never mentioned him in any debate on disability.

Mark invoked the second Person of the Trinity and Claire, who had been listening in steadily growing disbelief on the hall extension, said surely they could sue. Sally let their outrage run on for some minutes and then offered calm, practical advice.

Tomorrow, she predicted and neither of her listeners had any difficulty in believing, would be decidedly difficult. The news media might decide to pontificate about privacy or simply to join in the story. Either way there was likely to be more personnel, possibly with rolling cameras, outside the Wellingses' house. If there were still interest in the afternoon, then Jeremy's birthday would be a gift to anyone still there. It might well scotch the rubbish about Jeremy's being hidden away but it would also upset an awful lot of the parents, who might well cancel their offsprings' attendance. They must now decide whether to go ahead or not. Then they should put on the answerphone and get a good night's sleep.

'It's all very well for her,' observed Claire when the call was ended and she had come upstairs again. 'She started this nonsense and now we're all suffering.'

'Damn Barton,' said Mark. 'It has to be he who supplied all those pictures. Rags, Rags, bloody Rags.'

'What shall we do about the party?' Claire had climbed back into bed and was watching him as, out of habit, he stared out over the dark garden.

'We shall go ahead. We cannot have our lives run by the press.'

'Is it wise? I mean, this can't go on for ever, can it? We could just postpone the party, perhaps just for a week?'

'No.' He knew that to Claire's ears he must sound like Pippa in one of her stubborn moods.

'And if parents start cancelling?'

'Tell them how disappointed Jer – Pippa will be.'

'As you have just accidentally pointed out, Jeremy won't mind, and it is his party.'

'In name only. It's Pippa who will suffer.'

Claire let the silence lengthen and he knew she

242

expected him to apologise for his casual dismissal of his son's ownership of the birthday party. When he did not she put out the light and settled down under the bedclothes with her back to his side of the bed. He ignored the gesture and went on looking out over the garden long after she had slid, exhausted, into sleep.

His resolution held the following day, and after he had taken Pippa to school, where he warned the headmaster about the coverage in the tabloids he was certain few parents would have read, Claire blew up balloons in a variety of colours while Mark retired to his study and relieved his feelings by writing angry letters to editors. The telephone rang steadily and Mark listened to the messages as he wrote, ignoring those from the media together with most of those from friends calling to sympathise, and answering only those from parents enquiring about the party, from the police reassuring him that someone would be there that afternoon, and from various members of Claire's family.

Shortly before lunch the front door bell rang and Mark went to answer, wondering if the press had decided that the mountain must go to Mohammed. A young woman of about twenty-five stood there. She wore a short skirt and a casual top, her hair looked several days overdue for a wash, and several pairs of cheap-looking silver earrings hung from her pierced ears. The tabloid press, thought Mark.

'Mr Wellings? I'm Janie Moss from Social Services. May I come in for a moment?'

Mark stood aside and she entered as Claire came out of the kitchen into the hall.

'Indeed?' Claire made little effort to conceal her hostility as the girl introduced herself. Memories of the disastrous respite episode still rankled, and the social worker's appearance was against her. 'A rare honour. What can we do for you, Miss Moss?'

'Janie, please.'

'I'm old-fashioned, I'm afraid.'

'Won't you sit down?' Mark hastily intervened, gesturing towards the lounge.

'I'm afraid we're very busy today,' said Claire, uncompromisingly standing as the others sat. 'I'll just get on in the kitchen while you talk to my husband.'

'Oh, I can come into the kitchen,' replied the girl at once, and before Mark could stop her she was following Claire.

It was Mark who offered coffee while Claire went on turning out jellies. Janie Moss accepted and there was a short, awkward silence.

'We just wondered if you needed any help with Jeremy,' began the visitor nervously.

'Why?' demanded Claire just as Mark was beginning to realise the answer.

Miss Moss prevaricated. 'It can be very difficult...'

'Would you like to see Jeremy?' asked Mark tightly, aware that it could only be seconds before the truth dawned on Claire and, despite his own rising fury, anxious to avoid a scene.

She assented quickly, too quickly, and followed Mark to the playroom where Jeremy, recently bathed, in bright new clothes presented to him for his birthday, lay on his activity mat, surrounded by the family's presents. Two balloons tied to his wheelchair handles waved gently in the breeze from the window, which was open only slightly in deference to the small but discernible chill in the weather. At the end of the mat a video played, Walt Disney characters dancing and singing; above it swung the new mobile given by Pippa.

'Oh,' said Miss Moss.

'What were you expecting?' Mark spoke quietly despite himself. 'Dickensian neglect behind closed curtains?'

'Of course not,' she rallied quickly. 'We just wanted to know if you needed any help.'

'And if we did? You won't have the nerve to suggest we might get it?'

Miss Moss's reply was cut off by the sudden venting of his pent-up rage.

'Social Services have given us damn-all help for seven long years. We asked you for respite care and you dumped Jeremy in bed for three weeks, thinking your duty done just by keeping him alive, and then had the gall to say we should have "specified" otherwise. Because we have money and don't need grants you've left us to do everything ourselves and haven't been near us. As far as you are concerned, Jeremy doesn't exist and Claire can just get on with it. All we get is the Snoezelen, and come to think of it, that's probably the Health Authority rather than your lot. We know why you are here. It's because you read the lower end of the tabloid newspapers and

245

you think you might be accused of neglect or better still that you might accuse us of neglect.

'Just in case there is still any doubt in your mind, I will give you the names of our doctor and vicar and then I must ask you to leave. I hope you never have the gall to come here again, but if you ever do perhaps you will pay my son the compliment of looking clean and tidy when you visit him.'

Mark knew he was being unfair and probably cruel, but he could not repent nor stop himself shutting the front door unduly loudly behind her.

'Your mother phoned,' said Claire as he came back into the kitchen. 'I just caught the end of her on the answering machine. What a nerve that woman's got.'

'Miss Moss or my mother?' grinned Mark and as she gave him a rueful smile he went to her and held her close. 'She's gone and my bet is she won't be back. I was unbelievably rude.'

'Good!'

'Probably not very good. After all we never ask Social Services for anything so we can hardly complain that they leave us alone. Let's just forget the benighted Janie.'

'Are the press out there?'

'Not visibly. I suppose they could be hiding in bushes.'

'They've given up pretty quickly.'

'They've got their story – but my bet is they know about Jeremy's birthday and they'll be here in time for the party. They've been ringing all morning.'

'It's a pity my sister did not use her place in the

246

Private Members' ballot to promote a privacy Bill.'

'I can take advice, but we will probably find no rule has been broken. They haven't come to the door or accosted Pippa, and Barton must have volunteered photographs which were lawfully his. That reminds me, do you think we should mention it to Barton?'

'I should like to do a lot more than mention it, but what is the point? He's getting on and doubtless he meant well. Even if he's seen that awful paper he won't realise the damage he did. After all he certainly won't have given them all that stuff about "hidden from the world". No. Leave well alone.'

'Thanks,' said Mark. 'I hoped you would take that line. The last thing I want is a scene with the neighbours.'

'Anyway, I don't want to upset Mrs B. She's a handy soul in an emergency with Jeremy.'

When Sam arrived there was still no sign of the press and Mark began to hope he might be wrong about its likely interest in the party. Sam himself looked and sounded uncharacteristically tired and Mark, who had never known him other than hale and hearty, felt a tinge of worry. Perhaps the flotation was putting more strain on him than had been expected.

They decided it was just about warm enough to have some games outside before it got dark. Sam put twelve blue candles on the cake.

The one o'clock news threw some light on the sudden dying of press interest in their affairs. A minor member of the Royal Family was getting

247

divorced and the details promised to be interesting, a member of the shadow cabinet had resigned in equally compromising circumstances, the interest rate had been put up unexpectedly and a hedgehog had survived three spins in the washing machine of an unsuspecting suburban housewife.

It looked as if peace and normality were once more to break out in their lives, but Mark was sobered by the reflection that there were many more significant stages through which Sally's Bill must pass, and that the interest which had died so suddenly was more than capable of as sudden a resurrection.

15

Despite the inauspicious events which had surrounded it, Jeremy's birthday party was unanimously voted the best yet. All the guests turned up, in the shape of eight of Pippa's friends and two children of Jeremy's own age, former kindergarten and Sunday School friends who had kept in touch throughout the past seven and a half years. They provided a good deal of pleasure to Claire and Mark not least because both were convinced that the continuing friendship was of the children's volition and not a product of their parents' insistence.

Wholly unexpected but hugely welcome were Ruth and Paul Wellings, who appeared halfway through, wanting to show solidarity with their press-beleaguered brother. It was the first time Mark could remember his own relatives out-numbering Claire's at a family gathering.

Ruth had the glow of a woman in love and Paul looked fit and tanned as if he had just enjoyed a spell in a hot climate, although it was now some time since he had returned from Australia. Only Sam gave Mark any cause for concern as he noticed his father-in-law's pallor and suspected he moved with forced rather than natural energy.

The weather was chilly but dry and the children played games in the garden, organised by Ruth and Paul, with the older children pushing Jeremy's wheelchair, the balloons on its handles waving madly.

'He'll be sick,' said Sam affectionately.

'Nope,' said Mark. 'Claire says the same every year and so do you, but he never is.'

'Famous last words,' muttered Sam ominously, remembering an experience with Pippa at a funfair.

'Right,' called Claire. 'Time for the egg and spoon.'

Riotous cheers greeted the announcement which, by tradition, presaged not only the last of the outdoor games but the feast to come. The adults distributed chocolate eggs precariously perched on spoons. Jeremy's was placed on his lap. Sam lined everyone up on the top of the bank and the children raced downhill towards the stream, Mark accompanying the wheelchair pushers to avoid any accident. Soon eggs were rolling everywhere with children screaming delightedly as they chased them. Some stayed on the spoons till the last minute and then fell in the stream with loud splashes, Jeremy's wheels ran over one provoking happy cries of 'ugh', and as usual Pippa's best friend, Ellen, won by walking rather than running down the steepest part of the slope.

Nobody argued because each was too busy either hunting the fallen eggs or eating those already found. Mark pulled wet ones from the stream and then helped to push the wheelchair back up the slope. By the time they had achieved this the rest of the guests were seated and enjoying Sam's amateur magic show, which kept them entertained until Jeremy was wheeled into place at the table and Pippa, with an expression of mixed self-importance and embarrassment, said grace.

Sandwiches, cream cakes, blancmanges, jellies and ice-cream disappeared with the usual rapidity while party poppers popped and the noise level rose. Mark marvelled that they had any room for the birthday cake which followed as Sam led the singing of 'Happy Birthday' and one of the older boys led the cheers.

Indoor games followed, with Jeremy winning pass the parcel as it lingered in his lap as the music stopped. Pippa opened it for him and uncovered a set of crayons. Sam calmed them all down with some more magic until the parents began to arrive.

'I'm glad we didn't cancel,' said Claire happily when the last guest had departed and Ruth had made a start on the clearing up. 'You were right.'

'I might just as easily not have been. Your father looks tired. Can you persuade him to stay the night? I've a feeling he ought not to drive.'

'I know. I've just sat him down in the lounge with a drink. Pippa is opening all the presents and showing him as well as Jeremy.'

It was a ritual. Each year Pippa sat in the lounge opening the presents and showing each one to Jeremy, while faithfully keeping gift tag and present together under threat of not being allowed to open any present ever again if Claire could not work out who had given what.

Claire and Mark would look at them later. There would be clothes designed for children of Jeremy's age but not his size, a game he could never hope to play, a toy he could never manipulate, but each year there were six or so well chosen gifts. Each year also there were one or two so obviously bought with Pippa rather than Jeremy in mind that they hurt and angered Mark and Claire.

To Pippa each parcel was a source of fresh excitement, and this year it was even more fun because Sam produced a pencil and paper and relieved her of the tedium of matching present to donor by making a list.

Sam declined the offer of a bed for the night, but he did agree that Paul should drive him to Sussex and then return to London by train while Ruth would return in the car she and Paul had arrived in. It was not until after all three had left and the children were in bed that Montefiore emerged from his refuge under the sofa, and with a reproachful look at Mark made it clear that he alone had not enjoyed the festivities.

Inglis gave him a similar glance when he arrived for work the next morning and Mark, already irritated by a bad train journey, looked forward to the day when the flotation was over and he could carry out his intention of setting up his own business. Like a child bored with school, he also found himself looking forward to Christmas as the next legitimate break. It was now less than three weeks away.

They were weeks which passed quickly. Parliament rose with Sally's Bill having had its first session in Committee. Term finished with Pippa's having played the Angel Gabriel in the nativity play and sung a verse of 'Away in a Manger' solo at the carol concert. Her examination results were less encouraging and Mark felt obscurely guilty.

They gathered in Sussex for New Year and Mark was pleased to see Sam looking better. Sally looked younger than ever despite all the pressure, but Claire commented in private that her striking red hair was less striking than it used to be. Aunt Isobel pronounced Pippa to have grown though it was only a couple of months since she had last seen her and asked if she would be staying up for New Year, but Claire firmly put an end to any such hope. As the adults clinked glasses at midnight and welcomed the new year in, Mark contemplated the passing of the old one without regret.

Within two months he was viewing the new one with even less enthusiasm. In January Jeremy stopped swallowing and this time it was not a false alarm. He was fitted for a tube and Claire began to feed him separately from the rest of the family. She became tired and depressed, and the closeness which had warmed their marriage in the last months of the previous year evaporated.

Inglis and May completed the firm's input into Sam's flotation but the last few weeks of the exercise were overshadowed by a bitter argument with another firm of accountants handling Sam's business and some of Mark's work was to blame. Inglis began to drop hints about the difficulties of Mark's home life and Mark, with more pique than preparation, handed in his notice. He was now faced with establishing himself in his own business against the background of a deteriorating domestic atmosphere, augmented by Claire's seemingly ceaseless recriminations over what she described as his precipitate folly.

Aware of the strain between her parents, Pippa reverted to the tantrums out of which she had once seemed to be growing. Both Mark and Claire were glad to receive a letter from the form mistress announcing a school visit to France in the Easter holidays, which they believed could do her nothing but good.

In March Sally's Bill emerged from a marathon session in Committee to an acrimonious Report Stage and Third Reading. Fortunately the argument this time was less the danger to categories of person not covered by the Bill and more the problems which would confront the medical profession. The BMA and GMC together with the Royal Colleges mounted an impressive onslaught against the legislation, which by a majority of less than twenty was sent to the House of Lords where even fiercer opposition was promised.

The new focus of the opposition at least led to the family being left alone but Sam, who attended the Third Reading, appeared personally affronted at what he considered the crass stupidity of those who sought to thwart his younger daughter's endeavours. He was particularly angry at the efforts of one Charles, Earl of Yetminster, who was making a very effective job of stirring up their Lordships against the Bill, and he had a great deal to say about the effete nature of hereditary peers. He and Claire had many an argument on the subject.

There had been one such argument not half an hour ago, and Claire had replaced the receiver with unnecessary force before coming into the lounge to lament the substance of Sam's comments to Mark, who preserved a diplomatic neutrality which served only to enhance her anger.

'Why don't you say something?' she demanded when he let one of her observations drop into silence.

'Because there is nothing to say,' he retorted wearily but without acrimony and, when she began her argument again, he rose and walked out of the room, away from the comforting fire blazing and the comfortless monologue of complaint. Presently she would cry and he, knowing it, would not return to comfort her.

She had not come up to bed when the telephone rang at gone one o'clock, waking Mark from a dream-ridden sleep. As he groped for the bedside extension the ringing stopped and he realised she must have picked up the receiver downstairs. He looked at the illuminated digits on his alarm clock, realising Claire's side of the bed was cold, before rolling over to resume his interrupted sleep, vaguely aware he should instead be resisting the tide of drowsiness which now engulfed him.

Her call, as she came running up the stairs, caused him to wake again with a start and by the time she reached the bedroom he was already sitting on the side of the bed, fumbling his feet into his slippers. He had not switched on the light.

As she burst into the room it was flooded with light and Mark groaned, putting up a hand to shield his eyes.

'Daddy's been taken to hospital. I must go. Will you take Pippa to school in the morning? I'll ring you at work.'

'Are you all right to drive? What's happened to Sam? Is he OK?'

She pulled an overnight case from the wardrobe and began to pack distractedly. Mark waited till she came back from the bathroom clutching a small floral bag of toiletries before trying again.

'I said what's the matter with your father and are you OK to drive?'

'Heart attack and yes. It isn't I who has been drinking. Goodnight.' She left the room abruptly, switching off the light.

'For pity's sake!' exploded Mark, groping for

the door. As he reached the landing Claire switched off its light from downstairs and slammed the front door shut. Pippa woke and called out.

Incredulous that she could prolong their argument at such a time and in so childish a way, Mark ran down the stairs, ignoring Pippa and calling after his wife. He caught up with her at the garage door as she struggled with the key. Gently, remembering her furious exchange with Sam earlier in the evening, Mark took the key from her, inserted it in the lock and pushed up the overhead door. The sound was loud in the night air and he subconsciously waited for the Bartons' light to illumine the back garden.

Unprotesting, Claire let him drive the car from the garage and bring down the door again. He told her, quietly, that she should not drive.

'I'll be OK. Will you do the gate for me? Really I'll be OK.' She sounded calmer.

'Well go carefully. It won't help anyone if you have an accident.' He knew it was useless to attempt to persuade her to wait for the morning. He guessed that Sally and Aunt Isobel were already heading for Sussex. It was the Renwick way. For all he knew, the Fiske branch of the family was even now setting out from Yorkshire.

'How bad is it?' he asked as he opened the back door of the car and put her case inside.

'Bad enough for the Fiskes to have been alerted.'

'Then I may need to bring the children down? You'll let me know?'

'Yes. Now please just let me go.'

He did, but when he walked back up the drive he found he had forgotten to pick up his front-door key and he was locked out. It took him half an hour to persuade Pippa to feel brave enough to creep out on to the dark landing and come down to see who was ringing the bell in the middle of the night. Frightened, she asked to sleep in her parents' bed and although he assented Mark, motivated by some obscure taboo or possibly by the modern emphasis on child abuse, was embarrassed that she should be there in Claire's absence. He slept badly and was already up when Claire phoned at six.

Sam was very ill and still in Intensive Care but was expected to recover. There was no immediate danger. Relieved, Mark sent his father-in-law his best wishes and asked to be kept in touch. When Claire's attention turned to domestic arrangements he assured her he had already thought of everything. He would ring Mrs Barton as soon as it was decent to ask if she would sit with Jeremy while he took Pippa to school and, of course, he would not go to work. He reflected with satisfaction that in four weeks' time he would never go to Inglis and May again, but it was not a reflection he could share with his wife.

In the event the break with his employers happened much sooner. Inglis telephoned later on that morning to say how sorry he was to get Mark's message, that it must be a very worrying time for him and Claire and that he hoped Sam would make a full recovery ('I'll bet you do,' thought Mark as he reflected on the likely impact on Inglis and May of the death or incapacity of

257

their most important client). However there would be a lot for Mark to do at home and, now that the flotation exercise was complete as far as Inglis and May was concerned, there was increasingly little for him to do at work. Clearly he could take on no new clients. Perhaps therefore it would be sensible if they were to dispense with the period of notice. Mark could collect any personal effects from the office when next in London...

Mark forced himself to sound soberly grateful rather than elated. Indeed, so unready was he to produce any alternative source of income that he knew his elation to be irresponsible, but such self-reproach could not stop him drinking a solitary toast to freedom when he had bid a courteous goodbye to Inglis and thanked him, hypocritically, for his understanding over the years.

Mrs Barton returned to sit with Jeremy while Mark went to fetch Pippa from school. Both he and Claire had marvelled at the lack of embarrassment on the part of either Barton following the events of the end of the preceding year. Either they really did not realise the damage they had done or did not consider it damage.

'Do you suppose they are waiting for us to say "thank you"?' Claire had giggled after one encounter.

Mark had merely shaken his head in bemusement.

He smiled at the memory of this exchange as he sat in the school car park waiting for Pippa. Getting out of the car to stretch his legs he inhaled the brisk March air, still savouring his unexpected freedom from wage slavery. Already Inglis and May seemed a far-off memory, as if he had worked there long ago. There had been no mention of any leaving ceremony but Mark's reaction to this had been mirth rather than any sense of insult.

His mirth faded as there came unbidden to his mind the wish to be as easily rid of his marriage. He reminded himself of Pippa's vulnerability, of Sam's illness, of Ruth's forthcoming nuptials. It was not a time to rock the boat. Uneasily he recognised that Claire's feelings, which should have been the paramount consideration, did not feature in his reasoning at all.

He forced himself to think instead of the steps he must now take to set up his own business, to weigh the merits of working from home against those of taking premises immediately, to decide the balance he should seek between personal and business accounts, to determine whether he should be a specialist or a generalist.

His thoughts would not be so readily channelled, and in the end he abandoned his attempt at self-discipline and allowed his mind to worry instead at the likely consequences of a divorce or even a period of separation.

Suddenly, into the clear air of the afternoon came the sound of very young voices singing. A piano, amateurishly but vigorously played, sounded the notes of 'Michael Finnegan', a song Mark had hardly heard since his own schooldays. Voices – pure, clear, obedient – joined in.

There was an old man named Michael
   Finnegan
He had whiskers on his chinnegan
The wind came out and blew them in again
Poor old Michael Finnyinnyinnygan.

To Mark's amusement the song, a different version from the one he had learned as a child, was repeated several times. After a brief pause the voices rose again but this time in a very different theme.

Peace, perfect peace, is the gift of Christ our
   God.

Mark wondered if Pippa were among the singers and if so whether she understood what she was singing, whether she believed it. He found himself hoping that she did. She would need something to rely on if he were to leave his family and it would be something she could share with the believing Claire, a bond between them in adversity.

Then came a solo – thin, wavery, perhaps a little uncertain as if the singer lacked confidence – and Mark recognised his daughter's voice.

Love, perfect love, is the gift of Christ our God.

A lump rose in Mark's throat as she continued the verse, ending with an almost perceptible note of relief. He found he had been holding his breath which he now expelled very slowly. Love, perfect and unconditional, was what she offered them all – Claire, himself, Jeremy, Montefiore. Only Jeremy would never reject her, would never walk away from a kiss or a hug as Montefiore did when he was hungry, or receive one impatiently as he and Claire did when worried or pressured by time.

He hated himself for his proposed betrayal but knew that now it was only a matter of time before it came.

His guilt was not lessened when he saw Pippa running towards him, swinging her school bag and calling something to Ellen as she ran. There was a general air of excitement, for the school broke up the next day and the one after that saw three classes depart for France. He wondered how on earth they would manage all the arrangements with Claire unexpectedly away.

Mark supposed he would never be free of arrangements for the care and organisation of his offspring. In most families the children grew up, took responsibility for their own lives, acquired their own bikes and cars. For Jeremy there was no such prospect. Their lives would always revolve around his need for a constant adult presence, for adequate transport, specialised feeding and increasingly he would become – was already becoming – too heavy for Claire to manage him as she would have managed a baby. He, Mark, would be walking away from the day-to-day burden of most of those responsibilities, and his conscience condemned him even as his resolution held firm.

Claire rang that evening with minute instructions and Mark found himself in an unfamiliar world of the laundering and packing of Pippa's clothes, the purchasing and assembling of last-minute items and the rather easier task of locating and checking travel documents and obtaining currency. Nurse Allen and Mrs Barton took it in turns to sit with Jeremy.

Throughout it all the thought nagged him that Claire's continued absence was ominous, and this suspicion was reinforced when he learned on Friday evening that the Fiskes were still in Sussex, together with Aunt Isobel, and that Sally was commuting from there to Westminster and to her constituency engagements. He was fond of Sam and anxious to see him, angry and disgusted when the Judas voice told him that if Sam died his daughters would be rich and independent and his own departure would be easier as a result.

On Saturday he drove Pippa to the school where two coaches were drawn up in the car park. Throughout the journey she chattered excitedly to Jeremy, whom he had brought along not only because he felt he had imposed enough on Mrs Barton but because Pippa had promised her brother that he could 'see her off and wave'. Accordingly, as the coaches drew away, Mark lifted Jeremy's hand and tried to make it wave as energetically as Pippa's was doing from the rear window.

The other parents waved also until the coaches were out of sight. As he dropped Jeremy's hand back into his lap and wiped away a dribble of saliva Mark heard one call, 'Safe journey, darling, safe journey' and felt a shaft of unease. Hitherto he had not felt any concern at all for his daughter's safety, trusting the school implicitly, taking the trip for granted, pleased for Pippa. Now a doubt niggled. He tried to laugh at himself. Were two days of running the home and children without Claire's aid really enough to turn him into a mother hen? He shrugged away the doubt and drove home to put into action a plan he had conceived in the night.

Once again he plunged himself into the task of packing, but this time for himself and Jeremy. He hoped he had left nothing vital from his son's luggage. As usual, when they took Jeremy away on a rare overnight stay, his equipment and necessities filled the boot. In her hurry Claire had taken the first car in the garage which was Mark's, her own being behind it. That at least was a blessing, as hers had been bought with the need to accommodate Jeremy's wheelchair in mind.

The journey which should have taken an hour took nearly two owing to an accident and an unrelated diversion. The traffic news told him a coach had broken down on the M4. For some reason it caused him to remember the mother who had called 'Safe journey, darling', and unease stirred again.

The Sussex house was deserted when he arrived and he was momentarily taken aback. They must all be at the hospital, which did not bode well for Sam but also presented him with unforeseen difficulties. He could not get in and even if he could there would be no one to sit with Jeremy while he visited the hospital. There was nothing for it but to take his son to the hospital, unpack half the contents of the boot to free the wheelchair and take him on to the ward.

Claire had told him that Sam was in Fleming Ward, but from there he was redirected to a private ward, and Mark hoped this was a good omen.

With the exception of Claire, the small band of Renwicks gathered at the bedside greeted him with surprised enthusiasm. His wife fired off a list of questions about the arrangements he had made, especially about contact with Pippa and the care of Montefiore. When he had answered each one patiently and satisfactorily she appeared not relieved but resentful. It was clear she considered his actions precipitate and irresponsible.

While Claire's inquisition was in full flow Sally and Rupert Fiske manoeuvred Jeremy's wheelchair near the bed so that Sam could touch him in greeting, and when it had finished he found that Sally had also vacated her seat so that he too could be close to Sam.

He studied the older man carefully. Sam looked and sounded weaker than the initial news had led him to expect, but he answered Mark's gentle enquiries with optimism and clarity.

'I turned t'bugger's boat upside down,' said Sam with satisfaction.

Mark, uncomprehending, blinked and momentarily feared for Sam's mind.

'Charon,' sniffed Claire, her tone appropriate to the instruction of a rather slow child.

Mark, enlightened, relaxed as he recalled the

264

ferryman of classical myth who took the spirits of the dead one by one to the underworld.

Later Claire took Jeremy to Sam's house and the older Fiskes went with them to help. The others stayed until a nurse gently hinted that Sam needed rest after which Mark, Rupert and Sally also left but Aunt Isobel stayed behind, with Sally promising to return for her later. It was obvious to Mark from this last arrangement that the family had a policy of an all-day presence at the hospital, and on the way out he asked Sally the question he could not have asked in Sam's presence.

'We think it's all right. They would not have let him move otherwise. Still, they're a bit cagey.'

'Have you noticed an improvement?'

'Yes, but it's slow. It wasn't a minor attack.'

'He seems in good spirits underneath it all.'

'What else would we expect? There are some people so optimistic that if they found themselves in Hell they would think it was Heaven with the central heating system gone wrong.'

Mark laughed but wished she had drawn a metaphor from something other than the after-life. He remembered Sam's own joke about Charon and wondered if the Renwicks realised their preoccupation with the subject.

Nevertheless on the following day the Fiskes embarked on the long journey back to Yorkshire and, after visiting Sam early, Sally left for a long-standing engagement in the constituency – from all of which Mark deduced a degree of confidence in Sam's recovery. He and Claire took it in turns to sit with Jeremy while the other visited

Sam. Aunt Isobel remained at the hospital until the evening, when she and Claire went to church.

Because it was not her usual church Claire did not take Jeremy, in case an outbreak of grunting disconcerted the congregation or caused a reaction not entirely compatible with good Christian charity.

Despite this precaution, neither Mark nor Claire was certain that Jeremy could still grunt. The last occasion either could remember preceded the cessation of swallowing, and they feared that the one had gone with the other. Neville Harris and the expensive London specialist had reassured them that all else was as well as ever but occasionally when he looked at his son Mark felt a chilly doubt, although he could produce no reason for it.

He could conceive of no logic either to support the recurrence of the same chilly doubt when, two days later, Aunt Isobel waved them off on their journey home with a cry of 'Safe journey! Drive carefully!'

16

Throughout the week the news from Sussex was good, and by the end of it they were able to speak on the telephone to Sam, who with deepening satisfaction told them once more the treatment he had meted out to Charon which in turn Mark repeated to members of his own family, mimicking Sam's Yorkshire accent. He had been grateful for their enquiries, as Ruth's wedding was fast approaching and his mother was immersed in preparations, seemingly enjoying her role as mother of the bride and producing an astonishing degree of organisation.

On Friday, as she set out for the three o'clock service, Claire remarked regretfully that it would be their first Easter without Pippa, so on the Sunday Mark accompanied her to church as if that might somehow make up for the loss she obviously felt.

As he reflected on the theme of resurrection Mark thought of Jeremy's and Sam's recoveries. Surely he had much to be thankful for, but he could not repress the feeling that there were still more personal Calvaries ahead. It had been a bad year, but he could not yet rid himself of his unease and believe the worst over.

Throughout the Bank Holiday Monday he and Claire argued and bickered as his wife left him in no doubt of the light in which she viewed what she continued to term his irresponsible and precipitate behaviour. He had left a perfectly good job with nothing else to go to and there were four mouths to feed and a roof to be kept over their heads. He need not think she would ask Sam to help.

He had expected no different a reaction, and might have borne it more philosophically but for a gradually growing self-doubt which had begun to torment him. He could not pretend he had been a great success at Inglis and May and it was no good trying to shelter behind Jeremy, the ever-ready, all-purpose excuse for whatever was going wrong in his life. If he had been a really valued employee producing much-respected work, Inglis would not have objected to the constraints produced by the demands of Jeremy's condition. His periods of unforeseen absence from the office would have aroused sympathy and concern, not irritation and resigned shrugs.

Mark could not disguise from himself that he had survived only because Inglis would not offend the man whose business accounted for so much of the firm's turnover. It was ironic, then, that his most unsatisfactory work should have been for Sam's flotation, and amidst the guilt he could not help but wonder if Sam himself had lost respect for his son-in-law as a result.

Unwisely he voiced a part of his thoughts aloud and wondered if he should give up accountancy altogether, raising Claire's exasperation to a pitch of fury unusual even in her worst of moods. Demanding to be left alone, Mark announced an intention to attend to some long-neglected tasks in the garden but as he was pulling on old shoes at the kitchen door she told him to change Jeremy's pad instead 'as he now had so much time he might as well spend some of it helping her'. He refused blasphemously, deriving some vague satisfaction from his bad behaviour towards both son and wife.

Emerging into the garden, he was relieved to see Barton aloft his stepladder clipping his hedge for the first time that year. It meant Claire would resist any impulse to follow him and renew the argument outside. She had the reticence of her class towards scenes in public, even had she not felt a particular distrust of Barton since the incident with the press.

Alone with his thoughts Mark found scarcely more comfort. His marriage was a failure, his job was a failure, his future uncertain. Even his pathetic attempts to seek solace outside his marriage had failed. His family's security rested as much, if not more, with his wife's father as with him. His relationship with his small daughter was erratic. It would not have surprised him if the cat had turned against him.

Rags ambled through the Hole and sat down wearily.

'You and me, both,' Mark told Rags. 'Ageing, fed up and sorry for ourselves.'

Rags looked up at the sound of Mark's voice, then put his head on his paws and went to sleep. Absurdly, Mark wished he could do the same.

The distant sound of lawnmowers, children's voices, a barking dog, drifted towards him on the light afternoon breeze while Barton's shears plied their rhythmic task. England was on holiday, and with the optimism of a warmish April was preparing its gardens for summer. Everywhere he looked spring bulbs blazed in a riot of colour, testimony to Claire's work over thirteen years.

What should have been a scene of peace and satisfaction instead appeared to his tormented eyes a mere mockery. His son would never run and shriek with childish glee on a warm holiday afternoon and there was no soul mate with whom to share the glorious beauty of this small corner of creation. In his mind's eye he saw the colour of

269

a Portuguese garden and the soul mate he had found there, fleetingly experiencing the balm she had brought his tortured spirit.

Mark did not return indoors until the darkness and chill of approaching night sent him there. Finding the kitchen in darkness and with no indication of cooking, he cut himself a sandwich and retired to his study where he proposed to draw up the plan which would ensure a steady enough income both to maintain his family and to part from it, but with frustration and helplessness he went to bed having spent the intervening hours brooding miserably and ineffectively.

In the morning he covertly examined the appointments pages of the *Daily Telegraph* until he remembered that if he sought to be employed by anyone other than himself he would need a reference from Inglis. Though he had no doubt that Inglis would write nothing which might offend Sam, the prospect was still humiliating and he spent some minutes bitterly amusing himself imagining to what euphemisms Inglis might resort in dismissing twenty years' work as inadequate and unreliable.

In a mood of resolution which even he recognised to be quite spurious, Mark devised advertisements for his accountancy services and sent them to the local papers. He did not expect such token activity to mollify Claire, and it was in strained silence that he drove her and Jeremy to meet the returning school trip. He had insisted they all go, remembering the small figure waving to Jeremy with affectionate vigour from the rear window of the coach and determined that Jeremy should be there to have his hand waved on her return. Anyway, as he had pointed out to Claire, this was her first holiday abroad without her family and it was important they should all be there to welcome Pippa home.

The school car park was full and parents were standing around talking, occasionally looking towards the drive, waiting for the two coaches to materialise. It was no very great surprise that they were late and, as he and Claire appeared to have little to say to each other, Mark got out of the car and began to chat to a father with whom he had spoken before on school occasions and who was standing alone admiring the particularly spectacular sunset.

They discussed sunsets around the world until that topic dwindled and the other man looked at his watch. Around them the inconsequential conversations continued. A mother lamented the speed with which her daughter grew out of her uniform, another hoped her son had profited academically from the trip and not merely fooled around 'as usual'.

Mark went and spoke to Jeremy, relieved to find that Claire too had now left the car and was talking to other parents, rather than sitting tight-lipped and alone. As he turned away from talking to his son he surprised an expression of sympathy on the face of a nearby parent and felt the resentment well up. How dare she patronise Jeremy – or him?

Parents were now glancing at their watches every few seconds and muttering their discontent. The children were bound to be impossibly excited and difficult to get to bed; suppers were spoiling in ovens; babysitters had been told it would only be an hour at most.

When Jake James appeared in person and the school was opened up, complaint gave way to faint alarm. Had the coaches broken down? Where were they? This was the age of the mobile phone, surely the drivers could let them know? Mark felt his stomach sink, the old premonition returning. From the faces of other parents he knew he was not alone, and took brief refuge from his fears by debating with Claire whether to bring Jeremy in.

James gathered them in the assembly hall and told them there had been an accident to one coach. The other had stopped to help. They would have more news shortly.

Immediately voices rose in a concerned babble. 'Which coach? What sort of accident? Was anyone hurt? Where? How? It wasn't serious, was it?'

Of course it was serious, thought Mark impatiently. Otherwise James would have suggested they all go home and wait for further details. He would have said 'A slight accident' or 'Absolutely nothing to worry about' or 'Nobody's hurt'. But he had said none of these things and if anyone doubted what that meant then the anguished look on the Head's face would have removed that doubt. He was controlled and competent but he was suffering under the burden of the information he was going to have to impart.

There was silence now, all eyes fixed on Jake James, eyes which begged for reassurance, eyes which pleaded that whatever had happened had not happened to one particular child. Claire's grip on Mark became painful, momentarily distracting him, and in that moment he noticed that other members of staff had arrived, and so had the vicar of the nearby church who acted as school chaplain. As Mark's glance rested on the vicar, ice moved inside him.

James spoke quietly and firmly, staying in command of every Head's worst nightmare. It was Coach A which had met with the accident and there was the possibility that some of the children were injured. Ambulances were at the scene and everything possible was being done. The incident had occurred less than half an hour from Dover but because a number of vehicles were involved the emergency services might have to use the offices of more than one hospital in more than one county. For the time being, therefore, the police were asking the parents to remain at the school and further details would be relayed as soon as possible. Meanwhile Coach B was once more on its way and expected in just over an hour. Children who did not require any medical assistance would be brought back to the school and transport was being arranged.

James asked the parents who had children only in Coach B to make their way to another school nearby, the Roman Catholic primary school of St Joseph's, which was opening up to look after them until the coach arrived. Parents with children in both coaches should go along the

273

corridor to the library where arrangements...

'Which coach?' Claire was demanding urgently. 'Which coach?'

Mark shook his head in misery, unable even to say 'A', as if by doing so he would confirm Pippa's fate. He was seeing again a small hand waving, a small mouth forming 'Goodbye', excited faces bobbing up and down, pressing themselves to the rear window of the coach, on the pane of which was pasted a large, black, single letter. A.

Abruptly he thought of the children of Dunblane, of the photographs that he could not look at, remembering how he had left the front page of his paper unread rather than risk seeing those rows of innocent faces in the school photograph, with so many ringed. Sam had said he felt the same way and recalled the Aberfan disaster of thirty years before.

The parents of Coach B children were leaving, quietly, ashamed of their own good fortune, embarrassed to show relief, still shaken by what might have been for them, by what would yet be for others. The rest stood or sat in numb horror, only the occasional sob or flash of defensive anger rising above the subdued murmur of fear.

'Come on, let's get Jeremy,' urged Mark, pulling Claire towards the door. It made sense, as they were likely to be in that wretched hall for a long time, but he also had another plan and, as if sensing this, Claire did not protest.

Once at the car Mark switched on the radio and fumbled between stations until he found one broadcasting news. They had missed the opening and sat in miserable impatience waiting for the headlines to be repeated at the end.

'Several children are feared dead,' announced the impersonal voice, in faultless BBC English, solemn-toned as befitted the sombre nature of the announcement, 'after a head-on collision between a coach and a lorry on the M20.'

Claire moaned helplessly, standing by the open door of the car on which she now leaned for support.

'She was in the rear of the coach,' said Mark, praying that the children kept the same seats throughout the trip. He thought it likely. Friends sought seats together, they left small personal items on them when they had to leave the vehicle temporarily and the seats became their own. Of course there were reasons they might change seats with each other: a childish quarrel or the sudden burgeoning of a new friendship, perhaps, or one of the teaching staff might move a sick or misbehaving child.

As Mark was helping Claire get Jeremy into the wheelchair, a departing car stopped and a Coach B parent put his head out of the driver's window.

'Hope it will soon be all right. I'm sure Pippa will be OK.'

He had no basis for any such certainty, thought Mark as Claire thanked him and said she was glad his child was unaffected. Clearly she knew who he was as further, brief conversation took place. The driver called 'Good luck!' as the car moved down the drive, in the slow procession which was now leaving Valence Towers and heading towards St Joseph's.

Mark stood, waiting for a convenient gap between the moving cars before wheeling Jeremy to the school entrance. A Ford Escort with a weeping woman at the wheel stopped for them and Claire waved their thanks as they crossed in front of it. Mark wondered if the woman wept from relief for herself and her child, or for those who still waited at the school until he recalled that some parents had children in both coaches...

'No. No. No,' muttered Mark to the Deity he did not acknowledge.

'What?' asked Claire, startled.

'Don't tell me there's a God,' said Mark.

'There is,' said Claire calmly. 'And I pray He will preserve Pippa.'

'And what will you say to Him if He doesn't?' retorted Mark, conveniently overlooking the fact that he himself had prayed for Pippa to have stayed in the rear of the coach.

Claire did not reply and together they began to lift the chair up the steps of the entrance. There was disabled access at the rear of the school, but they could not be sure it was open tonight. A man hurried up to them and began to help. He too had gone out to listen to the news on his car radio but he too had only caught the headline summary at the end.

Back in the assembly hall the news of death had already spread. Some of the nuns from St Joseph's had arrived and were dispensing hot drinks. Where only one parent had come to meet the returning child the other was now arriving too so that couples might endure the nightmare together, and the hall was filling. From time to time Jake James came back into the hall and sought out a particular couple. Other parents watched their reactions with dread, aware their own turn must come.

Close to where Mark and Claire sat on chairs designed for children was an older man who, oblivious to what was going on around him and unseeking of news, had not once lifted his head from his hands. Claire wandered over to him and Mark watched her touch his shoulder and saw the man look up. They began to talk and then Claire fetched him a hot drink. Mark pushed Jeremy over to join them.

Claire introduced Bertie Wells, grandfather of seven-year-old Leslie. He was bringing the child up because his grandson's parents had been killed in a car crash together with his, Bertie's, wife. An older child, also in the car, had survived but had died of cancer two years later. Mark saw the tears in Claire's eyes but she blinked them away and began to offer what little comfort she could. Wells asked about their own situation and they told him of Pippa. He glanced at Jeremy and asked if they 'had others'.

Mark shook his head.

'Then she'll be all you've got. Just like he's all I've got.'

Neither Mark nor Claire responded. If both were angry neither showed it, in Claire's case because she felt too sorry for the older man, in Mark's because he recognised with guilt a reflection of his own feelings. He recalled his terror and grief when he thought Jeremy was dying last year but he knew that what he was feeling now was different. If they lost Jeremy the loss was solely theirs, but if they lost Pippa the loss was hers too: loss of hope, happiness, children of her own.

Claire whimpered suddenly and, following her glance, Mark saw Jake James approaching. Frantically he tried to read the Head's expression and found he could not.

'Mr Wells,' began James.

Briefly Mark tried to convince himself that James had said 'Wellings' not 'Wells', but it was to Bertie he was now speaking, not Mark. He saw Claire's sudden tension relax into emptiness and reached over the seat Wells had vacated to hold her hand. Wells, Wellings. The coincidence was just one more small cruelty to add to their torment.

Wells left with James, forgetting them in the urgency of whatever news James had imparted.

'I hope that was good news,' whispered Claire.

'I think he would have told us if it were. I think he would have told the world.'

Claire's shoulders sank in defeat.

Presently the vicar wandered over. He had no more news than they. It was true that fatalities were feared but he did not know how many among the children. It seemed unlikely that the driver could have survived. Shocked, Mark found he wanted to brush aside the news of the driver as if it were unimportant.

As Claire and the vicar talked he thought of Ben, his future brother-in-law, and of how he had lost his first wife and children in a road accident, and of Bertie Wells. The old adage that accidents

278

were always someone's fault entered his mind, and for the first time in months he thought also of Robert Cooper. Cooper would read of this night's tragedy and be glad he had not sent Philip to Valence Towers, although he would have been too young to have been on the trip. He would search the papers in dread for mention of Pippa's name, ridden by the guilt of what he had done to Jeremy.

The vicar's voice rescued him from thoughts of Robert Cooper. 'I think Jake is about to tell us something.'

Mark saw the Head was now on the stage and he and Claire joined the agonised rush to the front of the hall, afraid to miss a syllable.

The Head read out a list of twelve names of children who were now on their way to St Joseph's in a minibus. He read in alphabetical order, slowly, giving the full name of each child to avoid any confusion or false hope. Alexandra Jane Bell, Zoe Harriet Curtis, Karen Margaret Francis, Jason Matthew, Claude Kenny... Mark cursed the position of their own name. He began to count the names: nine, ten, eleven, there was still hope; but the last name was plain Mary Yates and not Philippa Isobel Graine Ruth Wellings.

Beside him he felt the hope die out of Claire and he realised she had been counting too. Again his mind showed him the Dunblane picture, but this time the children wore the uniform of Valence Towers and one of the ringed faces was Pippa's. This time he would not be able to escape by turning the page.

'There must have been more than forty

children on that coach,' he said to Claire. 'The odds are still with us.'

Jake James next read another, shorter list of children detained in hospital but with minor injuries and shock only. They might well be released in the next few hours and if those parents would make their way to the Library they would be given the contact numbers of the hospitals. He and Claire clung to each other as the list was read. Again there was no mention of Pippa. Eighteen out of forty children accounted for, plus those whose parents had already been spoken to individually by Jake James... The odds were now much less favourable.

The fortunate parents left and soft chairs were wheeled in from the staff room for the remaining ones, together with some more appropriately sized hard chairs which had been gathered from around the school. The nuns produced another round of hot drinks.

Mark fell into conversation with Ellen's parents. They had three children on the coach – Ellen, and twins in the class above. Neither had the red-rimmed eyes of those who had wept; their faces were masks on which suffering had etched deep, terrible lines. Three children on the coach.

A rumour swept the hall that two members of staff had been killed.

'They would have been in the front,' said Claire.

Mark tried to recall which teachers had been on the trip. The two French teachers, of course. The Deputy Head. One class teacher for each of the four classes involved but one of those was one of the French teachers and another the Deputy Head. That made five. He thought of one of the French teachers, young, pretty, a French girl married to an Englishman. The Deputy Head had five children but Mark found himself resenting the loss of the younger teacher's life more. If they had died. If either had died.

Suddenly Claire was nudging him and he saw James once more approaching them. He was smiling. Dear God, he was smiling.

'Good news,' said James quietly, indicating that they too must be quiet in deference to the other parents. 'Pippa was on Coach B.'

He had just begun to explain when Claire fainted in Mark's arms.

Jake James dealt with the situation as competently and discreetly as he had dealt with so much that evening. A nun brought a glass of water and a nearby parent, a nurse, came to their assistance. Mark found himself torn between concern and impatience. He was in a fever to be at St Joseph's, where the coach would have arrived ages ago. Pippa would be distressed, wondering where they were, frightened by the night's events.

As soon as Claire recovered he tried to move them off but Jake James detained them. He explained that one of Pippa's class had been taken ill just before they left France. Accordingly when they boarded the coaches again on leaving the ferry one of the teachers suggested the child's older sister from Coach B should come and sit with her. Pippa had been next to the sick child and was therefore asked to change places with the older child and rather than leave her alone in a strange class the teacher had sent Ellen with her to Coach B, moving a friend of the older child to Coach A. That was why Jake James now detained them.

Ellen was naturally still at St Joseph's with Pippa but her parents would wish to stay on here for news of the twins. Could Mark and Claire look after Ellen for the night? Could they give Ellen's mother a lift to St Joseph's so she could explain what was happening to Ellen?

The arrangements stretched Mark's nerves. He wanted to be at St Joseph's with Pippa and he found himself positively clenching his teeth as James moved to explain the situation to Ellen's parents. Ellen's mother's response was surprisingly practical. There was no need for her to go to St Joseph's. Ellen was safe and well and could have very little idea of the magnitude of what was going on. It would be cruel to enlighten her until they knew the exact situation of the twins. If she, Ellen's mother, were to go to St Joseph's she would not trust her own reactions and if she were to break down in front of Ellen that could only scare the poor child and it would not then be fair to hand her over to Mark and Claire for the night.

Mark listened with a mixture of admiration and disbelief.

'She's right, of course,' said James as he saw them to the door. 'The children on Coach B won't have much idea what's been going on.'

Mark knew he was warning them not to alarm Pippa and Ellen, and reassured him accordingly.

Pippa and Ellen were the only ones left at St Joseph's when he and Claire arrived. The nun waiting with them explained that it had taken a long while to realise why they were not being collected. There had been two members of staff on Coach B but both had stayed at the scene to help with calming the children and identifying others. (Mark noted that word 'others'. She was avoiding saying anything about death or serious injury in front of the children.) This was only possible because one of them had brought along her student daughter who was studying to teach primary school children. It was therefore decided to leave this girl in charge of Coach B children. Unfortunately she simply took Pippa's and Ellen's presence on the coach for granted, not having been briefed by her elders.

The girl had waited with them for some time before the nun told her to go and that she would be responsible for them. After they had waited a bit longer the nun had asked the girls their telephone numbers and telephoned their homes. There had, of course, been no reply and Sister Agnes Xavier had not really been expecting one. When she learned that Ellen had a brother and sister on Coach A she thought she might have found part of the answer and telephoned the school.

Hours of unnecessary suffering, thought Mark. He thanked Sister Agnes Xavier and began to urge the children towards the door.

'We can't go yet,' wailed Pippa. 'Our cases are on the other coach and all your presents are in them.'

'William's there too,' said Ellen, her mouth beginning to tremble.

'Your brother?' whispered Claire.

'No. My bear. William. I can't leave William all alone in my case.'

Mark met Sister Agnes's eyes, an incredulous question in his own. The nun's were full of unshed tears, but it was she who said gently:

'There's been an accident and it will take a lot of time to sort everything out but there's lots of nice policemen about and I'm sure they will look after your cases. William will have quite a story to tell.'

Ellen sniffed, unconvinced.

'Home,' said Claire firmly. 'Cocoa and chips.'

The children whooped with delight and sped for the door while the adults stared at one another, dumbfounded.

'They don't know,' said Sister Agnes sadly. 'The driver of the other coach stopped some way off so they didn't see anything. When their parents arrived here the children were embarrassed by the effusive way they greeted them. They've simply no idea.'

'Ellen Eames has twin siblings on the other coach,' Claire pointed out. 'Surely she's worried?'

Sister Agnes Xavier shook her head. 'Why should she be? Children of that age have no experience to alarm them or on which to build in their imagination. A child at this school died last term and we clubbed together for a present for her younger sister. One or two of the children were actually jealous. We forget how a child sees these things. Perhaps it's just as well. If anything

284

has happened to one of the Eameses then Ellen will suffer soon enough. Meanwhile where ignorance is bliss, 'tis folly to be wise.'

Mark thought of Gray's poem from which Sister Agnes Xavier had quoted so aptly. Later that evening he extracted a small volume from the lounge bookcase and read it aloud to Claire.

17

The late-night news showed pictures of the aftermath of the crash. A lorry, travelling towards the Channel Tunnel and unlawfully in the fast lane, had gone out of control and crashed across the central reservation, colliding head on with a coach carrying forty children between the ages of seven and nine. Two cars behind the coach had failed to stop in time and piled into the accident. The drivers of the lorry and the coach had died instantly, as had the driver of one of the following cars.

The school was identified merely as a private preparatory school in Surrey. It was believed the children were returning from a visit to France. Two teachers had died and there were reports of fatalities among the children but names and addresses were being withheld until the next of kin had been informed. An emergency number, for the use of worried friends or relatives, was then both read out and shown on the screen.

Immediately the telephone started to ring.

Mark spoke first to Sam and then to Sally. Claire rang Aunt Isobel. There was no point in seeking to reassure his own family, who were scarcely aware that Pippa had made such a trip. That task could wait till the morning, when the school was likely to be named, but he still took the precaution of recording a message to calm callers with news of Pippa's non-involvement with the coach concerned.

Claire was the last to retire to bed, by which time it was one o'clock but they had still received no communication from the Eameses. Exhausted, neither slept and at dawn they went down to the kitchen together to make a pot of tea. Mark checked the answerphone to find no message.

'Ring the school,' said Claire, yawning as she set two mugs on the table.

A fresh-sounding female voice answered, which did not suggest its owner had been up all night. Clearly Jake James had drafted in reinforcements. Mark enquired about the Eames twins.

'Are you a relative?' asked the voice.

Mark gave his credentials.

'Just a moment, please,' said the voice in a tone more appropriate to the checking of a minor piece of clerical information than the life of a child.

Mark grimaced to Claire. 'The admin. brigade have arrived,' he told her without bothering to cover the mouthpiece, and was immediately disconcerted to hear the voice again.

'Sorry to keep you waiting,' it said conversationally as Mark ground his teeth.

Then another voice spoke, tired, drained, dispirited. Mark only just recognised it as the Head's. The Eames twins were fine. Stephanie had been detained with concussion and Zachary had broken both feet but otherwise it was just cuts, bruises and a good deal of shock.

'Thank God,' said Mark, simultaneously signalling reassurance to Claire, who mouthed 'Wells' to him. He put the question to Jake James.

'Not so good. Leslie is hanging on, but I got the impression from the hospital that it's in the balance whether he lives. His grandfather is distraught, of course. You know Bertie Wells?'

'Since last night. Jake, how many dead?'

'Three drivers of the various vehicles, Mr Robinson, Miss Clark, Mrs Davis and so far four children.'

Mark closed his eyes as he heard the Head's voice waver. 'I don't know what to say,' he muttered helplessly. 'Can you tell me who the children are?'

'Two have been named overnight: little Christina Bright and Sebastian Lucas. For your information only, the others are Chloe Strange and Caroline Kay.'

Three of the names meant nothing to Mark, but Christina Bright had been one of the children Pippa had invited to Jeremy's birthday party. Mark remembered how he had rescued her chocolate egg from the stream after the egg-and-spoon race.

'Jake, what about the kids from Coach B who changed with Pippa and Ellen?'

'Both all right, and you can hardly be gladder

about that than I am. When the parents came back from St Joseph's I said it was sure to be all right – they couldn't possibly have been on Coach A. I actually got one of the staff to start ringing round to see which of their friends they had gone off with.'

So he and Claire – and when they grew older, Pippa and Ellen – were spared the illogical guilt they might otherwise have felt.

'And the others?'

'Twenty-five children completely OK or with very slight injuries. Two in Intensive Care, including Leslie Wells, eight very badly injured but not in danger, one poor mite has had an arm amputated.'

'Is it all right if we phone again later?'

'Yes. We'll be here.'

'You need sleep, Jake. Is there anything we can do? Do the nuns need help?'

'No. There are no parents here now – they're all at the hospitals – and the nuns have gone home. It's just a question of obtaining and relaying information now.'

'The press?'

'Are using a different line. Mr Wakefield is doing a magnificent job with them.'

Startled, Mark thought of Mr Wakefield, the drama teacher. He was in his early twenties, with long hair and a habit of addressing the parents as 'man'. He taught drama twice a week at Valence Towers and once a week at a pupil referral unit. In between he wrote his own plays but when one was accepted for television it was screened late at night and was of a kind which no Valence Towers parent would have allowed a child to watch. He survived because the school productions were always first class and children rushed home from his classes with questions which proved disconcertingly difficult for parents to answer.

'Oh,' was all Mark could find to say before repeating his exhortation to the Head to get some sleep and ringing off.

He repeated the information to Claire, who knew Chloe Strange from Brownies but neither Sebastian Lucas nor Caroline Kay. She groaned when she learned about Christina Bright but most of her active concern was for Leslie Wells.

Mark thought mainly about Mrs Davis, the young French teacher, and Jack Robinson whose name had provided a ready source of amusement every time he urged pupils to a more expeditious approach. As Deputy Head he was respected by all, but it was as a father of five children that he would now be mourned.

'We had better work out what – and how – we are going to tell them,' said Claire at last.

'I think we should see what the Eameses say first. They're bound to ring as soon as they think it's decent.'

They rang shortly before eight when Claire and Mark were reading the morning papers. There were pictures of the wreckage and reports of the deaths of the three drivers – none named – and of two teachers. Clearly one of the three had died in the night. There was no exact figure for the number of children who had died nor much detail about the school, which remained unnamed.

Mrs Eames sounded very different from the haggard woman they had talked to at the school. Steph and Zach were recovering well, she told them, but were at different hospitals sixty miles apart. She had arranged for Ellen's aunt to collect her before lunch if they did not mind keeping her till then. Meanwhile she was very grateful for all they had done...

In the course of the morning the school was named and Mark telephoned his family before they should hear it on the lunchtime news. The Queen, Prime Minister and Leader of the Opposition sent messages of sympathy to the school. The Bartons called on Mark and Claire.

Pippa watched the news with them and they told her that some children and teachers had gone to Heaven and everyone would miss them and feel upset. Meanwhile lots of Mummies and Daddies were happy because their children were alive.

'Will they be like Jeremy?' asked Pippa matter-of-factly.

Mark drew in his breath with shock, but Claire's eyes signalled to him and he answered 'No, not as far as we know,' in as even a tone as he could manage.

'It's all she knows about car accidents,' Claire reminded him when they were alone. 'A naughty man drove his car too fast and hit Jeremy and that's why he is like he is. Ergo, children who get involved in road accidents end up like Jeremy.'

'She's eight in a couple of weeks.'

'A young eight, but I suspect she may start to grow up next week when she goes back and there are empty desks.'

Mark ran his hands through his hair as he observed, 'Jake might well decide to postpone the start of term. Doubtless the press will want to cover the first day back.'

'They won't come here, will they?'

'I imagine not. Pippa might rate a mention as Sally's niece and the brother of Jeremy, but they will have all the drama they want without needing to risk intrusion here. The public tend to be sensitive about things like that at this sort of time and the editors will know it.'

'I keep thinking about Leslie Wells and that poor man.'

There was a short silence.

'Poor Jake! What a way to end his teaching career,' Claire lamented.

'Still, he's the ideal person to see the school through it all. He'll get things back to normal quicker than most.'

Back to normal. They were easy words to say, but he was no longer sure what constituted normality for him and his family. Working, earning, a daily routine had been his normality for two decades, but for the foreseeable future he was neither working nor earning and the days offered nothing but uncertainty. For Pippa normality had been the routine of home and Valence Towers. If, as he increasingly yearned for, he were to leave she would find neither home nor school the safe, secure places they had once been, where adults protected her against all evil. As yet his daughter did not fully realise the enormity of what had happened the previous night but, when she did, some of her innocence would be lost, some early – too early – sense of her own mortality inculcated.

Ever since he could remember Sam had represented their background security. It was he, Mark, who kept the roof over their heads, food on the table and two cars in the garage, but it was Sam who had made sure they were able to leave no stone unturned when it came to coping with Jeremy's disability. The early visits to doctors in the States, the alterations to their house, the state-of-the-art wheelchairs, the Stannah, the bathroom hoists, were all provided by Sam. Now Sam had suffered a heart attack sufficiently bad to have put his life in danger. True, if Sam were to die, the money supply would be greater, not less, but there was more to the security Sam gave them than just money.

He was good with Jeremy and Pippa loved him. He and Aunt Isobel were always the first to be called on when help was needed, and they always rose to the occasion. Mark had been relying on both to provide the self-isolated Claire with the moral support which would be necessary if he were to leave. If Sam were not around and he, Mark, were to break away, there would be no rock left in Claire's life.

Jeremy alone was unaffected by events, unable to dread, unable to know desertion or disorientation, unable to feel loss or sorrow, impervious to the wounding debate which surrounded the Euthanasia Bill and which for months had clouded the background of their lives.

Back to normal.

For one more day the crash dominated the news. Photographs of the dead teachers, tributes to their work, details of the drivers and their families, accounts from the survivors and praise for the emergency services filled both broadsheets and tabloids. Parliament returned for the summer session and more than an hour was taken up with expressions of sorrow and with tributes from Members of Parliament, including Sally.

On the Saturday Claire took Pippa to buy new items of uniform and the shop assistant said how terrible it all was. Pippa explained that she had been on the other coach, but the assistant told her anyway what a brave little girl she was.

Pippa began to wear a more sober air and to ask both Mark and Claire questions about the crash at unexpected moments.

On the day the school returned the picture Mark dreaded appeared in all the papers. He recognised last year's school photograph and this time forced himself to look at the happy, innocent faces in the four large rings, then at the three adults in the front row encircled with smaller rings. With futile rage he cursed Fate.

Pippa returned, subdued, and informed them that she had spent the English lesson writing letters of consolence.

'Condolence,' corrected Mark.

'It's console,' insisted Pippa, but without much spirit.

'Yes, but it's condolence, not consolence. I can show you in the dictionary.'

'Apart from the letters, how was it?' asked Claire, irritated by the argument.

'Sad,' said Pippa.

Jake James had eschewed professional counselling for his pupils. Not all parents shared his view but Mark and Claire did. New staff were already in place and James settled his school down with a sensitive but determined hand.

Several pupils missed the start of term due to their injuries. Leslie Wells was at last removed from the critical list and his grandfather rang up Mark and Claire to tell them and to thank them for their interest, which had been relayed to him by the Head.

Leslie was lucid but had suffered internal injuries of some magnitude and would be weeks, possibly months, more in hospital. It was a mercy he, Bertie, was retired and could look after him.

'But at least he won't be a cabbage. I'd rather he died than have him a cabbage.'

This time Mark was less forgiving, but he gave the older man the benefit of the doubt. He might just have forgotten about Jeremy, although, as he remembered Wells' comment when they were sitting together in the school hall, Mark did not believe this to be the case. The other's next words dispelled any remaining uncertainty.

'You see, I couldn't cope like you do. I wouldn't want to see him like that every day.'

Mark heard the break in Wells' voice and understood. This, then, had been Wells' private dread over so many days while the fate of his grandson hung in the balance, and probably it had haunted him because the last child on whom he had focused before receiving news of his own was Jeremy. Mark was glad it was he and not Claire who had taken the call.

'You would be surprised how you cope when you have to,' he said, not in defence or self-deprecation but to encourage the other. Wells had difficult days ahead.

He found Claire in the lounge, and was telling her the news when his attention was distracted by the television screen. 'Who's that?' he asked as the screen was filled with the remarkably good-looking features of a man in his thirties talking about the Euthanasia Bill, to which he referred by its correct title of the Terminally Ill Persons Bill.

'The Earl of Yetminster, no less. He's leading the opposition to Sally's Bill in the Lords. Isn't he a dish?'

'Hmmm,' muttered Mark dubiously, and resumed his narration of Leslie Wells' progress, carefully censoring the conversation which had actually taken place. Claire gave him her attention but kept her eyes on the screen. With amusement Mark recollected how she usually turned off the set at the first hint of such debates.

Sally was next to be interviewed. She was, as ever, calm and impressive, but he got the impression she was tiring and he reminded himself that it was an immense undertaking for a new MP in her first year. She was courteous to Yetminster but unyielding and held her ground well.

It was the first of many such televised confrontations as the Bill endured a fierce passage in the Lords, and so eminently televisual was Yetminster that he was on the screen night after night, even when it was the bishops arguing amongst themselves which produced the day's headlines.

He was even a topic of conversation at Ruth's wedding, where Pippa, much to her embarrassment, received almost as much attention as the bride herself. Mark was watching his daughter extract herself from yet another over-exuberant adult embrace and wondering if she found the fulsome thanks for her safety more disturbing than flattering, when Rachael, Ruth's twin, commented on Yetminster.

'Brains, film-star looks, land, money, title, got it all, and gives the impression of being as nice as the chap next door. If he were in the Commons he could be Prime Minister. Everybody is talking about him.'

'Shall I ask Sally to arrange an introduction?' asked Mark, amused. 'He's still single.'

'Not for long, I bet. But no thanks.' Her gaze strayed towards the young man who until now had shared a flat with her, Ruth and the other girls.

Mark looked too but was not impressed. He wondered what the new arrangement would be.

His family was so rarely gathered as one that each member of it made the most of the occasion to comment on the others. Ruth was radiant, Ben happy, his mother in her element despite the necessity for so much organisation. His father was ageing and Christopher was increasing around the girth but it was at John that he looked most closely, at John who struggled with a modest job, a working wife and a mortgage.

Mark fancied he could see signs of strain and wondered how he would make out if he were to leave Claire while having no job – or, for that matter, if he did have one.

The children congregated around Jeremy once they discovered they were allowed to push his chair, and made a great deal of noise while the grown-ups talked animatedly, kindly and even maliciously until the time for speeches. His father revealed more wit than Mark had previously credited him with and Ben proved a competent but shy speaker. Mark warmed to him and knew his sister in good hands. Mellowed by such happy certainty he drank more champagne than he should.

When the time came for departure, Claire insisted on driving, and by the time they arrived home his mood was spoiled.

'Why?' demanded Claire. Why was it always she who abstained and did the driving? This was his sister's wedding not her sister's wedding. So why had it to be she who bought the present, made all the arrangements and drove them home? He had not lifted a finger with Jeremy all day. He had left it all to her while he stood about talking and drinking too much...

Receiving no response she began to shout at him, and stopped only when she remembered Pippa was in the back. She was still angry when they arrived home because Mark had slept most of the way and not taken his share of distracting Pippa, who was still apt to grizzle on long car journeys.

As he staggered, still half asleep, from the car,

Mark wondered if it had really been so recently that they had clung to each other, wondering if Pippa were alive or dead, believing that, if only she were spared, they would never worry about small things again, never argue over trivia, never feel burdened by the petty weights of the day. It had not taken long, thought Mark grimly.

Back to normal.

18

The morning sun shone on St Joseph's school as Mark drove slowly past, his eyes seeking the church of the same name, its rays falling on the children running or standing in small groups in the playground, in the charge of a lay teacher whose brightly-patterned floral frock would not have been out of place on a beach. The everyday scene made a poignant contrast with that which he had last witnessed there and superstitiously he averted his eyes, as if to banish what he now saw would also somehow make the darker memory miraculously disappear.

The church came into view on a bend some hundred yards further on, an old one, unlike most Catholic churches, its stone mellow in the sun. Mark parked and retrieved two large sacks from the boot, jumble previously destined for their own parish but now at Claire's instigation being given instead to St Joseph's as a token of their gratitude. Sam had sent a cheque which

Mark suspected was less token.

In the porch he set down his burden and turned the large ring which was the handle of the church door. At once he was struck by the strange scents. The church he attended with Claire smelled of old wood, polish and flowers; this one exuded the sweet, slightly cloying aroma of incense and candles. It was, he realised, some time since he had visited a Catholic church and for a moment he stood, looking at the banks of candles which lined the side aisles and at the small handful of people praying.

He could see no priest to whom to deliver the bags and he was wondering whether he should just leave them with a note when Sister Agnes Xavier emerged from a door at the front of the church near the altar, recognised him and hurried across to ask after Pippa and Ellen. In her eagerness for news she barely noticed the sacks he offered.

He assured her both girls were well and as she enthusiastically thanked Mary, Mother of God, she turned her attention at last to the large dustbin bags at Mark's feet and invited him to the convent for a coffee.

The convent, situated behind the church in a large and well-kept garden, had been on its present site since the middle of the last century and housed some thirty nuns. Mark, who knew about the falling off of vocations in both the Anglican and Roman Catholic Churches, marvelled that this convent appeared untouched by the trend. St Joseph's primary school was a rarity in that nuns outnumbered the lay staff by a very large margin.

When he commented on this Sister Agnes Xavier looked sad, explaining that two other Houses belonging to the Order had closed in the last five years and the nuns were now concentrated here. Ten of the sisters were over seventy years of age and there had been no more than four novices in the last three years. A life of poverty, chastity and obedience had little charm for the young, and she believed the monastic way of life would have disappeared altogether in the next few decades.

Mark responded with an expression of sympathy but he could feel no real sorrow. Sister Agnes Xavier must once have been a beautiful woman and, as she was also a very kind one, he would have preferred her to have been a wife and mother, not an ageing member of a declining group in a dying world. He could not wish her fate on any young woman.

Yet as he entered the convent he was aware of a great peacefulness, of timeless serenity, of deep calm. He thought of Smith and could picture her here in this quiet place where, as he sat and waited for Sister Agnes Xavier to bring in the coffee, only the gentle ticking of the old clock on the mantelpiece made any sound. He wished he could stay in this room – the nun had called it the parlour – for a very long time.

After savouring the peace for a while he began to look about him. A large crucifix hung in the centre of one wall. Strangely he found it soothing and familiar. His eyes wandered over the bowl of summer roses in one corner to the next wall on which were a pair of pictures, one portraying the Last Supper, the other the Resurrection. He stood up to study the first, to see what expression the artist had given to the face of Christ, wondering would it be sadness at His betrayal or fear of the dreadful fate to come. A few hours after this supper the man in the centre of the table breaking bread would be so unnerved He would sweat blood in the garden of Gethsemane. Had the artist foreshadowed the horror?

He had not. The Christ in the picture had the holy expression of the saint, untroubled, mystical, prophetic. The apostles were similarly bland, with nothing to suggest the impetuousness of Peter, the snobbery of Philip, the cynicism of Thomas. It was impossible to guess which might be which, and Judas was distinguishable not by furtiveness but by a scowl. Disappointed, Mark turned away.

The other walls offered photographs of sundry Mothers Superior of the convent, some sepia, some fading, two recent. In the earlier ones the nuns wore long habits and their wimples allowed not a wisp of hair to escape. In the contemporary ones the habits were shorter and in the most recent the head was completely uncovered. Mark was studying their faces for the secrets of their vocations when Sister Agnes Xavier returned with a tray bearing two china cups, a matching milk jug and sugar bowl, a plate of chocolate biscuits and two shiny teaspoons. The traycloth was embroidered with flowers, reminding Mark of one they had at home but never used, a present from Aunt Isobel.

They talked of Valence Towers and the aftermath of the tragedy and how lucky Pippa and Ellen were in escaping not only injury but also horror. 'They didn't see a thing and therefore didn't fear anything and there haven't been any nightmares,' observed Mark. 'No mental scars as far as anyone can see, but I don't suppose we'll put it to the test by asking Pippa to travel on a coach in the near future.'

'Buses? Cars?'

'No problem. She takes them for granted, but this was only her second time on a coach and she may just associate coaches and death for a while. Though I can't even be sure that either she or Ellen really understands it all. When she first went back to school she was very thoughtful and a bit withdrawn, but then only the other day I heard her and another girl discussing with some disdain whether some of the children cried or not. I don't think they could understand why Claire got angry.'

Sister Agnes Xavier smiled and shook her head. 'Think back and ask yourself how much empathy you had at that age. I expect some of the boys boasted they didn't cry and some of the others disputed it. The child who lost an arm is just as likely to show off her false one as to feel self-conscious about it. I'm afraid that, poor soul, will come later.'

Mark thought of Portugal, of Sarah and the child who had swum away from her screaming.

'I hope she finds a good man to look after her when she grows up,' continued the nun. 'More coffee?'

Mark accepted in order to postpone the time of departure.

'Did you see the lady praying at the candles of Our Lady of Sorrows?' asked Sister Agnes Xavier as she refilled his cup.

Mark tried to recollect the handful of people he had seen in the church but could not recall noticing anyone in particular.

'She is Bridget Bright.'

'Christina's mother? I know her but I didn't see her there.'

'She's carrying a terrible burden and she comes to light a candle every day. You see Christina was the youngest of six, born ten years after the next youngest, and all the other children came here to St Joseph's, but by the time Christina was old enough to go to school Patrick Bright was very successful and making a lot of money so they decided to educate Christina privately. When they decided on Valence Towers, Father Michael tried to talk them out of it and told them it was their duty to send Christina to a Catholic school where she would be taught the faith. I think Bridget thinks it's a judgement on her...'

Mark closed his eyes against the horror. 'I'm sorry,' he said. 'I wish I'd realised who she was when I was over at the church. I'd have spoken to her. She shouldn't torment herself like that.'

He wondered how many other parents were torturing themselves. Perhaps there was a child whose parents had disagreed over whether to send it on the trip, another whose parents had originally said no and later changed their minds. There would be bitterness and perhaps recrimination as well as bereavement to bear and overcome.

Sister Agnes Xavier nodded. 'Of course not. They were doing what they thought best for Christina, but she may need a lot more support before she comes to believe that.'

'I'll make sure we don't lose touch with her,' promised Mark. 'Christina used to play with Pippa from time to time.'

He rose reluctantly, finding himself oddly attached to that peaceful room. Sister Agnes Xavier smiled. 'Thank you,' she said, 'and of course if there is anything any of us can do just let us know.'

Mark said he would, although he could not tell whether the offer was in respect of Bridget Bright or Pippa or merely a general one. It occurred to him that it might refer to Jeremy who had, of course, been with them that night when they met Sister Agnes Xavier for the first time.

The nun walked with him as far as the church, where Mark stopped and suggested he might see if Mrs Bright were still there, but Sister Agnes Xavier shook her head.

'She'll have gone by now to help out at the school. She's been doing that ever since Christina died. But if you would like to light a candle of your own...'

She was looking at Mark, and suddenly her voice trailed off. 'Oh, I'm sorry,' she stammered, colouring.

It was the first time Mark had seen her peacefulness disturbed, and he hastened to restore it. 'There is no need to be. My mother rejected it and married out. I'm not anything. I'm afraid I don't believe at all.'

'Then I'll pray for you,' she said briskly, and he glimpsed steel beneath the gentleness.

They talked a little longer then, as they were finally parting, she asked, 'Do you know Rabbi Cohen?'

Mark said he did not, forbearing to add that he did not want to and nor did he want to know Father Michael who had inadvertently added to Bridget Bright's grief, nor Chris Sands' successor, nor the pompous priest who currently stood in for him nor anyone else who might have an interest in his soul. Except perhaps Sister Agnes Xavier.

Impulsively he said, 'Will you pray for my wife?'

'Of course.'

She did not ask why but, when he arrived home with the peace of the convent still soothing him, Claire did not ask why the simple task of delivering jumble to St Joseph's had taken so long.

After lunch he retired to his study and went through the Appointments pages of three national papers, drafted letters to send to local businesses and read his bank statements with growing alarm. Sam rang, proposing to come down for the weekend. It was the first time he could remember expecting a visit from his father-in-law with less than enthusiasm, as he suspected Sam had been drafted in by Claire to do what she would almost certainly have described as talking some sense into him. He was sure that Sally's intended visit for two weekends hence might well have been instigated for the same reason – after all, they had seen her in the Whitsun Recess and it was rare for her to take time off in Session even at the weekend, especially with the Euthanasia Bill back in the Commons – and wondered what Claire supposed either Sam or Sally might achieve which his own acute awareness of his predicament might not.

His tasks in the study completed, Mark looked for other reasons to stay there, not wanting to face the inevitable and repeated questions from Claire about what he had been doing, what chances he thought he had and what progress he was making. Nor did he want to face the list of uncongenial jobs she produced each day with the observation that now he was around all the time he might just as well make himself useful. He had begun to take on all the shopping, errands and school runs and to make them last as long as possible before reluctantly returning to the house and to Claire. He was surprised at how sociable some of these occasions were, and at first wondered how Claire had remained so resolutely isolated, until he was sobered by the reflection that Claire so often had Jeremy with her when she left the house.

He turned over the pages of the *Financial Times*. Even the paper irritated him and, deriving some vague satisfaction from deliberately increasing his ill-feeling and misery, he re-read what he considered a lamentably ill-informed view of the appropriateness of increasing incentives to leave the State Earnings Related Pension Scheme after the age of forty. The author had a touching faith

306

in the regulators.

On a sudden inspiration Mark spent the next two hours penning a withering rebuttal. He was rather pleased with it when he had finished, so he wrote a covering letter and addressed an envelope to the *Financial Times*. He placed the letter and article inside and sealed the envelope before he could re-read his work and lose confidence in it. He was still not convinced he would actually post it, but he had undeniably enjoyed himself writing it and it had kept him in the study with the irregular staccato of the word processor enough to convince Claire that activity was in progress and to discourage her from disturbing him.

At seven she did put her head round the door to enquire in tones of surprise if he wanted supper, but by then he was engrossed in his third article and he shook his head irritably. He emerged at ten, exhausted, with three envelopes addressed to the *Financial Times*, *The Times* and *Investors' Chronicle*.

'What on earth have you been doing?' asked Claire as she came out of the kitchen with her sleeves rolled up and wearing a dough-covered apron.

'Writing.'

'At this hour?'

'Is it any odder than baking at this hour?' countered Mark with a grin.

Claire smiled back at him and he marvelled that a few hours of quiet industry and purpose should so quickly have restored domestic peace.

'I've written three articles for three prestigious

newspapers on the operation of the private pensions industry,' he announced, and waited for the peace to shatter under her sarcasm.

'Then post them *now*,' said Claire, 'before you change your mind.'

Mark stared at her.

Claire walked up to him, removed the envelopes from the hall table where he had just placed them, took his hand and placed the packets firmly in it before turning him round and propelling him towards the front door with her hands against his back.

'OK, OK, I give in, but why now? The post has gone.' Mark turned on the doorstep and faced his wife in wonder.

'Which is what will have happened to your confidence in the morning. You'll want to revise them, or you will want to counter this or that argument or something, and then you will spend too long doing it and decide it's all too late because someone else has got in first.'

'How do you know?'

'Because I've done it myself.'

Mark looked at her in surprise. 'You too have written three articles on the private pensions industry?'

'No. One story for a woman's magazine. While you were in Portugal.'

'Have you still got it?'

'No. I was so embarrassed by it that I scrubbed it from the word processor, but since then I've seen worse in print. Now go, or I'll drag you to the postbox by force and that will give the Bartons something to talk about for weeks.'

How little they shared, he thought, as he walked, savouring the scents of the summer night, to the postbox. He thought of the shopping trips and of how she had nursed for so long the shame of hitting Jeremy, of his own weariness with Inglis and May and sudden resolution to resign. Two islands, buffeted by life's waves, enduring the impact alone.

Returning, he was amused to see Barton at his bedroom window, ostensibly in the act of drawing curtains, and Pippa in the kitchen claiming to have been woken by the smell of baking. Claire gave her a warm chocolate bun, warned her it was bad for the digestion and sent her back to bed with the further warning that with exams coming she must not be tired.

Jake James made every class, other than the kindergarten, undergo the ritual of a full set of summer exams. At the age of eight Pippa already understood the rigours of revision, and Mark had refreshed his own memory a great deal in the last week about Kings and Queens and varying climates, found himself struggling with the binary system and reading *The Wind in the Willows* with new eyes. He intended to let Sam take over at the weekend.

Deciding to get the conversation with Sam out of the way at the earliest opportunity rather than have it hovering over him, Mark invited him into the study after dinner on Friday on the pretext of wanting his views on a job application. They settled into two old chairs, long since discarded from the lounge where the infancies of Jeremy and Pippa had ruined them. Through the open window they could hear the song of a thrush.

'She's up late,' remarked Sam as he packed tobacco into his old pipe. The study was the only place where Claire allowed any smoking indoors, conceding that the more tolerant Mark rather than she had to bear the ill-smelling aftermath.

Mark placed two brandy balloons on the small table between them.

'It probably means Pippa has switched her light on. Whenever she does that bird produces a dawn chorus. It must be the dunce of the nest.'

Sam laughed and Mark said no more, leaving the first move to his father-in-law, knowing that Sam would want to get the discussion out of the way as much as he.

'T'lass is worried,' said Sam.

'Understandably. So am I.'

'So what did you have in mind when you did it?'

'Nothing other than getting out of Inglis and bloody May.'

If Mark were now confirming his worst fears, the older man gave no sign of it.

'Claire tells me you want to work for yourself. Can't say I'm against it, but it takes time and grit to build up summat and there's three beaks besides your own open while you do it.'

'Time, grit and support,' amended Mark, this time without heat.

A shadow crossed Sam's face. 'She's worried,' he repeated.

Mark did not respond. Outside the window the thrush had ceased and the only sound now was that of Claire calling Montefiore in for the night.

310

Mark got up and drew the curtains to discourage insects from the light. As he did so he noticed the next-door garden was still illuminated by downstairs lights. The Bartons were up late.

Sam tried again. 'Well, how long do you reckon before t'work comes in?'

Mark shrugged. 'It's slower than I thought even in my most pessimistic moments. Two old ladies and one abandoned wife in a tizz about their income tax forms, a second-hand car outfit who want professional endorsement of a crooked VAT return, and two small businesses who have recently lost their regular accountants for perfectly respectable reasons but who are approaching several others before making up their minds.'

Sam gave a grin which Mark reluctantly returned.

'Sounds par for the course,' said Sam. 'I once had only three jobs in as many months, but once it started it never stopped and six months after that I had to take on an extra pair of hands.'

'Of course there'll be more work after September when people who have failed to get their tax forms in want help with doing their own assessment, but I won't survive just on that.'

'Then you need a stopgap. Summat to keep you going while you build it up. I know a firm who want someone for six months. Special project. Own hours.'

'What sort of firm?'

'Lawyers. Not mine, but I know one of t'partners and he were telling me he needs a figures chap for a while to help them with a job.'

'Which firm?'

'Etheridge, Etheridge, Barnes and Ampthill.'

'Where?'

'London.'

'No.' He watched the hope die out of Sam's face and, knowing he was being irrational as well as ungrateful, hated himself.

'Because it's London? I know commuting's what you hate but it would be over by end of t'year.'

'Also because it's Etheridge, Etheridge, Barnes and Ampthill.'

Sam raised his eyebrows. 'Know summat I don't?'

'No,' Mark shook his head. 'Nothing like that. I had never heard of them until two minutes ago. It's just that they sound too much like Inglis and May – stuffy, old-fashioned and downright tedious.'

Sam stared at him incredulously. Mark looked back without defiance but seeing no need to amend what he had just said.

'This isn't like you, lad,' said Sam sadly.

'No,' agreed Mark, aware, if Sam were not, that by addressing him as 'lad' he was summing up his view of his son-in-law's conduct.

'I'm sorry,' he added. 'I know it's not fair to you, Sam, especially when you've been ill, and I know it's not sensible either, but you can forget Etheridge, Etheridge, Barnes and Ampthill.'

Unlike his elder daughter, Sam knew both when to give up and how to keep his temper. He stared gloomily into his brandy for a while and then changed tack.

'Gather you've been writing?'

'Yes. Claire seemed to like the idea too.'

'She tells me this morning t'editor rang up?'

'One did. Yes.'

'And is paying you a good sum?'

'Good relative to the time it took to write the piece, but it would hardly keep us.' Mark stood up to refill their glasses but, when he held up the decanter, Sam shook his head and he poured more into his own glass than he had intended.

'But it's still summat. Claire says they were good pieces, that you explained it so even she could understand. Not all technical and boring.'

Sam waited and Mark became aware that the older man attached significance to what he had just said, that it implied something he had not yet grasped, that it had not just been an attempt to soothe a battered ego. Whatever meaning Sam intended, it eluded him and all he could do was look quizzical, resigned to the belief that Sam, who must already consider him thoroughly irresponsible, would soon consider him stupid as well.

'So you can teach.' Sam's voice was heavy with the weariness of explanation. 'You have a gift for making hard things easy to grasp. You know how to make the technical stuff interesting. What I'm trying to say is that accountants have to be taught and you could teach 'em.'

'You mean polytechnic lecturing? Something like that? Or tutoring for professional exams?'

'They don't call it a poly any more,' pointed out Sam. 'But that's the sort of thing I mean. Part time. And coaching students and even small boys who can't get as far as the six times table. And writing. Maybe you'll pick up a regular column on some professional rag. And meanwhile the old ladies and the income tax and anything else that's not cheating the VAT. Anything. Lots of things. And then you can drop 'em one by one as the business builds up. Write a textbook and ask Sally to illustrate it with funny cartoons – you know how well t'lass draws – and do anything else you can think of. None of it'll make you rich, but it will be summat until you know whether you can survive on your own and it's better than sitting here all day not able to make up your mind whether you want to work for someone else or just for yourself.'

Sam stopped at the end of the longest speech Mark had ever heard him make, including his effort at Mark's wedding to Claire.

'And,' continued Sam, with his first display of asperity that evening, 'If you don't like it because it doesn't come with a guaranteed executive income and a salary-related pension scheme, you had better make up your mind to the likes of Etheridge, Etheridge, Barnes and Ampthill.'

The thrush once again began her song, suggesting to Mark that Pippa must have switched on the Paddington Bear lamp by her bed, but now it was he who felt like the dunce of the nest.

Claire was already in bed when he went upstairs to find Montefiore occupying the pillow on his side. Half asleep, she mumbled that the Bartons were still up. When he returned from the bathroom he heard a car turn into the Bartons' drive, and going to the window he watched the

314

light stream out of Barton's front door as he opened it to his late-night visitor. Mark recognised the local vet and his heart sank, but by then Claire was asleep and he made no comment. Pippa had known enough of death recently and he did not want her facing it yet again, whether in human or animal. He went to bed, willing Rags to be all right.

He dreamed Sister Agnes Xavier invited him into the convent but when he was inside he found himself facing rows of desks and he began to teach the employees of Etheridge, Etheridge, Barnes and Ampthill to say their six times table. Inglis applauded him and all the rest joined in. Elated, he bowed and left the room and walked into the stock cupboard at Inglis and May. Ginny was there, reaching up towards something on the top shelf. He stared at her legs, his eyes moving up towards her short skirt. The door of the stock cupboard banged.

He woke to hear the vet's car start up and vaguely realised it was the car door which had disturbed his dream. He was sure it had been a pleasant, warm, reassuring dream with some new quality about to enter it which he wanted to experience. He tried to sink back into it, but the vet's car was still running, the engine growing louder. In mute protest he woke again to find the engine was Montefiore purring. He tried to hold on to the fleeing dream, feeling an undefined sense of loss.

The vet, in a long white coat and wearing a stethoscope, was sitting in the study telling him Rags had three months to live and Sister Agnes

Xavier walked out of a hospital ward to say it might be for the best. Claire told him it was disgusting as she pulled weeds from the garden and placed them neatly in her make-up tray. He asked her where Pippa was and she said of course she was on the coach. He asked if it were Coach A and she said it might have been H or J. Barton's shears began clicking and Mark asked them if it were H or J. From the top of the hedge Sam said Polly would know. Then he and Claire were crawling along the bottom of the hedge looking for the Hole, which had disappeared. They could hear Rags barking but there was no Hole for him to come through.

Mark knew only that he must wake up before they found the Hole, that when they found it some horror would confront them. He began to struggle with increasing desperation, knowing they were about to find it and then he was through, to the other side of the hedge where four small figures in Valence Towers uniform waited for him. They reached towards him and he shouted at them to go away, but they just smiled and then he saw Pippa floating towards them with a large ring round her head. He shouted again and again, feeling Claire beginning to tug him back through the Hole. He kicked back at her as he tried instead to go forward and reach Pippa. Then the scene disappeared in a blast of blinding light.

He woke gasping, still wanting to shout. The bedroom light was on and Sam was standing at the door by the light switch. He disappeared as Pippa started screaming. Montefiore tore after him. Claire was bending over him and he became aware that he was entangled in bedclothes, that half the contents of his bedside table, including the lamp, were on the floor and that his pyjamas, soaked in sweat, were clinging to him.

'It's all right, it's all right,' Claire was saying, 'but I've got to go to Pippa. She's probably terrified. Just lie still.'

For a while that seemed the easiest thing to do and he lay there, feeling his breathing return to normal and the relief flood through him as the nightmare receded and reality took over. By the time Sam reappeared at the bedroom door he was sitting up, trying to free himself from the sheet.

Sam looked tired and worried and Mark felt an unreasonable guilt, but most of all he felt resentful. He saw himself through Sam's eyes: selfish, rash, stubborn and now needing to be rescued from nightmares like a child. It did not help when Sam came up to the bed and deftly released him from the sheet. Together they began to pick up the lamp and other items and to restore the room to its normal appearance.

'Sorry,' said Mark eventually.

'Must have been a bad one,' observed Sam.

'Yes.'

He did not comment further and Sam was worriedly asking if there was anything he could do when Claire came back to say she was going downstairs to make Pippa a hot drink and did anyone else want one? Sam shook his head but Mark contented himself with glaring, resenting the fuss being made, and when his father-in-law took the hint and returned to the guest room he switched off his lamp and resolutely closed his eyes as if to announce the subject closed.

Claire returned to it at once when she came again to bed and told his unresponsive form that Pippa was now settled.

'You haven't had one like that for years.'

Mark grunted. He had not told her about the one last year in Portugal, but in any case she was right. Then he had merely dreamed of struggling and shouting but had woken to a smooth bed and a quiet room.

'Did it have something to do with your quarrel with Daddy?'

'We didn't quarrel. Sam doesn't quarrel.' Mark forbore to add that his life might be easier had she inherited that particular trait from Sam. Instead, he thought, she was like Aunt Jane, and was immediately shocked by the reflection as he visualised his wife in twenty years' time. His imagination could provide no place for him at her side.

'What then?'

'Nothing. Everything. I want to sleep.'

Huffily, sighing with exasperation, Claire extinguished the lamp on her side of the bed. They lay silent, each pretending to seek sleep, both hag-ridden by racing thought.

'I'm sorry,' said Mark into the darkness, knowing she was still awake and brooding.

'So am I. I don't seem to know how to reach you any more. You were shouting about ghosts and telling them or someone to get back.'

'I don't remember much about it,' lied Mark as,

318

fleetingly, he reviewed the dream from the safety of wakefulness.

Claire did not press him but presently, as he was beginning to feel the first heaviness of sleep, she remarked that she suspected Rags was ill, that she thought the vet had called next door.

Mark mumbled confirmation, thinking of the small terrier with affection, in his mind seeing him play with Jeremy when both were eight years younger. The dog was still on his mind as he drifted into sleep but when he woke next day he thought not of Jeremy but of Pippa, who had spent so much of last night's supper telling Sam about Rags and Montefiore.

His worst fears were confirmed when Claire visited the Bartons after breakfast and returned to tell him and Sam that Rags had died in the night. Later, when a tearful Pippa asked him to give Mr and Mrs Barton a letter of consolence, he simply smiled and put it through his neighbours' letterbox.

Mrs Barton called him as he walked down the drive a few hours later and showed him the letter.

'Dear Mr and Mrs Barton,

'I am sorry to hear about Rags. I shall miss his fir and his barks. I liked the way he used to beg. I consoul.

Love, Pippa.

P.S. Montefiore is sad too.'

Mark started to grin, noticed Mrs Barton was near to tears and assumed a more appropriate expression as she told him how lucky he was to have such a delightful little daughter. Recollecting her childlessness, he could feel real pity.

At lunch Pippa asked what would happen to the Hole. Privately he hoped another dog would one day emerge from it to befriend his daughter, but that was not a hope he could share with her now. He chose instead to tease her about the misspelled words and she indignantly insisted she did know the difference between fir and fur.

19

As soon as Mark had suspected why Sam had been invited for the weekend, he had embarked upon a strategy to minimise the opportunities for the subject of his employment to be discussed. Without first consulting Claire he had invited Neville Harris and his wife to dinner on Saturday, knowing that their presence would inhibit any inclination on the part of family members to raise the subject. Claire saw through the ruse but liked Neville and Daphne Harris too much to feel really resentful.

While Claire supplied Daphne with a large gin and tonic, Mark took Neville Harris upstairs to examine Jeremy. The doctor went through his usual routine and then stood up smiling.

'All seems fine,' he pronounced cheerfully.

'Are you sure?'

The doctor's smile faded and he turned to look down at Jeremy. 'Is something wrong?'

'Not that I can put my finger on,' admitted Mark, 'but there is something. A minutely subtle change in expression perhaps, or a different sheen to the skin, but something.'

'Hmm. I can't see anything, but in my experience parental instinct can usually be relied upon in this sort of situation. What does your wife say?'

'I haven't mentioned it. I don't want to alarm her unnecessarily.'

Harris received that with a mental shrug. 'When are you next due to see the specialist?'

'In a few weeks.'

'Perhaps you might bring that forward and, if I may be permitted to say so, I think you should tell Claire. If there really is any cause for concern you may be certain she will have noticed too and be worrying accordingly. It would be silly to be so busy protecting each other that you merely each bear the anxiety alone.'

Ruefully Mark appreciated Harris's tact. He did not for one moment suppose the doctor was fooled over the situation between him and Claire, any more than Chris Sands had been. He murmured something noncommittal and suggested they return to Sam and the ladies.

Harris bent to pick up his bag and asked if Pippa would be staying up. Mark shook his head and told of the letter of 'consolence', and they both laughed.

'She's been much better lately,' Mark added, describing how Pippa's tantrums had decreased both in frequency and volume. 'I think she appreciates getting more attention at mealtimes now that Jeremy is fed separately. He still sits with us, of course, but we don't spend half the meal seeing to his needs. I suppose we should have done it before.'

'Easier said than done,' commented Harris. 'I once had a patient who had been blind since birth but her husband and children could see. She was always complaining to me that, even though they were going through a bad patch with money, she could never get her family to switch off the light when they left her alone in a room or the house. She saw it as a quite meaningless waste of electricity but none of them could leave her reading braille or doing the chores in the dark. They said it wasn't natural.'

Mark nodded, grateful for the other's understanding.

'Claire won't hear of Jeremy sleeping downstairs. Hence the Stannah lift,' he said. 'It just proves your point. Making them conform to our way of life denies there's any difference. We call it respect but, when you think about it, patronising might be a better word.'

Them and us. He could never remember using those terms before but he felt no remorse.

'No.' Harris looked down at Jeremy. 'Not patronising. Not even respect. Just love. You can't bear to exclude those you love. That's what's behind it.'

'Pippa has felt excluded,' observed Mark with a belated flash of insight, and this time found Harris had no ready simile with which to soothe the wound of reality and self-recrimination. He remembered Bertie Wells' hostile honesty and resented it less.

Just as the weekend when Marianne and Peter had come to stay had produced a leavening effect on Claire, so now she came alive in the company of the Harrises, and the evening passed pleasantly. Afterwards she sent Sam to bed while Mark helped her clear up. Locking up before they retired he saw that the Bartons' house was in darkness. Sapped by grief, they must have gone to bed early. Mark mourned with them and for them, deciding not to call in Montefiore in case they heard him and were reminded of their loss.

Waking in the early hours, Mark thought he heard a fox bark in the garden and hoped Montefiore was by now safely in. As he dozed off once more he heard the creature bark again. Something tugged him back towards consciousness and reluctantly he struggled to wake up properly. The sound came a third time, and this time he scrambled out of bed with a gasp, fumbling towards the door, entering Sam's room without knocking and, in a role reversal of the previous night, snapping on the light.

Sam's anxious eyes registered relief, but he scarcely moved and when he spoke the sounds made no sense. Reassuring his father-in-law that help was on the way, Mark hastened to the telephone where, remembering the problems he had encountered the previous year, he was careful to leave no room for doubt about the urgency of the situation.

Back in his own room he looked pityingly at Claire's sleeping form. A few hours ago she had seemed almost happy. He recalled Hardy's vicious reflection on the President of the Immortals and bitterly wondered how much more sport He would have with Claire. Then he thought of Smith and Sister Agnes Xavier and their serenity rebuked his blasphemous rancour. For a second longer he shirked the task of waking his wife, until the fox sound came again and the emergency steeled him to the task.

While Claire moved about between reassuring Sam and getting dressed, Mark checked Pippa and Jeremy, but both were sleeping soundly through the disturbance so he went downstairs, ready to open the front door before the ambulance crew should ring the bell and wake them up. He suspected that it was a futile gesture and that the necessity for the crew to walk upstairs and bring Sam down by stretcher would certainly mean that Pippa at least would wake and wonder what was happening.

In the event she slept on and Mark was glad, for Sam had lost consciousness and Claire was finding it hard to hide her fear. As she climbed into the ambulance he promised to join her later in the morning. He watched the vehicle disappear, its light flashing, then returned inside to ring Sally.

A man answered the telephone and Mark was both surprised and embarrassed, immediately seeking for innocent explanations and failing to find them. He thought the voice was vaguely familiar but could not place it.

'We think a stroke,' he told the sleepy-voiced Sally. 'I'm afraid Sam is very poorly, whatever it is. Claire thinks you should get to the hospital as soon as you can, otherwise I'd have left it till morning before calling you.'

'I'm on my way,' said Sally. There was no hint of sleepiness now.

'Claire also thinks Aunt Isobel should know.'

'And you?'

Mark hesitated, then said gently: 'I think so too. Sorry.'

'I'll call her now and pick her up in half an hour. We should be at the hospital in under two hours at this time of night.'

'Drive carefully. Give me a call when you have some news.'

He rang off and stood at the foot of the stairs listening. There was still no sound from Pippa's bedroom. Relieved, Mark went through to the kitchen and made tea. Montefiore wandered in from somewhere in the house and sat looking hopeful. Mark rewarded him with a bowl of food, uncertain when the cat would next be fed, before going upstairs and dressing in the certain knowledge that he would get no sleep even if he went back to bed. Already there was a hint of dawn in the sky.

Mark made plans for the morning. Nurse Allen could feed Jeremy but Mrs Barton was afraid to use the tube and he had no idea which of them would be free to help. He resolved to feed his son himself anyway before he set off for the hospital.

When Pippa finally woke at seven he explained what had happened, that Mummy had gone to the hospital with Grandad and she could sleep in if she wanted to and she would not have to go to church or Sunday School. He expected her to rejoice in the unaccustomed freedom but instead she seemed disappointed. She was not, however, unduly perturbed about Sam, and for that he was grateful before it occurred to him that she might well herself be required at the hospital before the day was out.

There was no answer from Nurse Allen's telephone so with some reluctance he rang the Bartons. Five minutes later Mrs Barton appeared at the back door and took over, apparently glad to be dealing with an extremity so much greater than her own.

Church bells were ringing as Mark got into the car, mentally preparing himself to tread once more the corridors which led to Peter Langley Ward. He had gradually forgotten Nurse Kenward, Dr Bonneaud, Mr Trotter and Nurse Leahy, but now they sprang up in his imagination and he saw again the huge Beatrix Potter figures over the beds in the children's ward. He found it strange that the hospital routine had been going on all this time without his being aware of it or affected by it, when once their lives had seemed to consist of little else.

So used was he to his father-in-law's healthy strength and resilience that, notwithstanding his warning to Sally, he expected Sam once more to greet him with a gloat at Charon's expense. It was a shock, therefore, to find Sam barely conscious, his face shrunken, his skin unhealthily pallid, his body covered with wires and his arm connected to a drip. Mark's eyes travelled over the white faces of Sam's daughters and sister and came to rest again on the sick man.

326

Mark felt his spirit rise in revolt. No. Not Sam, who was so full of life, who had a well-earned retirement ahead of him, who had hardly ever been ill or irritable, who had done no harm to anyone despite the power of his wealth and success. Not Sam, who still preferred a pint of beer to the best champagne, who followed every stroke of Yorkshire cricket, who made Pippa laugh till she could laugh no more.

A consultant, named Oscar Kitcatt, said Sam was stable. Mark did not believe him simply because he could not take the name seriously.

There were too many of them on the ward and they had to agree a rota, so Claire, Sally and Aunt Isobel took it in turns to retire to the canteen or the corridor. Occasionally they were all requested to leave the ward and Mark began to feel superfluous and a nuisance. He decided he would believe Oscar Kitcatt after all and go home. The Fiskes were due later that day and he had no idea how so many would manage without incurring the displeasure of the hospital staff. It was, however, safe to assume that they would be using his home as a base, so he excused himself on the grounds that he should go and get the house ready, a task he would not have achieved so competently had he not had Mrs Barton's help.

Sam regained full consciousness that evening and to the family's relief was lucid, no longer babbling the jumbled nonsense which had characterised what little speech he had uttered while drifting in and out of coma. The ward sister suggested the entire family go home, assuring them there was no immediate cause for worry. Mark was not surprised to hear they had resisted and that Sally had stayed.

Claire's arrival home was hailed by Mark as the relief of Mafeking.

'Why?' she managed a weak smile.

'I've put Sally in the playroom with the camp bed, Aunt Isobel is in Pippa's bed and Pippa is in ours as is Montefiore, the Fiskes senior have the guest room and Rupert will camp out on the sofa downstairs. Mrs Barton thawed a few things from the freezer but the milk supply is low and I can't find enough sheets.'

'Never mind. The Fifth Cavalry is here now.'

'We're mixing up our history. How's Sam?'

'Vastly better. Sends his love. Sally will stay till breakfast so Ru might as well take the playroom.'

Mark shook his head sadly. 'No go, I'm afraid. I've put the pink floral sheets on the camp bed.'

Mark watched his wife laugh with genuine amusement but little energy, the lines around her eyes crinkling into haggard canyons.

'It's not fair,' she said at last.

'He'll be all right. He's got all the fight in the world.'

'Someone died on Peter Langley tonight.'

'But he won't. He's tough.'

Claire gave a small shrug of helplessness but swallowed further comment as Aunt Isobel came from the kitchen to say she had opened four tins of soup and would that be enough?

It was. Each member of the party was tired, anxious and dispirited and Sam was the ghost at the feast, their thoughts never far from the frail wraith of the man who had for so long dominated the background of their lives. Aunt Isobel was distracted and occasionally tearful, Claire preoccupied with thoughts of what to tell Pippa, the elder Fiskes vaguely wondering for how long they might have to stay in the South.

Guiltily, Mark found himself silently speculating that Sam's business affairs were now in a state of such flux that they would take some time to sort out were he to die. He repressed the thought that this must necessarily delay his own bid for freedom and was startled when he saw Rupert watching him as if reading his thoughts. As their eyes met, Rupert flushed and he turned to engage in determinedly energetic conversation with his father.

Rupert too, thought Mark with bitter amusement. He was still in his twenties but of an age to be thinking about families and mortgages, of an age when glittering prospects are irritatingly of less interest to the bank manager than present limitations, of an age when hope leavens necessity and ambition still lends excitement to daily toil. Sam was loved deeply and would be achingly missed, but he was a rich man and when rich men are dying their wealth is seldom wholly banished from the thoughts of those preparing to mourn.

Suddenly Mark feared the Terminally Ill Persons Act. Such were the affections around that table for Sam that any one of those present would willingly enter beggary rather than see him die, but there were many more old men much less well loved: old men in pain and fear and tempted to end it with unending sleep, happier perhaps for knowing that their families would be better off materially without them, especially as those families seemed so understanding about it...

Mark shrank from the thought, taking refuge in plans for the next day, making them the subject of general discussion. Claire was to take over from Sally early next morning. Mark drew the evening shift. In between there would be much to do with so many unexpected guests for whom he must provide.

When he finally arrived at the hospital Mark found Aunt Isobel sitting outside Peter Langley Ward. She told him they were 'seeing to Sam', and Mark wondered if that were a euphemism for Sam's relieving himself or if there were complex medical procedures under way.

'Mr Kitcatt is there,' pronounced Aunt Isobel worriedly, enlightening him.

The reports all day had been good, so good that the Fiskes were now proposing to go home on Wednesday or Thursday and Rupert was returning to work the next day. Only Sally and Aunt Isobel, the much nearer relatives, felt it not yet safe to leave. Now Sam's sister appeared not merely anxious but agitated, despite assuring him that there had been no change and that Kitcatt's examination was routine.

'It's the way he's talking,' she suddenly broke out, and then as suddenly fell silent as if she would have taken back the words.

'Is he confused again?'

'Not exactly confused.'

Mark waited, puzzled, for further explanation, but none came. He decided not to press Aunt Isobel further, reasoning that he would find out soon enough when he was allowed to see Sam or talk to Kitcatt. Gently he reminded her that Sally was waiting outside in the car and she began to gather up her handbag and umbrella, avoiding his eyes.

'I know what you think about it, but you mustn't let him think it,' she said with conviction.

Mark stared, repressing exasperation and a sudden unease.

'Don't worry, Aunt Isobel. Whatever it is we'll sort it out.'

'I hope he doesn't say it to Claire. You know how it would upset her.'

'Yes,' soothed Mark, feeling as if he were playing a bit part in *Alice in Wonderland*. 'We won't let him say it to Claire.'

Aunt Isobel snorted. 'You can't stop Sam doing anything. But he mustn't. He really mustn't, dear.'

As he watched her walk away without her normal bustle and purpose Mark wondered, not for the first time, how anyone so hopelessly vague had managed to raise the determined, often headstrong, Sally. Usually such speculation amused him, but tonight he felt burdened. There would come a time when Aunt Isobel would no longer be able to look after herself. He comforted himself with the thought that at least Fate had spared any of them having to look after Aunt Jane. Surely even the Renwick devotion to family duty must have buckled under such a prospect.

He had waited more than half an hour when he saw Kitcatt approaching. The consultant was smiling, and Mark remembered how Jake James had smiled as he approached to tell them Pippa was safe.

'It's looking OK,' he said, 'but it will take time and he's going to have to be careful. Get rid of all that business stress for one thing, and get some exercise for another.'

'How long will he have to stay in Intensive Care?'

'Not too much longer, but I want to be sure before I move him. He's had a massive stroke and that's on top of a heart attack not so long ago. He's a tough one, though.'

'Long-term effects?'

'Too early to say. His speech is fine, but he has no movement at all in his left leg and only a little in his arm.'

'But he is lucid?'

'Gracious, yes!' Kitcatt smiled wearily and Mark wondered if Sam was proving disconcertingly demanding for a patient in Intensive Care.

When he was at last allowed on the ward he found Sam weak and tired. The nurse told him he could not stay long: Mr Kitcatt had said Mr Renwick should not have any more visitors today. It was important he should rest. Mark nodded meekly and sat down by the bed.

'Bossy lass, that one.' Sam's voice was strong enough to carry and the nurse turned and shook her head, but Mark saw she was amused, not angry, and knew that he had guessed rightly about Sam's behaviour.

It was all Sam said that evening, and he had been drifting in and out of sleep for hours when Rupert arrived to spend the night on the seats outside the ward.

'They'll probably tell you to go home,' said Mark. 'Sam's stable and I should think they all long for the days when visiting hours were severely restricted and relatives knew their place. They only let me stay in there twenty minutes.'

'Aunt Claire says if anything happens one of us must be here. Aunt Izzy was in a bit of a state when she got back so they're a bit worried. There was some discussion about ringing the hospital but I said you were here and would let us know.'

Mark blessed the younger man's common sense, but Rupert could provide no enlightenment as to why Aunt Isobel was so upset.

Enlightenment came the following afternoon when Mark entered Peter Langley Ward to find Sam arguing weakly but persistently with the nurse he had called bossy but whose identity tag proclaimed her to be named Halsey. She rolled her eyes at Mark in mock despair before moving to attend to another patient. He liked her and knew Sam to be in good hands.

'They'll not tell you owt about anything,' Sam complained as soon as her back was turned. 'Reckon how I am is my business, but they reckon it's theirs and theirs alone.'

'Oscar Kitcatt can tell you all you want to know,' pointed out Mark with a smile.

'She knows.' Sam pointed with a feeble finger at the nurse's back. 'Knows but won't tell.

'Do you know?' asked Sam suspiciously, while

Mark was still thinking of a diplomatic reply to his father-in-law's last observation.

'I know you're doing very well. Kitcatt says you're tough.'

'He can say that again,' muttered Nurse Halsey, and Mark knew that Sam was supposed to hear and that the two had established a comfortable reassuring rapport.

'So what about my left side then? That tough too?' Sam's eyes were bright with perspicacity.

Mark hesitated, then repeated what Kitcatt had told him. Sam absorbed it in silence for a while before commenting in a complaining whisper that he was getting rid of the business anyway and it was hardly his fault the preparations for flotation had proved so complex. As for exercise, what use was that to a man with only one half of him functioning?

Mark was uncomfortably conscious that Nurse Halsey could hear and he half expected her to take him aside and reprove him for alarming the patient. He waited till Sam's querulous monologue ceased then quietly pointed out that lots of stroke patients recovered full movement. Sam received that with the judicious air of a schoolmaster assessing the contribution of a not very bright pupil.

It was when Nurse Halsey's back seemed somehow to be subtly suggesting that it was time he left his father-in-law to rest that Mark heard Sam suddenly mutter, 'Lass is right.'

'Sorry, Sam?' queried Mark, uncomprehending.

For a while Sam did not reply and Mark began

to think he was tiring and that the remark had meant nothing, when the older man began an explanation which left Mark in no doubt as to what had frightened Aunt Isobel into incoherence.

'She got it right. Life's not worth having if thou's not enjoying it.' He looked up at Mark piteously. 'I want to go quickly, lad. Not like wife. It were hell to watch.'

'It won't come to that, Sam. Kitcatt was right about your being tough.'

'Listen, lad. 'Twere two men went out of this ward since I been here. Two. One went feet first and one went in wheelchair. First chap were luckier. Our Sally's right.'

Mark met Nurse Halsey's eyes as she turned round, a kidney dish in her hand, professional competence in her face. Her eyes warned more clearly than words, 'Don't argue. Don't get him worked up.'

Mark, lost for words, looked back at Sam who had begun to speak again.

'I saw their faces. T'wife of first one were crying fit to break your heart just watching. But second chap, his face were already dead though wife were smiling as if it were Christmas morning. I don't want to be like it, lad, I don't right want to be like it. He didn't neither. He wanted his grave.'

Mark had to strain to hear. Sam's voice was barely above a whisper now and the Yorkshire accent stronger than Mark had ever heard. He was glad that no one else on the ward could hear, not even Nurse Halsey, who had in any case moved to a patient on the other side of the room.

335

Another nurse was moving towards them purposefully and Mark got up, relieved by the knowledge that he was about to be asked to leave and let the patient rest. He patted Sam reassuringly. 'It'll be all right, Sam,' he said vacuously.

He had almost reached the ward door when Sam called to him, hoarsely but audibly: 'You'll see to it then? You or Sally? You'll do it for me, lad, won't you?'

Mark turned. 'Don't worry, Sam,' was all he could manage as he made his horrified escape.

Nurse Halsey caught up with him in the corridor.

'Has he been talking like that a lot? He upset his sister, but she wouldn't or couldn't tell us what had gone on.'

'Sometimes he gets very exercised by it, Mr Wellings, but other times he never even mentions it. I think he has only told you and the elder Miss Renwick. He was confused and briefly mistook her for your sister-in-law. When he's tired he does get muddled.'

So she knew who Sally was and what her Bill proposed. It was probably widely discussed in hospitals up and down the country, thought Mark.

'Did he ask her to – help?'

'I don't know. I wasn't on duty, but from what Nurse Davis told me, it's quite possible.'

'My God! Aunt Izzy!'

'He'll forget these ideas once he's stronger. And you were right to tell him he can recover his movement. He must just be patient.'

'Not his forte.'

'No. I imagine not. Please don't be too worried, not even if he asks you again.'

'The Bill hasn't even passed into law yet, and even when it does it won't come into effect for months. Aunt Izzy must realise that, and anyway he doesn't fall into the right category to be covered by it.'

'If I had my way it would never come into effect, Mr Wellings. But we're certainly getting a foretaste of what's to come.' There was a short silence before Nurse Halsey added, 'With all due respect to your sister-in-law.'

Mark was thankful when she returned to the ward, but when Sally arrived a couple of hours later he felt obliged to tell her what had happened, omitting only the reference to Graine, who, ironically, was the subject of Sally's first comment.

'Of course he remembers Mummy. Poor Aunt Isobel.'

Later that evening she arrived home without having seen her father. Sam was asleep and was to have no more visitors that day. However Kitcatt had appeared while she was there and had assured her that all was well and that Sam should soon make good progress. And, by the way, she had bumped into that nice Irish nurse called Leahy, who had looked after Jeremy last year, and she sent her love.

The good progress which Kitcatt predicted came slowly and Sam remained in hospital, eventually transferred to a private ward, while his family gradually resumed their normal lives. As he grew stronger and his left arm regained half its normal strength and mobility Sam grew more hopeful but, contrary to Nurse Halsey's forecast, he persistently returned to his theme of a voluntary death, though now envisaged as an event for the future rather than as an immediate escape from his incapacity. Claire became upset by it and Mark knew that once Sam was strong enough she would argue bitterly with him. At least now he had regained his normal sensitivities he did not raise the subject in Aunt Isobel's presence, but there was a discernible, though not easily defined, mood of favouritism towards Sally, which Mark resented on Claire's behalf at the same time as understanding how it had come about. If Claire noticed she did not comment, and continued to bear most of the responsibility for visiting Sam now that Sally had returned to London and was once more immersed in politics.

The Terminally Ill Persons Bill, now awaiting royal assent, began once again to dominate the press and when, during one of Sally's weekend visits, Mark returned from the hospital to hear the sisters arguing he presumed the disagreement to be about that. As he stood in the hall dealing with a wet umbrella he mentally braced himself for whatever battle was being waged so vigorously that its participants had not even heard him arrive or were too engrossed to care that he had. It occurred to him that he had never heard Sally and Claire raising their voices in dispute with each other – not even when Sally was a child – and while he was becoming aware of this he also realised, with shock, that the quarrel was not about the Bill but about him.

'You're losing him,' Sally was saying urgently.

Automatically Mark glanced towards the head of the stairs, but there was no sign that Pippa was around and he wondered if she were at a friend's house.

'I know.' Suddenly Claire's voice was quieter, heavy with defeat. 'I'm sure something happened in Portugal. He said he had met a widow and made light of it, but I'm sure it wasn't so casual. There's no sign that he's still in touch. I've watched like a hawk. And then there was that awful secretary – Gilly or Jeanie or something. But she seems well and truly off the scene too.'

'You don't need to worry.' Sally's voice was brisk rather than sympathetic. 'Dad challenged him after she turned up here at tea that weekend. He said he had never played away and Dad believed him. He's a good judge. But Dad also said Mark was fed up with everything and I'm afraid that includes you.'

Mark stood stock still. He knew he was eavesdropping and that he should go into the kitchen now, heralding his arrival with loud steps. He went on standing still.

'Listen, men like Mark were just made for unending respectability, but instead what happens? He at least gets as far as toying with temptation and as if that were not enough he chucks in his job without having arranged any alternative.' Sally's tone was insistent.

'And when Dad found him work with a good firm he said no because the firm sounded boring. I know that isn't like Mark but it's happened and

I can't see why you think I'm to blame. It's probably the male menopause or something.'

'No. It's you, Claire. You don't try to lighten the load. You've cut yourself off from everyone and you nag the poor man half to death. Pippa doesn't need to find out that Mummy and Daddy don't love each other any more.'

'You don't understand. It's hardly easy being here all day responsible for Jeremy...'

'Spare me that nonsense. Jeremy deserves better than to be made the excuse for everybody else's messes.' Sally's voice was sounding increasingly angry and now it was contemptuous too. The Renwick unity had cracked. 'He'll leave you as soon as he feels he decently can, and I don't think that means when Pippa has her eighteenth birthday celebrations. If anything happens to Dad, Mark will reason you'll be well enough provided for to make it safe for him to go.'

So his sister-in-law had read his mind, and Claire had guessed far more about his near infidelities than he had realised. Her powers of observation and her intuition had not become as dull as she had.

As Mark absorbed this he became aware that Sally had changed tack.

'He needs to feel his roots, something solid to anchor him. You should get him to see a Rabbi.'

'What on earth for? He's never had time for any of that.'

'I saw how he looked at Ruth and Ben at their wedding.'

'He was probably envying them their happiness.' Claire's voice wavered, and Sally's was gentler when she next spoke.

'No. I overheard him talking about how they would have Friday nights, and his tone said it all.'

'I don't believe it. He could have tried it any time he wanted. I wouldn't have minded. I mind much more that he doesn't believe in anything. Anyway he probably meant Friday nights in the family sense. That's scarcely Torah and Talmud type of thinking.'

'Perhaps what he has seen of believers hasn't encouraged him.'

Claire did not rise to that but instead began to muse about how impressed Mark had been with Sister Agnes Xavier. 'After all, he was baptised as a baby,' she observed.

It was time to interrupt the quarrel. He opened the front door and shut it loudly before heading for the kitchen where he found a seemingly peaceful scene in which only he appeared to feel ill at ease.

Two hours later Aunt Isobel telephoned from the hospital and asked him to come without telling the others. Making an excuse to take the car out he arrived to hear Sam shouting, and when he reached Sam's room he found two nurses and a white-faced Aunt Isobel trying to calm him down.

'My own daughter! My own daughter trying to kill me!'

Mark raised an interrogative eyebrow at Aunt Isobel. She crept close to him and they both turned so Sam could not read their lips.

'He's wandering,' she whispered. 'He thinks Sally is trying to kill him.'

'I'll not let them,' shouted Sam. 'They've no right.'

'They can't,' said Mark firmly, approaching the bed. 'It's not law.'

Sam looked at Mark, now aware of his presence, dimly realising that he should not be there. The older man made a visible effort to return to his normal perspective, to leave the world of half-understood horrors in which his mind had been wandering. The puzzle was too much for him and he sank back against the pillows, muttering in morose confusion.

Sam continued staring at Mark, trying to make sense of what he had just said. 'They can kill you now. When you're a nuisance.'

'No. Only if you're so ill that you want them to, and they can't even do that yet and won't be able to for a long time. It's not law.'

The words made no sense to Sam. He merely knew that Mark was arguing with him and he was convinced that whatever his son-in-law was saying was wrong. Briefly he struggled to find the right way of expressing this before giving up the attempt. He looked around the room and focused on Aunt Isobel. Isobel would sort it out. She had always been there when he needed her. Reassured, Sam slid into sleep.

When Sam next woke his daughters were by his bed. He did not know them, nor the old lady who held his hand, nor the middle-aged man who sat further back by the television. He looked straight ahead at the one who mattered, smiled with relief and gently called 'Graine!' as he died in Aunt Isobel's arms.

20

'I am the Resurrection and the Life, saith the Lord.'

The chill rain tore through the small group as they buried Sam Renwick in the graveyard of the tiny church on the Yorkshire moors next to the wife he had never ceased to miss. There would be a memorial service later in Sussex, but Claire and Sally had restricted the funeral to family only. Aunt Isobel wept and Pippa jumped up and down in a forlorn effort to combat the cold as Claire threw the first piece of earth on Sam's coffin.

Aunt Jane had been buried here too, but Mark noticed that no one felt obliged to pause dutifully by her grave as the family left the churchyard to take comfort in the warmth of the Fiskes' house.

'You would never think it was summer,' Aunt Isobel shivered, and Rupert Fiske put his arm round her. Another gust of rain driven by a bitingly cold wind made them all hasten to the waiting cars. Jeremy's wheelchair briefly got stuck in a rut and everyone was obliged to come to a sudden stop. Pippa barked her shin on the back of it and protested bitterly. She reflected the thoughts of all when she announced she wished she were at home by the Aga with Montefiore.

His daughter had taken her grandfather's death badly, but with the resilience of childhood she was soon preoccupied with other things, and Mark had not wanted her to come to the funeral. His tentative suggestion that she should remain in Surrey with a schoolfriend was repelled as firmly as he had expected it to be and Mark was glad that Pippa remained in good spirits. When they were assembled at the Fiskes' house she spent a great deal of the time entertaining an increasingly amused vicar with schoolgirl jokes.

At least her jokes were still innocent, mused Mark, although possibly that was just for the vicar's benefit. Her simple sense of humour and the immoderate laughter it provoked from her would be among the things he would most miss when he left.

Mark knew that it must be a little while yet before that parting could take place. He could not inflict it on Claire so soon after Sam's death, and certainly not on Pippa after the events of the last year. His daughter must have a period of stability, yet he yearned for the much-postponed crossing of his Rubicon.

In the interval there would be practical matters to attend to, including sorting out Sam's will and business affairs and finding long-term gainful employment. Neither was likely to prove either quick or easy. He remembered the quarrel between Sally and Claire and he wondered if, in the coming months, his wife would make efforts to save herself and her children from desertion or whether her will were now too thoroughly sapped for her to care. He found himself hoping she was resigned to their parting and vaguely dreaded the more active intervention of his sister-in-law.

Somehow it seemed to him unlikely that the Renwicks would let him go without a fight. He began to imagine life without them and to consider how he might draw closer to his own siblings and relatives and particularly to Ruth and Ben, but even as he contemplated this he knew that his real need was simply to be alone.

Such efforts as he himself made stemmed merely from duty, and he was glad when they were repulsed. When he proposed a family holiday to Claire she observed that as he was not working he had no need of a break and should use his time to find work.

In the event it was no living Renwick who tried to detain him, but Sam from beyond the grave.

The will was read formally in the drawing room of the Sussex house which had for so long been Sam's home and in which Sally and Claire had spent so much of their childhoods. The room was filled with the expectant, and the family was considerably outnumbered by representatives of the causes to which Sam had devoted much of his wealth. Mark listened to a string of bequests to charities, a major benefaction to one of the universities, minor legacies to friends, a decidedly generous one to the housekeeper. There was the occasional muted gasp of gratitude as Sam's largesse exceeded hopes tentatively, perhaps fearfully, nurtured. The local church was especially well treated, as was the one in Yorkshire where Sam and Graine lay buried.

The Fiskes exchanged glances as their inheritance secured a comfortable retirement, Rupert brightened as he came into a sum it would have taken half a working lifetime to earn, Aunt Isobel wept as the largest bequest yet was announced in recognition of 'the years of sacrifice and selfless love of my beloved sister'. Mark put an arm round her as the solicitor announced the setting up of a trust for Jeremy and another one for Pippa to be shared with any issue from Sally.

Jeremy would be safe and secure after he and Claire died and although he had expected no less Mark felt relieved, as if a shadowy burden had suddenly been lifted. As for his daughter, whatever other hardships life threw at her money worries would not be among them.

'Well, then, Mark, you can leave, can't you?' said Ginny's light, mocking voice, so real that he momentarily doubted it was only in his imagination he had heard it. Appalled, he sought the serene tones of Smith, but she was silent. Then Sam spoke:

'And to Mark Edward Wellings, my son-in-law, one hundred thousand pounds as a mark of my admiration and gratitude for the way he has looked after my family, especially Jeremy...'

Mark saw a fleeting smile of satisfaction cross Sally's face, but also surprise. Claire looked briefly perplexed and Aunt Isobel pleased. For once he was quicker than they, understanding immediately what Sam had intended, admiring the dead man even as he mentally rebuked his shade.

A man could do a lot with one hundred thousand pounds. He could set up a business, supplement a temporarily unsatisfactory income,

346

pay off his mortgage, assist friends or relatives, choose expensive schools, make wise investments. A man might do any of these things with such a legacy, but if that man were Mark Edward Wellings he could not leave home on the strength of it, could not use Sam's money to betray Sam's daughter, could not desert Jeremy while keeping the money which rewarded his past fidelity and devotion. His father-in-law had left him a choice between rejecting his wife and rejecting the money or keeping both, in death offering a bribe he would not have had the effrontery to offer in life.

Mark wondered when Sam had written this provision into his will, if perhaps it had been after their conversation following Ginny's visit or whether it had been long ago before even he, Mark, had begun to question the future of his marriage. Whenever it had been done the result would be the same, vowed Mark. He might hate himself on behalf of both the living and the dead but he would still go, and the money would be added to the children's trusts. He gave himself twelve months. By next summer he would be free.

He caught Sally's eye and quickly averted his gaze lest she read his thoughts. His wife seemed untroubled by what those thoughts might be.

'...and the residue of my estate...'

Mark looked not at the solicitor but at Sam's daughters as all remaining money, property, the business, goods and chattels were left between them. As they came into legacies worth several millions of pounds both women looked sad and blank, as if the very receipt of the money confirmed the passing of Sam's spirit. He wondered how Pippa would react to his own death when it came, if she would have forgiven his betrayal or perhaps shared what should have been unique to him with a stepfather. The latter was not a comfortable thought and nor was the rude reality which suddenly occurred to him as he realised that from now on Claire's attraction to any man would be her money. Mark mentally shuddered, not for his wife but for his daughter, knowing it would be hard to protect her, that she might not want his protection, that Claire might teach her not to want it.

At least there would always be Renwicks while Pippa was growing up. Surely the clan would protect her if he could not. His resolution held. Twelve months.

After the storms which had so badly shaken their lives, those months brought calm. Pippa cried for Sam at Christmas – their first without him – but was consoled at being allowed to stay up and see in the New Year, also for the first time. She announced gravely that champagne was quite nice but not as nice as *7Up*.

Sam's business was at last floated and both his daughters sold their shares. The Sussex house remained unsold and unoccupied while Claire and Mark discussed whether to sell their own and move into it. Mark would have been glad to see Claire settled there and it would have been possible for Pippa to have stayed at the same preparatory school as the journey would have

348

been manageable. Yet it would take her away from Neville Harris, the Bartons, Nurse Allen and such few friends as still made any impact on her life and so, reluctantly, he would not be persuaded.

In January the Terminally Ill Persons Act came into force and the first people to take advantage of it extolled its virtues while others forecast abuse and horror. Mark found himself profoundly disturbed, remembering Sam, and surprised both Claire and Sally when he expressed his reservations. The Pope himself condemned the Act in advance of a tour of Europe, and Sally found herself once more arguing vigorously in the limelight, frequently with Charles Yetminster. Claire became fraught-nerved and irritable as the controversy raged.

In February Mark accepted a partnership in a firm near Godalming and began again the routine of a daily task. It proved as unexacting as he had hoped, and he still wrote articles in his plentiful spare time.

In March a small Cairn burst through the Hole and Tatters entered their lives. Pippa was ecstatic and Montefiore disdainfully resigned.

Jeremy grew heavier but was otherwise unchanged. The specialist was reassuring.

At Easter the new vicar arrived, was inducted and generally liked. He came to dinner and was an instant success with Pippa and Montefiore, causing Mark to feel a very small lightening of his burden. He had still not discussed his impending departure with Claire.

The Easter holiday also marked the first

anniversary of the deaths of the children in the coach, but the parents of those unaffected were almost more saddened when Jake James announced his retirement. Pippa showed little reaction to either event.

Life was settling down, routine re-established, Pippa happy and demanding that her plaits be cut off because they were old-fashioned. With admirable self-restraint Claire forbore to comment on this *volte face,* but insisted the plaits remain until Pippa was sure as they could not be grown again overnight. Their daughter returned from a weekend in London with Aunt Isobel displaying a short, modern hairstyle and a collection of brushes with which she played for hours in front of a mirror.

'She's only nine,' wailed Claire. 'And she would be into makeup as well if I let her.'

The passion for hairstyles and make-up was succeeded by importunate demands for a pony.

'Daddy's house has a paddock,' observed Claire guilefully.

'It's under offer,' said Mark, 'and not before time. The market's dreadful.'

'They withdrew,' announced Claire triumphantly.

'I'll think about it,' prevaricated Mark.

'Ellen has a pony,' pressurised Pippa.

'Let's see your exam results at the end of term,' retorted Mark.

It was a conversation oft-repeated, and as the summer term wore on and Sam's house remained unsold Mark wondered if his resistance to the move was still justified. He suspected

Claire might well be instrumental in the failure to sell, and if her heart were that set on the Sussex house she would move there after he left. Surely it would be better to settle her there first, try and establish some local friendships, take from her the responsibility of selling their present home and get their affairs properly sorted out before any divorce.

Divorce – and still the word had not been spoken between them since Sam's death. Mark was sure his wife knew his intentions, but so steadfastly was she ignoring the consequences that sometimes he was obliged to doubt whether the knowledge did in fact exist.

Outwardly life was tranquil and that was the signal for them all to consider Jeremy, the all-too-ready focus for anxiety when none other was on offer. Yet here too was little cause for concern. The vague fears which Mark had harboured the previous year did not prove justified. Gradually Claire became less able to lift him unaided and Nurse Allen visited more often to help, but otherwise Jeremy's routine was undisturbed, with his parents and Nurse Allen taking turns to feed him, Pippa continuing to float yellow plastic ducks in his bath, and the moving images of his mobiles, friends and television still parading before uncomprehending eyes. Both Neville Harris and the specialist were satisfied that everything was in order.

'Be careful where you put him,' warned Claire one Sunday as they wheeled Jeremy into the back garden. 'The sun is very strong.'

'Don't worry. I'll see he stays in the shade. The

others will be out soon anyway.'

It was Whitsun and both Aunt Isobel and Sally had arrived for the long weekend. For the past week Britain had basked in sunshine and the beaches were full. Mark had decided to spend the weekend getting on with gardening tasks which had been sadly neglected since he had begun to work again. Such horticultural success as they had enjoyed that year had been almost entirely due to Claire's efforts.

Barton's shears clicked their way along the top of the hedge as Tatters appeared and flopped down beside Jeremy's chair. Montefiore eyed him from the safety of the kitchen step. Otherwise Mark was alone in the garden and he savoured the peace as he fetched a stepladder from the garage and prepared for an assault on the honeysuckle at the side of the slope. He could still just see Jeremy in the shade of the lilacs at the top of the slope on the other side.

It took Mark a while to position the ladder firmly on the sloping ground. Before climbing it he glanced at his son, who appeared to be fast asleep. Soon Mark was absorbed in his pruning, oblivious of the world around him, his thoughts peaceful, considerations of the future comfortably suspended. Out of the corner of his eye he saw Aunt Isobel come out to check on Jeremy before returning indoors to where he assumed Claire and Sally were still clearing up after lunch.

Barton's first shout did not register with him. The second did and he looked up to see Jeremy's wheelchair gently rolling down the slope towards the stream. Horrified, he made too rapid a descent of the awkwardly balanced stepladder and fell, bringing it down on top of him. He lost precious moments disentangling himself, and as he gained his feet he saw the wheelchair gathering speed. Mark raced after it as nine years before he had run after the four-year-old boy who in turn chased a white rabbit.

He grabbed the wheelchair but its momentum carried him forward, causing him to fall. Mark clung on and the chair tipped sideways, throwing out its precious cargo who began to roll down the steepest part of the slope. Mark was not yet standing when he heard the splash as Jeremy hit the water.

He was there in seconds, surely less than seconds he told himself afterwards, kneeling by the stream, staring at his son in the water. Jeremy had rolled in face up, but the water was well over his head. No reflex had closed his mouth which yawned slackly open. His eyes too were open and, through the distortion of the water, he looked serene and peaceful. Mark went on staring, unwilling to disturb his son's peace.

For perhaps two seconds. No more, please God, no more. Then he recollected himself and began to pluck Jeremy from the water, cursing his son's increased weight and the steepness of the slope around the stream, despairing at the thought of how much water had poured unresisted into Jeremy's lungs.

Artificial respiration, mouth-to-mouth resuscitation. Regardless of what it was called, Mark could only make an amateur attempt. He turned Jeremy on his stomach and began to press down on his back in an attempt to force the water from his lungs.

As he did so he glanced up and saw Barton, frozen into immobility, his shears poised but utterly motionless, staring at him from the top of the hedge. Then, as if from nowhere, Claire appeared beside her son and announced with suppressed hysteria that Sally was calling an ambulance and Aunt Isobel was keeping Pippa out of the way.

Mark went on ineffectually pumping water.

'Has he stopped breathing?'

Irritated, anxiety-ridden, desperate, Mark did not answer.

Claire repeated the question and he looked at her.

'Yes. His mouth was wide open.'

'Is his heart still working?'

'I don't know, for God's sake.'

Claire was silent. Then in little more than a whisper she said: 'If he's not breathing and his heart isn't working, he's dead.'

'He might not be brain dead.' Appalled, they stared into each other's eyes, then Mark's hands ceased their futile work and reached out instead to Claire. In each other's arms they wept over the body of their son.

21

The paramedics tried where Mark had failed, but his son was pronounced dead even before he was lifted into the ambulance.

Barton gave a detailed account to the inquest. He had been clipping his hedge, he told the Coroner, and had seen it all. Mr and Mrs Wellings had pushed Jeremy out into the garden and stationed him in the shade. Mrs Wellings was most particular about making sure the brake was firmly on. When she had applied it she always gave the wheelchair a little push to make sure it would not move. He was quite certain she had done so on this occasion, he remembered it very clearly. Mr Wellings was in the garden but on the other side up a ladder. After a while Miss Renwick came out and went to check on Jeremy. Miss Isobel Renwick, the senior Miss Renwick, Mrs Wellings' aunt, not Miss Sally Renwick who was Mrs Wellings' sister and the famous MP.

The Coroner bore it all with patience, including a defensive statement that Tatters had sat only beside the chair. Certainly he had never ventured to the back of it. Tatters could not, absolutely not, have accidentally knocked the brake off.

It was an idea that had never entered the heads of those present, and Mark felt a stab of pity for the Bartons that such a thought had occurred to torment them.

Barton proceeded to tell how he had seen the wheelchair suddenly roll forward. It was very slow because at that point it was not on the slope proper. Mrs Wellings was most particular about its never being on the slope. Indeed at first he was not sure if it really were moving. Then he saw it was and called Mr Wellings, who did not appear to hear. So he shouted again and by then he was most disturbed because the chair was on the slope, but Mr Wellings heard and he, Barton, was much relieved.

Unfortunately in his haste Mr Wellings fell off his ladder... Barton took the Coroner through the ensuing agonising events. Mark held his breath as Barton reached the point where he, Mark, had arrived at the stream.

'He started pulling him out,' said Barton, and launched into a description of the awkwardness of this exercise.

Only Mark noticed the absence of the word 'immediately'. Barton had glossed over those few seconds when he, Mark, had knelt by the stream doing nothing but wonder at the peace on his son's face. It was impossible that he had not noticed from that high vantage point, even though Mark's back would have been turned to him. As he had cursed his neighbour's garrulity to the press when they had gathered outside his home during the passing of the Terminally Ill Persons' Act, so now he forgave him and was grateful for the protection he was being offered.

Claire said in evidence that she had been upstairs in the bathroom when she heard shouts. By the time she reached the stream her husband was giving Jeremy artificial respiration. Her son was no longer breathing and they were not sure if his heart was working. Mark was not using mouth-to-mouth, he had Jeremy on his face and was trying to force the water out of his lungs. It did not appear to be working terribly well.

'And then?' prompted the Coroner gently.

'We knew he was dead.' Claire's voice wavered.

The Coroner looked sympathetic but he did his job. 'You stopped trying to resuscitate him?'

'He was dead,' repeated Claire with dull obstinacy.

Mark took her hand as she returned to sit beside him.

Sally testified that she had seen nothing of the accident until she arrived at the top of the slope to see Mark pulling Jeremy from the stream. She had gone inside to phone for an ambulance and asked Aunt Isobel to keep Pippa indoors.

Aunt Isobel testified that when she had gone to check on Jeremy the brake of the wheelchair was fully engaged. Jeremy had been asleep.

A representative of the company which had made the wheelchair testified that upon examination the brake was found to have been seriously weakened, probably by a heavy knock. It was unlikely to have happened in the course of the accident and the condition was almost certainly the cause of the tragedy. It was not possible to say how the weakening had occurred but it was significant that this was the indoor wheelchair and therefore the family did not have it regularly inspected as they did its outdoor counterpart. The brake could have been damaged by a collision with furniture or childish antics or some other unnoticed mishap. Unfortunately because the weather was so fine there had been a decision not to transfer the boy to the outdoor chair. The analysis was supported by an independent expert who assured the Coroner that no possible blame could be attached to the company.

The medical evidence showed that Jeremy had taken a very great deal of water into his lungs. His mouth had stayed fully open, his reflexes ruined by his condition. He had sustained a heavy blow to the head when he was thrown from the chair but there was no suggestion that he was actually unconscious when he hit the water. His heart had stopped well before the time the paramedics arrived. The failure of the lungs and the twin shocks of being precipitated from the chair at speed and then hitting water had all taken their toll on an uncertain constitution. The paramedics had attempted resuscitation but to no avail. It was difficult to argue with Mrs Wellings' assessment of death within minutes of being pulled from the water and the probability was that Jeremy was dead before then. In all the circumstances the odds were heavily against success coming from the sort of amateurish attempts Mr Wellings had made to revive the boy.

The Coroner probed only a little further and half an hour later the family left his court with the expected verdict of accidental death.

'Murder by neglect,' whispered a ghost in Mark's ear.

'Only a few seconds, not even that,' cried back

Mark's spirit in agony.

'So why did Barton cover up?' demanded the ghost.

'You look just about all in,' commented Paul, breaking in on the terrible conversation and temporarily banishing the ghost.

'It's still all a bit grim,' agreed Mark, irrelevantly remembering the same brother's presence during the case against Robert Cooper and mentally observing that the Wellings could be relied upon to turn up to support each other at law if not on other occasions. The reflection made him smile.

'That's better,' said Aunt Isobel, who had been watching him closely as he fought his ghost.

'You should get away for a while,' put in Sally, to be immediately supported by Mr Barton, who offered his wife's services in looking after both house and cat.

The words mocked rather than comforted Mark, whose tortured spirit yearned for permanent absence and whose conscience told him that there could be no question now of meeting his timetable for abandoning his family. Pippa had begun to cling to him and Claire as if fearful that they might follow Sam and Jeremy out of her life. She had become withdrawn and this time was slow to adjust, tormenting Montefiore with extravagant affection, irrationally resentful when her pet struggled from her grasp.

At the service of cremation she stood woodenly, half-heartedly joining in 'Jesus wants me for a Sunbeam', her small face pinched and unhappy.

I am the Resurrection and the Life, saith the Lord.

'Take her out,' said Mark to Ruth as the congregation began to sing 'Jesus loves me, this I know'.

Shortly the coffin would be hidden by the curtains as it began its journey towards the flames. He was unsure how much his daughter understood, but she would realise her brother's body was being taken for destruction, not buried whole like Sam's. But Pippa did not know Ruth well and would not leave Mark's side.

Afterwards Aunt Isobel took her home while the others waited in the garden of remembrance, looking at the wreaths and flowers which had garlanded the coffin. The sun blazed down in sharp contrast to the cold and rain which had made Sam's funeral such a misery.

Only a little while ago life had seemed once more tranquil, perhaps even promising, and now they had sunk again into horror. Mark began to wonder if his family was cursed.

To Mark's surprise it was Claire who rallied first, planning for the future between intervals of grief. Mark no longer resisted a move to Sussex, and a middle-aged couple with elderly parents showed an intense interest in buying their house with its chair lift and bathroom hoists. Claire pursued the sale with steady determination and Pippa told everyone that they were moving in the summer holidays. To Mark's relief the prospect excited rather than daunted her, doubtless due to Claire's observation that no paddock was complete without a pony and that it would be nice to have a swimming pool.

Yet beneath the excitement his daughter was wary, reverting to a babyish dislike of her parents being in different rooms at home or separating on different errands when out. She cried if Montefiore stayed out all night and felt rejected when Tatters did not appear at the Hole.

Each night Mark looked out over the darkened garden postponing until the last moment the time when he must get into bed and risk the sleep which was now rarely untroubled by the ghost of his son.

Always the dream started with the singing, the clear childish tones and the notes of Michael Finnegan. In real life Mark could not recall ever having heard Jeremy sing that particular air, he could only recall hearing the children of Valence Towers sing it as he waited one day for Pippa. But it was Jeremy who sang it now, compelling him to look down into the clear water where the small four-year-old boy smiled up at him as he sat cross-legged on the shingly bottom of the stream where the weeds trailed and goldfish incongruously swam. The smile accused Mark and threatened him.

In vain did he reason with himself on waking. The stream had a muddy bed not a shingly one, as well he knew from the occasions when Pippa had dropped something in and clamoured tearfully for its retrieval. No fish swam in it. He was haunted by guilt, not ghosts. Defying his logic the dream still came, the detail unchanging. He found himself looking forward to the move to Sussex, hoping to rid himself of the small, reproachful spectre and of the memories which lived in his present home.

The move took place towards the end of September when instead of wanting his help Claire banished Mark for two days and sent Pippa to stay with Ellen. As his firm wanted him to do some work in London he decided to stay with Aunt Isobel. Sally, still in Parliamentary Recess, invited him to dinner so that they could sort out some of the remaining financial issues over their decision that Claire and Mark should take over Sam's house, buying out Sally's share.

Sally looked radiant when she opened the door to him and for a moment he could not decide what was different, then he realised that the long flame-coloured hair had been cut and bobbed, no longer settling at the back of Sally's neck in a plaited bun. Its colour had some time ago lost its youthful glory, but the hair was still thick and luxuriant as it shone in its new style.

'Very nice,' Mark complimented her. 'Did you have it done anywhere famous?'

'Yes, Michaeljohn.'

Mark was surprised. Sally, for all that she had grown up moneyed and wanting for nothing, despised what she described as conspicuous consumption and laughed at people who patronised establishments for their names and labels. He had been expecting her to say 'I had it done in that little shop down the road' or some such thing.

Her flat, a large one in Westminster, was as he remembered it, furnished with antique and modern furniture which should have clashed but

362

did not, the carpets and curtains of colours which should have competed but instead seemed complementary, as Sally's red, rust and orange clothes so often seemed with her hair. It took an artist's eye to bring it off. Few could have produced such combinations without risible results.

His eyes wandered to the large mantelpiece which should have been too ornate but was not and stayed there.

'That's Charles,' said Sally unnecessarily as she saw him staring at the photograph. Yetminster's good looks were not easily forgotten.

Mark switched his gaze to his sister-in-law, absorbing not only the new hairstyle, but the elegant figure which seemed now more elegant still, the expensively casual clothes – and the radiance. Her radiance told him before her words.

'We are going to be engaged.'

After he had kissed her, she went to fetch champagne while Mark sat and wondered.

'But he hated your Bill,' he said as Sally came back with the bottle and two long-stemmed flutes.

'And as a consequence it is now a very much better Act than it would have been. Their Lordships' amendments were better than anything our House produced. So, thanks to Charles, it is as watertight as it can be against abuse and laxity. I sleep better as a result.'

Mark remembered the man's voice he had heard when he telephoned Sally to call her to the hospital. Yetminster, of course, now he thought about it. Then it probably was innocent. Yetminster was a renowned and vocal Catholic. He felt obscurely relieved.

Sally read his thoughts. 'You spoke to him once on the phone. He was staying here with his sister and niece. He had a large family invasion that weekend and his house caught fire. He had to scatter them everywhere, poor chap.'

Yes, thought Mark. The fire had made front-page news.

'You'll be a countess,' he said, grinning.

'Sally Yetminster. But his family name is Treduggan.'

'What will your constituents think? Will they like having a countess for an MP?'

'If they don't they won't have to put up with me for long. I'm not standing again.'

Mark, his champagne glass halfway to his mouth, gasped and lowered the drink. 'Why ever not?'

'I've done what I went there to do.'

'Euthanasia?'

'The relief of the wretchedly dying. Yes.'

'Of course it's a major achievement,' observed Mark, suppressing his own doubts. 'Many people will be grateful to you...'

'I doubt it,' interrupted Sally. 'Are you grateful to Alexander Fleming every time the doctor gives you an antibiotic?'

'But there will be other achievements. Other things to fight for.'

'Then others must do the fighting. There isn't even any guarantee I would be elected. My majority isn't exactly large and an awful lot of people hate the Act.'

'So what will you do instead?'

'Marry and have half a dozen children, draw and paint. Do good works. Help Charles with the estate.'

The words had no trace of irony and Mark found himself floundering for a reply. It occurred to him that Claire would be disappointed, that she derived satisfaction from the career of her sister, even when she disapproved of the causes Sally sometimes adopted. Aunt Isobel might well be glad: she found the fierce criticism of her niece difficult and she would certainly consider a happy marriage a satisfactory substitute. Poor Aunt Isobel.

'I've managed to do some painting this recess. The results are in the dining room.'

Carrying their glasses, they walked through the large glass doors which connected the two rooms and stood looking at the canvases.

The largest bore a painting of a very old lady holding a baby on her lap. The elderly figure was bathed in twilight, the baby in the red light of dawn. Moving nearer Mark appreciated the detail: the weary slump of the woman's shoulders, the eyes which sought the long rest of the dead, and the hope and expectation which shone from the face of one as yet too young consciously to know or appreciate such sentiments.

The next painting was of the same theme. A very old, wrinkled, arthritic woman stood naked in front of a mirror from which a very young and beautiful woman gazed back. Again it was the detail which held Mark. The older woman's head was half turned to present a glimpse of its profile and the face was quite unmistakably the aged version of the young woman's. They might have been two photographs taken seventy years apart.

The third showed a schoolgirl of ten or eleven working worriedly at a desk while on the wall above her a woman in the robes of a don looked down with a look of wistful indulgence mixed with quiet satisfaction.

'That one does not work so well,' observed Sally. 'Less dawn and twilight and more elevenses and teatime. It lacks the force of the others. Different message.'

'You have huge talent,' said Mark in wonder, 'but we've always known that. When you can give it real time you'll make a big name for yourself.'

'Six children won't leave much time.'

'You're serious?'

'Yes. Charles wants a big family too. Sadly Ozzie hated the idea.'

Ozzie? Ozzie Something-Something. The one who had been there at the accident. Although he could not recall the surname he could recall Ozzie very clearly, and shuddered. So Sally had been serious about him. He wondered if she had grieved for him in the many intervening years, years which had produced other men but, until now, not one with whom she wanted to spend her life.

'I hope you'll be very happy. You and Charles – and the children. I thought you were such enemies, I suppose it's funny.'

'Not enemies, adversaries. He was a capable opponent and, as I say, he made it a better Act.

Anyway we agree on so much else – abortion, eugenics, genetic engineering, sexual mores.'

'Yes, he's a Catholic.'

'I won't be, if that's a disguised way of asking, but the children will.'

Mark thought of Sister Agnes Xavier. He would miss St Joseph's which, since their meeting there, he had visited on the odd occasion. He was surrounded by certainty: Ben and Ruth, Charles Yetminster, Claire, Sister Agnes, the vicar, all drawing comfort from their different faiths. He pushed the thought aside, not ready to confront his own sense of emptiness.

Instead he returned to something Sally had now mentioned twice. 'You were worried that your Bill had loopholes?'

'Of course. Guy Mortimer was quite right about the way we've let other laws get beyond control. You remember him? One of those who spoke in the debate at Second Reading?'

'I don't remember him very well but I do remember his argument. He was the one who said "No granny will be safe".'

'That was him. It was the only thing that gave me any pause for thought. Even now I wonder if there is something we haven't seen. Some un-intended effect, as the Parliamentary draughts-men call it. I wouldn't want to go down in history as the woman who made it lawful to finish off anyone over the age of seventy-five.'

She was asking for reassurance, Mark realised with a small frisson of shock. Tough, independent Sally was not so sure of herself, and he could not give her the bland comfort she sought. Once he might have done, but not since Sam had raved on his deathbed, afraid he was to be killed. She must never know, he thought urgently, never. As far as he knew only he and Aunt Isobel, other than the nurses, had heard Sam's fear. Sam's daughters must not be allowed to stumble on that terrible secret.

While he was still seeking the right words, Sally continued: 'But if I had my time over again, I would still do it. If people decide to abuse the Act, that's up to them and if society condones it there is nothing I can do about it.'

Mark heard the defensiveness in her tone. 'What made you take that risk?' he asked gently, and knew the answer even before she gave it.

'Mother.'

'Claire told me she suffered. I'm sorry.'

'Suffered! She lived in hell and went on living in it. I heard her tell my father she wanted to die and I heard him tell a nurse that it would be better for her when it was all over. In the last two months they kept me away from her room.

'I was four and I wanted Mummy but they wouldn't let me go in, said she was too poorly. Then one day the nurse was called to the phone and I crept up to her door. She was cursing, moaning out loud and sobbing. She kept crying out that she wanted to die. I was frightened but I went in because I missed her so much.

'At first she didn't hear me, and I got right up to the bed where I got the most almighty shock. You see, I was expecting Mummy and instead there was this skeleton. She had no hair, was thin to the bones and writhing in pain. Then she saw me and smiled but it just made her look like a death's head. She held out a hand to me and it was just like a claw. I was only four. I screamed and screamed and backed away. By the time half the household had come running she was crying and still trying to beckon me over to the bed. As they took me out she was again saying she just wanted to die.

'Even at that age I could work it out. She loved me and wanted me but they wouldn't let me see her like that. But I had seen her and I began to feel braver. A little while after I went to her room again but she was barely conscious. After a bit she did focus on me and she said, "Soon, I'll be in Heaven where there is no pain. But Daddy will miss me so you must be very brave and grown-up and look after him. Promise."

'So I promised, and when they found me there that time they let me stay a bit before taking me out. I never saw her again, but I heard her once when I was in the garden and the windows were open. She must have been in agony. Daddy and I never discussed it but he knew well enough why I was determined that those who want to die in those sorts of circumstances should be able to. No one should go through that. Claire is luckier than I. She can remember our mother as she once was. The only memory I have is of that skeletal wreck. It wiped out everything else.

'I'm sorry it has caused so much pain to you and Claire. I did realise, of course, that the debate was never going to be contained and that all sorts of issues about quality of life would arise and that Jeremy might be dragged into it. But I had to do it and it has given some meaning to Mother's suffering. Indirectly it spared others.'

So in revolt against one parent's wretchedness on her deathbed she had inadvertently scared the other on his. Mark closed his eyes. When he opened them, a response on his lips, Sally had gone and his gaze fell instead on a twilight-swathed old woman clutching a dawn-bathed child.

His eyes switched to the table, and as he noticed it was laid for three the doorbell rang and he heard Sally greeting her future husband in a bright, untroubled voice. Curious, he went through to the hallway of the flat, wryly reflecting that he and Sally were unlikely to discuss Sam's house tonight.

Arriving back at Aunt Isobel's he was unsurprised to find she had gone to bed, unsurprised and relieved for he had yet to work out how much of what he had learned might be safe to discuss with her. Izzymum might know all or she might know nothing.

Breakfast was rushed as he overslept. Aunt Isobel had dithered between not wanting to disturb him and wondering if he might get into trouble if she did not. Between mouthfuls of toast Mark promised he would be back by seven.

He walked in with the *Evening Standard* under his arm. Rumours of a closer-than-supposed friendship between Sally Renwick and Charles Yetminster led the diary column. He guessed there would now be a formal announcement fairly soon, and wondered that they had kept it quiet for so long. Aunt Isobel already had the news and was proposing they should celebrate with a small sherry.

Mark put the *Evening Standard* face down on the table, embarrassed because the front page was given over to revelations of the lively extramarital sex life of a Government Minister. He was quite certain that Aunt Isobel would not know what some of the things mentioned meant. He was disconcerted, therefore, to see her pick up the paper as he went through to the hall to ring Claire.

His wife was irritable and petulant. She was the last to know about Sally's engagement. She could not understand why no one had told her. When Mark said he did not think there had been any formal announcement she said they were talking about it on the radio. For once the Renwick communication system appeared to have broken down. Furthermore Pippa had been sick and the Eameses had rung up to tell her. Surely they could cope with a sick child without bothering her when she was so busy. They had twins, after all.

It was impossible to imagine Sally carping at Yetminster in such a fashion. Mark felt a wave not of envy or irritation but of self-pity. He wanted escape with all the intensity Graine Renwick had once wanted it. The thought shamed him but he refused to repent.

When he returned to the kitchen, Aunt Isobel put down the *Evening Standard* face up. Mark gave the front page an uncomfortable glance. 'I don't know why they do these things,' he muttered censoriously.

She looked at him, amused. 'Oh, I don't know, dear. They probably find it quite gurgle-making at the time. But they ought to know by now that they'll get caught.'

Mark spilled his sherry. Gurgle-making? Aunt Isobel?

'Oh dear,' she said, absentmindedly wiping up the sherry with her apron instead of a cloth. 'Aren't I supposed to know these things? Poor Aunt Isobel.'

Mark stared at her, wondering if the last words were a coincidence or sarcasm. Did she know that was what they called her? To cover his confusion he began to talk of Sally's engagement and at once felt on safer ground as Aunt Isobel began to describe Yetminster as 'a nice young man'.

'She'll give up Parliament of course,' pronounced Aunt Isobel confidently, and Mark could not be sure whether her certainty sprang from definitive information or merely from her knowledge of Sally's character.

'She has very strong views about full-time motherhood,' continued Aunt Isobel, 'and anyway, she's done what she went there to do.'

'Was she right to do it?' asked Mark.

'Oh yes, dear. I know you and Claire had a lot to put up with while it was going on, but just think of all those poor people.'

'Aunt Izzy, what about people like Sam? Very rich people and very sick? Or perhaps not rich at all but a tremendous drain on the family? Not everybody is loved as Sam was loved.'

'Oh, Sally provided for all that in the law. I thought you supported it, dear?'

'I did, but now I'm not so sure. Nor am I so certain you can provide for that sort of thing in legislation. Look at the 1967 Abortion Act.'

'Well, yes, but Charles put in all sorts of safeguards. That's how they fell in love, you know.'

Mark let her ramble on for a while about Sally's future happiness. They would marry at Westminster Cathedral because Charles was a Catholic but sadly they would then see much less of Sally because Charles lived in Dorset, although she supposed they must come to London quite a lot when the House of Lords was in session, but perhaps Sally would remain in Dorset once there were children...

Mark had ceased to pay attention. He was thinking of Pippa and wondering how soon she would rally and of Jeremy and how much he missed his son. He became aware that Aunt Isobel's prattle had ceased and forced his mind back to the present.

'Penny for them?' Aunt Isobel was saying. 'You were miles away.'

'I was thinking of Jeremy,' said Mark.

The smile faded from the eager, innocent face.

'You mustn't torment yourself, dear. You did all you could.'

Mark thought she meant that they had exhausted every remedy known to modern science in the quest to cure or palliate Jeremy's condition and he prepared to agree dismissively. Her next words turned him cold with shock.

'Those few seconds wouldn't have changed anything.'

'You mean when I fell off the ladder and...'

'No, dear. By the stream. When you didn't do anything.'

He looked at her, seeing the knowledge in her eyes.

'Mr Barton told me,' she enlightened him. 'When you and Claire had gone off with the ambulance and Sally was trying to reassure Pippa, he came round and went through the whole thing. He was terribly shocked and I think he was near to tears. When he came to how you finally arrived at the stream he said that you just knelt there frozen with shock. For several seconds, he said, and then you went frantic, pulling Jeremy out.'

'He didn't say that at the inquest.'

'I asked him not to,' said Aunt Isobel calmly. 'I said you were probably so shocked you hadn't even realised you had hesitated. It would be cruel to suggest to you that there was something more you could have done.'

'And he accepted that?'

She refused to spare him. 'He accepted that we shouldn't say anything.'

'He looked so peaceful.'

'He is at peace, dear. I know you would much rather have him around, just like I would rather have Sam around, no matter what sort of state the stroke left him in, but they are at peace. Both of them. So if there were a couple of seconds when you preferred him to have that peace, don't blame yourself. If you are telling yourself that you would have done more had it been Pippa, that is because Pippa would have had so much more to lose and so you would have been even more desperate. Also because she would have stood more chance of survival.'

Mark, appalled by the extent of her knowledge, did not answer.

'Anybody at that inquest must have realised that you and Claire gave up before you were quite sure he was dead, but he was dead. The pathologist said so. You have nothing to feel guilty about, either about stopping the artificial respiration when you did or about hesitating so briefly when you saw him in the stream. We all loved Jeremy, but now he's at peace.'

22

Mark leaned back, feeling mentally drained and exhausted. He had finished work at lunchtime and was now on the train home, looking unseeingly at the trees, fields and cattle which told him that the train had now left the suburbs behind and was speeding through green belt. In the last two days his world had shifted like a kaleidoscope and nothing was quite as he had once seen it.

Sally, who had once appeared so cool, clever and independent with a glittering career ahead of her, had been unveiled as a psychologically-damaged child who had embroiled a whole nation in the resolution of her trauma. Aunt Isobel – poor Aunt Isobel – had changed from a vague, elderly, innocent maiden aunt into a sharp-witted, worldly-wise woman who knew those around her better than they knew themselves.

He searched for clues that he had missed in the past. Aunt Isobel's insistence on quitting Sussex for her own independent life in London as soon as she was sure Sally had settled at Cambridge was surely one. For what had she come back to London after all those years? Mark, remembering her unexpected comment on the Minister's sex life, wondered now if she might have had one of her own. He thought it improbable, but then the entire conversation had been improbable.

She had effectively, if with great gentleness, told him that it was quite in order to let his child die. He remembered now her response when Claire had raged about Nurse Kenward. 'Well, it wasn't very kind of her, dear, but there are people who think like that.'

Suddenly a fresh thought struck him. Aunt Isobel alone had gone to the wheelchair that afternoon. He could see her now bending over Jeremy. Had her foot slid unnoticed to the brake?

Reality arrested the mad whirl of his thoughts. Dear God, first he was casting Aunt Isobel as a seductress and now as a murderess. He laughed aloud and a fellow passenger walking along the train, thinking him amused not tormented, smiled at him.

Whatever happened in the future he could never again be surprised by one of the Renwick women, thought a bemused Mark, but in this, as in so much else, he was to be proved wrong.

The train arrived on time and Mark alighted at his usual station. He was glad to find the car both unvandalised and willing to start after its two nights in the station car park. He wondered if he would ever use this station again.

As soon as he turned into the drive he was struck by the empty aspect of the house, the curtainless windows, missing garden furniture, no hosepipe coiling from the outside tap. He carried out his mission of checking that nothing was left in house or garden, that the contract cleaners had done their work thoroughly (run your hand behind the radiators and check the Aga ovens and under the taps in the bathroom, Claire had ordered), that they had secured each window after cleaning and had left the keys with the Bartons.

Mark walked purposefully through the house. The incoming owners could have little cause for complaint. In the lounge a basket of dried flowers had been placed in the centre of the mantelpiece together with an envelope containing what Mark guessed was a 'welcome to your new home' card. In the kitchen the old kettle had been left with plastic cups, tea and coffee. Beside them was a typed list of local shops and potentially useful telephone numbers. By Neville Harris's name Claire had typed in capitals: VERY GOOD DOCTOR. STRONGLY RECOMMENDED.

Only in Jeremy's old room did he linger beyond the brief time necessary for his duties. For a moment he envisaged the room as it used to be, seeing again the activity mat and the mobiles. Saddened, he turned to go, shutting the door firmly behind him. He let himself out by the front door and went to the Bartons' house, where he was assured the spare keys were safe. He was to drop off his own at the estate agent's.

Mrs Barton produced tea and scones and he stayed an hour, feeding Tatters the odd piece of cake or sandwich as he talked to the elderly couple. He wondered if Barton had told his wife what he had not told the inquest.

When it was time to leave and he had retrieved his car from the drive, he glanced once more at the house as he shut the gates behind him. He hoped the next occupants would be happier there than he and Claire had been. A chapter of his life had closed and he did not intend the next – at the house in Sussex – to be a long one.

By the time he had found somewhere to park and visited the estate agent it was dark, and half an hour later rain lashed the windscreen as he drove to Sussex. When the tyre was suddenly punctured he slewed across the road and brought the car to a safe stop, cursing, remembering the damaged spare tyre he should have replaced months ago. He reached into the back for his briefcase and located his mobile, but when he dialled the RAC he heard only the bleep of a low battery warning. He had no mackintosh but there was a spare umbrella in the boot. Resignedly he got out and began to walk, his eyes seeking a telephone box.

It was gone ten when he arrived home, tired and irritable. He snapped when Pippa flew down the stairs to greet him and sent her back to bed. Refusing supper, glancing only cursorily at the substitution of their belongings for Sam's, he went up to bed. The room they always used was full of unpacked tea chests and he realised he and Claire would now be in the master suite which Sam had always occupied. He wondered if that might upset Claire and if it was one of the reasons she had sent him and Pippa away while she moved in and made Sam's home theirs. He was too bad-tempered to enquire.

'That wasn't very kind,' observed Claire as she came into the bedroom. 'She's been longing to show you her new bedroom.'

'I can see it in the morning.'

He glared at the bedside table and the tallboy, where his personal belongings had been arranged in the same order as in the previous house. Their presence suggested permanency.

'I want a divorce.'

The sudden, unplanned words shocked him. Claire sat down at the dressing table, picked up a comb and began to run it through her hair.

'Not now,' she said judiciously, as if responding to a request from Pippa for sweets before a meal.

They stared at each other's reflections. Incredulous, Mark did not know whether to feel hope or irritation. Was he being promised or just not believed?

'I realise we have to give Pippa time to adjust...'

'Before shattering her again. Thanks, Daddy.'

Mark sat down on the end of the bed. Before he could speak his wife said: 'We're having another child.'

Satisfied, she watched the shock enter into him and smiled at him through the mirror. She knew what his next words would be.

'Are you sure?'

'Very. The doctor says it's nearly four months.'

His mind rebelled against her words, denied them. Nearly four months. Whitsun, after Jeremy's death, when they had clung to each other, sharing unspoken guilt.

How soon afterwards had she realised that the last compelling moral demand on him to stay had died with her son in the water? So, she had set her trap and now it had closed on him. Sam's attempt to keep him with his family had been pathetic by comparison. He could turn his back on one hundred thousand pounds, but he could not turn his back on a pregnant wife. His very soul forbade it.

In his imagination the gossips revelled in his wickedness.

'And after all that and then losing that poor little boy he just walked out leaving her with a traumatised daughter and a new baby on the way... Must have been a woman somewhere. Something younger. There always is, isn't there? And they say his father-in-law was so taken in by him that he left him half a million or something like that...'

He did not need their spiteful censure to know it was impossible, and the empty years of duty and pretence yawned ahead.

'So she's won, Mark.' Ginny's mocking tones replaced the eager destruction of those of the gossips. 'But at least you get the hundred grand.'

Claire was still looking at his reflection. In her certain triumph she scarcely bothered to hide her amusement. So his marriage had come to this: that an unborn child, instead of bringing hope and joy and wonder, should merely herald a battle won. Sickened, repulsed, disgusted with them both, he momentarily resolved to go anyway. Nothing mattered but to regain some self-respect. He saw her guess his thoughts and the fear flare in her eyes.

'Mark, you can't leave me now.' Her tone had become pleading, frightened.

'What's left?'

'Pippa, the baby. Oh Mark, please. Surely it can be better now that ... that...'

Claire shirked the dreadful words. Mark did not.

'Now that Jeremy has gone. It was never Jeremy who was the problem: it was us, wouldn't you agree?'

Defeated, Claire sank her head in her hands. Presently she looked up and reached for a tissue. Then she turned to face him. 'But whereas poor Jeremy could not change, we can.'

'I'm no longer up to that challenge. It won't work.'

'But it did once. We used to be happy before it all happened.'

So let her try, he thought unkindly, let her make the effort for a change, but his reason opposed him. Freedom was years away and he knew it. They must both try to shape the intervening years or resign themselves to deepening unhappiness. He had come to maturity in the seventies but their ethos had passed him by. He would stay and he would try to make it work for all of them, especially for the new child, the innocent, helpless weapon in a long-drawn-out war of attrition. But this time he would not consent to try alone. He reached out to touch her stomach as he had during those earlier, happier pregnancies, but felt numb rather than rewarded when the hope entered her eyes.

When at last they went to bed Claire slept at once, while Mark tossed and turned on the horns of his dilemma, which his heart still denied was solved despite the insistence of his mind that it was. He thought of Smith and ached with longing and sadness. When at last he drifted into sleep he heard the singing and fell wretchedly towards the small, relentless ghost.

From beneath the water the child smiled up at him, the child he had last seen in real life more than nine years ago. He smiled back and waited, some small remnant of his conscious mind telling him that he had no choice, wondering if the ghost would ever become the teenager who had died.

The singing changed. The notes of Michael Finnegan were replaced by those of 'Peace, perfect peace, is the gift of Christ our God', but it was not his daughter singing as it had been when he stood outside Valence Towers. There were many voices, pure, childish, joyful. As Mark watched, other children surrounded Jeremy and he recognised Christina Bright and the others who had died on the coach. They were happy, reaching out to Jeremy, and beyond them he knew there were others, many, many others. The children of Dunblane, of Aberfan, of famine, of strife. Those he saw, the children of Coach A, were holding Jeremy now and taking him away. Mark peered into the water at the fading forms and saw his son give him one last smile. Mark waved and, singing 'Love, perfect love, is the gift of Christ our God', the small ghosts faded from his dreaming sight for ever.

Peaceful, forgiven, reconciled, he woke and stared into the darkness. Beside him his wife stirred and gently moaned as the child within her moved, proclaiming its life.

This Large Print Book for the partially sighted, who cannot read normal print, is published under the auspices of

THE ULVERSCROFT FOUNDATION